Special Edition

DEAR GRUMPY BOSS

JULIA WOLF

This one is for the women with plump asses and round tummies, who've been told to be something else one too many times. Fuck that noise. You are exactly who you are meant to be. Perfection.

CHAPTER ONE

Elise

THE CONFERENCE ROOM WAS packed.

Shoulder to shoulder.

Perfume clouds, not enough deodorant, elbows knocking.

I found a seat near the back, not around the long table in the center of the room but in a corner, my coworkers Lani and Brandon on either side of me.

"They're going to have to knock down some walls," Brandon drawled in his Georgia-met-Chicago accent.

"They like us being squeezed in here," Lani whispered, eyeing the people around us with suspicion. "It makes us remember how unimportant we are."

Richthink Marketing was not a good place to work. There was no trust between colleagues. In fact, we were encouraged to compete against each other. If our boss could have convinced us to Jell-O wrestle to get ahead, he probably would have.

"Nothing but sardines." I bit on my bottom lip, scanning the crowd. Half the faces were new. To a stranger off the street, it would have been obvious we were two distinct groups of people:

the hardened, beady-eyed veterans of Richthink and the optimistic, grateful-to-still-have-a-job newcomers from the marketing firm that had just merged with ours.

Needless to say, I was deep in the throes of searching for a new job. It wasn't easy. I was beyond entry level and wouldn't settle like I had with Richthink. I needed my next job to be something I looked forward to instead of just passing the days like I was now.

"Drinks tonight?" Brandon asked.

I nodded. "Patrick's out of town until Friday."

Lani bumped my elbow, drawing my attention. On purpose or not, it didn't matter.

"Didn't you vow not to vent to him anymore?"

"Yes. That's why I have you guys."

Patrick was patient. Patrick was a nice guy. Patrick wouldn't say it, but his nonverbal cues let me know in no uncertain terms he'd gotten tired of hearing how much I loathed my job. And since I had been making a valiant effort over the last year to help our relationship feel less like settling than my job, I kept my venting to a minimum at home.

Brandon bumped me from the other side. "I'm happy to play your therapist. You'll receive your bill at the end of the night."

I cocked a brow at him. "I'm not paying your bar tab."

He pretended to flip his hair. "Can't blame a girl for trying, right?"

The meeting got started and droned on and on. In my boredom, I let my gaze sweep over the new hires, stopping on a young brunette across the room. She was frowning at me. Not in an angry way. It almost looked like she was trying to figure something out. Figure me out?

I lifted a brow, and her eyes narrowed.

Did I know her?

I didn't think so.

She looked down at her phone, so I moved on to the people around her.

A minute or two later, Lani nudged me. I glanced at her, and she jerked her chin in the direction of the brunette. I swiveled my head back, and sure enough, she was staring again.

Strange.

Lani scribbled on her notepad: *Do you know her?*

I typed out a message on my phone and tilted the screen toward her.

No, but she's been staring at me like she knows me. What's that about? Do you think she's sussing out the competition?

Lani scribbled again.

Probably sussing out your boobs. Did I mention how hot they look today?

I tapped on my phone.

You did. Thank you for that. We'll discuss my boobs and the brunette with the staring problem later.

The meeting ended after an interminable hour. We were instructed to mingle, which was laughable. We all had deadlines—mingling hadn't been built into our time lines.

I headed back to my cubicle, my mind on all I needed to get done today. I didn't notice the person following me until I sat down at my desk and she was there, in the opening of my cube.

Startled, a hand flew to my chest. Her cheeks flushed.

"I'm sorry. I didn't mean to sneak up on you."

"That's okay. I wasn't paying attention." Letting my hand fall to my desk, I waited for her to say something. She kept standing there, shifting back and forth between her feet. "Is there something I can help you with?"

"Actually"—she peered at her phone—"are you Patrick Lincoln's girlfriend?"

The hairs on the back of my neck rose. "Yes. Why do you ask?"

"Well, we haven't met yet, but my name is Kara. I've been dating Steve"—Patrick's college roommate and best friend—"and they added me to the group text a while ago."

"The...group text?"

She nodded, taking a step closer, her phone clutched in her hand. "The one with all the guys from college."

"The Drunk Tank?" Patrick's special name for that particular group text, which, as far as I had known, was *strictly* guys he went to college with—no significant others.

"Yes. That's the one. I don't know why they added me since I've only met them a couple times."

My stomach lurched. "You've met Patrick?"

Her nod was slow, and in the space of seconds, she seemed to realize I hadn't known that either.

"Yes, I have. Steve brought me along to the bar. It was a mixed thing. Some of the other guys had their girls with them. Patrick said you were busy with work."

I couldn't quite process what she was saying. It felt like someone had draped fabric between me and the rest of reality, an invisible hazy gauze between us. I couldn't truly understand what was going on.

"How did you recognize me?" I heard myself ask.

This woman was a stranger, yet knew things about my boyfriend I didn't. She was in his group text—the one that was supposedly all "inside jokes" and "college references"—the one Patrick was always tapping away in when we were together—the one I'd never worried about because I trusted him.

"Well, that's what I wanted to tell you. I assumed you didn't know and couldn't in good conscience work with you and not tell you about this."

She held her phone out to me, and I took it, blinking a few times so I could focus.

There was a GIF. Not sent by Patrick, but his frat brother, Chance. That was normal, fine, no problem, except for the subject of the GIF.

It was me, bouncing on my knees, in a bikini.

Chance had sent it.

Not Patrick.

"What is this?" My throat had gone desert dry, my question coming out as a rasp.

"I don't know how it started or *who* started it, but all the guys use that GIF. If you scroll back, you can see—"

I shook my head. "No thank you. Listen, I appreciate you telling me, but I can't do this at work." The tears that had begun to form in my eyes evaporated. "That was very solid of you to let me know."

"Of course." She took her phone back from me. "Please, let me know if there's anything I can do."

She started to turn, and I called her name. She stopped, raising a questioning brow.

"This is a terrible place to work," I told her. "If you can get out, you should."

Her eyes went round. "Really? Oh god, I was hoping—"

"No." I stacked my hands on my desk to keep them from shaking. "Don't hope. You'll only be disappointed. It's a bad, bad place."

She slumped against the opening of my cube. "Damn. Well, thanks for telling me. Woman to woman and all that."

I lowered my eyes to my keyboard. "We have to look out for each other. Can you do me a favor and not tell Steve about this? I want to have the opportunity to figure out what I'm going to do before I talk to Patrick."

She reached out, like she meant to touch me, but stopped herself. "Of course. I hope you're okay."

Sucking in a breath, I flicked my gaze to the photo of Patrick and me at a wedding three years ago. He was holding me, nuzzling my neck while I laughed. Back then, I'd thought he was magic. Now, I wondered if he was nothing more than an illusionist.

"I will be."

Once I found out just how deep this betrayal went.

***

Lani and Brandon huddled around me at my place. Patrick was on a work trip in Boston and had conveniently left his iPad behind. Brandon had been prepared to hack into it, but it wasn't locked. He wasn't even trying to hide this from me.

Brandon took the iPad and began to scroll through the messages. I was too dizzy from heartache and two shots of straight vodka to be in charge of scrolling.

"When I sent him that video, he told me I was his sexy little treasure." I held my empty glass to my lips, rolling it back and forth. "And when I got home, he couldn't keep his hands off me."

Patrick Lincoln and I had been together for four years. We'd met at my first job post-college back in Denver. A whirlwind. Love at first sight. Something I'd never had.

When he was transferred to Chicago, where he'd grown up, there'd been no question I would follow, saying goodbye to my brother and college friends.

Two years in, the spark dimmed. He was busy. I was miserable at work. But I loved him and was determined to bring us back to the early days.

Sparks didn't have to dim, did they?

I thought not.

Lingerie, positions, spontaneity, toys—I did it all. I'd been an *awesome* girlfriend.

A year ago, I went on a girls' trip to Aruba with my college friends. One of them took a video of me in my bikini on the beach, down on my knees, sultry and sexy for Patrick. He made me feel that way. Always had. After growing up as the fat girl, having a man who appreciated each of my curves gave me confidence. It let me walk around on the beach in Aruba in a bikini, feeling like a damn goddess.

"I found it." Brandon's look was grim. "The first time he shared the video."

I swallowed hard. "When?"

"A year."

Oh god.

I took the iPad, reading the date first. He'd shared it while I was in Aruba.

Tyler: *I see why you call her JT.*

Chance: *She truly lives up to her name.*

Steve-o: *Does she know you sent that?*

Tricky: *She was in public wearing this. Who's going to tell her anyway? Not you.*

My eyes flicked to Brandon. "What's JT stand for?"

He grimaced.

Lani slapped his knee. "Just tell her. She's going to find out anyway."

Brandon wrapped his hand around mine. "It's really stupid, Lise. Frat boy humor at its finest."

Lani slapped him again. "Tell her!"

He huffed. "It stands for jiggle tits."

I couldn't even force myself to blink. My boyfriend, the one I trusted with my body, my sexuality, my everything, had turned me into a joke. He'd taken all my insecurities and GIF-ified them for his buddies' amusement.

I took the iPad out of Brandon's hands. I had to see this with my own eyes.

Chance was the one who took a clip from the video, slowed it down, and turned it into a GIF. Me bouncing, my tits, thighs, tummy jiggling in slow-mo. What I'd thought looked sexy now seemed utterly laughable.

The guys used the GIF for things like the stock market going down, news of a plane crash, Chance's bad date, Tyler's car getting sideswiped, to punctuate how hilarious a joke was.

They used it all the time.

They never called me by my name. It was JT or nothing.

I squeezed my eyes shut. It was like I was back in high school again. All the self-esteem I'd built, the love for my body, the confidence I'd gained over the years, deflated like a sad little balloon.

Love at first sight?

I huffed to myself.

The sight of me was a joke to him.

"Are you going to call him?" Lani asked carefully.

"No." I opened my eyes. "I don't want to look at him."

Lani gently slid the iPad out of my hands and placed it on the coffee table. "I don't blame you. If I saw him right now, I'd carve out his balls with a rusty spoon."

"Nice," Brandon scoffed. "That's helpful."

"I'm expressing my anger," Lani said primly. "It isn't good to hold it in."

Brandon patted my knee. "What do you want to do?"

"I think..." I sucked in a breath, "I want to get really, really drunk tonight. Tomorrow, I'll deal."

Lani, my dear sweet friend, held up the vodka. "That can absolutely be arranged."

———◆———

Twelve hours later, I was dealing.

I'd never been one to sit around feeling sorry for myself. At least, not for long.

I called my brother.

"Elliot."

"What's wrong?" It was seven a.m. in Denver, but Elliot was immediately alert. From the sounds in the background—voices, low music, metal on metal—knowing my brother, he was at the gym.

"I need to leave Chicago by tomorrow."

A pause. Something banging. "What did he do?" His jaw was clenched.

"He humiliated me. I don't want to see him. I need to be gone before he's back from Boston."

Another pause. Clanking that sounded like weights. "I'm coming. I'll be there tonight. In the meantime, I'll arrange movers and my assistant will book us a flight for tomorrow evening. Have you resigned?"

This was why I'd called Elliot. Not for his warm caretaking. Elliot was no-nonsense, all-action. That was what I needed. Action. Movement. Removing myself from this pitiful situation as quickly as possible.

I licked my dry lips. "No. That's my next plan. And so you're not alarmed, I'm going invisible."

He cleared his throat. All business. "Changing phone numbers?"

"Yes. I have to." Blocking Patrick wouldn't be enough. Not for me. I had to extract myself from his life completely.

"All right. That isn't a problem. I'll have a new phone couriered to you this afternoon. Is that soon enough?"

"Yes, I can't imagine you could have one to me any sooner anyway."

He scoffed. "There are ways." That, I believed. Elliot rose to challenges.

A man's voice was in the background. Someone familiar. I tried to block it out. I had enough to think about. He was demanding to know what was going on. My brother told him.

"It's Elise," Elliott murmured. "She's coming home."

I couldn't hear the other man's response, but then, I was actively trying not to.

We talked for another few minutes, which was rare. Elliot was more of a brief texter. Checked in a few times a week, made sure I was alive and well. We cared about each other but weren't siblings who chatted about the weather. Well...I could have. It wasn't Elliot's style.

Today, though, he didn't rush off the phone. He used his compassion, which he normally kept tucked away, and let me talk. He assured me I would be taken care of. I would stay with him until he found an acceptable apartment for me. Then he told me there was nothing for me to worry about anymore. He could shoulder my burdens until I was ready to take them on again.

My brother.

God.

Sometimes, I forgot who he was, but he always reminded me.

"Elise."

"Yeah?"

"Tell me the truth. I'll be angry if you don't. Did he hurt you physically?"

A loud grunt in the background. Another clang. That same man's voice, whispering viciously. I couldn't close my ears, so I shut my eyes instead.

"No. Not physically. I don't want to relive it. I'll send you the screenshots."

His intake of breath was sharp. "Will I need to hire someone to take him out?"

"Is that—you know how to do that?"

"Elise." An admonishment. Like I was stupid for asking. Of course Elliot knew how to do that. He knew how to do everything. If he didn't, he'd find out.

"Elliot, you're not hiring a hit man."

"It would look like an accident."

In the background, there was mention of taking out his kneecaps. I told myself the sound came from the television—not *him*.

"You don't even know what he did," I argued.

"I know it was bad. I know he hurt you. That's all that matters."

With that, a tear tracked down my cheek. The first one I'd allowed since Kara had walked into my cubicle. This wasn't for Patrick. He didn't deserve my tears and wouldn't be getting them.

Another tear fell.

For the way my brother loved me.

Elliot might have been cold. He might have seen the world in black and white. But when push came to shove, he excelled at being a big brother.

"I'll be there soon, Elise."

"Thank you, Elliot."

I put my phone down and stood up. There was a lot I had to do today—and sitting around feeling sorry for myself wasn't on the list.

It was time to become a ghost.

CHAPTER TWO

Weston

THE MOMENT I STEPPED into my condo, every last ounce of peace from the weekend was sucked out of me.

The stench of weed hit me as hard as the music blaring from my sound system. Thank Christ for being in the penthouse or my neighbors would have been up in arms. If the roles were reversed, I would have been too.

I tossed my heavy backpack down on the floor in the entry. Not my style, but I'd put it away after I dealt with the music. Then I'd deal with Miles.

Clicking the music off, I scanned my living room. Two glasses of wine on the coffee table, one with lipstick on the rim. The end of a joint in a Baccarat tumbler half filled with melting ice. Something pink and lacy on the carpet. A tie pointing like an arrow to the hallway.

This way to the asshole.

I'd left for the weekend, not telling anyone but my assistant I'd be out of reach. Camping on my own, something I'd done since childhood. I'd needed the quiet to get my head ready for what was to come, and there was nothing like being alone, under the stars, to make everything else feel small, including me.

In my world, where my role was *big*—the boss, creator, CEO—having the reminder I was nothing more than a piece of dust in the grand scheme of things kept me grounded. It gave me peace.

Miles was a peace killer. He had radar, sensing my empty condo from a mile away. It was a much more impressive location to take his hookups than his bedroom at our parents' in the suburbs. Or maybe he had an apartment now. It was difficult to keep track of my brother and his living situation. As long as he showed up to work and did his job, I remained hands-off.

Invading my home was unacceptable. Not that he cared. He'd been a loose cannon since birth. Our mother pinched his cheeks at his antics. Our father counted on me to keep him in line. A twenty-six-year-old man who needed to be kept in line.

It rankled.

"Miles!" I bellowed. "Get your filth out of my apartment."

A moment of silence then a feminine giggle. Down the hallway, where the bedrooms were, a door opened. It had better have been a guest room. If he'd fucked someone in my bed again, there wouldn't be enough camping trips in the world to calm my anger.

It took a solid five minutes for Miles to wander into the living room, still pulling his Henley over his head. His hair was sticking up in every direction, and there was a hickey on his neck.

A hickey.

Twenty-six years old.

Jesus.

He grinned. "Hey, man. I didn't think you'd be back this early."

My gaze swept the mess he'd left in my home. My brow winged, and I huffed. "Clearly. Get out."

"Calm down. My guest is getting dressed. Don't you want me to clean up?"

"I want you to leave. Take the sheets with you. I don't have the time nor inclination for a trip to the incinerator."

He picked up a wineglass and slugged back the contents. Wine as a shooter. Nice. Only my brother.

"Aren't you an environmentalist? Burning perfectly good sheets seems pretty wasteful."

I folded my arms over my chest. "They were perfectly good until your bare ass touched them. I don't want them in my house anymore."

He waved me off. "Dramatics. The sheets are fine. You probably paid a mint for them. Organic cotton, is it? Nothing but the best for Westie."

There was resentment there, and I'd never known why. Miles and I had grown up with the same privileges, the same opportunities. We'd both gone to Ivy League colleges. Never had to struggle. I'd launched my business while still in college. Miles had yet to even launch himself.

He took digs at me. Laughed at my successes. Acted like the most put-upon man in the state of Colorado. Yet he'd taken the job I'd offered. Had accepted the perks of being an Aldrich—of which there were many.

He was given respect simply because of his last name.

Still, the resentment festered.

"If you're interested in what the sheets are made of, why don't you grab them and your guest on your way out? Give me the key before you go."

He rolled his eyes. "Enough with the sheets. You wouldn't have known I was ever here if you hadn't shown up early. That's on you."

A shocked laugh exploded out of me. "That's on me? Where do you get off?"

It was then his guest emerged. She couldn't have been over twenty. I hoped like hell she was over eighteen. Miles danced the line of inappropriate, but if he was trolling the local high school for dates, I'd call the cops myself.

"How old is she?"

Miles turned to the girl. Small and blonde, her makeup was smeared and her minidress was inside out. A little girl playing dress-up and getting it all wrong.

"How old are you, sweetheart?" he cooed at her.

"I'm twenty-one." Her upper lip curled. "You said this was your place. What, do you like, live with your dad or something?"

That made Miles snicker. "My dad. Holy fuck, you're great." He turned to me, his forehead crinkled with amusement. "Did you hear that? That stick up your ass is aging you, bro. You look old enough to be my dear old father."

My nostrils flared. Not because I was insulted by some young girl who couldn't even put her clothing on correctly—no, it was because they were both still inside my home.

"Get out." My jaw was too tight. My dentist had already warned me I was bound to crack a molar. "Leave the key."

Miles sighed like I was asking a lot of him then ushered the girl out. While he dealt with her, I sat down on the couch and scrolled through my neglected texts. I clicked on Elliott's.

Elliott: *Elise is moved in.*

Succinct. That was Elliott Levy, my best friend since childhood. His younger sister, Elise, had needed a place to live in Denver, and I'd secured an apartment in my building. Although I hadn't seen her yet, she'd been back in town for a couple weeks and had moved in this weekend while I was camping.

Me: *Good. Does she like it?*

Elliott: *She's pleased. The building is secure, and most importantly, her ex has no idea where she is.*

Me: *Did you give her my number? In case she needs anything.*

Elliott: *I'm sure she has it.*

I wasn't so certain. If she did have it, she hadn't used it in years.

Miles plopped on the other end of the couch. He hadn't left with his guest. Hadn't even escorted her downstairs.

A gentleman, that one.

I raised a brow. "You're still here."

"Yeah." He slid down on the cushion, lacing his hands behind his head. "Think I'll stay for a while. How was camping?"

"How do you know where I was?"

"Context clues, Westie. The big backpack in the entry. Your absence all weekend. Oh, and your assistant spilled the beans."

"She didn't," I growled.

Renata had been with me since day one—when I'd barely been able to pay her. She was loyal to her bones and, unlike many of my employees, wasn't charmed by Miles. If I couldn't trust her, there was no one I could trust.

He held a hand up. "Whoa, whoa, whoa. No need to go postal. Renata is innocent. I might have told her there was a family emergency. Pulled at her grandma heartstrings. She finally told me where you were. I'll send her flowers to make up for it."

"*I'll* send her flowers as an apology for having to put up with my brother."

He flicked his fingers in my direction. "Fine, fine. I'm sure whatever you choose will be better anyway. Just sign my name to it." His hand went back to behind his head. "Anyway, you never answered. How was camping?"

I sighed. There was no reasoning with Miles. I'd tried for years, but it was an exercise in frustration.

"Good. I set up near Clary's Pass."

"I like it out there. You should have asked me to come."

"The point was to get some peace and quiet."

He turned his head toward me. "I can be quiet. Maybe I could use some peace too."

"Next time."

He chuckled. "That's not true and we both know it. When was the last time you took me with you?"

"I don't know." I scrubbed at my gritty face. After a four-hour hike back to my car this afternoon, I needed a shower. But that wouldn't be happening until Miles got gone and left my key behind. "Before I went to college probably."

"When Mom made you take me."

"When you thought it was a good idea to take LSD in the middle of nowhere, and I had to carry you, naked and singing the Beatles at the top of your lungs, back to my car. That was the last time."

A slow grin spread across his face. "Oh yeah. That was fun. We should do that again. I'll be your sober companion this time and carry your big ass like a backpack." He held up his arm and flexed. "I've been working out, Westie. I could do it."

I grimaced. The idea of putting myself in my brother's care was absolutely terrifying.

"No thanks."

He released a long exhale, his grin slipping. "Eh, it was worth a shot." He snapped his fingers. "I've been meaning to tell you, I won't be in the office this week."

I sat upright, my narrowed eyes focused on my hapless brother. "Why is that?"

He shrugged. "Mom asked me to fly with her to France. I couldn't say no, could I? I already let Renata know. My work is covered. I even sent an email to HR." He brushed off his shoulders. "Come on, you can say it. You're proud of me for being responsible."

The knot in my stomach loosened. I wanted to be angry at him. He certainly knew how to push the boundaries. But he'd taken all the right steps and there was really nothing to be angry about.

"Fine. Next time, give me more warning."

He had a goofy grin on his face again. "If you're jealous, just say that. I know it's tough not being Mom's golden boy."

I remained unaffected by his prodding. I'd heard it one too many times.

"Aren't you leaving?"

"Nah." He settled deeper into the couch. "Think I'll hang out for a while. You won't see me for a whole week, so I'll give you the opportunity to get your fill to tide you over until next time."

Exasperated, I pushed up from the couch and headed toward my bedroom. "I'm going to shower. You can go now. Leave the key on the counter on your way out."

Miles called out to me. "In your dreams!"

He truly had no idea how right he was.

CHAPTER THREE

Elise

THREE WEEKS POST-GHOSTING, POST-MOVE, post–new life, today was the day:

My first day at my new job.

In some ways, things were easier. My new apartment was gorgeous. Of course, there was nothing but the best for Elliot Levy's little sister. That was what his property manager had told me.

Downtown.

Views.

Spacious two bedrooms.

Check, check, check.

Saoirse danced into my bedroom without knocking. But then, we had an open-door policy: as long as our doors were open, either of us was welcome to dance on in. A throwback to our college days. We were picking up where we'd left off as roommates.

When I moved to Chicago three years ago, I never thought I'd be back here, living with Saoirse again. My feelings were still mixed about being back, but living with Saoirse? I wasn't ambivalent in any way. She was my favorite human. I counted myself lucky she was willing to be my roommate one more time.

"Oh, you look good." She circled her finger in the air. "Do a twirl for me, pretty."

Another tradition. Before going out, we'd always hype each other up. The same thing applied for job interviews, dates, first days...

I twirled for her, needing the hype now more than ever, and she wolf-whistled.

"Nice, honey. You look ready to go out and make that bank. Titties are tittying nicely."

I snorted a laugh and cupped my breasts. I'd gone somewhat conservative for my first day. Black cigarette pants, a white V-neck that barely showed a hint of cleavage but did mold around my ample chest, and an oversized, men's style tweed blazer.

"Do I want my titties tittying at the office?"

She arched a brow. "Come on, Lisie. We both know your boobs are always working overtime. They have no choice but to be banging."

She spoke the truth. My breasts entered a room before I did. As much as I tried to downplay it, there was no real way to disguise the roundness of my body. Not that I should have had to, but I'd need some time to get back to where I'd been before the GIF.

When I frowned at my reflection in my floor-length mirror, Saoirse stepped up behind me, wrapping her long arms around my shoulders, and pressed her face next to mine.

Saoirse Kelly was beautiful. Tall and lean, her blonde hair seemed to be permanently lit by the sun. She was the daughter of a California state senator and a Wyoming rancher. There were long, rich legacies on both sides of her family, but meeting her, you'd never know it.

Saoirse was peppy and kind, with a sunshine personality that was more contagious than irritating. We'd met at eighteen in the dorms of CU-Boulder and had immediately clicked. Besides Elliot, she was the person I'd missed most while I'd lived in Chicago.

Having her back in my life full time was more of a relief than I'd thought it would be.

"It's going to be great, Lise. I'll be here when you get home with wine and pizza. I can't wait to hear how impressed everyone was by you."

I smooshed my cheek into hers. "You're only saying that because you love me."

"That's true. But I also know you better than anyone, so my opinion should count the most."

It should, she was right. But that wasn't how it worked. A million compliments could be decimated by one insult.

I was still pretty decimated by the GIF. As much as I didn't want to be. But that had nothing to do with today. Today was about leaving behind the drudgery of Richthink and a career path I'd mistakenly stumbled down and establishing myself as a professional writer.

Elise Levy

Copywriter

Andes, Inc.

My new title was embossed on my freshly made business cards. I wasn't certain I needed them, but when Elliot had handed me a box containing five hundred, I'd gotten butterflies.

"Okay, I believe you." I met her eyes in the mirror. "I think I'm ready to go."

She smiled.

I smiled back.

Here it goes.

Andes, Inc. headquarters stood out from the high-rises around it. At eight stories, it had been built as an environmentalist's dream. A green space and solar panels on the roof, light shelves, and energy efficient window coating, its carbon footprint was lower than any building its size in the state.

I'd read this on the website before my first interview.

I always overprepared myself. It was a Levy trait. Elliot didn't meet anyone without compiling a dossier on them. Of course, he was CEO of a multibillion-dollar company and I was a simple copy-writer—the butterflies were still there just thinking about my new title—so our scales of preparedness were slightly different, but the point remained the same.

I walked into the lobby. Bright light filled the open, four-story foyer surrounded by windows. I was early, so it wasn't crowded, but it wasn't empty either. My heart was in my throat as I strode to the bank of glass-enclosed elevators. Nerves and excitement blended. I'd be fine once I got started. It was the unknown that had me on edge.

The elevator doors slid open, and I stepped in with two other women. Polite smiles were exchanged then they picked up their conversation on fall designs.

"Hold the elevator." A gruff command just outside the sliding doors.

My hand shot out, hitting the open button. I looked up, my breath catching at the man in a fitted suit, crisp white shirt, no tie.

Weston Aldrich stepped into the elevator, his head down, tapping on his phone.

It had been years since I'd seen him.

"Eight," he murmured, turning to face the front.

The women stopped talking, looking at me with expectation, but I was frozen in place. What could they possibly expect from me?

The elevator began to move, and Weston glanced at the panel of numbers closer to him than where I was, slightly behind his right shoulder. Had he wanted me to push his floor for him?

We ascended, and I studied Weston's back. I'd forgotten how much space he took up. Not just from his immense height and the breadth of his shoulders but his presence. He seemed to stretch the air around him.

We stopped on three, and the two women hurried off. Weston reached forward, hitting the eight. The doors closed, leaving us alone. He moved over, almost beside me instead of in front, leaving plenty of space between us. Always considerate like that.

I stared at my shoes. If he noticed me, recognized me, he didn't say a word. That was what I wanted. At least for today.

There was no hope I'd avoid Weston forever. This was his company, after all, *and* he was Elliot's best friend. Even if I managed to get out of socializing with him with my brother, I would be in the same building with him every day.

Day one—we were already sharing an elevator.

We finally arrived on the seventh floor, and in my periphery, Weston raised his head. As I stepped forward, he glanced at me. I held my breath, bracing myself, but he didn't say a word.

As soon as the opening was wide enough for me to fit, I was through the doors, charging forward like I knew exactly where I was going. Fortunately, I ended up at a reception desk, leaving Weston behind.

The receptionist for the creative floor, where I worked, showed me to my desk. There were no cubes at Andes. The entire space was open, some individual desks, some long tables meant for collaborating.

I spent the first part of my day reading through employee manuals, stopping every few minutes to meet new coworkers. I memorized a few of their names, but there were so many new faces, all young, fresh, outdoorsy, they blended together.

When I wasn't reading, I was watching the inner workings of the office out of the corner of my eye. Richthink had been quiet, people staying huddled in their cubes most of the day. Here, people laughed freely. They stopped by each other's desks, spoke, shared computer screens. It was early, but the striking differences made me optimistic about my future here.

Halfway through the day, just as my stomach started to growl, two people approached my desk. I looked up and blinked. A tall, lanky man stood beside a short, button-nosed woman I recognized as the receptionist from earlier. Together, they were strikingly similar to Lani and Brandon.

"Hey, newbie. We're going down to the cafeteria for lunch. Want to join?" The man's accent was half British, half Colorado.

The woman nodded, her curls bouncing. "Please come with us. I'm prepared to gossip about all our coworkers, if that's incentive to you."

With a laugh, I grabbed my purse from where I'd stashed it in my desk. I'd been braced to eat lunch on my own, but this was a much better offer. "That's definitely incentive."

In the elevator down to the first floor, I turned to the Lani and Brandon lookalikes. "I'm really sorry, but I have no idea what your names are. It's just...I met so many people—"

The man turned toward the back wall, attempting to hide his snicker. Lani Two stuck out her hand. We shook.

"I'm Rebecca. That wanker is Simon. Lived in the States since he was seven and still clinging hard to that accent."

Simon, in an Andes pullover and khaki pants, smoothed a hand down his chest. "Don't spill all my secrets, cricket. We're trying to charm the newbie so we're not stuck with just each other at lunch every day."

He winked at me in a way that let me know we were batting for the same team. I was beginning to suspect he and Rebecca really were the Colorado Lani and Brandon.

"Everyone calls me Lise, by the way. I dropped the *E* back in high school."

Rebecca bobbed her head. "Efficient. I like it."

The cafeteria, like the rest of Andes headquarters, was open and bright, with windows from floor to ceiling. I nabbed a veggie burger and sweet potato fries then found a seat with Rebecca and Simon.

Rebecca launched right in. "Okay, basics. I'm married to Sam, high school sweetheart. Simon is single and ready to mingle...with men, in case you were wondering. The best bathroom is on the third floor. The best snacks are in the fifth-floor common area—you just have to avoid Matilda, fifth's receptionist. If she sees you, you'll be stuck talking to her for a solid hour. Ummm...what else?"

She tapped her fingers against her temple. "Oh! You can get Andes clothes at cost from the company store." She gestured to her fitted hoodie and utility skirt. "Before I worked here, I wouldn't have been caught dead dressing like this, but in all honesty, it's incredibly comfortable."

Simon tore his roll apart and dipped a piece in his soup. "Yup. Everyone wears Andes around here. I know we all look like Lemmings, but I swear, once you've been here a little while, you'll *want* to look like Outdoor Barbie."

Rebecca agreed. "It's something in the air."

Weston had started Andes in college. He'd invented a filler for coats that was thin, more environmentally sound than down or cotton, yet trapped heat inside and kept cold out better than anything on the market. Over the last decade, Andes had expanded from coats to an outdoor lifestyle brand with standalone stores all over the world. Even the US winter Olympic team wore Andes. Weston had created something huge, all from an idea he'd had when he was twenty.

Aside from the coat he'd given me when I was still in high school—that I hadn't worn—I'd never owned a piece of Andes clothing. I wasn't planning to start now.

I tugged at the collar of my blazer. "I don't think I'm going to be able to give up business casual. It's too ingrained in me."

Rebecca tipped her kombucha toward me. "I'll be waiting with an 'I told you so' the first time you come to work in a puffer vest."

My nose scrunched. "No. There is absolutely no way I'm adding puff to myself. That won't be happening. I've already got enough going on."

That made them both laugh, but it was true. I'd spent my adult years honing my style. I could do casual, but hoodies and sweats made me look like I'd spent all day on the couch and didn't give a damn about myself. Then again, Andes hoodies were a lot more sleek than the ones I'd owned in the past...

I stopped my train of thought. Had I already been infected by the brainwashing air pumping in through the vents?

"Okay, okay. Enough about clothes." Simon patted his mouth with his napkin. "Let's discuss the real tea—you. Where are you from? Why are you so cute? What did you do before you joined us?"

Rebecca smacked his arm. "We're supposed to be dishing about Andes *then* prying into Lise's personal life. You're going out of order."

He rolled his eyes. "All right, fine. Here are the basics: most people are team players. If they're not, they learn pretty quickly Weston Aldrich doesn't play that game. There was this guy who joined the creative team last year, Dave from Canada—"

Rebecca groaned. "Oh, Dave from Canada, why did you have to give your homeland a bad name?"

"Right? Canadians are supposed to be friendly, then there was Dave. He was a squirrelly fellow, but we're naive little lambs drinking the Andes water, so of course we trusted him. After a brainstorming session with the visual team, Dave trotted up to Weston's office and presented the team's ideas as his."

I sucked in a breath. "Backstabber."

Simon picked up his knife and did a *Psycho* imitation. "Total *reh-reh-reh* screaming-in-horror moment."

"What did Weston do?" I asked.

Rebecca pressed on her freckled cheeks. "It was glorious."

Simon nodded. "He brought Dave back to the creative floor, forced him to tell everyone about *his* brilliant ideas, then gave him the dressing down of a lifetime. I wish I'd recorded it. Dave never showed his Canadian face at the office again."

Rebecca's eyes darted to the side. "Speak of the devil."

I turned—and there was nothing subtle about my movement. Weston Aldrich was walking through the cafeteria, an older woman on one side, a man around his age on the other. As far as I had seen, Weston and the man were the only people wearing suits in the building.

They were in conversation, but Weston paused each time he was greeted, giving nods or exchanging a few words.

"Do people like him?" I asked, my eyes still drinking in the man I first met when I was a little girl.

"He's well respected," Rebecca answered.

"It's hard to really like a man that...untouchable, I guess is the word," Simon added. "I don't mean that in a bad way. He's involved in the company on every level, and he's approachable. It's just that no one really knows him. Well, aside from his assistant, Renata."

Weston suddenly turned his head, as if sensing we were talking about him even though he was too far away to hear our quiet conversation. His searching gaze found mine easily. His eyes scanned from the top of my head down to the table, where my hands were clasped, then returned to my eyes.

My heart was trapped in my throat. I couldn't have looked away if I'd wanted to. Weston Aldrich had grown into a beautiful man, of that, there was no doubt. Then again, I'd thought he was beautiful when I was ten and he was fourteen and he sat with me in my family's den where I'd hidden during my father's Shiva.

His mouth moved, forming one word that made my insides revolt.

"Ellie."

His nickname for me. The one that had caught on—

No. I wasn't going to think about that now. Not with my new coworkers in my new life. I'd left that in the past.

I straightened in my seat, cutting off eye contact with Weston. Rebecca and Simon were both staring at me, their eyes wide.

"What was that?" Rebecca demanded in a gentle, joking way.

"So"—I tucked my hair behind one ear—"my brother and Weston were...well, *are* good friends."

"Oh shite." Simon scrubbed at his mouth. "Did I say anything bad? I don't think I did, but—"

I reached across the table to pat his hand. "Stop, please. I barely know Weston. I promise, I'm not reporting back what you say about him. And no, you didn't say anything bad."

Simon and Rebecca exchanged looks, like they didn't quite know what to believe.

Then Simon started mumbling, "Oh shite, oh shite, oh shite," before perking up into a sunny smile. "Mr. Aldrich."

Rebecca waved at the man standing right behind my left shoulder, his hand gripping the back of my chair.

"Hi, Mr. Aldrich."

"Rebecca, Simon. Having a good lunch?" His voice. I'd forgotten what it had sounded like in person. When I heard him in the background of my phone calls with my brother, distance dulled some of the effect. In person, it was rich and smooth, like the finest morsel of dark chocolate.

Simon blushed as he nodded vigorously. "We are. Rebecca and I are getting to know our newest employee."

"The kombucha is delicious," Rebecca added, her cheeks turning a deep shade of pink that matched Simon's.

"That's good to know." He turned, moving beside me, effectively blocking my view of my lunch mates. I had to tip my head back to see him. He was staring down at me with an impassive expression. "How is your first day?"

These were the first words he'd spoken to me in three years. I remembered the last ones. *"You're making a mistake."* He'd been right, of course, but I'd never admit that to him.

Putting on my best professional smile, I erased the past from my mind. This man was my boss, Elliot's friend—nothing more.

"My day has been really great so far. Simon and Rebecca are the best greeting committee ever." I held up a wilted sweet potato fry. "And these are delicious. I'll have to try the kombucha tomorrow."

From behind Weston, Rebecca let out a little snort.

Weston remained unaffected. But that was him, calm and cool.

"We should get back," I said. "I still have a lot to catch up on."

Weston's heavy stare grew pinched. He was so high up, my neck strained to keep looking at him. Lowering my chin, I grabbed my phone off the table. For a moment, no one moved, then I felt a subtle drag of Weston's knuckles along my shoulder blade. I stiffened at the surprising contact, and his hand fell away in an instant.

"Have a good rest of your day," he said curtly before turning and walking away.

I plastered on a big smile for Simon and Rebecca. "Are you guys ready to go?"

The two of them were my new favorites since they didn't ask any further questions about Weston. Maybe it was obvious from our brief interaction we really didn't have a relationship of any sort.

I really didn't want to think about him anymore.

This was my new job, my new life.

Weston Aldrich was going to be a very, *very* distant part of it.

Chapter Four

Weston

Five days a week, at six a.m., I met Elliot Levy and Luca Rossi at our private gym.

If I wanted to be accurate, and I did, I should have said I met Elliot at that time. Luca making it anywhere when he should have was a crapshoot. Today, he arrived at six fifteen.

"Hello, gentlemen." Luca stopped by Elliot, who was doing leg presses, taking a swipe across his brow. "Working up a sweat already. Very nice."

Elliot grunted. He wasn't a big talker, especially so this early in the morning. Luca made up for his silence, regaling us with tales of his debaucherous nights out. He hadn't changed much since Stanford. Older, somewhat wiser, but still no intention of slowing down.

"How's Elise settling in?" he asked Elliot.

I dropped the dumbbell I'd been using and wiped my face off with my towel, curious about Elliot's answer. My first glimpse of Elise Levy since her going-away dinner three years ago hadn't told me much about her state.

"Fine. She likes her new place." He turned his head, glancing at Luca then me. "Patrick continues to call me. I would block him, except getting to hear his misery gives me a joy I can't seem to part with."

I huffed a dry laugh. "He still has no idea where she is?"

"Well…" Elliot's mouth hitched, "I think he has suspicions she's back in Colorado, but since I have continued to deny knowledge of Elise's very existence, let alone her whereabouts, he's fairly lost."

I stared at him, blinking, in awe of the depths of his duplicity. "You're denying her existence?"

Elliot nodded. "How can I know where she is when I don't have the faintest idea who he's talking about?"

I would have said I was surprised by Elliot's cunning—gaslighting a man into believing his girlfriend of four years was a figment of his own imagination—but I had known him most of my life. There was nothing and no one he cared more about than Elise.

Luca chuckled. "Can I just say how proud I am of your sister? Ghosting that dick is honestly the worst revenge. I wish you'd installed cameras so we could have watched his reaction when he came home and all her things were gone—that's the only thing that would have made this better."

Elliot didn't laugh. "She showed me the screenshots. He deserves every ounce of pain he's feeling."

Elliot refused to share exactly what Patrick had done to drive Elise away, and that was fine. Though I wasn't close with her these days, she was my best friend's sister, so I was naturally protective. And since my investors wouldn't take kindly to me murdering a man, even if he deserved it, it was better I didn't know.

"If he shows, let me know." Luca cracked his knuckles. "I haven't scrapped with anyone in too long. I'm feeling bloodthirsty."

Elliot got up from the leg press and wiped the machine down with his towel. "He won't show. He didn't work for her when he had her, so I'm certain flying across the country is too much effort now that she's gone."

I climbed onto a treadmill. Luca hopped on the one beside me. While Elliot stayed mostly quiet during his workout, Luca liked to engage. I was somewhere in the middle, at least with them. I had no desire or need to have small talk with anyone else. Fortunately the few other people who were here at the same time kept to themselves.

"Yesterday was Elise's first day, right?" Luca asked.

I narrowed my eyes at him. He pushed buttons on the display of his treadmill.

"Why are you asking so many questions about her?"

He turned, his brow pinched. "Why shouldn't I? She's Elliot's sister. I care about him, so by extension, I care about her. Don't you?"

"Of course."

He tilted his head. "Then tell me how the fuck her first day was, West. It's not a trick question, I can promise you that."

I increased the speed on my treadmill. "I saw her once. She seemed to be settling in."

"Seemed to be? Did you ask?"

"I asked her how her day was going when I saw her in the cafeteria."

"Hmmm."

My eyes slid sideways. "What does that sound mean?"

"I don't know." His feet clapped on the belt of his machine. "If she were working for me, I'd like to think I'd take greater pains to welcome her, not leave our meeting to a chance run-in at lunchtime."

"Interesting information. Fortunately for Elise, she doesn't work for you."

Luca's family owned motorcycles. And by that, I meant they owned the company that manufactured the top-selling motorcycle brand in the US. One day, when his father stepped down, he'd take over the business. He rued that day, since it meant he'd have to grow up, be responsible, actually show up at the office daily. For a man who was chaos incarnate, his future was a nightmare for him, so I imagined even attempting to work for him would be equally hellish.

"No doubt. But don't you think you should reach out? Maybe invite her to lunch with you? If you had a sister, Elliot would do that."

We both glanced at Elliot, who'd moved on to leg curls, and laughed. The idea of Elliot Levy going out of his way for anyone but us or Elise was unimaginable. He barely acknowledged I had a brother. I couldn't see him ever taking Miles to lunch.

"Elise...doesn't like me."

I felt him looking at me but kept my eyes straight ahead as I jogged.

"Elise Levy? Elliot's sweet little sister with the big dimple in her right cheek?"

"Left." I cleared my throat.

"Yeah, left cheek." He reached over and backhanded my bicep. "There's no way she doesn't like you. Not that you're immensely likable. You could do with lightening up every once in a while."

"Thank you," I intoned.

"No problem." He slapped me again. "What I'm saying is, Elise is a nice girl who's been through the wringer. If she wasn't overly friendly yesterday, it's probably your fault, not hers. Maybe you could tone down the big, bad, grumpy CEO vibe and invite her to lunch like a guy who's known her since she was a kid."

I smacked the control panel, raising my incline. "I'll consider it."

"Consider it then do it. Elliot will appreciate her having another big brother looking out for his sister."

He would. That was true. If he thought he could get away with bodyguards surrounding his sister, they would have been hired years ago. That wasn't a role I was willing to play. The days when I looked at her as my little sister and she looked back at me like I could do no wrong were long, long gone.

But she was my employee.

I would welcome her to the company like I would anyone else.

It was the least I could do.

⚬

The day started off wrong and had only declined from there. I rubbed my temples after hanging up from a call with one of our suppliers in California. That wasn't something I normally had a hand in, but I had been working with this particular factory since the very beginning and refused to relinquish my personal relationships simply because my company had grown beyond what I'd projected.

But those personal relationships could be a detriment. My supplier seemed to think our business friendship meant he could delay our delivery with a simple apology and a few stuttered excuses.

No.

I let him know that was not acceptable.

We were not friends.

I would find a new supplier if this happened again.

Now, I was rubbing my temples, not understanding why it was difficult for some people to do their jobs. Why bother doing it if it's not done correctly? I couldn't wrap my head around shoddy workmanship in any arena, much less when millions of dollars were at stake.

Renata knocked on my open door. "West."

"Yes?"

"You have a half hour in your schedule. You should grab lunch."

Exhaling, I glanced at my computer screen then back to my assistant. Renata would never dream of cutting corners. That was why she still had a job.

Tapping my forehead, I remembered what I'd promised a few days ago. "Do me a favor and call Ellie. Ask her to join me for lunch."

Renata's brow crinkled. "I have no earthly idea who that is. Is she in your contacts?"

It wasn't like her not to know a name. Even a new one.

"She's our newest employee. She started on Monday. I've been meaning to ask her to join me for lunch all week, but...well, you know..."

She rolled her eyes. Renata was the only person who could get away with that around me—and she knew it.

"You're too busy for your own good. Yes, I know. What I don't know is who Ellie is. The only new employee who started this week is Lise. She works on the creative floor doing copywriting."

My head jerked forward. "Lise?"

"Lise Levy. Is that who you mean?"

Lise. Hmmm. "Yes. She's Elliot's sister. She was always Ellie to me. I suppose times have changed."

Renata didn't move. She stared at me. I blinked back at her. "Yes?"

She folded her arms across her chest. "You didn't mention Mr. Levy's sister was working here. I wonder why."

I glared at her. She didn't flinch. "I don't tell you everything, Renata."

"Yes you do," she scoffed, waving me off. "I'll go call Ms. Levy for you, though it would probably be nice if you did it yourself."

In her sixties, Renata had no-nonsense, short, silver hair and an impudent regard for my authority. Ten years ago, she'd shocked me with her blunt assessments of me and how I did things. Now, I counted on her to tell me the absolute truth, even if it was a blow to my ego.

I wouldn't say she was like a mother. She wasn't warm and cozy enough for that ... and would probably storm out if I ever implied it. Renata was the aunt who came to visit once a quarter, pointed out every one of your flaws, then gave you the building blocks to make yourself better, all while cleaning up your messes.

Needless to say, I would have been lost without her.

She popped her head back in my office. "She said no."

"No?"

There was a fire behind Renata's steely eyes. "Lise Levy said no thank you, she's too busy to stop for lunch. I asked if there was a better time, and she said she'll be busy all day."

My brow dropped heavy over my eyes. "What?"

Renata's thin lips pursed, most likely to hide her merriment. "I don't think Ms. Levy wants to have lunch with you."

What the fuck?

One thing about me: when I made a promise, I stuck with it. Elise may have been too busy to stop working, but she had to eat, and so did I.

Ten minutes later, I arrived on the creative floor, a paper bag of sandwiches specially made for me by the cafeteria in hand. Wandering the floors wasn't uncommon for me, so while people looked up from their desks to nod or greet me, no one ducked for cover or seemed alarmed.

That was how I liked it.

I never wanted to lose that.

Elise was sitting at her desk, headphones on, typing on her keyboard. When I stopped in front of her, it took her a few moments to look up. Her pink lips parted when she realized who was standing there.

She pushed her headphones back. "Weston."

I held up the bag. "I brought lunch. Take twenty minutes to eat with me."

"Um..." She chewed on her bottom lip. "Okay. I can—"

"That's right. You can."

Knowing she had no choice but to follow me, I started for the break area on the opposite side of the floor. Everything was open on this level. There were no walls surrounding the four tables, snack bar, and refrigerator. One table was occupied, the rest free. I sat at the table closest to the windows, away from the other group.

Turning my head, I watched as Elise wove through desks, smiling at her coworkers. It had been a long time since I'd seen her in person and social media only showed so much. She was the same yet entirely different. Words couldn't quite capture the changes.

She slid into the seat across from me, and I took a quick, cursory sweep of her. Unlike most people in the office, she wasn't wearing Andes clothing. Instead, she wore black trousers and a white top with a little black tie around the neck.

Professional.

All of her was. Even her sleek, black hair.

"You cut your hair."

Her lips parted again, and she smoothed a hand over the ends. "Yes. A few months ago."

"Oh." I pushed the paper bag to her side of the table. "Take your pick."

"Um…" She opened the bag and took the sandwiches out one by one. "This is a lot."

"I wasn't sure what you liked. I noticed you were eating vegetarian in the cafeteria, so I ordered meatless and ones with meat."

She selected a sandwich and pushed the others back to my side of the table. "I'm not a vegetarian. Thank you for being so thoughtful."

"Of course. It's not a big deal."

Like always, Elise ate her pickle spear before she did anything else. On her last bite, her mouth pulled down into a frown.

I placed mine on a napkin and slid it to her.

Her brow furrowed. I shrugged. She took the pickle, just like the hundred other times we'd done this dance.

"How are you settling in?" I asked.

"Really well." She took a bite of her sandwich, indicating that was the end of her answer.

"We're not keeping you too busy?"

Swallowing, she wiped her mouth with her napkin. "No. I like what I'm doing. Though there's a lot of work, it's interesting."

"Good. I was concerned since you didn't have time to stop for lunch."

"Oh." Her shoulders lowered. "Did Elliot ask you to do this?"

"Do what?"

She rubbed her lips together, her eyes flitting to the side. "Babysit me? Check to make sure I'm not going off the rails? That kind of thing."

"Actually, no, he didn't. But considering you work here and he's my good friend, I feel somewhat responsible for ensuring you're doing well."

Elise raised her chin. She had always had a cute chin, with a cleft right in the center, like someone had pressed their thumb there and left a print behind. There was something elegant about it now. Elegant and stubborn.

"I'm doing well, which I've told my brother many times. He didn't have to send you to double-check."

"I told you he didn't send me. This was voluntary." I took a sip of water. "I'm relieved to know you like working here."

"I do."

We were so stilted. It hadn't always been this way. I was four years older, so we hadn't been best friends or anything, but up until I left for college, Elise had been something close to a little sister to me. When I came back for Thanksgiving break, she'd barely spoken to me. She'd shut down on me, though I kept caring about her.

"And...how is everything else?" I asked carefully.

She clasped her hands together on the table. Her nails were short and painted baby blue. She'd always kept them painted, usually some shade of blue. A lot had changed, but some things never did.

Lips rolling inward, her long lashes brushed the apples of her cheeks when she lowered her eyelids. "Being back here, for the reasons I came back...it's taking time to adjust to."

That was all she gave me.

Shut down.

She was reminding me of Elliot.

The Levys were experts at blocking out their emotions when they needed to.

"You're unhappy."

She raised her eyes to mine. Mostly brown with generous flecks of green and gold. In the sunlight, they sparkled. This wasn't the first time I'd noticed the captivating color. It had just been years since I'd been close enough to really appreciate them.

"I'm adjusting to being single after four years in a relationship. So sometimes I'm unhappy, but not always. I know I'll be better soon."

I didn't like that answer. "Does Elliot know this?" It came out gruff, but that's how I was feeling.

A tinkling laugh burst out of her. "That I'm unhappy sometimes?"

I nodded.

She tilted her head, and the sun caught in her hair, turning it reflective. Almost too shiny to be anything but glass.

"Well, I haven't explicitly told my brother I'm not always happy, but since he was the one who helped me move and knows what ended my relationship, I think he could guess I'm not sunshine and daisies every minute of the day."

I folded my napkin into a square and tossed it on the table. "He should do something about it."

Another laugh. "It's going to take time. Contrary to what Elliot believes, he doesn't actually control every element of the universe. This is something that has to work itself out."

That answer was unacceptable, but Elise was laughing, so I wouldn't argue with her. Laughter was a lot better than the flat nothing she'd been giving me.

"Renata tells me you go by Lise now."

Again, her pink lips parted. Was I that shocking?

"Yes. Most people call me that. Elliot refuses to change, which isn't surprising, knowing him. Elise or Lise is fine."

"No Ellie?"

Her eyes met mine. There was something there, beneath the surface, but she blinked, and it was gone before I could catch it.

"No. You were the only one who called me that, you know. I haven't gone by that since high school."

She pushed back her chair and gathered the remnants of her sandwich. "Thank you for taking the time out of your day to check on me. You can tell Elliot you did your duty and I'm fine."

I stood too, perplexed at the sudden ending of our lunch. Granted, it hadn't been the most comfortable time of my life, but I hadn't been ready for it to end.

"I told you, Elise, it wasn't my duty. I *wanted* to have lunch with you."

She tucked her thick hair behind her ear. "That was very nice of you, Weston. I appreciate it. I have a lot to get done today, so I'll just—"

I held my arm out. "Of course." She passed me, and I followed her out of the break area. She glanced over her shoulder at me.

"You're coming with me?"

"I'm escorting you to your desk."

"Oh." Turning around, she wobbled on her booted feet, righted herself, and marched the rest of the way to her desk. Then she swiveled around, her cheeks flushed. "Here we are."

"Yes." I picked up her pink headphones. "These are cute."

She took them from me, holding them against her middle. Her shoulder lifted. "I like them."

"Pink's still your favorite color?"

Her chest rose as she sucked in a breath. "I guess it is since I keep buying pink things. I'm surprised you remember that."

"I haven't forgotten a thing about you Elli—Elise."

She glanced at her desk. "Well, thank you for lunch. I should get back to work."

I tucked my hands in my pockets, rocking back on my heels. "I should too. Renata's probably seconds away from sending out a search party."

Given I was ten minutes late for a meeting and had been ignoring Renata's calls, it wasn't an exaggeration.

"I'll see you around, Weston." Elise sat down at her desk, her hand going to her mouse to turn on her computer. "Thanks again."

Dismissed.

Just like that, Elise ended our encounter.

I had a thousand things to do before I went home for the night. I should have been relieved our lunch had been brief and my promise had been fulfilled. But as I rode the elevator up to my floor, Elise's admission of unhappiness clung to my mind.

Problems were like puzzles to me. I had to solve them before I could relax.

If Elise Levy wasn't happy, I would find a way to make her so.

CHAPTER FIVE

Elise

"Ms. Levy!"

The front desk clerk of my apartment building, Terrence, waved me over. "You have a delivery."

"Oh! Okay." I stopped at Terrence's desk as he disappeared through the door behind him.

It was the end of my first week of work. All I wanted was to go upstairs, put on yoga pants, pour a glass of wine, and have a debriefing session with Saoirse. But I could slow my roll for a delivery, especially since I had no idea what it could be. Surprises were my favorite.

Terrence reappeared, carrying a sweet little bouquet of pink flowers. He placed them on the desktop in front of me.

"Here you are, Ms. Levy."

"Oh wow, these are so pretty."

He grinned. "They are. Enjoy them."

I picked up my flowers, telling him to have a nice weekend. By the time I made it up to my apartment, I had checked every place I could for a card. Like the previous three weeks, there wasn't one.

Saoirse spotted the flowers right away when I walked in. "Oooh, another bouquet from your secret admirer?"

I placed them on the kitchen island and laughed. "I'm sure Elliot had his assistant send them to me then forgot he told her to do it. It's a 'welcome back to Colorado, please don't jump off a mountain' gesture."

She swung the spatula she was using to cook around in the air in front of her. "Isn't it more fun to imagine they're from someone other than Elliot?"

I shook my head. "I'm not quite ready to romanticize my life again. My feet are stuck to the ground."

There was also the fact that I hadn't been in this state long enough to have acquired any admirers, secret or not. And if I had one, I wouldn't know what to do with him. The only reason I was functioning like a semi-normal human every day was out of necessity and spite. I wouldn't let my broken heart break the rest of me. When I was ready to one day use my heart again, I needed the rest of me to be whole so I could put myself back together.

She blew out a puff of air. "Fine. Be practical."

I laughed on my way out of the kitchen, retreating to my bedroom. Slipping into yoga pants and a purple hoodie, I mused to myself that I really should stop by the Andes company store so I'd have at least one piece in my wardrobe.

I could hike. I used to love going on hikes. My Chicago life had been a world apart from how I'd grown up. Patrick wasn't very outdoorsy, so I became not very outdoorsy too. But I was getting back to me.

And I needed hiking apparel.

Next week, I'd buy some cute hiking gear from the shop and take myself on a hike.

I still had at least a bottle of wine to drink before I thought about that.

⸺⬥⸺

We were eating the dinner Saoirse had made—chicken fajitas, fresh guac, homemade tortillas—and I was on my second glass of wine in addition to the edible I'd had before dinner.

"Weston made me eat lunch with him today."

Her eyes went wide, and she started coughing, her hands flying up to cover her mouth.

"Oh my god, don't just blurt things out like that when I'm chewing," she admonished. "Give a girl a chance to swallow."

Our eyes met, and because we both had a twelve-year-old boy inside us, we snickered.

Saoirse wiped her mouth. "Okay, tell me everything."

I shrugged. "His assistant asked me to join him for lunch, I politely declined, so he brought lunch to me."

She sucked in a sharp breath. "You politely declined."

"Yes. I knew it would be awkward, and he was only asking out of obligation, so I tried to pass to save us both. But, of course, he's stubborn and egotistical, just like Elliot, so he had to have his way."

"Or maybe he wanted to have lunch with you."

I picked up my wineglass, swirling the amber liquid around. "I doubt it. Anyway, it was strange and uncomfortable. I'm almost certain he felt the same way too. Hopefully that will be the last time we put ourselves through that."

She put down her loaded tortilla. "How did he look?"

I rolled my eyes.

Saoirse cackled. "*That* good, huh?"

Admitting defeat, I nodded. "He's more beautiful than he ever was. It's sick."

Weston had the immaculately dressed, artfully scruffy tousled-hair thing down to a science. He walked the line of high-powered CEO and sexy outdoorsman. He had always been handsome. Strikingly so. But as he'd gotten older, his attractiveness had been honed to something hard to look at straight on.

Saoirse sputtered. "Sick? You're crazy, Lise. If he insists on being in your face, enjoy the view."

"I told you, he's not going to be around. He did his good deed, which I can admit was very nice of him, but I'm sure I won't see much of him anymore."

◆

Saoirse and I made the most of the weekend. We'd gone to a farmers' market, loitered at a coffee shop for a few hours, then hit a pub with a few of our college friends Saturday night. Sunday, we did an easy hike and lazed about. It was perfection.

Monday started filled with optimism—until I got to the elevator bank and a familiar face was waiting there.

Not Weston.

Worse.

Miles.

The elevator came. I didn't move. He stepped on, and when he turned and faced the doors, his eyes lit on me. With recognition?

It was hard to tell. I hadn't moved, and since there was no one else around, it was even more obvious I was resisting boarding the elevator with him.

He grinned and beckoned me with his hand. "Come on. I don't bite."

Oh jeez.

Trapped, I got on.

The seven was already lit up.

Oh no.

"What floor?" he asked.

"Um. Seven."

He swiveled around, taking me in. His fingers snapped. "Are you kidding me? Ellie Levy?"

I forced a smile. "Hi, Miles."

I barely got his name out before he was hugging me tight. My arms stayed limp at my sides, but he kept on hugging. If I wasn't mistaken, he was sniffing my hair too. His nose was definitely firmly buried somewhere behind my ear.

Finally, he pulled back, cupping my upper arms.

"What in the world are you doing on this elevator with me, Ellie Levy?"

Miles was a less refined version of Weston. Still as handsome as the devil, but where Weston was chiseled, Miles was more roughly hewn. If he'd been born in the eighteen-hundreds, he could have easily slid into the role of a cowboy, bandanna, fancy hat and all. These days, he reminded me of an overgrown frat boy, which he probably was.

My eyes darted to the climbing numbers. "It's Elise or Lise, please. And I work here now. On seven."

His hands squeezed my arms. "What the hell? Does Westie know about this?"

I breathed out a laugh. "Of course he does."

Miles let go of one of my arms to smack his forehead but quickly returned to hold me again. "What am I even saying? Westie knows all. He just forgot to mention one of my best girls was going to be working on the same floor as me. That troublemaker. He probably wanted me to return from Paris to a surprise."

The elevator doors slid open. Miles slipped his arm around my shoulders, pulling me out with him. If he hadn't, I probably would have stayed all day, riding up and down between the floors aimlessly.

"What brought you back to Colorado, Ellie?"

"It's Elise or Lise," I answered rotely.

"Oh, right. Sorry. It'll take me some time to get that through my thick skull."

My mouth quivered. "Please try."

"I will. Scout's honor. Now, answer the question. Tell me everything that's happened to you since high school."

When we neared my desk, I managed to duck under his arm and spin away from him, putting the desk between us. His jaw dropped. I supposed I *had* moved quickly.

"This is me." I curled my fingers around the edge of the desk. "I have a lot to do, so…"

His dark-blond brow winged. "Unfortunately for both of us, my desk is all the way across the space." He wagged a finger at me. "Don't think I didn't notice you dodging my questions, Elise."

His eyes rounded on my name, making sure I noticed he'd gotten it right that time.

Sucking in a breath, I decided to answer him now rather than revisit this conversation later. Hopefully, he'd move on to someone more interesting.

"I moved back to be closer to Elliot. Plus, my job in Chicago wasn't what I wanted to be doing. So, here I am. There isn't much to tell about my post–high school years, honestly. College, work, that kind of thing. Probably the same as you."

He winked at me. "I have a feeling you're holding out on me. Let's have lunch and catch up."

What was it with these Aldrich men and insisting on having lunch with me? Jeez.

"Actually, I have plans. We'll catch up another time."

He shoveled his fingers through his overgrown hair. "I'm holding you to that, Lisie." He cocked his head. "Actually, I like Lisie better than Ellie. It's going to stick. I feel it."

Miles wandered away without a goodbye, and I collapsed into my chair. So much for my Monday morning optimism. Working with one Aldrich brother had been trying. Two? I wasn't certain it was going to be possible.

CHAPTER SIX

Elise

AFTER ONE WEEK AT Andes, my lunch dates with Rebecca and Simon had become an unspoken given. I'd slotted in with them easily. They were gossips but not malicious, which made them fun to be around.

My phone vibrated as we were finishing up. I checked, finding a text from Lani.

Patrick caught me as I was walking into the building this morning. He looks terrible. I laughed in his face then told him I had no idea who Elise was, never heard of her, and he should probably seek help. Did I do good?

Tears sprung to my eyes, and I quickly blinked them back. I didn't even know what they were about. Obviously, I wasn't over the way my relationship had ended. Did I care that Patrick looked terrible? A little. But the spiteful monster that apparently lived inside me enjoyed my brother and friends stonewalling him so completely.

I texted her back.

You did amazing, friend. Thank you for having my back, as always.

I pushed thoughts of Chicago aside as we rode the elevator back up to seven. Simon and I split off from Rebecca, leaving her at reception. Nearing my desk, I almost tripped over my feet at the sight of Weston Aldrich working at the long collaboration table nearby.

"Oh yeah, he likes to work on all the floors," Simon murmured. "He's a man of the people, you know?"

I snorted. Simon was sarcastic but not derisive. From what I'd gathered over the past week, Weston was generally liked, but more than that, he was well respected. I suspected Simon might have a tiny crush, but that was understandable.

"Really?" I whispered.

"I think that's the vibe he's going for. It keeps us on our toes, that's for sure."

Weston lifted his eyes from his screen, catching me staring. His lips curved at the corners, and he nodded. I barely managed to nod back, but he continued to watch me walk to my desk.

He was in my periphery when I sat down. My stomach plummeted. How was I going to do my work with him right there?

The next time I glanced his way, his attention was back to his computer.

I shifted the few papers on my work surface around and something yellow caught my eye. A Post-it had been stuck between two printouts. Brow pinching, I read the neatly printed words:

When elephants are stressed or having hard times, they hug and comfort one another by putting their trunks in each other's mouths.
Miles.
This had to be from Miles.
His sense of humor obviously hadn't matured since high school.

I tucked the Post-it in one of my drawers, ignoring the swirl of nausea in my stomach and knot of hurt in my chest. The four years Miles spent teasing and bullying me during school, I'd learned if I ignored him, he'd move on. For a while, at least. A reaction was exactly what he wanted, and he wouldn't be getting that from me.

My guard was down when I arrived at my desk on Tuesday.

Stupid.

I should have known better when Miles was involved.

Baby elephants suck their trunks like baby humans suck their thumbs.

When they get mad, they throw tantrums.

I tucked that one on top of the other one. Waves weren't my thing, but I'd come from an office where making waves meant drowning under them. I could safely take these Post-its to HR here, surely, but then what? Miles was Weston's brother. He wasn't going to be fired, probably not even reprimanded. Not that I wanted him fired. I simply wanted him to forget I existed.

I sucked up my anger. There was nothing I could do today, and there was too much work to be done to spend time thinking about Miles Aldrich and his immature antics.

After lunch, I went to my first creative department meeting. Weston attended, but he didn't lead. He sat on the side of the room, his tablet in his lap, seemingly taking notes as the heads of each team spoke.

Andes put out a quarterly catalog that was more like a magazine. In an age where most things had gone digital, the Andes catalog was something consumers regularly requested to have sent to them in the mail. Not only were the photographs beautiful, the short articles never failed to be interesting. I was guilty of being one of the hundreds of thousands of people who read it cover to cover.

When my editor, Salma, spoke about the topics of the articles planned for the next edition, Weston interrupted her with a wave of his hand.

"I'll be visiting some of our factories in California in a few weeks. Let's do a write-up of that. You choose the angle." He scribbled on his tablet like now that he'd spoken, it was a done deal.

Salma's brow dropped. "That's a great idea, Weston. The thing is, it's been decided for months we're focusing on lifestyle."

He cocked his head. "I understand. As I said, you choose the angle."

He put a period at the end of his sentence that was so firm it was almost audible. Salma, a woman in her forties who carried an air of having her shit together, seemed flustered by Weston's abrupt demand. He wasn't cruel about it, but he wasn't leaving this topic open for discussion.

Salma's fingers worked the screen of her tablet up and down, up and down. "I don't see how we can fit in a story about a factory—"

I cleared my throat, crossing my fingers my interruption would be appreciated. "What if we interview factory workers who wear Andes on their off days? The audience might be interested in how the people who make their coats and hiking gear use those products in their everyday life."

Weston's expression started out annoyed with Salma's reticence, but as I spoke, he slowly slipped into a half smile. Salma wasn't shooting death glares at me like Dick the dick would have been. She was nodding, glancing from Weston and back to me.

"Actually, that would be fresh." She tapped her stylus on her chin. "Why don't you take that, Elise?"

From across the room, Miles started a slow clap. He looked around, but no one joined him, which didn't seem to affect him in any way.

"Nice job, Lisie."

Weston gave his brother a sharp look. Miles grinned at him, unfazed, but at least he stopped clapping.

"You'll travel with me to California," Weston clipped at me. "Renata will send you the details."

My lungs squeezed in my chest. When I spoke up, I hadn't imagined I'd be given the assignment. I'd only just started here, and now I'd be traveling?

That was...

Better than I could have expected.

All the more reason to ignore the Post-its.

Except they weren't so easy to ignore. Wednesday and Thursday were more of the same. Seemingly harmless facts about elephants scrawled on yellow Post-its.

Fifteen years ago, these little notes would have made me smile.

Now, they brought back really crappy memories.

I spilled everything to Simon and Rebecca at lunch on Friday.

"Can I tell you guys something?" I asked.

They stopped eating, their attention immediately rapt.

Simon swiveled his wrist. "Please do."

I sucked in a breath. "It has to remain between us, though."

Rebecca mimed zipping her lips. "As long as I can tell Sam, I'm a vault."

That made me laugh a little. "Spousal privilege. I'll accept that."

Simon lifted his shoulders and held his hands out. "The only people I gossip with are you two. I'm not going to tell anyone. You can trust me, Lise."

I wanted to be able to trust these two. My confidence had been shaken by Patrick and his buddies, who I had considered my friends as well, but I wouldn't allow what they'd done to keep me from forming bonds with other people. Simon and Rebecca struck me as straightforward and no bullshit. They were my allies at Andes, and right now, I needed them.

"Miles Aldrich and I went to school together. We weren't friends, but we were in the same grade, so I've known him forever. He was always just...there. I never paid attention to him. But then we got to high school and everything changed. He teased and taunted me and riled the other kids up to join in."

Rebecca and Simon's expressions had gone from interested to horrified.

"That little twerp," Rebecca ground out. "He bullied you?"

I lifted a shoulder. "I don't know if I'd call it that. He started something and it grew like a wildfire." Tucking my hair behind my ear, I swallowed down the lump in my throat. "When I was little, I was kind of obsessed with elephants. So much, Weston used to call me Ellie. I loved it back then because it was special between us, you know? But I guess he told Miles about it, and when he started calling me Ellie the Elephant in high school...well, it wasn't so cute."

Thick thighs and big butts hadn't been in style back then—there'd been no chance of escaping school without being teased. Having it come from Weston's brother while using his special name for me had been a unique kind of betrayal that had knocked me to my knees.

Simon's expression turned thunderous. "What an idiot. As someone who was relentlessly bullied in school, I'm taking this really personally, Lise. I'd go homicidal if I had to work with any of those guys. I don't know how you're doing it."

"I didn't know he worked here when I accepted the job."

Rebecca winced. "Yeah, I can see how that might have affected your decision."

"I wouldn't have taken it." I rubbed my lips together. "I haven't been thinking about him all these years, you know? And when I realized we'd be coworkers when we shared an elevator on Monday, I was prepared to suck it up. It's been eight years since high school. I've matured and moved on. I was hoping he had too. But…"

Simon angled forward, his eyes narrowed into slits. "What did he do?"

I blew out a slow breath. I absolutely hated this. "All week, someone has been leaving Post-its with elephant facts on my desk. They're anonymous, but it has to be Miles. It really couldn't be anyone else."

Rebecca and Simon exchanged angry looks with each other. Simon fisted his knife. Rebecca's cute face was glowing red.

"That asshole. You should tell Weston," Rebecca said.

Simon nodded. "Put that little shite on blast. No one deserves to be harassed at work—and that's what that is."

I cupped my forehead, looking up at them from under my lashes. "I don't want him to be fired, I just want him to leave me alone. And if I don't react, maybe he will. He eventually stopped in high school, so maybe…"

"I get that." Rebecca reached across the table to squeeze my forearm. "The situation has all kinds of layers that make it complicated. The bottom line is: you should be safe and comfortable at work. If Miles isn't capable of allowing you that, his stupid ass needs to get the boot."

Simon nodded. "I'll back you up, whatever you decide to do. If you want me to go with you to talk to HR, I'm there."

"Me too," chimed Rebecca.

Feeling ten times lighter, I grasped some of the optimism I'd started the week with. But the moment I arrived back at my desk and spotted the small yellow square stuck to the front of my drawer, all of it evaporated.

Done.

I was done.

This was not how professionals behaved.

I wasn't going to tattle on Miles. We were going to have a long-overdue conversation.

Yanking open the drawer, I plucked out the other Post-its and strode to Miles's desk, the stack clutched in my hand. When I approached, his brows lifted.

"Hey, Lisie." His grin faltered at my expression. "What's up?"

I waved the Post-its. "Can we speak in private, please?"

I'd let him get away with this behavior in school. Never once had I confronted him, fearing I'd only add fuel to his inexplicable fire. But I was an adult. Letting things like this slide wasn't something I could do.

"Uh"—he pushed back from his desk, rising to his feet—"sure. There aren't a lot of places that are private around here."

I nodded toward the stairwell. "There will do. This won't take long."

"Oh. Okay." He seemed perplexed, but he shouldn't have been. He was being a deliberate asshole to me. He should have expected to be confronted.

When we were both on the stairwell landing, the door firmly shut behind us, I held up the stack of Post-its.

"This stops now or I'm going to HR."

Any trace of humor slipped from Miles's expression. He held his hands up, palms out. "Whoa, whoa. What's going on?"

"Don't, Miles. We both know what you've been doing. It's insulting for you to play dumb."

He scratched the side of his head. "I'm not playing dumb, Elise. In this case, I'm actually dumb. I have no idea what you're talking about."

I stared hard at him. "Ellie the Elephant." Then I picked up his hand and slapped the notes on his palm.

He frowned, looking from me to the Post-its, reading the elephant facts one by one. When he finished, he handed them back to me.

"I can see why you would think these are from me, but they're not."

My fingers curled around the slips of paper. "I don't believe you, Miles, but whether you admit it doesn't matter. I'm asking you to stop so I don't have to escalate this. This isn't high school. I won't put up with this treatment."

He reached for me then seemed to think better of it at the last moment and dropped his hand.

"Elise, come on. I barely even remember the whole elephant thing from when we were kids. Do you honestly think I'm going to be looking up elephant facts to…what? Torment you? I'm happy you're here. I have no reason to torment you."

I blinked at him, gutted by his dismal recollection of some of the worst years of my life. He wasn't exactly shrugging his shoulders, but it felt that way. "You don't remember what you did to me?"

He cocked his head, studying my face. "Well, I'm not going to deny I was an idiot back then. I did anything for a laugh and probably hurt your feelings. For that, I'm sorry."

Probably? This wasn't the confrontation I'd dreamed about as a teen. But it was Miles. I should have predicted he wouldn't drop down and beg for forgiveness.

"Miles, *you* come on. You did a lot more than hurt my feelings. You can at least acknowledge you spent four years with a very specific agenda. You wanted me as uncomfortable as possible. And you succeeded."

His brow furrowed, and he cupped the back of his neck, seeming genuinely worried. "I told you I'm sorry. I can't take it back. What else can I do?"

"Stop leaving notes on my desk!"

He threw his arms out. "I'm not! I swear on my dick, they're not from me. You want to fingerprint me? Do a handwriting analysis? Game on, Lisie. I'm innocent."

I sputtered. "You're not innocent."

His arms fell heavily to his sides. Contrition weighed down his features. "No, I was a bad guy to you a long time ago, and now I see I did more damage than I ever cared to acknowledge. Lisie, for that, I swear, from the bottom of my heart, I'm sorry, but I didn't leave those notes."

"Well…"

I was stumped. I believed he'd locked away the things he'd done to me to keep the weight of remorse away all these years.

So, I had a choice to make. I'd gotten my apology from Miles. It wasn't the pretty package of soul-deep regret and pleas for forgiveness I'd wanted back then, but it was something. Probably as good as I'd get from Miles.

"Look, I know it's really crappy to hear, but until you just brought it up, I had completely forgotten about the elephant thing. When I see you, I see my old classmate, Elise, who turned into a pretty woman I now work with. I have no reason or desire to hurt you. It's easy for me to say I let all that stuff go a long time ago, but it's true."

There was no guile behind his pleading eyes. Miles wasn't trying to pretty up our past or sell me lies about living with regret for years. He'd done something bad to me and moved on from it.

It hurt.

But it was believable.

My grudge against Miles Aldrich was so long held, it would be difficult to let it go. But maybe I could.

"Lisie." Miles came for me, moving in slow motion so I could dodge him if I wanted to, but I didn't move away. He wrapped me up in a hug, and after a moment, I hugged him back. "I'm really sorry I hurt you," he murmured.

In my mind, I was stomping and yelling, demanding to know why he treated me that way, scratching and clawing so he would feel the same pain he'd inflicted on me.

But where would that get us?

Miles Aldrich was standing here, hugging me, earnestly apologizing, and I believed him to be sincere.

"I forgive you," I whispered, and it was a relief to mean that.

He lifted his head and pulled back slightly. "Yeah?" His green eyes were alight with mischief. "For real? Did we just become best friends?"

With a breathy laugh, I shoved him away from me. "Don't push it."

"Fine, fine. One day, you and me, Lisie, we're going to be besties." He patted his chest. "I'll earn it, though."

He opened the stairwell door for me, allowing me to walk ahead of him, then stopped me by grabbing my wrist.

"Do you want me to find out who's been leaving the notes?" he asked quietly.

"Um..." I glanced around, but no one was paying attention to us. No one except Weston. Standing beside the collaboration table on the other side of the room, he watched us through narrowed eyes. "No. I think I know who left them since you didn't. I don't know why but—"

He grimaced. "Westie, huh?"

I nodded. "It kind of has to be him."

He rubbed his scruffy jaw with two fingers. "Westie wouldn't do anything to hurt your feelings. I don't know why the hell he'd be leaving you elephant facts, but I guarantee his intentions aren't malicious."

"I don't know." I shrugged, suddenly wishing it was the end of the day. There were still hours to go. "Look, I have a lot to do—"

"Yeah. Me too. I'm glad we cleared the air, though."

I tipped my chin. "I am too."

Weston had taken a seat but was still watching as I strode back to my desk. Sitting down, I opened up my email, composing a new one.

To: westonaldrich@andesinc.com

From: eliselevy@andesinc.com

Dear Mr. Aldrich,

Please refrain from leaving any more elephant facts on my desk from now on.

Sincerely,

Elise Levy

CHAPTER SEVEN

Weston

My fingers hovered over the keyboard.

I shouldn't have been on seven.

My to-do list for the day was longer than my arm.

I'd rescheduled a call.

Renata was going to murder me soon.

I'd wanted to see her reaction. If the note had made her smile. Instead, I witnessed what looked to be a special moment between her and Miles *then* received a terse email.

I wrote back.

⁂

To: eliselevy@andesinc.com

From: westonaldrich@andesinc.com

Dear Ms. Levy,

Please refrain from calling me Mr. Aldrich. That's my father.

Do you hate elephants now?

Curiously,

Weston

—◆—

It didn't take long for me to receive a reply.

To: westonaldrich@andesinc.com

From: eliselevy@andesinc.com

Dear Mr. Aldrich,

I don't hate elephants. Only a sociopath would hate them. I'd simply rather not receive Post-its with facts on them anymore. Isn't that a waste of company resources?

Indifferently,

Elise

—◆—

I growled to myself. Elise was fifteen feet from me, typing away on her computer like I wasn't in the room. She'd spent years ignoring my existence from afar, but up close was harder to deal with.

—◆—

To: eliselevy@andesinc.com

From: westonaldrich@andesinc.com

Dear Ms. Levy,

Is it the Post-its that offend you or the elephant facts?

Please note I requested you not address me as Mr. Aldrich. I'm neither a stranger nor old enough for it to be required.

Thoughtfully,

Weston

———◆◇◆———

She stopped typing and used her mouse to click on my email. It only took a second for her lips to purse and her forehead to crinkle. Then she started typing again, and a thrill shot up my spine, anticipating what she would send next.

———◆◇◆———

To: westonaldrich@andesinc.com
  From: eliselevy@andesinc.com
  Dear Boss,
  The only thing I'm offended by are the trees being chopped down to make the Post-its you wasted.
  Do your investors know all the time you spend googling elephants?
  I have a lot of work to finish. If that's all...
  Busily,
  Elise

———◆◇◆———

I tapped out my reply, vowing it was the last one. I had to retreat to my office to get actual work done. There was no chance it would be happening here, where distractions abounded.

———◆◇◆———

To: eliselevy@andesinc.com

From: westonaldrich@andesinc.com

Dear Elise,

Please note my objection to being addressed simply as "Boss." You could be addressing anyone, as it is not specific to me.

You'll be pleased to know all the paper used at Andes, Inc. is 100% recycled. No trees were harmed in the writing of said Post-its.

Environmentally,

Weston

Elise continued typing for several minutes. The entire time, my eyes flicked from her to my screen. I nearly gave up and retreated to my office when my email notification lit up.

I clicked on her message.

To: westonaldrich@andesinc.com

From: eliselevy@andesinc.com

Dear Grumpy Boss,

Is that better? Anyone reading this would know I was addressing you.

I am extremely relieved for the trees. Still, the Post-its are un-necessary. Ages 10-13, I spent studying elephants and have retained everything I learned.

Expertly,

Elise

I bit my lip to hold back a laugh. *Grumpy Boss*. Only her. She told me once I was Elliot's grumpiest friend. It hadn't seemed like an insult, merely an observation.

To: eliselevy@andesinc.com

From: westonaldrich@andesinc.com

Dear Elise,

I'll inform human resources of the change in my name. It may cause some confusion, but in the end, cutting to the chase will be much more efficient.

On a different *note*, what did you have to discuss with my brother in the stairwell?

Notably,

Weston

To: westonaldrich@andesinc.com

From: eliselevy@andesinc.com

Dear Grumpy Boss,

Can you also report to HR that my boss is prohibiting me from getting my work done? If you send your name change and my complaint in one email, your efficiency level will rise exponentially.

That is between Miles, the stairwell, and me.

Have a good day.
Conclusively,
Elise

Though Elise was done with this interaction, I still wanted an answer. I started to formulate a reply when Renata sent me a message through the internal system.

You have a call in five minutes. If you're not up here to take it, I'm officially taking over your position. I'll have you know, I've always thought Andes should start using more polyester. Like leisure suits. That will be my first decision as CEO. Disco wear.

I grimaced at her threat and shut down my laptop. I'd played around enough. I was responsible for too many livelihoods to loiter on the seventh floor, waiting for a glimpse of a smile from a girl who could barely deign to acknowledge me.

It was six on a Friday. Most of the staff had left for the weekend. I was sitting at my desk, catching up on work I'd neglected the past two weeks.

Distracted.

That didn't happen often.

In fact, my single-mindedness had ended several of my relationships, including one with a woman I had almost gotten engaged to. Women had told me even when I was with them, I was at work. My focus would stray. The truth was, when it came down to it, Andes had always been more important to me. They had been right to leave me.

Yet, here I sat, mountains of responsibilities, and I wasn't even attempting to take any of it on. While I should have been returning calls and going over a cost analysis report, I was watching a recording of the security feed of the seventh-floor stairwell.

No sound.

I could only imagine what Elise and Miles were saying to each other. Intense. Emotional. Miles looked serious for once in his life. Elise passionate.

I'd watched it several times, and it always ended the same: him hugging her, her melting into him and hugging him back.

There was no possible way they were a couple.

But why not? They were the same age. Elise was beautiful. Miles...well, he had his charms which seemed to land him women by the droves. Why wouldn't they be interested in each other?

Disgusted at myself, I hit the keyboard.

The recording started over.

I watched it again.

CHAPTER EIGHT

Elise

ELLIOT WAS GOING TO murder me. He hated when anyone ran late. Fortunately, my brother loved me and would forgive me...after he eviscerated me. It was the eviscerating part I wanted to skip.

Brunch wasn't supposed to be stressful.

But when I arrived at the restaurant, Elliot wasn't alone, nor did he look angry. He was laughing at something his friend, Luca Rossi, said. I approached the table, tentatively smiling, and they both rose. Elliot gave me a quick hug and a kiss on the cheek. Luca grabbed me in his arms, dipped me back in a purely dramatic fashion, then pulled me up to kiss my forehead.

"Bellissima!" He smoothed his palm down the crown of my head, beaming at me. "It's been too long. I'm offended you've been back in Denver for weeks and this is the first I'm seeing you. I had to beg Elliot to let me come along today."

Luca Rossi was one-hundred-percent bullshit. But he was charming and made me laugh, so I let him get away with it.

That was a thing for him: women letting his caddish behavior slide. Along with the charm, he was devastatingly handsome, his

Italian roots coming out in his sleek, ebony hair, golden complexion, and intense brown eyes. Add in his height and gym-refined body, and Luca made panties drop wherever he went.

It was impossible not to flirt with him. From the moment he came home with Elliot on a break from Stanford, we'd fallen into a teasing kind of friendship. We both knew it was harmless, but it drove Elliot mad.

All the more reason to do it.

"And I'm offended I've been back for weeks and you haven't even called me," I shot back as I took my seat.

Luca grabbed my hand, rubbed his thumb over my knuckles, and gave me puppy-dog eyes.

"I would have, my sweet Elise, if your selfish brother had given me your new phone number. He actually told me if I wanted it, I'd have to do the work to find it myself. Can you believe that?"

Elliot rolled his eyes. "Get your hand off my sister."

With a smirk, Luca lifted my hand to his mouth, giving it an over-the-top, noisy kiss.

"Elise, tell Elliot to stop interfering with our relationship," Luca pleaded.

I lifted Luca's hand to my mouth and gave him the same kind of kiss. "Elliot, stop interfering. Don't you want Luca as a brother-in-law?"

Elliot's upper lip curled in disgust. "Why would you even joke about that? Now I've lost my appetite."

The fourth chair at the table was suddenly pulled out, and Weston Aldrich folded himself into the seat.

"Sorry." He placed his phone face down on the table and turned his head to greet me. "Hello, Elise."

"Oh. Hi. I didn't know you would be here."

Dear god, my cheeks were on fire. I let my hair fall forward, hopeful it would cover up some of my embarrassment. I'd been so brazen yesterday, emailing him all sorts of snarky remarks. It had been easy from behind a screen. Facing him again was a whole other ballgame. If I'd known, I might have changed out of my hiking gear. The leggings and long-sleeve T-shirt weren't exactly my best look.

Elliot cleared his throat. "Neither of them was invited. At the gym this morning, I mentioned I would be having a quiet brunch with my sister and they glommed on."

Luca lifted his glass. "I never turn down bottomless mimosas."

Weston opened his hands. "I couldn't be left out, could I? I would have been utterly grumpy."

Dear. Freaking. God.

Why?

If it had been possible to douse myself in water and melt into a puddle like the Wicked Witch of the West, I would have. Weston, Elliot, and Luca would have been left gawking at the pile of clothing and gelatinous goo in my chair, but I would have been dearly departed, away from this awful moment.

Luca guffawed. "Like you're not always grumpy." He grabbed my hand again. "Anyway, you interrupted our discussion. Elliot objects to taking me on as a brother-in-law. Can you believe that shit? I'm offended."

Weston cocked his head. "Wouldn't you have to win Elise over first? Actually, you might want to stop sleeping with any woman who's sentient before you do that. An STI test would be a good next step. I don't know, it seems like you're putting the cart well before the horse."

There was something harsh in Weston's tone and mocking in his smirk. In all the years I'd known him, or watched him from a distance, I'd never seen him with an expression like that, much less directed at his good friend.

Luca kept my hand in his, but his humor fell away. "That's a low blow, West. What crawled up your ass?"

I glared at Weston. His smirk had fallen flat. "That was unnecessary," I admonished.

His eyes landed on me. "It's unnecessary for Luca to shamelessly flirt with you when it obviously makes Elliot uncomfortable."

Elliot lifted his coffee to his mouth. "Speak for yourself, West. Although the idea of my sister succumbing to Luca's flagrant advances is repellant, I do have a sense of humor. They've been playing at this same joke for years. I'm not worried about my friends going after my sister. We all know she's a no-go zone."

I rolled my eyes. "I didn't realize I was a zone. I was under the silly impression I was a woman who could make my own decisions."

Elliot put his cup down, his movements casual and easy. "You can. I trust that you find the idea of succumbing to Luca as repellant as I do."

I snorted, goading him a little more. "I don't know…" I lifted Luca's hand to my cheek, pressing it there, "Luca's looking awfully good today, and I'm single now. It might be our time."

Luca shot me a wink. "Is it? Jesus, Elise. Give a guy some warning. I haven't had the chance to have a full-body wax." He gestured to his T-shirt and jeans. "I'm basically a human sweater under my clothes."

I bit my bottom lip and let my lashes flutter. "Oh, keep talking, you filthy, fuzzy bear."

Our waitress stopped at our table, taking our orders, and I climbed aboard the bottomless mimosa train with Luca. Based on Weston's permanent scowl, I was going to need to drink to get through this brunch without snapping at him.

Must not tell grumpy boss he's a dick.

Elliot leaned forward, his elbows on the table. "Don't think I didn't notice you were late. What were you doing this morning?"

"Saoirse and I were supposed to go on a sunrise hike this morning, but she was too hungover to get out of bed."

Weston let out a low growl. "You went out alone before sunrise?"

"No." I shook my head. "I'm late because I waited until it was daylight to go on the hike and misjudged how long it would take to get here. And honestly, Elliot, I was ten minutes late. Is that really a crime?"

If I'd told them my Uber driver had taken the long way and driven fifteen miles under the speed limit, all while turning around in his seat to speak to me, he probably would have found a way to block my account so I could never order another rideshare.

Which was why I wasn't going to mention it.

I wanted to continue being able to drink bottomless mimosas and not worry about driving my tipsy self home.

Elliot raised his chin. "It's not a punishable crime, unfortunately. You know how I feel about prioritizing commitments." His fingers steepled. "West raises a good point, though. You went hiking alone?"

"In the daylight," I replied.

Weston angled his body toward mine. "By yourself."

"Yes." The weight of their glares had me sinking in my chair. "It's a busy trail, though. I passed people every few minutes. Plus, I had my phone and bear spray. I wasn't being stupid."

"You're a young, pretty woman. You can't go on hikes alone," Elliot said with a sense of finality.

"Thank you for saying I'm pretty. However, I lived in Chicago for three years. I'm not some naive little lamb taking myself out for slaughter. I made sure I was on a safe trail and Saoirse knew where I was."

"It's an unnecessary risk," Weston added.

"Do you go on hikes alone?" I challenged.

"Of course. But since you're not naive, you know it's different, as maddening as that is. You shouldn't be anywhere secluded by yourself."

I frowned at Weston, hating that he was right about the state of the world, but I'd taken precautions and kept my wits about me. I wasn't arguing to be stubborn. They were simply wrong.

"I think we'll have to agree to disagree."

"I don't love it, *bella*," Luca added soothingly.

I winged an eyebrow at him. "*Et tu, Brute*?"

"We want our Elise to be safe."

I rolled my eyes, though I couldn't help smiling at him. His friends could really take some lessons from him on bedside manner.

Fortunately, our food was delivered, putting a pause to them ganging up on me. And since they were three large men who'd undoubtedly put in some hard work at the gym this morning, they dove into their food, letting the topic slip away.

When they emerged from their scraped-clean plates, conversation focused on Elliot's forthcoming trip to Dubai to visit a property his company was considering investing in. He hadn't traveled in the month since I'd moved back, and I suspected that was purposeful.

He'd been keeping an eye out for me, and I supposed he'd decided I was steady enough to leave for a week.

The men grappled over who would get the check, Weston being the most adamant. I didn't bother trying. Not that I couldn't have snuck in and beaten all of them, but all three would have held a grudge forever if I'd paid for them. It was not worth the trouble.

It was raining by the time we were ready to leave. We lingered under the restaurant awning, saying our goodbyes.

I took out my phone to order an Uber. Weston watched over my shoulder.

"You don't need to order a ride." He pressed on my screen, exiting the app. "I'll drive you home."

"No thank you. I don't want you to go out of your way."

Luca barked a laugh. "It's not out of his way." His eyes flicked to Weston's. "She doesn't know?"

Weston's headshake was subtle. Elliot groaned.

"Oh, for god's sake. You live in the same building as West." Elliot pulled me into a hug before I could wrap my head around what he'd just said. "Be good while I'm gone. West and Luca are here if you need them. I'm allowing Luca to have your phone number on the caveat he doesn't send you dick pics."

Luca's brows waggled. "Sexting at nine?"

I let go of Elliot to fist Luca's T-shirt. "Come on, Grandpa. No one sexts before midnight."

Elliot shoved a cackling Luca away from me. "No sexting. Don't even joke about it or you'll be getting a front-row view of my breakfast splattered on the ground."

Weston's palm pressed gently on the center of my back. "Wait here. I'll go get my car so you don't have to walk in the rain."

"You don't have a driver?" I was only slightly teasing.

His hand slid up to my nape and gave it a quick squeeze. "I don't. What kind of environmentalist would I be if I was driven around in a big gas guzzler?"

Weston disappeared into the rain, and it was times like this it was easy to forget he was the CEO of a very successful company.

A large black SUV pulled up to the curb. Elliot had a wry expression. My brother wasn't nearly as environmentally minded as Weston and had no qualms about being driven around in a big gas guzzler. He and Luca both hugged me again before climbing in the back of the SUV.

A minute later, Weston pulled up. I was prepared to run out to him, hoping not to get too drenched, but he hopped out of the Tesla and strode across the sidewalk, holding a large umbrella. *He* was drenched, but he made it look good. His shaggy hair was dripping wet, like he'd gotten extra sweaty doing things. Most likely sexy things. And the way his shirt was plastered to his chest was obscene. Every square, taut muscle was on display, small, tight nipples stabbing at the fabric.

Reaching me, he gathered me under his arm, ensuring all of me was beneath the umbrella and walked me to his car. I managed to climb in without getting a drop of rain on me.

What a gentleman.

I twisted in my seat as Weston pulled out into traffic.

"We live in the same building?"

"Mmmhmm. I'm in the penthouse."

"Naturally."

His mouth quirked. "I suggested the building to Elliot."

"Good suggestion. Did you also have the rent magically de-creased? Saoirse and I are paying well below the market value."

He shrugged then completely dodged the question. "Why were you and Miles in the stairwell yesterday?"

Sighing, I sat back in my seat. "I thought he was the one leaving the Post-its, so I was speaking to him about it."

His head jerked. His hands tightened slightly on the wheel. "Why would you think it was him?"

I was unwilling to delve into my high school trauma. If he didn't know how Miles had treated me, I wasn't going to be the one to break it to him. Not that he would have cared. What was done was done.

"It seemed like a prank. Miles is known for doing that type of thing." I stacked my hands in my lap. "How did he know the nick-name you used to call me?"

"Hmmm?" His brow dropped. "Ellie? I don't know. Back then, Elliot and you were kind of my whole life outside of school. It wouldn't surprise me if he'd picked up on it when I was prattling on about you."

"Oh." I slumped, somewhat lost for words. Of course, to any-one with eyes, it was obvious Weston and Elliot were joined at the hip and had been since elementary school, but I never would have guessed he'd include me as part of his *whole life.*

"Why was he hugging you?"

I turned sharply toward him. "What? How do you know that?"

He grumbled, tapping his thumbs on the wheel. He didn't seem keen to answer me, which meant I wasn't answering him either.

"You're really not going to answer me?"

Since he chose to stay quiet, I did as well. But while I was silent, I chewed on the possibilities. There was really only one that made sense, but I couldn't imagine why Weston would go out of the way to watch the security feeds.

He pulled his car into the underground parking below our building. I couldn't quite figure out the door, but that was fine since he pressed the screen in the console, opening it for me.

Weston plugged the car in to charge then we headed to the elevator.

"The penthouse?" I pursed my lips.

"Where else?" His eyes danced over me. "Do you like your apartment?"

I nodded. "I do, though I'm suspicious about the rent."

"Just accept your luck. Don't question it."

"Do you know anything about the flowers I've been receiving every week?"

Another bouquet had been waiting for me Friday when I got home from work. Just as sweet and pretty as the previous week. Terrence had had no clue who they were from, and of course, there'd been no card.

"No." He tucked his hands in his pockets. "Do you want to come up to my apartment?"

"No." My nose twitched. "Do you want to come to mine?"

"Yes."

My stomach tilt-a-whirled at his immediate response.

He followed me off the elevator, hovering behind me while I opened the door. It was quiet, so Saoirse was probably still sleeping. Alcohol hit her hard. She was going to spend her Sunday in bed, and knowing her, wouldn't feel the least bit guilty about it.

I held my hand out toward the flowers sitting on the kitchen bar. "These aren't familiar to you?"

He slowly shook his head. "I haven't seen them before. Though, they're the perfect size for a bedside table. I wonder why you didn't put them there."

I beckoned him to follow me down the hallway. "We have to be quiet. Saoirse is sleeping off her Saturday night."

"Still?"

I glanced at him over my shoulder. "That sounded judgy."

"It was."

I bit the inside of my cheek to keep from laughing. He had no right to know I found him funny.

Just inside the doorway of my bedroom, I pointed out the flowers on my nightstand.

"Those are last week's. They're still really fresh. I've been rotating them so Saoirse and I can both enjoy them."

I looked up at him. He was close. Despite his damp clothing, his body heat radiated out of him. It occurred to me then we were alone in my bedroom. Why had I invited him here? I couldn't recall the thought process.

It also occurred to me how exposed I was in my leggings. They were fine for hiking, not for wearing in front of Weston Aldrich and all his perfection.

"You're a good friend to share even though your roommate is lazy."

Snorting, I shoved at his chest. "She isn't lazy. Saoirse is the busiest person I know. Sometimes it catches up to her."

He wandered more deeply into my room, picking up a picture from my dresser. Elliot, my mom, and me at his high school graduation. A couple years later, she was gone, and our family was down to two members.

"She couldn't even pretend to be happy," I remarked.

"No." He traced his thumb over the picture. "Elliot was leaving. It was probably a hard day for her."

"Every day was a hard day for her."

He set it down and turned to me, his hands back in his pocket. "You're nothing like her."

"Good. I like when people say I'm just like my dad. When they compare me to my mom, it feels like an insult."

"It probably isn't, but I can understand why you feel that way." His mouth set in a firm line. "The circumstances aren't ideal, but I'm glad you're back in Denver. Elliot's relieved to have you home."

Having him in my room was strange, and he was standing there as though completely comfortable among my things. There had been so much distance—distance I had imposed and he'd added to—being in close proximity now was admittedly jarring.

"Thank you. The circumstances are actual shit, but being here isn't. The swanky digs definitely ease the pain."

He chuckled, his perfect pink lips tipping into a beautiful smile, and my insides knotted. Why did he have to look like that and have a laugh I could imagine hearing in the bedroom while losing my mind with him?

"That's good to know." He walked forward, to where I stood by the door. "I should go. I'm probably getting your floor wet."

I stepped aside to let him pass. "It was incredibly gentlemanly of you to fetch the car for me, you know."

He rubbed his hand down his front, still smiling softly, both of us in the doorway.

"If I don't practice once a year, I'll forget how to do it."

I gasped, my hands on my cheeks. "And you practiced on me? Wow, what did I do to deserve this honor?"

He reached out and tugged the end of my hair, giving me a long look. "You came back."

"That simple?"

The corner of his mouth hitched. "Yes. That simple." He raked his hair away from his face. "I really do need to go. I have a few hours of work ahead of me, and again, my clothes are soaked."

After Weston was gone and I had time to go over what we'd talked about in my head, I realized he'd never explained why he'd been leaving the Post-its.

I made a mental note to ask him at work.

And for once, I was looking forward to seeing him again.

CHAPTER NINE

Elise

CEOs WERE BUSY. I knew that.

But after seeing Weston around so often during my first two weeks at Andes, I supposed I had developed false expectations. This week was a different story. I hadn't even caught a glimpse of him in the elevator.

That was why I smiled so big when I arrived at my desk on Thursday and a Post-it was waiting for me.

Alfred Hitchcock was frightened of eggs.

I sputtered a laugh. Now that I knew these were from Weston, though he hadn't admitted it explicitly, I looked forward to receiving them. He'd left me one each day this week, each with a random fact that had nothing to do with elephants.

Miles strolled by, whistling softly. He stopped in front of me, rapping his knuckles on my desk. "What's that little smile about?"

I crinkled my nose. I'd forgiven him, sure, but we weren't friends. I wasn't certain I even wanted to be friends with him.

"Nothing." I tried to hide the Post-it under my hands, but he spotted it.

His brow lifted. "I didn't leave that one."

"I know you didn't."

"Who did?"

I shrugged. I was working on regaining my ability to trust people but really doubted I'd ever trust Miles Aldrich. If I did, it would certainly take more than a few days to happen.

He clutched his heart. "I'm wounded you're keeping secrets from me, Lisie."

"Maybe I don't know who left them. They *are* anonymous."

He staggered back, drama king that he was. "You're killing me here. I feel the pain from your withholding deep in my bones."

"I hope you're not hanging around for an apology."

"I'm not." He straightened his tie. It was a skinny one, straight from the nineteen-sixties. "How are you settling in?"

"I like Andes very much."

He grinned, twinkling his eyes at me. "My brother gave me the third degree about what we were talking about in the stairwell. I told him I didn't even realize this building had stairs."

Despite myself, I sputtered a laugh. "Did he take that well?"

"He did not, which made it even more fun."

I found myself grinning back. "Call me crazy, but I think he watched the security feed. He's *that* nosy."

"A control freak is what he is. That's why he's always working on different floors, keeping watch over everyone. Does Elliot hang out with his employees?"

My eyes bulged at the preposterous idea. "I can't imagine that he does. That doesn't mean he's not just as much of a control freak as Weston. He just doesn't care about his employees' personal lives.

They could be banging in the stairwell and Elliot wouldn't blink as long as they were doing their jobs."

Miles shook his head, murmuring, "Banging in the stairwell..." Then he perched his butt on the edge of my desk. "I suppose Westie isn't a complete carbon copy of Elliot after all. I'm shocked."

I crossed my arms, leaning back in my chair. "Did you think they were?"

He rolled his eyes. "Weston has been obsessed with the Levy family since the moment he met Elliot. He's always wanted to be like him. I was honestly astounded they didn't go into business together."

"Or do you think it's possible they were always similar and that's why they became such good friends?"

"Sure, anything's possible." He scrubbed his scruffy jaw. "Did Weston ask you about the stairwell?"

I nodded. "He did. I saw him over the weekend when I was out to brunch with Elliot. I didn't give him a straight answer because it wasn't really his business."

He clicked his fingers. "That's why he accosted me first thing Monday morning. Nosy bastard."

I moved my mouse around to turn on my computer screen. As Miles and I had been talking, other employees had filled up the surrounding desks, starting their workday. Miles seemed to be in no hurry to leave, but I had a list of tasks a mile long.

"Don't you have work to do?" I asked as sweetly as I could.

He grinned at me and ignored my question. "We should have been friends back in the day. I always liked you. I should have tried harder to make you like me." Shrugging, he hopped up. "Good thing I have a second chance to lure you into a lifetime of friendship. How am I doing so far?"

"Subpar."

"Fuck," he hissed under his breath. "Well, don't worry, Lisie. I'm in it for the long haul."

Then he wandered away, whistling as he went.

———◆———

I worked without a break until my stomach started to growl. My eye caught on the yellow sticky note still sitting on my desk, then my thoughts drifted to Weston's lunch invitation during my first week.

If he could invite me to lunch, I could invite him.

I picked up the phone and dialed his assistant. I didn't have his direct phone number and we weren't quite in the place to text each other. At least, I didn't think so.

"Weston Aldrich's office. This is Renata, how can I help you?"

I cleared my throat. "Hi, Renata. This is Elise Levy. I work on seven. Anyway, I'm calling to see if Weston would like to join me for lunch today."

A long pause.

So long, I thought she hung up.

Finally, she spoke. "He's incredibly busy this week."

"Doesn't he have to eat?"

"Well…"

"Can you ask him? I can grab something for him and bring it up there if that's easier."

She sighed. "Hold on, Elise. I'll check." She didn't sound too optimistic.

I clicked around on my computer while I waited. It didn't take long for her to come back.

"Elise?"

"Yes. I'm here."

"I'm sorry, but Weston isn't open for lunch this week."

"Oh." My stomach dropped with disappointment. "Did you tell him it was me?"

"I did. The answer is the same. Mr. Aldrich doesn't normally take a formal lunch break. If you have something you'd like to speak with him about, I suggest email."

The sting of rejection smarted. "Thank you. I'll remember that."

I hung up, embarrassed for thinking I could just call up the CEO and invite him to lunch. Weston obviously didn't see me as anything other than an employee and his friend's sister. I didn't know why I'd thought anything had changed.

⊷⊶

The workweek that never ended finally did. Simon, Rebecca, and I were out for drinks with Saoirse, whose office was nearby. This week it was, anyway. She was a temp for now, not ready to settle down and choose one job.

Rebecca glanced around the bar brimming with office workers looking to put a cap on their week.

"There are some tasty men here tonight," she remarked.

Saoirse giggled. "I'm sorry, but aren't you married?"

Rebecca arched a brow. "Married, not dead. It's not like Sam doesn't check out tits and asses on a regular basis. I'd be worried if he didn't. He's good at doing it subtly when I'm around, just as I eye up all the suit porn in my proximity."

"It's a shame they're all chronically straight." Simon leaned forward in his club chair to pick up his drink from the small round table in the center of our group.

Rebecca elbowed him. "We can be wingwomen tonight. Let's find boys for Saoirse and Lise."

I held up my hands. "I don't want a boy. I'm still mangled from the last one."

Rebecca rolled her eyes as if I was saying stupid things. "Obviously, the next one will be purely physical while you unmangle your poor heart. No need to wear out your batteries while you're healing."

Saoirse nodded. "There *is* an awful lot of buzzing coming from your room at all hours. It's distracting if you must know."

A surprised laugh burst out of me. "Oh, shut up. That isn't true and you know it."

She shrugged, her eyes darting to the side. "I'm not judging. I'm just saying, the real thing might be more satisfying than silicone."

As the three of them plotted to find me a real-life man to get the job done, a group of suited men entering the bar distracted me. Weston was surrounded by some of the suits who'd been visiting Andes headquarters this week. As he took a seat, his eyes flicked up, searching. They landed on me and flared.

I nodded. He nodded back, his full lips tipping into a small smile. I took a long pull from my drink, attempting to pay attention to my friends, not Weston Aldrich. He wasn't looking at me anymore, anyway. The men had pulled him into conversation.

Rebecca leaned into me, tipping her drink toward a group of men standing together at the bar. "What about that one? He keeps looking over here."

I glanced that way. "Which one?"

"The tallest one, with the beard. He's cute."

Saoirse twisted around to check out the guys, not even trying to be subtle about it. "Oooh, yes. He's a little bit ginger, Lisie. Have you had a ginger before?" She turned back in her seat, her pretty face alight with excitement.

"You know every guy I've been with," I reminded her.

She nodded. "True. No gingers in the bunch."

Simon angled toward her. "How big of a bunch are we talking here?"

I pointed at Saoirse. "If you tell him my number, I'll cut off your hair in your sleep."

She grabbed the end of her blonde ponytail protectively. "Wow, living in Chicago made you ruthless. I wasn't going to tell him about the seventeen guys you've slept with."

Simon's jaw went slack. "Seventeen? And that was all before you got with the douchelord. By the age of twenty-two, you'd had seventeen? Why you little hussy!"

I rolled my eyes. "She's pulling your leg. My number's nowhere near that. It takes me much too long to be comfortable enough with a man to get naked in front of him to have that many notches."

"Damn," Rebecca cursed. "I was about to high-five you."

Saoirse waved them off. "Let's get back to the cute ginger at the bar. Is he looking this way?"

I lifted my eyes and was met with a friendly gaze and a soft smile. The ginger businessman was watching me. Feeling brazen for no particular reason, I lifted my drink to him, and his smile widened.

Then I realized I had no idea what to do next and had no game at all.

"Oh my god, he's staring hard at you," Simon cooed. "Get it, girl."

"I have no clue how to get it. I've been out of the flirting game for too long." I kept my eyes down so I didn't accidentally clash with the ginger again.

Rebecca plucked my drink from my hand, tipped it back, and swallowed it down before handing me my empty glass.

"Oh dear, you need a new drink. Our waitress is dismally slow. You should probably go to the bar and order one before you get too thirsty."

I stared at her, blinking slowly. "You're maniacal."

"That's what Sam says." She tossed her hair behind her shoulders. "That's why he loves me so. Now, get to the bar and let ginger make his move."

Nerves were tossing the contents of my stomach around in wild waves. But I told myself all I was doing was walking to the bar. If this man was actually attracted to me and interested in knowing me, he could come talk to me. Otherwise, I was just buying myself a new drink. No harm, no foul.

Of course, I nearly stumbled on my way there. I righted myself, finding Weston looking at me again. Biting down on my bottom lip, I carried on my mission, finding an empty spot at the bar.

The bartender took my order, and I waited, butterflies committing violence in my stomach. They had to be swashbuckling in there. There was no other explanation.

"Hello."

I looked at the man who'd stepped up beside me. Tall was my first thought. Lovely beard was my second.

"Hi. Your beard is lovely." Oh Jesus. Who'd allowed me to speak?

He grinned. "Thank you. You're lovely overall."

I couldn't hold back a smile. "Thank you." I held my hand out, confidence blooming. "I'm Elise."

"Thomas. Can I buy your drink?"

"You don't have to."

"I'd like to. That way, when I ask for your number, you feel obligated to throw me a bone."

He took me off guard, making me laugh. "That is quite the plan. And since you're being so honest, I may feel obligated to give it to you."

We chatted for a few more minutes, the usual getting-to-know-you things. When he took his phone out, I happily gave him my number. Aside from his height, there was nothing intimidating about Thomas. He seemed nice and wasn't overly handsome or buff, which for me, was a plus. In fact, he was a little soft around the middle, which I found attractive on him.

I wasn't in any way ready for something serious, but if Thomas contacted me, I would go on a date with him. He had a really great beard and a charming smile. Deeper qualifications weren't required.

We parted, and I started to go back to my group when the hair on the back of my neck rose. I turned my head, finding Weston glaring at the men, his jaw clenched. Poor guy. He couldn't even have a relaxing evening out. Though I wondered if he ever truly relaxed.

Probably not.

When I sat back down with my friends, they played it cool, but I could tell they were bursting with giddiness for me. Rebecca made a few fire engine jokes, and Simon told us about the one redhead he'd dated. Saoirse grabbed my hand and gave it a hard squeeze. More than anyone, she knew what a big deal it was for me to open myself up to possibly moving on.

We were all a little bit tipsy when we left the bar. Rebecca had big plans of going home and seducing Sam. Simon's night was just getting started. He was meeting his real-life friends. Work wasn't real life, and I wasn't even a little insulted. Saoirse and I waited by the curb for our Uber.

Behind us, bar noises grew louder as someone exited. Boisterous voices carried loudly through the night. Saoirse and I huddled closer.

"Elise." A bark so commanding, both Saoirse and I immediately twisted around to see the source. Weston had parted from his group and was striding toward us. "I'll drive you home."

Saoirse's hand tightened on my waist. I shook my head just as a car pulled up in front of us.

"No thank you. Our Uber is here." My gaze lingered on his. He seemed angry. His week had probably felt much, much longer than mine. "Have a good weekend, Weston."

His head dipped, and he stayed planted there on the sidewalk as we climbed into the back of our ride. I waved as we drove away.

Saoirse let out a whoosh. "That man is so frigging intense."

I giggled. "I know, right? He's always been that way."

"Hot, though."

"Yeah." He'd always been that way too, even as a lanky teen.

"Let's talk about Thomas." She took my hand, wrapping both of hers around it. "How did it feel to be hit on by a cute guy?"

"It felt...like maybe Patrick's opinion of me isn't the end all be all."

Her face went soft. She pressed my hand to her cheek. "It isn't. Remember how sexy you felt in Aruba? That's what matters. Patrick couldn't handle you feeling yourself that way. He was a small man with a small mind and a small prick."

I snorted a laugh. "Unfortunately, his prick isn't small."

She snapped her fingers. "Drats. Well, I hope he and his big dick are enjoying all the time they're spending with his right hand. He's never going to find a woman sexier, funnier, or more wonderful than you. And I am one-hundred-percent certain he knows that and it's killing him."

"I don't know if that's true, but honestly? I don't really want to think about him anymore."

"You're right."

My phone lit up in my lap. I had a new text. Saoirse and I both read the screen.

"Thomas," she whispered.

Hi, Elise. Sorry I'm not playing it cool, but I really enjoyed meeting you and would love to take you to dinner tomorrow night. Are you available?

I gasped. Saoirse squealed.

I was going on a date. With a man.

Holy frigging crap.

Chapter Ten

Weston

Luca kept giving me the stink eye for tagging along with him, but he could go fuck himself. As if he didn't invite himself everywhere Elliot and I went.

"What if this was a date?" he grumbled as we were seated on a patio with mountain views.

I opened my menu, peering at him over it. "You're not dating Elise."

"Well, obviously not when you're getting between us."

I gave him a droll look. "You don't date. If you gave Elise the Luca Rossi treatment, Elliot would have your head on a pike."

He sniffed. "She's beautiful. Don't you think she's beautiful?"

"Of course she is. She always has been."

He snapped open his menu. "I never noticed before. Shame. I could have been looking at her instead of you and Elliot. It would have made all those drab dinners you guys forced me to a lot more entertaining."

Before I could use my menu to brain him, Elise came rushing through the restaurant. Thank Christ she wasn't wearing those obscene leggings. They had been a second skin, revealing every one of her curves. I'd barely survived walking behind her into her apartment.

Luca rose before I could, helping her into her chair and made a big show of kissing her cheek, winking at me when his lips were on her. When she was seated, I realized this week's brunch outfit wasn't any better.

"Weston," she breathed, her cheeks flushed. "Luca didn't say you'd be here."

I couldn't take my eyes off her. "What on earth are you wearing?"

She reared back, her hand flying to her chest. There was so much bare skin. Her tits were practically on a serving platter, shoved up and out by a corset contraption beneath an open flannel top. It was a bewildering combination that had clearly scrambled my brain.

"I'm wearing clothes, Weston." She started to pull her flannel closed, but Luca caught her hand.

I scoffed. "Barely."

"You look perfect. Don't let this jackass bring you down," he murmured gently.

She sighed, turning her hand over to wrap her fingers around his. "Thank you. Saoirse and I went to the farmers' market this morning and she wanted to be my stylist. I have all this pretty lingerie I never had the chance to wear and she claims it's a crime, so we both went out in lace and flannel. I felt good. Had I known my *boss* was going to be here, however, I would have changed."

Luca rolled his pretty boy eyes. "West can get up and leave if he's making you uncomfortable. *I* invited you to lunch. *He* invited himself."

She waved him off. "It's fine. Honestly, I don't know what I was thinking running around like this. I'm sure I look ridiculous." She started to button her flannel, and *I* reached out, catching her hand. It took all my willpower not to get stuck on how unbelievably soft her skin was.

"You don't look ridiculous. I apologize for making you feel like you did." I forced myself to drop my hold on her.

She was still clutching her shirt. "Why *did* you?"

"I—" I rubbed my chin, searching for a suitable excuse for behaving like a jackass. "I'm not used to seeing you dress like this. It took me off guard and I reacted poorly. Luca's right. You're perfect. Lovely. Don't change a thing."

She lowered her hand, attempting to hide her smile. "Well, then I guess I forgive you. It's a good thing too, because I would have hated to tell Elliot my boobs took you off guard."

Luca let out a raucous laugh. "Oh, fuck. Please do, but make sure I'm there to witness the atomic bomb when it goes off."

She laughed with him. "He still thinks I'm a child."

"He's protective," I corrected. "Don't you think that's understandable, given your circumstances?"

"It is," she admitted. "And I'm protective of him for the same reasons. But I've never once had anything to say about the women he dates, nor have I sicced my friends on him to make sure he doesn't get lonely when I'm out of town."

Luca held his hands up. "Now, now, I asked you to lunch of my own volition. I happen to like your company."

"Thank you," she said sweetly. "I enjoy your company too."

I interrupted the lovefest.

"Your roles are different, though." I placed my menu on the table, squaring my attention on Elise. "He's four years older, yes, but Elliot was your guardian. I don't think that responsibility ever ended for him."

Elise and Elliot were orphans. Their father had died from a brain tumor when she was ten and Elliot was fourteen. The tumor had taken him within months of diagnosis. No one had been prepared. Least of all, their mother. After losing her husband, Elaine Levy fell apart. As a constant visitor to the Levy household, I'd witnessed her steady and rapid decline. Elliot had almost turned down Stanford, but Elise hadn't allowed him to.

Two years in, he'd ended up dropping out anyway. Elaine had wrapped her car around a tree and Elise had needed him. Whether he'd move home had never been a question. Me following, on the other hand, *he* hadn't allowed.

"And I love him for it," she said. "But that responsibility doesn't extend to you guys, you know. Can't we just be friends without all the big brother stuff coming in to play?"

Luca raised a brow at me. "I can cut out the big brother stuff, sweetheart. I don't know about West. He's been doing it for a lot longer than me, and now he's your boss."

"We can be friends," I snapped, annoyed Luca was speaking for me.

The waiter came by for our order then, eyeing Elise's cleavage. His gaze kept returning, the art of subtlety completely lost on this douche. Fortunately for him, she seemed oblivious.

Luca and Elise settled into an easy conversation about the farmers' market and upcoming weekend activities. I listened to them both but chose to stay quiet. For one, I'd already put my foot in my mouth one too many times this afternoon. For another, it was nice to watch Elise laugh and enjoy herself.

Her happiness wasn't a puzzle I'd been able to solve, which nagged at me. If I hadn't been stuck in meetings all week, I would have worked harder at it. My daily Post-its had probably been more annoying than anything.

"Oh, Luca." Elise perked up as if just remembering something. "Can you suggest a good place to grab a drink near my apartment? Somewhere not too busy where we can speak to each other?"

"Of course I can, *bella*." He reclined in his chair, draping his arm over the back. "Tell me the occasion. That will give me a better idea of places to suggest."

She cupped her cheeks, doing nothing to hide her rising blush. "I have a date tonight. He asked me to dinner, but I said drinks instead in case it's awkward and I want to bail."

His eyebrows shot up. "A date? Way to bury the lede. I think you need to start at the beginning."

I sat up straight, interested in her answer.

"It's not a big deal. Last night, I was out with my coworkers and this guy approached me. He seemed nice, and he was very straightforward and eager, which I liked. Anyway, his name is Thomas, he works in finance, and he confirmed our date first thing this morning. According to Saoirse, that scores him top marks." She gestured toward me. "Weston was there. He saw me talking to him. You can ask him what he thinks."

I crossed my arms over my chest. "Wait a minute. You're going on a date with that redheaded lumberjack in the ill-fitting suit?"

Luca choked on his water, sputtering into his fist. Elise, meanwhile, did not seem amused. Then, neither was I. Last night, I *had* noticed some big guy chatting her up, but I'd missed a number exchange taking place.

"His name is Thomas, Weston, and I found him very good-looking. Not everyone can look like they stepped out of a magazine, but that doesn't mean they aren't worthy of respect."

I chuffed. "I didn't say that, so don't put words in my mouth. I'm only talking about the man I saw you with last night. You can, and should, do a lot better."

Her eyes narrowed. "You know nothing about him other than what he looks like. Who knew you were so shallow?"

"Yeah," Luca chimed. "Who knew? I'm ashamed of you, West."

I picked up my glass, ignoring Luca. "I'm simply saying you shouldn't rush into a date with the first man who asks."

She folded her arms under her tits, and I nearly swallowed my tongue. They were so fucking round and right fucking there. Were they always there, just like that, under her clothing?

What was I thinking? Of course they were. She walked around with those round fucking tits every day. She sat in my building, typing on my computer, doing work for my company, those big, beautiful tits beneath a measly layer of clothing.

"Why are you presuming Thomas is the first man to ask me out? For all you know, I could have been sleeping my way through Denver the past month."

Luca chuckled. "My god, Elise. We have to hang out without Elliot more often. You're even more fun without your ball and chain dragging you down."

That made her laugh. "He would definitely *not* appreciate me banging my way through the city, and if you tell him I said that, I'll shave your head."

"You cruel mistress. My lips are sealed." Luca mimed tossing her the key to his locked lips. Elise caught it and tucked it in her cleavage. I wondered what the fuck I'd done in my life to deserve this form of torment.

She turned back to me. "Honestly, Thomas is going to be my first date. I don't have very high expectations, and I'm definitely not looking for a new boyfriend. But like I said, he seems nice and nonthreatening, so I'm going to give the whole dating thing a whirl. It could be fun."

Our waiter returned, setting down our plates while I mulled over her words. As soon as he left, I asked, "What does nonthreatening mean?"

She picked up her pickle. Always the pickle first.

"It means I don't think he's the type to twist me into knots and spit me out all tangled up when he's through. Nonthreatening."

"Then he does sound like a good dude to practice your dating skills on," Luca agreed. "I'll text you some recs for tonight. You want low key, not too romantic. Our boy Thomas doesn't need to get any funny ideas."

When Elise's pickle was gone, I put mine on her plate. We'd never eaten a meal together where I didn't give her my pickle. There'd also never been a time when she hadn't beamed at me for doing so.

"Thank you, Weston. You're my favorite person to eat sandwiches with. I always get double the pickles."

I wiped my mouth with my napkin. "I like how happy a pickle makes you."

Her cheeks flushed. "It's the little things, you know?"

Luca's head cocked, his eyes darting from me to her. I could practically hear the gears of his mind turning, but whatever he was thinking, he chose not to speak it out loud.

To: eliselevy@andesinc.com

From: westonaldrich@andesinc.com

Dear Elise,

As one of my newest employees, I'm checking in to see how you're doing.

Did you have a nice weekend?

On the elevator this morning, you appeared rejuvenated.

Are you that thrilled to be back at work?

Inquiringly,

Weston

To: westonaldrich@andes.com

From: eliselevy@andesinc.com

Dear Grumpy Boss,

Do you send this type of email to all your new employees?

I had a lovely weekend. Are you asking about any specific moments?

As for your question regarding my rejuvenated appearance, that is neither due to my nice weekend nor the thrill of returning to work. My secret is bathing in the blood of virgins once a week. If you're nice, I'll share my source.

Sanguinely,
Elise

------◆◇◆------

I tipped my head back and groaned. She couldn't make things easy, could she? If Elise had realized I was ignoring hundreds of emails to read hers, maybe she would have gone easier on me.

I wanted to know how her date with fucking lumberjack Thomas had gone.

------◆◇◆------

To: eliselevy@andesinc.com

From: westonaldrich@andesinc.com

Dear Elise,

While your bloodbath sounds fascinating, and is clearly working, I don't think I'll be partaking in the ritual.

As for which specific parts of your weekend I'm referring to, I'll be honest and say I'd very much like to know if I should be hiring someone to make redheaded Thomas disappear.

Homicidally,

Weston

------◆◇◆------

To: westonaldrich@andesinc.com

From: eliselevy@andesinc.com

Dear Grumpy Boss,

I don't know if I should be using company time to discuss my dating life. You should probably rethink putting your murder plans in a company email as well.

I'm very busy today. Aren't you? It's strange you have all this time to email me when you couldn't fit me in for lunch last week.

Hmmm…

Concernedly,

Elise

⎯⎯❖⎯⎯

Lunch? What was she talking about? If she'd wanted to have lunch with me, I would have found a way to make that happen.

"Renata," I called out.

My assistant took her time making her way into my office.

"Yes, Weston?"

"Did Elise Levy call to invite me to lunch last week?"

She nodded. "Mmmhmm."

"What?" I rose from my desk, my chair rolling backward. "And you didn't think to tell me?"

She cocked her head. "Actually, I did tell you. You were in meetings with the Sava Group last week, as you recall."

My brow pinched. I wasn't amused by Renata's tone. "Yes. I am well aware. What I do not recall is you telling me Elise Levy phoned for me."

"I did, Weston, and I don't appreciate you implying I'm a liar." Her hands went to her hips. "You were in your bubble and nothing exists outside of it. I didn't press the issue because I know how you get when you zone out the rest of the world. I also didn't realize Elise

Levy's calls should be put through, considering you never told me that."

Exhaling, I stared at my assistant. She was right. Last week, I'd had meeting after meeting. When I wasn't in meetings, I was responding to emails and making budget decisions. All my weeks were hectic, but last week had been especially so. I'd done nothing but work and sleep. Everything else had fallen by the wayside.

"Elise is Elliot's sister."

"I'm aware." Renata's mouth twitched. She wasn't happy with me.

"Unless I tell you otherwise, put Elise through when she calls."

"Please," Renata added dryly.

Lifting a brow, I wondered if anyone else in my position was reminded to use their manners by their assistant.

Probably not.

"Please, Renata."

She smirked. "Of course, Weston."

I nodded. "Mark off some time for me around lunchtime today." She glared at me. "Please," I added.

"All right." Then she wandered out with a carefree wave over her shoulder.

To: eliselevy@andesinc.com
From: westonaldrich@andesinc.com
Dear Elise,
Would you join me for lunch today?

I'd like to apologize for neglecting you last week, *and* since we technically won't be on company time, we can discuss the murder of redheaded Thomas.

Professionally,

Weston

———◦———

A minute later, her email pinged in my inbox, and a stupid grin spread across my face.

———◦———

To: westonaldrich@andesinc.com

From: eliselevy@andesinc.com

Dear Grumpy Boss,

I'll accept your invitation under two conditions:

1. You can't glare, frown, or scowl at me.

2. There is no mention of murdering or maiming my dates.

Since I'm doubtful you can meet those conditions, I'll write your name on my calendar in pencil so I can erase you at any moment.

Skeptically,

Elise

For the first time, probably ever in this office, I tossed my head back and laughed. Elise Levy had just laid down a challenge, and I was more than willing to accept it.

———◦———

To: eliselevy@andesinc.com

From: westonaldrich@andesinc.com

Dear Elise,

Mark me down in pen.

Confidently,

Weston

CHAPTER ELEVEN

Elise

WESTON TOOK ME TO a sushi restaurant a few blocks from Andes headquarters. We'd just placed our orders, and so far he had managed to keep his facial expressions on an even keel.

He clasped his hands on the table. "I'm sorry again for last week."

He'd always had nice hands. Long fingers. Neatly trimmed nails. But now, they were essentially hand porn. Veins stood out like wild rivers running beneath his skin made golden by the sun. The calluses on his palms and fingers belied his position as CEO. Weston must have still loved spending time outdoors.

"It's fine. It was presumptuous of me to think you'd have time for me." I was completely over the rejection. When I'd had time to reflect on it, I'd felt a little stupid for calling. His schedule probably had next to no flexibility.

"No, it wasn't presumptuous at all. I'll always make time for you if I can, Elise." He picked up his hot tea and took a slow sip before placing it on the table. "I have this problem. Well, I should say I've been told it's a problem even though it's always worked to my benefit."

"Who told you it was a problem then?"

His mouth twitched. God, were his lips sexy. I'd forgotten how full the bottom one was. Full and pink. He was probably a great kisser, with that anatomy and his perfectionism.

"Ex-girlfriends," he answered, pulling me right back to reality. Weston had a lot of ex-girlfriends.

"Okay, now I'm intrigued. Spill what your problem is."

His lips pulled into a half smile. "I've been told many, many times I can be single-minded. When I'm concentrating on a project or deep in my work, I'm not aware of anything outside of it. In the past, I've missed reservations and forgotten plans for days because of my hyperfocus."

"Ahhh…" I picked up the wrapper from my chopsticks and began folding it into a small square. "Yes, I can see why that would be a problem for your plethora of girlfriends."

A deep, full laugh burst from him. "Plethora? Really?"

"Yes, Weston. Every time I saw you after you went away for college, you had a different woman with you. I think that qualifies as a plethora."

His humor fell away. "Not all those women were girlfriends. In fact, most weren't."

"Yet you felt compelled to bring them to our family dinners."

There had been a point in my life I'd considered Weston Aldrich my friend. Back then, I never questioned that he cared for me.

When he went to college and I started high school, things had changed. I'd been miserable, and deep down, even though it hadn't been fair, I'd blamed Weston for what Miles had put me through. So, I'd stopped talking to him, and once I'd shoved that wedge between us, Weston had added to it by rarely coming to visit alone. He'd almost always had a girl with him—even at my going-away dinner before I moved to Chicago.

"I'm surprised to hear you'd noticed since you barely spoke a word to me," he intoned.

"Just because I wasn't speaking to you doesn't mean I didn't see you."

His attention was on his teacup. He rotated it until it was in a position that seemed to satisfy him and looked up. "*Why* weren't you speaking to me?"

I lifted a shoulder. "I don't know, Weston. Does it really even matter? We're here together now. I'm speaking to you, and you no longer feel the need to bring one of your plethora with you, let's just leave it at that."

His brow started to lower, but I wagged my finger at him. "If you're about to scowl at me, think again. You gave me your word. No frowning."

His expression smoothed, the corners of his mouth hitching. "So, we're never going to discuss how you went from my little buddy to a stone-cold bitch at the flip of a switch?"

I had to laugh. "You're calling fourteen-year-old me a stone-cold bitch? Isn't that illegal?"

He didn't join me in laughing. "I guess that's a no."

My eyes rolled. "I wasn't a bitch, West. I was having a tough time with self-image, my mom was going off the rails, high school sucked most of the time, and you kept getting more good-looking every year."

His head cocked. "What does that mean?"

"It means I didn't like myself back then, so I pushed everyone away."

You. I pushed you away.

He went still, his gaze heavy and searing. "But I liked you enough for both of us."

I sighed. He truly believed that. "I know you did."

"You were like a sister to me."

I cringed for my younger self. "And I had a massive crush on you, you oblivious man. The ingredients for disaster were there. My low self-esteem, your hotness, our age difference, your parade of gorgeous girlfriends. Once you went away, you came back as not mine anymore. I don't know. Looking back, it's silly, but at the time, it felt so big."

He blinked at me a few times, slowly, as if trying to decipher what was real.

"It isn't silly, Elise. Your feelings have never been silly to me. I wish I'd known back then."

"I never would have told you any of that. Besides, it took me until adulthood to really understand why I was so mad at you. If you'd pressed me on it then, I would have either run away sobbing or cussed you out."

He shook his head. "You never would have cussed me out. You're too sweet for something like that."

That made me laugh and raise a brow. "I thought I was a stone-cold bitch?"

"I only made that judgment because I didn't have all the information. Now that I know how hot you think I am—"

"Oh my god!" I tossed my folded-up chopstick wrapper at him. "That was when I was basically a child, Weston. I obviously don't think that anymore."

His mouth curved into a smirk. "Am I hideous now, Elise?"

That was a fishing expedition if I'd ever heard one. Weston Aldrich was a lot of things, but hideous wasn't one of them, and he was too smart not to be aware of it.

I wasn't taking his bait.

"Oh, yes. I'm surprised you even go out in public."

He inhaled deeply and rubbed his chest. "It's tough, and takes a lot of courage, but I manage to leave my cave a few times a month."

I clapped my hands. "Very brave."

Our waiter brought our food, and we both went quiet. This wasn't the topic I'd expected to talk to him about, but I guessed it was time to somewhat clear the air, and I was glad we had. Hopefully we could lay the past to rest.

Weston decided to ask me a question after I had just popped a California roll into my mouth.

"How was your date?"

I held up a finger, chewing, and then swallowing. I made him wait a few more seconds while I drank some water.

"It was strange to be with someone other than Patrick." I crinkled my nose. "It struck me during my date with Thomas that I'm really, really single."

"It only struck you then?"

"Don't be purposely obtuse. It's one thing to declare yourself single, it's another to act on it. I've spent so long in a relationship, it's strange to even consider letting another man touch me."

"And did he?"

I picked up a tuna roll, my eyes flicking to Weston's. "Did he what?"

He tapped his chopsticks on the table. "Touch you."

"Oh. No. Well, he kissed me, but—"

His upper body lurched forward. "He *kissed* you? That's touching."

"It was a peck. And a hug," I explained.

His upper lip curled. "I'm trying really hard not to scowl at you."

I laughed. "Why would you scowl at me? You should be happy I'm moving on."

"Isn't it too soon to be kissing random lumberjacks?"

"No, I don't think so. It's the exact right time for me to be kissing random redheaded lumberjacks. Besides, Thomas isn't that random. He went to CU-Boulder too but was two years ahead of me. We have mutual friends."

Weston speared his chopsticks into his pile of wasabi, peering at me from beneath furrowed brows. His expression was dangerously close to a glare. "Did you like it?"

"Kissing him?"

He lowered his chin.

"I've never kissed a guy with a beard. It was...different."

He chuffed dismissively. "Sounds like a disaster."

I snorted. "It wasn't at all. I actually expected to feel like I was doing something wrong, which is ridiculous. I was pleasantly surprised to find I didn't feel guilty in the least."

"You have nothing to feel guilty about."

"No, I know I don't." I shook my head. "Anyway, I might see him again. Some friends of his are going to see a band play on Friday night. He asked me to go out with them."

The droll look he gave me said he was totally unimpressed. "He should be taking you out to dinner somewhere nice, where reservations are required. It's too soon to just 'hang out' with his goonie friends."

I burst out laughing. "You sound so frigging old, I can't even believe it. Is this what happens when you turn thirty? You turn into some uptight elitist?"

"I've never changed, Elise."

I pressed my lips together, amused. "So, you admit to always being uptight?"

He jabbed his chopsticks at me. "I'm beginning to think it was better when you were a stone-cold bitch. No insults flying my way."

I leaned forward, grabbing his hand. "Come on, Westie. You don't mean that."

He flipped our hands over so his were on top. "No, I don't mean it at all." His fingers tightened around mine. "Jesus, the virgin blood is doing you well. Your skin is like brand new, out of the package. So soft."

"One good thing my mother taught me was to always moisturize." I dragged my index finger down the side of his thumb. "Your hands are rough. If they were chopped off and found in a ditch two states away, no one would believe they could belong to you. These aren't the hands of a man who works at his computer all day."

His sexy lips were parted, and probably not from desire. "That was macabre. Should I be worried for the safety of my hands?"

My teeth dug into my bottom lip. Teasing Weston had always been so fun. He was so serious but never failed to play along with me.

"Oh, so you're selfish?"

His eyes flared. "How's that?"

"When I told you about the virgins, you never batted an eye. But one mention of chopping off your hands and you're calling the police."

"I need my fucking hands, Elise." He glared at me like *I* was the nut when he was the one practically shouting about his hands.

"The virgins need their blood, Westie!"

He clucked his tongue. "You've been spending too much time with Miles. He's the only one who calls me that."

"I don't know why. It's catchy."

He gave me another long, considering look. "Do you see him outside the office?"

"Who? Miles?"

One brief nod. He still hadn't let go of my hand.

"No. I only see him at work. But he's decided he and I should have been friends back in school, and he missed the opportunity, so he's making up for lost time by perching his ass on my desk every day."

His mouth pulled down. "I'll tell him to stop."

"Why? He's annoying, but he usually goes away when I tell him to." After the fifth or sixth time.

"Has he been hugging you?"

He was fully frowning at me, breaking the first rule. But he'd put me in such a good mood I decided not to call him on it.

"All the time. We call them hug breaks. We take five minutes out of our day and hug it out. I'm surprised you haven't noticed us on the security cameras."

Grunting, he pulled his hand back and swiped his mouth with his napkin. "I don't know what you're talking about."

"Sure."

His eyes narrowed. "Don't hug my brother."

"I'll try not to."

He grunted again. "You know how to piss me off, Elise."

I giggled at how easily riled he still was. God, I'd missed this man. "It's like old times."

And just like old times, when Weston gave me the full force of his attention, something inside me blossomed, awakening a craving for more attention, more long looks, more Weston. Fortunately, I was older and wiser.

Developing a crush on this man was a loser's game.

We weren't the kids we'd been when he'd held me as we watched elephant documentaries during my father's Shiva. We could never go back to that easy innocence or casual closeness, not because of Weston but because of me. My heart was attuned to adoring this man. If I let myself, I could easily slip back into pining over him.

So, we'd have this: occasional lunches, silly emails, nothing more.

The walk back to the office was quiet, and that was my fault too. I was busy firming up my boundaries in my mind as Weston snuck questioning glances at me.

In the lobby, I stopped near the company store. Weston turned to me, his forehead crinkled.

"I'm going to check out the shop before I go up. I need some Andes gear for my hike this weekend." I jerked my thumb over my shoulder.

"All right. I'll come with you."

"That's okay. I'll be quicker on my own."

He was openly scowling at me, but I supposed we were finished with lunch, so there was no longer any need for him to follow my rules.

"Okay...who are you going on this hike with? Not the lumber-jack."

"No, not the lumberjack." I lifted a shoulder. "Probably Saoirse."

"Not alone either, Elise."

Sharp. He meant it.

I shook my head. "Not alone."

Probably.

Maybe.

There would for sure be other people on the trails.

He studied me for a drawn-out moment. My cheeks heated. His gaze traced over my face, lingering on the hottest parts.

"All right. Thank you for joining me for lunch." He stepped forward but didn't reach out to touch me. Instead, he leaned in, putting his mouth near my ear. "I'm really fucking glad you're back."

I turned my head, and our cheeks brushed. We both went still. I sucked in a breath. He exhaled warm air onto my skin.

"Me too, Westie."

He let out a low chuckle. "Goddamn Miles."

"Go to work, Mr. Aldrich."

"Don't call me that, Elise."

He pulled back, but only far enough for me to see his fiery hazel eyes.

My lips tipped.

His gaze fell to my mouth.

My stomach tied itself in a knot.

Oh jeez.

"Good day, grumpy boss," I whispered.

His eyes flicked back to mine. "It's been a great day, sweet Elise."

This man couldn't play fair if he tried.

Chapter Twelve

Elise

Since moving back to Colorado, I'd become addicted to my weekend hikes. I was on my own since Saoirse was currently skydiving with a new friend she met in a coffee shop last week, but I didn't mind.

I'd spent the last few hours hiking through meadows and then a canyon. The sun was brighter here, so when I came to a thick copse of trees after four miles, I breathed a sigh of relief.

Okay, I panted.

In my defense, the air was thinner and the trail was on an incline.

Who was I defending myself to? I was out here panting and sweating and having the time of my life. Each time I pushed myself, I took ownership of my body.

I remembered why I'd loved my thick thighs and soft stomach before Patrick made me believe there was something wrong with me.

These thighs carried me over rocks and hills.

My stomach was round, but my core was solid.

I was solid.

My body might not have been everyone's ideal, but it belonged to me. If I didn't love it, who would?

There was more to love than hate.

No one got to tell me how to feel about myself.

Those were the things I told myself on a continuous loop, and I was doing so much better than I had been when I'd first arrived. But I sometimes faltered. Memories of the GIF and Patrick's nickname liked to swing back and flatten the progress I made on good days.

The point was I was getting there. It would take time, but I had time.

I walked off the trail, following the sound of the nearby creek. When I found it, I sat down on a flattened boulder and stared in awe at the scenery. I couldn't believe I'd left all this behind.

I'd liked living in Chicago, but this…

There was nothing like it.

I was where I was supposed to be.

I didn't know how much time had passed. One moment, I was resting beside the creek, and the next thing I knew, I opened my eyes, disoriented. I guessed I'd fallen asleep.

Taking out my phone, I checked the time, surprised to find an hour had passed.

Saoirse had texted me a picture of her in her skydiving gear with the message: "I survived!" I grinned at my brave, crazy friend. She never said no to a challenge and didn't let fear stop her from having new experiences. It was part of why I loved her.

There was another text from Thomas. Oh, sweet, redheaded Thomas.

Hey! I'd love to see you again this weekend. Text me if you can fit me in.

I sighed.

Jeez.

We'd gone out last night. Music, drinks, his friends. There hadn't been a huge opportunity to talk since we couldn't really hear each other. I'd had fun, though. The band had been outrageous, and the vibe had been pretty chill.

Until he held my hand. I hadn't been able to stop noticing how soft his was.

Like sinking into warm butter.

I'd let him kiss me when he took me home, and it had been nice. His hug had been even nicer. I wasn't sure I could picture myself in bed with him, though.

Still, he was a nice guy. A good guy. I'd give him one more try. If I still wasn't feeling it, I'd let him down easy. I'd never be the girl to drag things out just to have someone in my life.

I sat up, taking a deep pull from my water bottle. It was time to start heading back. I had a long walk ahead of me.

Climbing to my feet, I stretched my arms over my head. That nap had been exactly what I'd needed.

I leaned down to grab my backpack, but a band of iron caught me before I could grab it. No, not iron. Strong, unyielding arms wrapped around my shoulders from behind and yanked me backward into something hard. Alarm bells rang in my ears, but before I could scream, a big hand covered my mouth.

"Elise," a low voice gritted in my ear. "Stop. Look in front of you. One o'clock."

My brain raced to catch up. It was Weston holding me, not some crazed rapist or cannibal from the hills. His tall, lean body pressed into mine, crushing my backside against him.

"Are you stalking me?" I mumbled from behind his hand. "Let go of me!"

He gave me a shake. "Look in front of you, baby. Stay calm."

He turned my head slightly to the right, and though everything inside me wanted to ignore his orders, I focused on the spot.

And nearly pissed my pants.

No more than twenty feet away stood a mountain lion. Stock-still, it watched us both, standing in the exact path I would have taken had Weston not stopped me.

My muscles locked up the very second I understood the situation. Mountain lions didn't normally come out at this time of day. If they did, and they saw a human, they'd usually run and hide.

This one wasn't hiding.

"Don't look away," Weston said firmly, raising his voice. "Keep your eyes on that cat, baby. You're going to be fine. We're going to stay big, make some noise, and scare that kitten away."

I whimpered against his hand. My heart thundered in my ears. What was happening? How could this be real?

"Come on, Elise." He took one of my hands and raised it up so our arms were straight out to the side. "Make yourself big and scary. Let's be loud."

He could be loud. I couldn't do anything but suck in strawfuls of oxygen and try not to pass out.

Weston moved our arms around and talked to the mountain lion while I trembled helplessly.

"Get the fuck out of here, cat, or I'm going to make a rug out of you," he boomed. "You'll look nice at my front door. I'll wipe my boots on you every fucking day."

The mountain lion licked its lips.

"Yeah, you don't like that idea? Then run along now, kitty. We know you're big and bad, we get it. But we're bigger and badder, you fuck."

Head tilt.

What did that mean?

Oh god.

"You're not even a real lion. Nobody's scared of you. You're just an overgrown house cat. Did you lose your ball of yarn? Go cry to the other kitties about it and leave us the fuck alone!"

Weston kept on, threatening the dangerous animal while it calmly stared back at him, unfazed by the madman in its forest.

Sweat pricked my forehead. My heart thrashed, more wild than the murderous kitty. My knees were so weak, I could barely stand. But Weston held me up. His arm kept me secure against his chest, lending me the smallest, barest sense of safety.

Weston continued yelling about the violent plans he had for the mountain lion while stroking my cheek with unimaginable gentleness.

We were going to die a horrible, painful death. Every second that passed and the mountain lion remained unbothered, the end crawled closer.

The mountain lion took a step.

My breath caught.

Weston's arm tightened.

Another step.

Then another.

But not toward us.

Slowly, lazily, it slinked across our path, its ears twitching as it listened to us. It disappeared into the trees, but I didn't feel any relief.

"We need to go," Weston ordered. "Start walking, baby."

"It could be out there," I whispered.

"It could. But we can't stay here. We need to start walking."

He had a point. Staying here wasn't a good idea. We were probably in the mountain lion's turf or something.

Somehow, I got my feet to work. I trudged forward, on high alert, my head whipping back and forth, searching for the mountain lion. How was this real? This couldn't be real.

Weston stayed behind me, holding my shoulders. He kept talking to me, making noise. I knew I should have been helping, making us louder, but that wasn't happening. Fear had clogged my throat.

He squeezed my shoulders. "I'm not going to let anything happen to you, Elise. You're safe with me. All you have to do is keep walking. Just keep walking. I've got you."

In the recesses of my mind, I remembered reading that mountain lions liked to attack from behind. They usually went for the back of their prey's neck. That was why Weston was staying behind me and not leading me out. He was protecting me, putting himself between me and potential danger.

"Thank you," I whispered.

"Don't thank me now. You're in deep trouble when we get out of here. And we *will* be getting out of here, Elise."

Suddenly, I wished for the mountain lion to reappear. A nice, deep puncture wound was preferable to a lecture from Weston on how stupid I'd been to come out here on my own.

When we made it out of the trees and into the canyon, I should have felt safer, but I couldn't bring myself to calm down. My body was on high alert, fight or flight activated.

For miles, Weston held on to me. He talked to me, not just about the mountain lion, but about the scenery, his favorite spots to camp, random tidbits about Andes, anything and everything.

Once we reached the meadows, he made me stop to drink water and tugged my hat down on my head. The sun had moved across the sky, slowly dipping at the horizon. Soon, it would be dusk. We needed to be out of here.

"We should keep going."

Weston stepped forward and cupped my face in his big, rough hands. "We will. I need you to catch your breath, though. Calm, baby. Everything is all right."

I turned my face to the side, breaking his hold. "I'll calm down when we're in the parking lot."

Palming the top of my head, he searched my sweaty, overheated face. For the first time ever, I didn't care how I looked to him.

"Then let's get going." He grabbed my hand, keeping a firm hold, and started off down the trail again, pulling me with him.

Eventually, purpose took over, moving my legs faster. I stayed at his side, and we were able to pick up our pace. Dusk was coming, but we would beat it. We were going to get out of here.

The parking lot was ahead. A few cars were left, including Weston's, right beside my SUV.

"Almost there, baby. Almost there."

It was then I noticed the tremor in his hand. My eyes flicked to the side of his face. His jaw was clenched tight, the muscles flexing over and over.

"Weston—"

"Not now," he gritted.

As soon as our feet hit the gravel parking lot, Weston tugged me toward my vehicle.

"Keys, Elise."

"They're in my backpack."

I'd intended to swing my backpack around to dig them out, but Weston was faster, unzipping the front pocket before I could move. Metal clinked, then he had them in his grasp, using the remote to unlock my doors. He opened the back seat, tossed my backpack in, and stuck my keys in his pocket.

His arms folded across his chest. He stared at me without speaking, moving toward me until my back hit the driver's side door.

Leaning forward, he braced a hand on the glass beside my head. "What the fuck were you thinking? If I hadn't been there—" He broke off, his eyes slamming shut.

"I know, I know. I don't know what would have happened." I raised my shaking hands to his heaving chest. "Thank you for being there."

His eyes flashed open and zeroed in on me. "I've never been more pissed off at you."

"I wish you weren't." My fingers balled his T-shirt in a tight grip. "Please, Weston, don't be mad at me."

He bent down, his nose almost brushing mine. "I'm so fucking angry, Elise. You have no idea what I want to do with you right now."

I inhaled. His hot breath hit my lips. A wild, frantic current flowed in the narrow space between us. Adrenaline coursed through my bloodstream. My mind scrambled.

Then he was on me, or I was on him. There was no telling who moved first. We collided, our lips suctioning to one another, his tongue delving into my mouth. Fingers threaded through my hair, tugging my head back. He kissed me hard, violent, and I clawed at him.

Shoving up the back of his shirt, I dug my fingers into his bare skin. The muscles alongside his spine were taut and defined, and his skin was slick with perspiration. He grunted into my mouth and pushed me harder into the door.

I sucked on his bottom lip until he tore it away and bit at mine. My knees threatened to buckle, but I had nowhere to go. Weston had me pinned tight. He wasn't letting me fall.

His hand traveled from my hair to my throat as he ravaged my mouth. I sucked on his tongue and tilted my pelvis toward his, trapping his erection against my stomach.

With a groan, he grabbed my breast, kneading it hard, vicious, then let it go to slip into the V of my shirt and under my sports bra. He took my nipple between his fingers, pinching and rolling it. There was nothing gentle about his touch. He was greedy and angry and taking it out on me.

Without warning, he yanked me forward, walked me to the side, and pushed me into the open back seat. As soon as I was flat on my back, he fell over me, wedging his hips between my parted thighs, his solid weight settling on me.

My shirt was rucked up, sports bra next, and his mouth was on my breasts, taking my nipple between his lips and sucking.

Wet heat surrounded my nipples. My mouth dropped. My lashes fluttered as I threaded my fingers through his sweat-dampened hair. He sucked hard but licked soft. He groaned against my flesh, like just the taste of me was getting him off.

My back arched and hips rose, further wedging his cock against me. He rocked as he sucked, hitting my clit through the thin fabric of my leggings and underwear.

We grappled with each other, exploring skin that had been forbidden. We'd been unleashed, and there was no place off-limits anymore. Our cores were locked together, grinding and seeking heat, friction, *more*.

My hand ventured down the back of his pants, and I grasped his flexing ass, pressing him into me. Thick and hard as steel, I ached to know what he would feel like sliding into me. Would it hurt?

Hurt so good.

Weston made claiming sucks all over my breasts and chest. Hard enough to surely leave marks behind. And I *wanted* it.

My heart raced. I was frantic, buzzing, crazed for him. He was just as crazed, touching me, rutting against me, kissing me everywhere.

"Weston," I murmured. "Please, West."

"You have to tell me what you need," he ground out.

"I need you inside me."

He shoved his face into my throat and dragged his tongue from my collarbone to my earlobe. "Take your pants off, baby, but don't expect me to be gentle."

"I don't want gentle."

He pulled back enough for me to lift my hips. My thumbs hooked into the waistband of my leggings, my hands shaking from the anticipation of having him inside me for the first time. The sound of his heaving breath spurred me on.

Then our eyes met.

And I froze.

He did too.

Reality snuck between us.

What were we doing? This was *Weston*. I couldn't have sex with him in a parking lot. Oh god. I stared back at him in horror. He flinched like he'd been slapped.

Somewhere behind him, voices carried through the early evening air.

With that very real reminder we were in public and nowhere near alone, we both sprang into action. Weston flew off me and out of the back seat. I sat up, yanking my shirt over my breasts and covering my mouth with my hand. What had I done?

This wasn't me. I didn't make impetuous decisions or lose control. I thought things through before I acted. If I'd thought, even for a second, about the consequences of making out with my boss, who happened to be my brother's best friend, my lips never would have touched his.

When I finally climbed out of the back seat, Weston was pacing at the back of my SUV, his hands clasped on top of his head.

I wished I could have driven off without saying anything, but since he was behind my car and still had my keys, I had no choice.

"I'm going to go."

He turned, facing me. Our gazes clashed, and I wanted to cower away from him.

"You can't do anything like this again." His hands were on his hips. "Do you have any idea how crazy you make me? You can't be out here by yourself. You were *asleep*. Anything could have happened to you."

He flung his arms to the side, pacing back and forth again. He was frustrated with me, but I was frustrated with everything. All I wanted to do was drive away so I could start thinking clearly, and maybe pretend the last fifteen minutes hadn't happened. It was kind of impossible with Weston's kiss-swollen lips and hair mussed from my fingers right in my frigging face.

He stopped two feet away from me. "I really fucking hope today illustrated my point. Promise me you won't do a hike like this alone again."

My breasts still ached from how hard he'd sucked on them and he was lecturing me. This man was a machine, shutting down his feelings without blinking.

"Your point has been made, I promise." I swiped my sweaty hands on my stretched-out shirt. "I'd like to go now."

His eyes narrowed on me, and for a long, drawn-out moment, he didn't move. Then he held his hand out, my keys in his palm. I snagged them from him, my fingertips grazing his skin. My breath caught, and he glared at me.

"Thanks for not letting me die."

His glare morphed into a deep scowl. "Go home, Elise."

That was exactly what I was going to do.

⸺ ◆ ⸺

Saoirse blinked at me. "No."

I nodded, picking up my second glass of wine. "Yes."

We were on the roof of our building with two bottles of wine and a pile of snacks. I'd just spilled everything that had happened on my hike today.

She shook her head. "Who would have thought being stalked by a mountain lion would be the second most outrageous thing to happen to you today?"

I snorted a laugh. "I can't believe I made out with Weston. What in the world was I thinking?"

I would have thought I'd dreamed it if not for the hickeys he'd left behind. My breasts were mottled with his marks. Why was that so hot?

"You weren't. It was one of those 'oh my god, I almost died, let me jump on this man to reaffirm I'm still alive' type of thing. It doesn't have to mean anything."

I gulped down more wine. This recap required a lot. "But it's *Weston*."

Her nod was solemn. "Yeah. I get it. Anything with Weston always means more." She piled two pieces of cheese on a cracker. "Well, was it good?"

I rolled my eyes and sank down in my lounger. "It was wild. He kissed like he'd die if he didn't."

She sighed, sinking down beside me. "Holy shitake, what's that like?"

"Like...I don't know, it took me over. I wasn't Elise. I was this sensual being who wasn't thinking about my rolls or if he could see my stretch marks. It was me and him, and nothing else mattered outside of our connection." I slapped my forehead. "Why did I have to kiss him? Now I have to live the rest of my life knowing kissing like that exists."

She raised an eyebrow. "You never had that with Patrick?"

Guilt swamped me. The answer was easy to give. I'd loved Patrick. I'd worked hard at our relationship, had given it my all. Our sex life had been hot, and he'd taken care of my needs every single time. But no, those out-of-control moments in the back of my SUV had been hotter than the four years I spent with Patrick combined.

"Never. Not once."

Her shoulders slumped. "Damn. And Weston's a no-go, huh?"

My mouth twisted, and damn if my eyes didn't burn a little. "Even if he and I weren't impossible, I truly think he got caught up in the moment. I've seen the women he dates. They're nothing like me."

She waved her cracker at me. "Go fuck yourself, Lise. He'd be lucky to have a woman as hot as you."

"He's had women ten times hotter. I promise you, he's not lacking beautiful company. Have you seen him?"

She gave me an incredulous look. "Have you seen *you*? Weston is hot, but honestly, honey, you might be hotter. With your tits titting all over the place, that ass, your stunning brown eyes, big puffy lips...come on."

"I'm a realist, babe. I know I'm attractive." Saoirse's eyes flared. Attractive obviously wasn't good enough for her. "Okay, I'm pretty. But I also know firsthand not everyone is into women with bodies like mine. Look at Patrick."

"Patrick was hot for you. He was also a dick."

I sighed. "Yeah, he was both of those things."

"You said Weston was hard as a rock."

I took another long pull of my wine. "So hard," I whispered, flashing back to the feel of him rocking against me.

She snapped her fingers. "So go fuck yourself with the 'not every-one's into bodies like mine.' As far as I know, you're not planning on gangbanging 'everyone.' Weston Aldrich is clearly into your body, honey. Don't try to talk yourself out of the facts."

My brow pinched. "I think...I don't want to talk about this any-more."

"Fine." She slapped her thighs. "Let's talk about your date with Thomas tomorrow night. Maybe you should make out with him too. For science."

I snorted a laugh, happy about the subject change. "Oh, well, if it's for science..."

Two bottles of wine later, I was happily tipsy and had pushed the hottest make-out session of my life out of my head.

Mostly.

Okay, not even a little.

CHAPTER THIRTEEN

Weston

"You need to relax." Luca pushed my drink toward me. "Drink up. You have another long week staring you in the face."

I picked up my glass. "I'm relaxed as I get."

Elliot chuckled and leaned back in his seat. "Which isn't relaxed at all."

Luca shot him a look. "Pot, meet kettle."

Elliot slung an arm over the back of his chair. "I'm relaxed. Just because I'm not out riding motorcycles and going to house parties like a fucking frat boy doesn't mean I'm incapable of relaxing."

It was Sunday. Elliot had just arrived home from his Dubai trip two days prior. He'd spent the afternoon with his sister. Tonight, the three of us had gone to dinner, and now we were having a few drinks at a bar we often frequented.

Luca held up his beer. "There's no need for you to be jealous of my active social life. Just because I have more than two friends doesn't mean I don't love you guys the most."

Elliot's eyes rolled. "As if I'm insecure about my place in your heart. I'm firmly wedged in there."

Luca winked at him and patted his chest. "For lifers, bro."

"Please don't say bro. Or lifers. It offends me." I tipped back my bourbon and soda, finishing it off.

"Speaking of." Luca nodded to someone near the bar. "There's Celeste. Looks like she's got some friends with her."

"Oh, Celeste," I said drolly. "I have no idea who that is."

Luca backhanded my arm. "I took her to the Saviano benefit. You met her. Auburn hair, hot body, sucks dick like she's being paid for it."

Elliot's brow winged. "Was she?"

Luca raised his glass in cheers. "Fuck off, old man. I've never paid for a lay in my life. That's a strictly volunteer position." He hopped up from his seat. "I'm going to bring them over."

I groaned. The women who flocked around Luca were always the most insufferable. Gorgeous, obviously, but I needed more than a pretty face to keep me interested, and that was all most of Luca's women offered.

Elliot angled himself toward me. "You never said, did you catch up with Elise on her hike yesterday?"

I happened to be talking to Elliot when Elise had texted where she was spending her day yesterday. Something had come over me—panic was probably the word—and I'd followed her. She'd been easy to find and hadn't noticed me behind her until I'd made myself known.

I didn't let even an ounce of guilt flicker across my face. "No. We must have missed each other."

If she hadn't told her brother about what had happened yesterday, I wouldn't be the one to do it. Not the mountain lion. Definitely not what had happened after.

He shook his head. "I can't believe she went out on her own again. Next time I see her, I'm going to throttle her. I'd intended to this morning, but she'd been so thrilled by the presents I'd brought back for her, I didn't have the heart to yell at her.

"What did you get her?"

"A little gold camel, a pink Pashmina, and some sand art. Nothing big, but you know Elise. Those kinds of things make her squeal. It's fun giving her presents. She always has these cute, over-the-top reactions."

It had been years since I'd openly given Elise anything, but I hadn't forgotten. Her face always turned bright pink and the dimple in her cheek popped when she beamed. There were hugs. So many hugs, and usually kisses on the cheeks.

I understood why Elliot hadn't wanted to ruin the moment.

Luca approached the table with an entourage surrounding him. Three women, the one with the auburn hair hanging off his shoulder.

He introduced us. "Elliot and Weston, this is Celeste, Mara, and Sarah. I begged them to join us for a drink. I basically had to promise my firstborn to get them to agree."

Mara, the brunette, took a seat beside me. Sarah, a blonde, sat beside Elliot, who admittedly took a vague interest. He didn't seem annoyed by the intruders.

Everyone paired off, so I was forced to make small talk with *Mara*, a twenty-three-year-old who worked in marketing. She had a lot to say on that topic. So much, she didn't notice I'd completely tuned her out, going over my weekly schedule in my mind.

"What do you do?" she asked breathlessly, as though she just ran a mile in her heels.

"I'm a garbage man," I deadpanned.

She blinked, her long, thick lashes casting weird shadows on her face. "Oh, really? Luca said—"

Tuning her out, I scanned the bar and landed on a big, redheaded lumberjack-looking fellow. Standing close to him was Elise Levy. He bent toward her, listening to her speak.

She had on snug jeans and a top that dipped low, revealing the upper swells of her creamy tits. There was not a chance this asshole wasn't trying to see what was beneath her top.

I smirked to myself. I knew exactly what was under there, and it was fucking glorious.

My smirk fell away when he brushed her hair back from her face and she leaned into him.

"Is that my sister?" Elliot ground out.

I turned back to the group. Everyone had stopped talking. Elliot was watching Elise and her lumberjack through narrowed, pissed-off eyes.

"Oooh." Luca covered his laugh with his hand. "Little Elise is on a da-ate."

Elliot whipped around toward him. "Why don't you sound surprised?"

Luca grinned wider. "Because your sister is a beautiful, grown woman and this isn't her first date with that gentleman."

Elliot's irritation at being out of the loop landed on me. "Did you know about this? Who is he?"

I turned my hands over, forcing myself not to clench them. "That's Thomas. They met a week ago. You should go check on them."

He shot to his feet before I even finished my sentence and strolled over to his sister with a false air of casualness. He was going to make a mess of things. He always did with guys she dated. Elliot had never liked any of them. And it wasn't some weird, incestuous thing. He wanted the best for her and had never once thought her boyfriends had qualified as that.

There was no part of me that wanted to watch this. Elliot and Elise were going to end up pissed at each other and he'd most likely push her further into the lumberjack's arms. It's what had happened when he'd disapproved of her last boyfriend.

We'd lost her for three years and were only now getting her back.

The girl beside me—god, I'd already forgotten her name—pressed her hand to my inner thigh. "You were kidding about being a garbage man, weren't you?"

I picked up her hand, holding it for a beat. "Why would I joke about that kind of thing?"

She curled her fingers around mine and let out a laugh that didn't come close to sounding real. "You're funny. Luca said you're funny, and you are."

I slipped my hand from hers and excused myself to the restroom. As soon as Elliot was finished with his intimidation tactics, I would be saying my goodbyes and heading out. I was getting too old and impatient to hang out with random, vapid women on a Sunday evening when I had no intention of taking them to bed.

Leaning against the wall in the bathroom hall, I replied to an email from Renata about my and Elise's trip to California at the end of the week. I had just hit send when someone rounded the corner.

My head shot up, and I locked eyes with a red-cheeked Elise. Her steps stuttered, and she slowed, wariness pulling at her soft features.

"What are you doing?" she asked.

I straightened, taking a step in her direction. "I could ask you the same. You're on a date?"

"Yes." She folded her arms under her tits, which did nothing to clear my head. I blamed that as I closed in on her until her back hit the wall, knocking a gasp from her chest.

"Why?"

She raised her defiant little chin. "Because he asked and I like him."

I tipped my head down, bringing my mouth beside her ear. Back and forth, I rubbed my lips against her velvet lobe. A shiver went through her, and her chest rose, pressing into mine.

"Elise..." My teeth nibbled along her lobe, then my tongue licked a path around the shell of her ear. Her arms fell to the bottom of my shirt, grasping it with both hands.

I drew my tongue along the soft line of her jaw. "Does your date have any idea you were writhing under me only yesterday?"

She sucked in a sharp breath. "Stop it, Weston. Don't talk about that."

Bracing my hand beside her head, I pulled back so we were eye to eye. The position reminded me of when she was trapped against her car.

When *I'd* trapped her.

"What did Elliot think of your boyfriend?"

Her nostrils flared. "You know he's not my boyfriend. You also know Elliot disliked him immediately."

"Maybe you have bad, bad taste in men, Elise." I picked up a piece of her hair. She'd made it wavy, but it was still as silky as always. "Why is that?"

She raised her chin a little more, bringing her mouth almost level with mine. I could have kissed her, and she wouldn't have stopped me.

That wasn't off the table.

"Maybe I've only known bad, bad men since my father died. Men who would stalk their best friend's sister, make out with her in the back seat of her SUV, then trap her in a dark hallway and lick her neck."

My free hand shot up to cup her jaw. "That's the thing, Elise. You could have moved away from me at any moment. You're choosing to stay."

I pressed my erection against her softness, pulling a raspy breath from her lips. Her eyes darted to the side then back to me.

"Why are you doing this?" she whispered.

"Why are you on a date tonight?" I shot back.

Her tongue darted out, licking her bottom lip, leaving it shiny. "I don't know how to handle you when you're like this."

"Like what?"

Her breath shuddered. She tried to turn her head to the side, but I tightened my grip on her, keeping her in place.

"Weston..."

"Like what, Elise?"

Her dark eyes flicked to mine. "Like you're jealous." She looked away. "As if you weren't just touching a beautiful woman. As if you weren't holding her hand a few minutes ago."

"What?" It took me a moment to understand what she was talking about.

Luca's girl.

It was on the tip of my tongue to deny it, but why? I was pissed she'd shown up here with that man. Why was she dragging it out? It was clear there was no chemistry there. If there was, she wouldn't have kissed me back yesterday.

But I had no room to be pissed. Elise wasn't mine, nor would she ever be.

"You're right. I was doing that, which means I shouldn't be here with you." A sense of honor finally came over me and I let her go. "You might think I'm a bad man, and maybe I am, but I would never be bad to you."

As I backed away from her, she pulled herself off the wall and smoothed her palms down her hips. "Weston…"

I jerked my chin toward the mouth of the hall, dismissing her. "Go back to your boyfriend. I don't have time for this."

She flinched at my caustic tone but didn't hesitate more than two heartbeats before scrambling away from me back into the bar, leaving a subtle cloud of her sweet, floral fragrance.

I finally got my head on straight.

I was being stupid, making thoughtless choices that would only end in disaster. That wasn't me, and it wouldn't continue.

Tomorrow, I'd set us both straight.

CHAPTER FOURTEEN

Elise

No Post-its were on my desk this morning.

Not that I'd expected any.

Kissing Weston had probably screwed up our chances of having a light, fun friendship like we used to. In my mind, I wanted to put the blame on him, but it was just as much my fault. Last night, when he had me pinned against the wall in the bar, I could have left. He hadn't been holding me captive.

Despite the fact that anyone could have seen us like that, including my date and my brother, those dangers hadn't crossed my mind until later. It had been all Weston's tongue on my skin, his dick prodding my belly, his body looming over mine. For those breathless moments, he had consumed me.

In the cold light of day, I understood how careless I'd been.

This was *Weston*. My boss. Elliot's best friend. Nothing like that could happen again.

As soon as I turned on my computer, I logged into my email. There at the top was one from Weston Aldrich, CEO.

To: eliselevy@andesinc.com

From: westonaldrich@andesinc.com

Dear Elise,

Please see me in my office at 9:30 this morning.

Thank you.

Cordially,

Weston

I groaned, cupping my face in my hands. I had fifteen minutes to ruminate and fret over this. It could be nothing. Our trip to California was coming up. Perhaps that was what he wanted to discuss. I hoped it was and we could get back to our professional relationship.

Please, please, *please* let this not be about the kissing. That was the last thing I wanted to talk about.

"What's wrong, Lisie?"

I looked up, finding Miles perched in his favorite spot on the edge of my desk.

"Headache," I answered. It wasn't untrue. It was his brother who was driving the ice pick into my head.

"Wild weekend, eh? I never took you for a party girl. You should have invited me out. I liven up every room I enter."

I squinted at him. "Really? Is that the only reason a person might have a headache?"

He tapped his chin. "In my experience, it's the most common reason."

"Which says a lot about you, Miles."

"You're sassy on this sunny Monday morning. It's very becoming on you." He waved his hand in a vague circle around me. "This whole thing is working for you. I like that you haven't succumbed to wearing Andes like the other carbon copies who work here."

I wore yellow today, hoping the sunny shade would put me in a better mood. So far, it wasn't working. It would take more than my favorite cardigan to pull me out of this slump.

"Thank you for saying so. If you want to know the truth, I *did* buy some things from the company store, but I can't bring myself to wear sportswear in the office." I grimaced. "I just can't do it."

Miles smoothed his hand over his tailored vest. "It's you and me to the end, Lisie. You won't catch me dead wearing Andes to work. It will never happen."

My phone started ringing before I could reply. Miles made no move to leave, so I answered it.

"Good morning, this is Elise."

"Hello, Elise. Weston asked me to remind you of your appointment," Renata breezed out.

My eyes closed, and I sighed. "I haven't forgotten. I'll be there at 9:30 sharp."

Her voice dropped. "He doesn't mind if you're early. In fact, I would suggest it. He's pacing inside his office like a lion in the zoo."

Another sigh. "Fine. I'll be right up."

With my agreement, she hung up without saying goodbye. I replaced my phone and pushed my chair back to stand.

"Have you been summoned?" Miles asked.

"I have." I started to touch my hair to make sure it was all in place but decided not to care.

"Is my brother giving you a hard time?"

I grabbed my phone, tucking it in the pocket of my A-line skirt. "He's just being Weston."

Miles scoffed. "So, that's a yes." He shoved off my desk, walking with me to the elevator. "Don't let him trod all over you, Lisie. When he gets in his moods, he forgets other people have feelings too."

He'd behaved that way last night, taunting me in that hallway. Jealousy, or something close to it, had driven him to piss all over me without any regard for how it would affect me.

"Don't worry about me." I patted his chest. "Don't you have work to do?"

He jumped back as if I'd scalded him. "Jeez, why do you have to remind me like that? I'm being all supportive and all you can talk about is work. What's up with that cruelty?"

I laughed even though I wasn't feeling particularly cheerful. "Shut up, Miles."

He stepped closer, poking my dimple. "Nice smile."

I gave him a shove. "Go away."

"You wish."

He stayed until I was on the elevator, waving at me as the doors slid closed. I shook my head, still smiling a little at his antics. When he was like that, it was easy to forget he'd made my life miserable for years.

Then again, I'd changed in the eight years since graduation. Miles obviously had too. Holding on to old hurts had gotten me nowhere. I had to let go of it for the sake of keeping the peace at work. It would do me no good to be angry at him until the end of time.

I hadn't been up to the executive floor. Here, there were offices instead of open spaces. The receptionist directed me down a quiet hallway. Weston's office was in the corner.

Renata's desk was outside his open door. Her serious mouth flattened as I approached. Though we'd spoken, we hadn't met in person yet. Looking at her, I realized she was the older woman I'd seen with Weston in the cafeteria on my first day here.

"Elise?" My name came out like a snap, sharp and precise.

"Yes, it's nice to meet you."

The corners of her eyes pinched. "That's fine. He's expecting you. Go inside and close the door behind you."

"Close the door?"

She gestured to her desk. "Please. I have a busy morning. I don't have time to listen to Weston expel whatever bug crawled up his butt today."

I sputtered, shocked at the way she was speaking about our mutual boss. She stared back at me with unimpressed, dark, beady eyes.

"Go on then." She nodded toward his door. "Don't keep him waiting."

Despite being directed to go straight in, I knocked first. From inside, Weston barked for me to enter. I was beginning to think Weston and Renata were a match made in heaven. They probably spent the day shouting back and forth at each other.

I slipped inside, shutting the door behind me. Weston stopped pacing behind his desk to stare at me. Glower, really.

This was a bad start.

"Good morning," I said.

Bracing his hands on his desk, he leaned forward. "Do you know why you're here?"

I twined my fingers to keep from fidgeting. I'd known this man most of my life, but he still managed to intimidate me. Under his relentless gaze, it was difficult to be still and not bow my head. I wasn't even a head-bowing kind of girl.

"Well, when I read your email, I assumed you wanted to discuss the California trip. Now, I'm not so sure."

"Sit down, Elise."

I walked forward and took a seat in one of the two chairs in front of his desk. He remained braced as if he was going to spring at me at any moment.

"Renata will email you the information about our trip." He straightened, crossing his arms over his chest. He'd removed his jacket and rolled up his sleeves. The muscles in his taut forearms flexed.

"I'm looking forward to it," I replied, determined to remain professional. At least one of us should have been.

"Are you?"

"Yes." I nodded. "Salma and I found three employees I'm going to interview while we're there. I've been trading emails with one. His name is Cameron and he's an avid rock climber. If we have time, I'd like to go watch him—"

"You won't have time." His brow dropped into a fierce line.

"Are you sure? I checked the schedule and—"

"I'm sure, Elise. My schedule has no leeway."

I tilted my head, confused. "I know that, but I was under the impression I'll be doing interviews on my own while you attend your meetings."

"That's true, but you're not going rock climbing with some guy named *Cameron* unless I'm there too. Since that's not possible, no, you won't be accompanying him."

My mouth dropped open. Weston continued glaring at me as though I'd done something heinously wrong.

"Weston—"

He scrubbed his hand over his mouth and stalked around his desk, coming to a stop at my side. "You see, *this* is why I wanted to see you."

"I'm here now." I nodded to the chair next to me. "Please sit. I don't want to speak to you while you're looming over me."

His ego was almost a tangible thing. He'd been a boss for too long. It was probably next to impossible for him to take orders.

Finally, he lowered himself into the seat, bracing his ankle on the opposite knee.

"I'm confused," I said.

"It's simple." He paused, raking his fingers through his hair, making me think it wasn't actually simple. "What happened this weekend can't happen again. It will get in the way of my relationship with Elliot and my working relationship with you. We barely kissed and I'm already having bouts of jealousy that are entirely unwanted and, frankly, I have no time for. We'll go back to how things were before and forget this ever happened."

I huffed a soft laugh. "We barely kissed?"

It was interesting that Weston was trying to rewrite history. Both times we'd crossed the line, he'd been the one to initiate, and he'd definitely been the aggressor.

He blinked at me. "Is that what you're stuck on?"

"I suppose so since I agree with the rest. Your jealousy is completely unwanted."

"You agree?"

I did agree. It was just…this felt an awful lot like rejection, and it stung. It hadn't been long enough for me to get over the way Patrick had eviscerated me, so I was being more sensitive than normal. Plus, this was *Weston*. The first keeper of my heart.

The first smasher too.

"Mmmhmm. We should absolutely go back to how things were before." I stacked my hands on my lap, smiling pleasantly. It was a show and a good one. "But wait, which 'before' are we talking about? The one with your plethora of women? When you pulled me aside to whisper in my ear that I was making a mistake moving to Chicago? How about the 'before' when my brother forced you to have lunch with me? Oh, wait, maybe when you sent me flowers every week and left cute little Post-its on my desk. Which one, Weston?"

"Elise—" He reached for me, but I drew my hands away, causing his frown to deepen. "There's no need to argue if we both agree."

"I'm not arguing. I'm asking how you would like me to behave toward you."

"Professional," he answered flatly.

My stomach lurched, but I made sure it didn't show. If Weston wanted professional, that was what he'd get. Later, when I was alone, I would have time to process this dagger in my gut.

"I can do that. Can you?"

His gaze remained steady and unaffected. "Of course."

"Good." I bobbed my head once. "Please remember if we run into each other socially."

His mouth twitched downward. "What do you mean?"

I flicked my hand around. Lackadaisical. Not a care in this brutal world. "You know, if I'm on a date and you happen to see me, don't corner me in a dark hall and carry on about my attraction to bad, bad men. That wouldn't be very professional."

He lowered his chin, fire burning in his dark eyes. He kept his tone flat, bored even. "You're right. It wouldn't. It won't happen again."

"Fine." Oh, I had to go before I got sad. Being sad over Weston was so five years ago. Now was definitely not the time. "Is there anything else?"

When he didn't answer, I hopped to my feet and smoothed my hand over the back of my hair. "I really should go. I have a lot to do before the trip."

I took three steps toward the door before my elbow was caught and I was yanked back against Weston's solid chest.

"I know you too well," he murmured beside my ear. "I've upset you."

"Stop it," I whispered.

"I don't want to hurt you." He nuzzled into my hair. "Don't you know that?"

I squeezed my eyes shut. "No."

"I don't, Elise. These last few days have driven me crazy and caused me to act outside of my character. I'm sorry for that. You just ended a serious relationship. The last thing I want to do is hurt you further."

I shook my head. "You haven't."

His mouth was beside my ear, which was the only reason I heard his soft groan. "I wish that was true." He let go of my elbow to wrap his arm around my middle, drawing me firmly against him.

"Weston..." I rasped, torn between pulling away and leaning into him. "Please. This isn't—"

"Once you leave this office, I won't touch you again. Let me fucking have this, baby. Let me hold you for a minute, then you can go."

It was stupid of me not to immediately walk out his door, but I didn't. I allowed him to turn me toward him. He took my face in his hands and covered my mouth with his. I held on to the lapels of his jacket, whimpering into his mouth.

He kissed me hard, backing me into his door. In that wayward moment, I didn't even care that Renata must have heard me clunk against it. Weston urged my mouth open and delved his tongue inside.

His kisses were deep, licking, and his hands were sure, roaming to my breasts, my ass, palming my pussy, before returning to my breasts again. He kneaded them, pinched my nipples, rocked his hips against me. It wasn't sordid or dirty, though it should have been given the location and who we were to each other.

What was happening between us was nothing less than desperate desire. At least now I could be sure I wasn't alone in these feelings. Weston must have carried the same attraction, one we could not act on.

We had this. These few minutes to taste each other, to touch and grasp, but this was it. It really had to be.

Weston reached down, gathering my skirt in his fist until he exposed my panties. His fingers grazed over the satin material to the elastic side, hooking inside. Calloused fingertips grazed my wet slit. Our groans twined together, low and breathless with surprise. I widened my stance, letting him in. This was happening. He was touching my pussy in his office. *My* Weston was sliding his fingers between my lower lips, finding my clit swollen and throbbing.

What was he doing to me?

This didn't feel like goodbye.

This felt like the beginning of something naughty and out of control.

In less than a minute, I was so close to coming I forgot how to breathe. He kept going, rubbing me with his thumb, the other fingers exploring my slick heat.

"Let me have it, baby," he murmured against my lips. "Give me this one time."

He was almost begging me, but he didn't need to. All he had to do was touch me like that, look at me how he did, and my pleasure was his for the taking.

"Give it to me," he demanded.

I was helpless to deny him this. My orgasm swept through me with the power of every fantasy and ounce of longing I'd carried around for Weston for years. I jerked and moaned into his licking mouth, and he held me through it, stroking my hair as he continued to stroke my clit.

"That's a girl," he praised. "So beautiful when you come."

When the last tremor abated, he let my skirt fall, and his mouth covered mine, this time kissing me slowly. The goodbye on his tongue was bittersweet.

We drew it out with languid, somber kisses and slow exploration of the places on each other we would never touch again. Every second that passed shook my resolve. Giving this up, now that I knew what he felt like and how tender he could truly be, would be difficult.

But necessary.

We were snapped back to reality by the soft knock on the other side of the door I was pressed against. Weston raised his head, his eyes glassy but wide. My breasts were in his hands. My hands were in the back of his pants.

He cleared his throat. "Yes?"

"Your ten a.m. meeting, Weston. It's time," Renata said.

"All right. Two minutes."

A long pause, then his gaze landed on mine. "*Fuck*."

"Yeah."

I slid my hands out of his pants, and he peered down at where he held me, a line between his eyebrows. I thought he'd let me go, but instead, he dipped his head. I gasped at the first touch of his lips on the upper curve of my breasts. He peppered kisses over my chest, paying special attention to the fading bruises he'd left two days before.

When he was finished with me, he carefully extracted his hands and righted my bra, then my blouse, arranging it neatly at my hips. He scanned me, and when he got to my hair, he combed his fingers through it until he was satisfied.

"Perfect," he whispered.

"Thank you," I whispered back.

"I have a meeting now. I'd like you to go so I don't have to walk into the conference room with an erection."

I laughed despite the pit in my stomach. "Okay." I glanced down at the tent in his immaculately tailored pants. "Good luck with that."

I rushed out of his office, avoiding eye contact with Renata. I had a feeling she'd had a pretty good idea of what had gone down. Luckily, I doubted I'd be spending any more time on the executive floor. I wouldn't have to face her again, and it was a good thing.

My strange...whatever that had been, was put to rest. My heart hurt, but since it had already been bruised, it was impossible to tell how much had come from Weston.

Then again, it was over, so it didn't really matter anyway.

Chapter Fifteen

I HAD FLOWN FIRST class exactly once, and that had been with Elliot when I left Chicago.

Needless to say, the possibility of flying first class on a business trip hadn't crossed my mind, so I was surprised to learn that I was when I checked in. I was also told I had access to the first-class lounge, and though I was curious what went on in there, I decided to hang out in the boarding area.

The people watching in airports was second to none. No way I'd give that up for a fancy lounge. Besides, I had a delicate text exchange to deal with.

Letting down Thomas gently wasn't fun. The worst part was how kind he was about it.

It had to be done, though. Prolonging the inevitable wasn't fair to either of us.

Staying out of the first-class lounge also meant avoiding running into Weston until we boarded the plane.

He was already seated when I boarded and his brow winged when I walked by him to take my seat on the opposite side, an aisle back.

If he had anything to discuss with me, he could send me an email. There was no need for us to be side by side for this flight. We'd be spending enough time together over the next few days as it was.

⚜

When we landed in California, I was relaxed and ready to work. Weston seemed quite the opposite, judging from his tight shoulders and pissed-off scowl. Without speaking, he stood by my row, gesturing for me to go ahead of him, then stayed on my heels until we were in the airport.

He stepped up beside me. "You changed your seating assignment."

I nodded. I'd learned ticket agents were a lot more accommodating when flying first class. "I like the window."

"I would have given you the window in my row."

I flicked my fingers. "That's okay. This way we both had the window."

"So, you were doing me a favor and not avoiding me?"

"Right. Exactly."

"I'm relieved, since avoiding your boss on a work trip would be both childish and pointless."

"Then it's good I just like the window seat," I answered. "From what I read on our schedule, we'll be visiting Simpson and Associates first. They produce outerwear, correct?"

"If the schedule says it, it's correct."

I nodded sharply, pleased Weston had reverted to his usual grumpy boss self. Grumpy Weston, I knew how to deal with. Sexy Weston was outside my paygrade.

"I'm looking forward to it."

I'd done my research on Andes' production practices. Andes didn't own its own factories. They contracted with factories all over the world, requiring them to adhere to Andes' strict labor and environmental rules. Four of the factories were in California, the others were spread around Asia, Mexico, and El Salvador.

It was honestly impressive how huge Andes had grown while still maintaining their strict production practices.

I shouldn't have been surprised when a Tesla was delivered to us at the pickup curb, and Weston climbed behind the wheel. He took environmentalism seriously, from his company, down to his personal habits.

Weston's thumbs tapped on the wheel as he sped away from the city. "Do you have questions for me?"

I looked up from my tablet, where I'd been reading up on our first stop. "Sure. Do you visit all your factories like this?"

He scoffed. "We work with more than seventy suppliers. I don't have the time to visit them all every year, though I've been inside each and every one at least once."

I waited for more of an answer. I had a feeling it wasn't so simple.

He exhaled, sliding his eyes to me. "Andes employs field staff who are inside the factories on a regular basis. Often, I'm taken on walk-throughs via videoconference, and those happen at random. I wouldn't be able to run this company if I had any doubt about *who* is making our products."

"Children?" I guessed.

He nodded once. "Exactly. Andes doesn't work with suppliers who have even been rumored to use child or forced labor. Our oversight is extensive, to some, over the top, but—"

"I don't think it's over the top. It's admirable."

"It's necessary." His jaw clenched. He continued tapping his thumbs on his steering wheel. Another few miles passed, thick silence filling the spaces all around us.

"Tomorrow, we'll be going to the mill that makes your filler?"

"Yes. They've been with me since the very beginning."

"Wow." I shook my head. "It's crazy to me that you started all this at twenty years old. When I was twenty, I spent most of my time either getting drunk at stupid parties, recovering from hangovers, or frantically studying for a test the night before."

He glanced at me again. "That's exactly what you should have been doing. Having fun, living. It's not like you had the chance to do that when you were in high school."

"Yeah." I sank into my seat. Weston didn't know the half of it, but the half he did know was bad.

My crazy mother. Her neglect, depression, violent mood swings...the car crash I never once doubted was intentional. The relief I never voiced when she was gone and I didn't have to take care of her. The solace when Elliot moved home and I could finally breathe again.

Weston had had a front-row seat to the madness of Elaine Levy.

"I shouldn't have brought that up," he gruffed. "I'm sorry."

I waved him off, even though he was right, he shouldn't have. "Don't worry. I know your boss hat is firmly in place, but it would be strange to pretend you don't know anything about me."

He cleared his throat, but his words came out with the same gruffness. "All of that is true, but now is not the time to press on a sore subject. It won't happen again."

"You're forgiven."

His jaw tightened. "That easy?"

"You're my boss, Mr. Aldrich. Of course I won't hold a grudge against you."

I swore I heard his molars crack.

<hr>

A team was waiting for us at our first stop. Two men and a woman in suits, and a man in khakis and a polo with the factory logo embroidered on his chest.

As we approached, the woman broke off from the group. The slow, perusing smile she gave Weston was in direct contradiction to the professional handshake she offered.

He took her hand in his, cupping it with his other. His eyes crinkled at the corners. "It's good to see you, Marisol."

She leaned in, her red lips glistening. "It's really good to see you, West. It's been too long."

This woman was stunningly beautiful. Tall and slender, with curvy hips and a tiny, nipped waist, she looked like the Hollywood version of a businesswoman. Her cigarette trousers and silky cream blouse could have come directly from the wardrobe department. Her glossy waves looked like they'd just been touched up by her beauty team. I wasn't even jealous. I was sort of dumbfounded this woman existed in real life.

"Far too long," Weston agreed.

After basically eye-fucking in broad daylight, they finally let go of each other, and he greeted the rest of the group. At the last minute, he seemed to remember I was there and introduced me to everyone.

They couldn't have been less interested in me, which was fine. I wasn't here for these suits anyway.

I spent the next two hours trailing behind the group, taking notes as we toured the factory. Weston stopped to talk to many of the workers, some he knew by name. The entire time, Marisol stayed at his side, finding every excuse to touch him.

I learned she was head of the West Coast supply chain for Andes. Obviously, she and Weston worked closely together. I idly wondered what else they'd done closely together. From her casual touches, I knew.

Interestingly, Weston had breached his own professional ethics to fuck *Marisol*. I supposed there were always exceptions to rules—especially when the exception looked like that.

When it was time to leave for the next factory, I headed toward Weston's Tesla, stopping in my motherflipping tracks when Marisol the Beautiful opened the passenger door and slipped inside, sitting in my seat like it belonged to her.

A throat cleared behind me.

I turned around, slamming my slackened mouth closed. Dev and Jeff, the other two managers, were next to their SUV.

Dev opened the back passenger door. "You're riding with us."

"I am?"

I glanced back to find the Tesla speeding out of the parking lot, and my stomach dropped. Weston had left me without saying a word. He'd actually abandoned me.

That asshole.

All I wanted to do was sit down on the curb and refuse to go anywhere until he came back and dumped Marisol out of my seat. Then I'd dump *him* out of his seat and leave him in the dust.

Instead, I pulled myself together and climbed into the back of the SUV with the two men who were strangers to me.

Nice. Really nice.

Several hours, another factory tour, and a tense, silent drive later, we arrived at our hotel. I was completely trashed, ready to curl up in my bed, order room service, and read smut until I passed out.

Because Weston was who he was, the hotel manager met us in the lobby and escorted us to our floor, stopping at my room first. As soon as I had the key in my hand, I ducked inside, leaving Weston with the manager in the hallway.

I was kind of done being around him.

Being ignored for almost an entire day would do that.

So, yeah. Boss Weston sucked. And seeing him with Marisol had brought me back to the days of his plethora of women. I wondered why I'd ever allowed him to touch me. This was who he was. He hadn't changed. He'd only gotten more discreet.

After ordering room service, I took a shower and put on the silk shortie pajamas Saoirse had bought me as a roommate gift.

It wasn't late, but I had no intention of leaving this room tonight.

I was towel drying my hair when there was a soft knock on the door. My stomach growled as if it knew my dinner was on the other side.

But it wasn't room service knocking. Weston stood there, his hands tucked in the pockets of his jeans.

"Oh." I was honestly taken aback to see him, especially looking so casual. "It's you."

His brow pinched as he took in what I was wearing. "Hey. I wanted to see if you'd like to grab dinner with me."

I tugged on my flowy camisole, wishing my shorts were a little longer. "These are my pajamas. I'm in for the night."

"You have to eat," he argued.

"And I will. I'm waiting for room service."

"Oh." He glanced down the hall as if searching for something to say. "I thought we could go over your thoughts on how today went and discuss the plan for tomorrow."

I shook my head. "If you'd like my thoughts, I'll email you."

Not all my thoughts. If I emailed those, I would be fired.

He dipped his chin. "Are you sure? There's a restaurant I like to eat at whenever I'm in town. It's walking distance and—"

"I'm sure, Weston. If you don't want to go alone, maybe Marisol will join you. I'm sure she'd be eager for it."

As he was about to speak, my room service arrived. Weston had to move aside to let the man carrying my dinner into my room. He placed it on the coffee table and thanked me when I tipped him.

In those thirty seconds of distraction, Weston had stepped into my room, closing the door after the server left.

I frowned at him. "What are you doing?"

"Are you angry at me?" he asked.

With a sigh, I sat down on the small couch and tucked my legs underneath me, holding a pillow in my lap. "No. I'm tired and don't want to work for the rest of the night."

"Being around me is work?"

"Why are you pressing this?" I held out my hand and let it fall heavily. "You asked me to dinner to discuss work-related topics. I'm not interested in doing that tonight. That has nothing to do with you and everything to do with me."

He pushed off the wall beside the door and strode toward me. "Is that right?"

"It is."

"Then why bring up Marisol?"

"Why wouldn't I? She's your colleague and you seem to have a lot to say to each other. So much so I had to ride in an entirely different vehicle with two men I was introduced to today. I'd think you'd have plenty to talk about over dinner."

He went still for two seconds, then his head bowed and he muttered a curse. "That shouldn't have happened. I shouldn't have let that happen."

"It's fine, Weston."

"No, it isn't. I asked you to come out here. I should have made sure you were comfortable riding with Jeff and Dev. That won't happen tomorrow."

It struck me hard that he didn't say he *shouldn't* have let Marisol take my spot in his car. Was I overreacting? I supposed it wasn't so ludicrous for Weston to drive his coworker while I rode with other coworkers.

But no. At the very least, he should have said something. Checked in with me. I wasn't going to gaslight myself into believing it had been okay for him to ditch me with Dev and Jeff, some of the least delightful men I'd ever met.

I put on my best smile. "I'll be prepared for it tomorrow. No biggie."

His eyes narrowed. "I don't like when you do that."

"What?"

"Act like you're okay when you aren't."

I shrugged. "I don't know what you'd like me to do."

Rounding the coffee table, he dropped into the armchair diagonal to me. He sat on the edge of the cushion, bracing his elbows on his knees.

"Elise." He pressed his palms together and leveled me with a direct stare. Then he spoke to me like I was a child having a tantrum. "If you felt neglected today, or you're angry at me for speaking to my managers and not you, you'll have to work through that. I made a mistake with the car situation, but the reality is this trip isn't about you and me. I'm here to touch base with my suppliers and my West Coast team. You're here to find content and conduct interviews for the catalog. That's it. This isn't a social trip. We're not on vacation. You get that, right?"

I blinked at him, unwilling to let him see his soft admonishment felt like a stinging whip across already tender skin. How dare he beg me to let him hold me one last time then behave like it had never happened.

"I do get that. Do you get that you're in *my* hotel room, pressing me even though I asked you to stop? I've told you more than once everything is fine, but you're still here, which I don't understand. Would you have forced your way into another employee's hotel room?"

"No," he uttered.

"Then why are you in mine?"

"Elise," he sighed. "Don't be difficult."

"Weston, don't be confusing. You drew a line with me, which I agreed with. If you want to be my friend outside of work, fine. Let's do that. But you can't be a total dick to me when you're being the boss. If we're not going to be friends, then you really shouldn't be in my hotel room."

His face had drawn into a displeased furrow. "I'm not sure what you want from me. Is there anything I can say that will be right?"

I crushed the pillow to my chest, tired and hurt and so completely done with this conversation. "Have you had sex with Marisol?"

He barely flinched, but it was enough.

"You can go." I turned away from him, staring at the far wall. This was the exact kind of drama I had no space for. And the wild thing was, I was half the cause of it. Me, the girl who had snuck out of Chicago in the middle of the night to avoid confrontation.

Weston Aldrich seemed to keep bringing out the worst in me.

It was maddening.

But when he got up and quietly left my room, I had to bite my tongue to stop myself from asking him to come back.

Chapter Sixteen

Weston

It was late.

Midnight.

Sleep eluded me.

I stood at the door separating my room from Elise's. Had she noticed we had adjoining rooms? More than once, I'd pressed my ear to the door to check if I could hear her moving inside.

Silence.

I rested my head against the door.

I'd screwed up today and hadn't even realized it while I'd been doing it. When I sank into work mode, personal relationships didn't really exist. Marisol riding with me to the second site had been natural. We'd been doing it that way for several years now. A habit.

That was no excuse.

Dev and Jeff were harmless, but they were also grade *A* assholes who talked shit about their wives and had no sense of humor. I'd bet anything the hour drive with them had been epically painful.

She deserved an apology.

Before telling myself the hundreds of reasons I shouldn't, I raised my hand and rapped on the door. Something banged in her room. Rustling followed, then her voice.

"What? Is someone there?"

"Elise, open the door. It's me."

The lock clicked on her side. She swung the door open a few inches, peering at me with sleepy eyes.

"What do you want?" she rasped.

I pushed the door open farther, enough to fit through. She staggered back until I caught her shoulder, pulling her toward me.

The lamp beside her bed was the only source of light in the room. Her sheets were wrinkled. Her cheeks were creased from her pillow. Warmth emanated from her soft, plush skin.

Blood rushed to my cock. I'd seen Elise many ways, but never sleep mussed, in little silky pajamas. One strap had slid off her shoulder, but I did nothing to right it. I had no desire to.

Holding my breath, I watched it slip even farther.

"Why are you looking at me like that?" she whispered.

"Because—" I squeezed my eyes shut. What was I doing?

"Do you…?" She placed a hand on my chest, over my pounding heart. "Why are you here?"

I opened my eyes, taking in the beautiful girl I should have stayed miles away from. That was a habit too. Whatever attraction I felt for Elise had been locked down tight for years.

Until now.

Nothing I did changed it.

Every time I saw her, it grew.

"I want you and pretending I don't doesn't make it go away. I fucking want you, Elise." My jaw was so tense my declaration came out tight and angry.

She sucked in a breath, her fingers curling into my chest. "You're an asshole."

"I know that. And wanting you is impossible, but there it is. I know you feel it."

Her chin went up. Defiant. Just how I liked it. "This will never work, you know."

"I know that. But we need to burn this…whatever this is between us. We have to burn it out."

Her brows winged. "Get it out of our systems?"

I took her face in my hands, rubbing my thumb along the cleft in her chin. "Exactly."

"While we're here?" she whispered.

"Only while we're here."

She rose on her toes, her mouth brushing mine. "I should say no."

My lips twitched. "You absolutely should." Then I slipped my fingers into the back of her hair and fisted it. "But you won't because I know you feel it too."

"You don't know anything," she hissed, leaning into me.

"I know I'm going to make you come until you scream."

She shook her head. "No."

I tugged her hair again. "No? Don't deny me."

Her lips ghosted across mine, and on the second pass, her tongue dragged lightly along my bottom lip. "The thing is, I don't scream when I come."

"Mmm." I caught her lip with my teeth, tugging gently. "I remember exactly how sweet you sound when you come. But I think I can do better when there's no one around to hear."

She shoved at me, but not hard enough to make me think she meant it. "I'm mad at you. You know that, right?"

"I'm mad at you too." I tipped her head back, licking a long line from her clavicle to her earlobe. "Still harder than I've ever been in my life. Still need to fuck you before I commit violence to rid myself of this insanity."

"Is it so insane to be attracted to me?" she asked in a shaky whisper.

"The way I am, yes. You have no idea what goes through my head when I'm around you." I sank my teeth into the tendon along her neck, sending shudders through her body. "When I see you, I want to eat you alive, spank you, suck your soft spots until I've marked every one of them."

She let out a breathless moan, her head lolling back. "I'm all soft spots, West."

"Then I guess I need to get started since I have a lot of work to do."

My mouth clamped down on the base of her throat, sucking hard until she groaned. My lips pressed on the same spot, kissing the pain away.

I pulled back to check on her. Her eyes were closed, lips parted as she exhaled a long breath. "Do you like that?"

"Yesss," she replied. "I don't like you, though."

I chuckled, ducking my face into her throat again. "I told you before, I like you enough for the both of us." I sucked her skin and cupped her breasts. They were heavy and round, spilling over the edges of my palms in a way that sent shots of agony directly to my balls.

I had to have her, to know this part of her, so I could clear the questions from my mind. I couldn't think straight anymore unless I was deep into my work, and even then, *even then*, my thoughts sometimes strayed to this woman.

As I sucked on her skin, I backed her toward the bed. She'd gone pliant, letting me lead her. When the backs of her knees hit the mattress, we stopped, staring at each other.

This was it.

Jump or turn back.

For me, there was no choice. My loyalty, common sense, and self-preservation had all been buried deep under my need for Elise.

Her fingers raked through my hair. She bit her bottom lip, her eyes trailing over me. Then one hand dropped, dragging down my abdomen to the waistband of my joggers. My cock was right there, pushing at the elastic. She pressed against it with her flattened palm.

"West," she breathed.

"You're going to take it, aren't you, baby?"

She nodded, biting down on her lip again.

"Say it, Elise. Tell me you want this."

"I want you"—her fingers wrapped around my cock, sliding down my length over my pants—"to fuck me with this. Do it hard and dirty so I forget every reason why you shouldn't."

A dose of pure adrenaline shot down my spine. Grabbing the neckline of her top, I yanked it so hard the thin straps snapped and her tits spilled out, creamy, capped with delicious, dark-pink tips.

"Oh, fuck yes," I growled. "Shorts off and get on the bed, baby. Let me see what I'm getting."

We both moved, tossing our clothes aside. Elise scooted onto the bed, her dark hair fanning across her white pillow. I braced one knee on the mattress, slowing to take her in.

"Jesus, West, you're hung."

That made me laugh. I gripped my cock in my fist, still looking her over. "And you're fucking pretty."

She writhed on the sheets, her arms crossing over her middle. Not happy with my view being obstructed, I reached down, taking her hands in mine, slowly coaxing her arms open again.

"I *have* to see you, Elise."

A little pant fell from her rosy lips. "Okay."

I started my perusal over. Taking in her full, round breasts and pebbled nipples. The little swell above her oval belly button. The gentle slope of her stomach below leading to a perfect triangle of dark hair.

My cock was throbbing, aching to get inside her, sink into all that heat and plushness.

Her curves were decadence personified. Not a single sharp edge or harsh angle. Her skin was tan and creamy, soft and smooth all over. Everything about her was feminine and sensual to the extreme.

I had to swallow hard, something a lot like nervousness clogging my throat.

Elise Levy was a dream I had never allowed myself to have.

"Come here," she demanded with honey on her tongue, holding out her hand. "Fuck me, West."

Kneeling at her feet, I slid my hands up the backs of her thighs to her knees, pressing her legs apart. I couldn't keep my mouth off her. She whimpered as I dragged my lips along the insides of her thigh.

My fingers were ahead of my mouth, trailing over her puffy, wet pussy, parting her slit to reveal her soaking pink folds.

"So fucking pretty, Elise." I slid two fingers into her, my eyes slamming shut as her heat enveloped me. Moving them in and out, I worked on making space to fit myself inside her. "So tight, baby. I need in there."

She held a hand out to me. "Come on, West."

"Not before I have a taste. Gotta have a taste."

I sank down between her thighs, brushing my mouth back and forth over her. She was fresh, clean, slick, hot. I buried my face in her folds, licking her all over, pumping my fingers in and out. The sound of her arousal was the sexiest thing to ever fill my ears. She was so swollen, her clit like a sweet little bead as I rolled it with my tongue.

"West," she moaned, her fingers weaving through my hair. "More, *more*." Her hips rose, bringing her pussy even tighter to my mouth. I gave her more, sucking on her clit, fucking her cunt with my fingers.

"So...good." She rode my tongue, her pussy vibrating on my lips. "I'm coming."

When she let go, it wasn't with a scream. Elise's cries were watery rainbows, vibrant but fleeting. Being the one to make her let go was achingly beautiful.

"Oh god, West, please."

I rose to my knees and sheathed myself in the condom I'd tossed on the bed when I'd gotten undressed. Elise was reaching for me, arching her hips in offering.

When I was covered, I fell over her, licking at her mouth. Her tongue clashed with mine, curling around it. Teeth nipping and sucking my lips between hers.

My cock prodded at her pussy, searching for entry. I reached between us, angling myself so the head slipped inside her opening.

Her mouth tore from mine as her neck arched. "West!"

"I know, baby." I slid in another inch, pushing up on my arms to watch. "Let me in."

Her body slowly opened, stretching to accommodate me. The sounds Elise made as I found my way into her a little bit at a time only spurred me on. I had to fuck this girl, and fuck her hard.

"You ready for more?" I gritted out.

Her eyes flared. "There's *more* of you?"

I chuckled, my head bowing over her. "Yeah, baby. I have more for you, and I'm going to give it to you. Let me in. You can take it."

Pushing her thighs farther apart, I snapped my hips forward until my pelvis met the cushion of hers. I saw stars. Never. It'd never felt this good, and we were only getting started.

"You feel way too good," I breathed out. "Way too fucking good, Elise."

"Move, West. I need to feel you move," she cooed, gripping my flexing biceps.

I repeated the snap, drawing out and plunging forward, over and over. Elise watched me, dragging her hands and nails along my arms and chest, letting out the sexiest little cries each time I bottomed out inside her.

My chest rumbled from an unfamiliar, deep, guttural groan. Each slam, her breasts shook. I took one in my hand, kneading it, rubbing her nipple with my thumb. Her fingers wrapped around my wrist as I touched her.

"Pretty tits, baby. Perfect, greedy pussy." I shook my head as I sank into her. "Can't believe I'm inside you."

She drew her knees up along my hips, taking me deeper. "You came here for this."

My mouth hitched. "Wanting something and getting it are two different things."

"Now you have me."

"Aren't I lucky?"

She brushed my hair off my forehead. "Stop talking to me and kiss me."

I smiled against her mouth, kissing her with the same thoroughness I'd fucked her. The deep, licking strokes of my tongue on hers matched the hard, powerful strokes of my cock.

Elise took it, rising to meet me, her arousal coating me from balls to tip. Her fingers were in my hair, her mouth on mine.

It was too much.

My hips jerked faster, powering into her. She moaned against my lips, arching her spine while I rode her soft, sensual body.

"So close," I grunted. "Want you to get there."

"Touch my clit so I can come with you," she rasped. "Bring me over with you."

My control was a razor's edge, but there was nothing that would stop me from giving her exactly what she needed.

Rearing back to my knees, I circled her legs around my hips so she was spread out in front of me. I held on to her hip, digging my fingers into the give of her flesh, and used the other hand to play with her clit.

"Yes, West. Keep doing that." She pressed her palm to the top of my hand, her back bowing to lift her ass off the bed. "I'm close."

"Get there."

The view of her all spread out, her pink pussy stretched around me, tits bouncing as I slammed into her, was going to be my undoing.

I loved the way her body moved with mine. I was mesmerized by it. We weren't even finished and I already knew I needed to do this again with her. Once wasn't going to be enough.

Her nails dug into my hand, and her mouth fell slack as her inner muscles went tight and fluttery, pulling me deeper.

"Oh, shit," I yelled. "Fucking hell, Elise."

Once she started, there was no holding me back. I fell over her, sealing my mouth to hers, needing that extra level of connection. My hips pistoned into her, over and over, racing toward the end. She held on to my shoulders, swirling her tongue around mine, kissing me with the same crazy fervor.

Building, building, pressure, need, madness until I made one final thrust and stilled at her deepest point. I panted into her mouth as I jerked my release, despising the condom blocking me from coating her bare inner walls.

I rocked and nibbled at her lips as aftershocks swept through me. She dragged her fingertips along my taut neck and sifted them into my hair.

"Oh god," she groaned. "I think you wrecked me."

Laughing somewhat deliriously, I rolled my forehead on hers. "I *know* you wrecked me. Fucking hell, Elise. What was that?"

Rolling to the side, I slowly pulled out of her. When my body had left hers, I stared at her, blinking hard. Her kiss-swollen lips tipped into a grin.

"That was really good sex." Then her teeth dug into her bottom lip like she was biting back another grin, but she lost. "Am I out of your system?"

Groaning, I shook my head on the pillow beside hers. "I feel like I just injected you directly into my veins." I cupped her breast and dipped my head to rub my mouth over it. "We've got two more days to find the cure."

She shoved at my sweaty chest. "Sure. Maybe. Now, go back to your bed. I'm tired."

I bit her nipple, making her squeal and shove at me again.

"Stop it." She kicked her feet wildly, nailing me in the shin.

I brought my head up, laughing. "You're really kicking me out?"

She brushed her hair away from her face and let her eyes move over me. "Yeah," she breathed. "Don't you think?"

Didn't I think it was a good idea to go? Didn't I think if we slept together, we might get confused? Didn't I think sharing a bed for more than sex could lead to feelings neither of us wanted?

Yeah. I did.

But my every instinct wanted to protest having to leave her.

"All right." I propped myself up on my elbow. "This isn't over, though."

She raised a brow, and the look she gave me was something new. In all the years I'd known her, she'd never once been coy or flirty, but that was what this was.

"We'll see." She shoved me again. "Now go."

With a huffed laugh, I cupped her cheeks and pressed my lips to her forehead.

"Good night, Elise."

"Good night, Weston."

I climbed out of her bed, grabbed my clothes from the floor, and started for the door separating our rooms. When I took one last look back, she'd already rolled to her side, facing the opposite direction, the blankets pulled up to her shoulders.

I forced myself to walk through the door, even though all I wanted to do was stay and soak up every minute we had until this was over for good.

CHAPTER SEVENTEEN

Elise

THE MORNING SUN SHONE like a spotlight on the unlocked door that separated my room from Weston's. I stared at it from my bed, my fluffy covers pulled up around my ears, willing myself to get up and lock it.

But it would be fruitless. If Weston wanted inside my room again, he would undoubtedly find a way, lock or not.

Last night had probably been a one-off anyway.

It was good that it was. Smart. The best decision.

That was what I told myself until I flung myself out of bed to trudge to the shower and the dull ache between my legs made my breath hitch.

Oh, Weston. Why did he have to be so...good?

It had been the best sex of my life. I couldn't remember a time I'd ever been so desired on a visceral level.

I brushed my teeth while the shower warmed up. The woman staring back at me in the mirror had been thoroughly fucked. My hair was in a rat's nest on top of my head. There were bite marks and bruises all over my chest, one dangerously close to my neck. My lips were still a little swollen and dark pink.

Weston Aldrich had marked me, and he'd done it with purpose.

He'd wanted me to see in my reflection.

It had been his intent for me to feel him when I walked.

Guys like him, with giant dicks and egos to match, were probably flooded with testosterone. It was all they could do not to beat their chests at every chance they got. Giving me hickeys and bowing my legs during sex was the socially acceptable equivalent.

I was glad I'd gotten to experience it once.

It would be silly to even think about doing it again.

The rain shower beat down on my head, and water sprayed me from both sides. This shower was more luxurious than any I'd ever been in. I stood there for a long time, my head back, eyes closed, muscles loosening.

A sudden slice of cool air brought me back to reality.

The reality of Weston stepping into my shower, naked and hard, his gaze trained on me.

He stopped in front of me, framing my face with his hands. "Good morning."

I straightened, sucking in my stomach. "Hi. You're in my shower."

"I am."

"I didn't invite you."

The corner of his mouth hitched. "You left all the doors between me and you unlocked. I took that as an invitation."

"Presumptuous," I muttered.

"Sexy," he muttered back as he dipped down to lick the side of my neck. "Did you sleep well?"

"I slept fine, thanks. You?"

He kissed up my neck to my jaw. My insides were waking up, showing interest in what this ridiculous man was doing to me at this ungodly hour.

"Terrible. I was hard all night. It was like trying to sleep on a log that kept stabbing me. Your fault."

I narrowed my eyes. "Are you trying to say I didn't satisfy you properly?"

"That's what I'm saying. Once wasn't enough and you sent me on my way with your scent all over me and the memory of your tight pussy. It was cruel."

He dragged his palms across my stomach. I sucked in even more. He grunted and squeezed my sides before slamming me against him, the air knocking loose from my lungs. My stomach went soft as his rock-solid abs pressed into it, and the look he shot me was nothing less than proud.

"What are you doing?" I uttered.

"I'm going to fuck you, then I'm going to take a shower and get dressed for a long day of work." He grabbed my ass with one hand, my face with the other and kissed me hard, all minty and fresh. It pleased me more than I liked that he'd brushed his teeth before coming to me. He'd put thought into this.

This was Weston. Of course he had. Weston didn't do anything without thinking it through.

He backed me into the wall, licking the inside of my mouth until I was breathless and panting. Sliding his fingers along the valley of my ass, he slipped forward to my core, found my entrance, and thrust inside. I sucked in a breath, and he took that as an opening to kiss me even deeper, stealing the little oxygen I'd gained.

I was dizzy from him. And needy. Every time I started to *think*, to question what we were doing or worry about how revealing the bright bathroom lights were, he rubbed a spot inside me that made all rational thoughts flee.

An orgasm washed over me in record time. Weston pulled back to watch me moan from parted lips. His fingers pressed and rubbed my inner walls, stretching my pleasure out until I needed more than fingers and he couldn't wait.

Cracking open the shower door, he grabbed the condom from the shelf where he'd left it, rolled it on with steady, urgent movements, then spun me away from him by my hips, molding his chest to my back. His cock fit between my cheeks, and he rocked, wedging it even more snugly while his mouth devoured my shoulder and neck.

I leaned my head back, kissing the side of his jaw, licking the rough stubble he'd yet to shave. His skin slid against mine, hot and slick.

"Need to get inside you," he murmured. "I have to know if you feel as good as I remembered."

"I do. I promise."

He breathed a laugh on my shoulder and pinched both my nipples. "I know you do. That sweet little pussy of yours is perfect, and I'm going to ruin it."

With that, he pressed on the center of my back, leaning me forward.

"Hands on the wall, baby. This is going to be hard and fast."

One hand, then the other, braced on the tiles. Weston held on to my shoulder, his index finger brushing my throat, and lined himself up with my opening. He nudged forward, slipping an inch inside me.

"West—"

Whatever I'd been about to say was swept away at the thrust of his hips. One powerful move and he was fully seated inside me, slapping against my ass. He gripped my hip, slid his other hand to the front of my throat, and fucked me hard and deep, his thick length igniting every one of the nerves inside me. My body had awakened and was finely attuned to this man.

Weston was on a mission, rutting as deeply as he could get, barely retreating before he buried himself to the hilt. His taut, muscular body slammed into my much softer one, groans rumbling from his chest.

He loved the feel of me.

I more than loved the feel of him.

He knew how to hold me, to make me forget my inhibitions and give myself over to this thing...this mistake we were going to keep making.

My back arched, and I used my arms to push myself onto his cock. We met, collided, retreated, and met again. Weston grunted, squeezing me, desperate and wild, bringing me back to last night, back to feeling his visceral desire and believing it to be true. For now, while it lasted, I believed I was the only woman Weston wanted.

The knowledge was heady.

"Come on, West. Come for me," I panted.

He leaned over my back, kissing my shoulder blade. "Can I come on you, baby? I want to paint your pretty ass, make it even prettier."

I clenched at his words, nodding vigorously. "Please, please."

"All right. I'm going to give you exactly what you want."

His movements sharpened, fingers digging into me. The air around us heated to a boil, and I could barely breathe. My head was light, floaty, and when his hand came down on my wet backside, my moans echoed off the tile. He slapped me three more times, enough to keep me with him but not truly hurt me, then yanked out of me with a sudden swiftness in time to see him ridding himself of the condom and tossing it aside.

"Changed my mind." He took his angry red cock in his fist, pumping it hard. "I want you to watch what you've done to me."

I wrapped my hand around his, moving with him as he stroked himself, and pressed my thighs together. This was too much. Too hot.

I cupped my breast and rolled my nipple between my fingers, making Weston grunt and shuffle closer.

"I'm coming," he gritted out.

The first splash of his release hit my stomach. I bent down, then dropped to my knees so the rest of it sprayed all over my breasts, catching a few drops on my tongue when I opened my mouth. Then I leaned in and wrapped my lips around his broad head, suckling the last of his release from his throbbing erection.

His hands went to my head, gripping the sides as I cleaned him with my mouth.

"Elise." He sighed my name. "You're too good to me. I'm going to get hooked."

I popped off the end of him and smiled up at him. "I thought I was already in your veins."

He ran a finger along my cheek and bottom lip, shaking his head. "You are." Then he took my hand in his, helping me to my feet. His mouth pressed against mine in a slow, melting kiss. "I'm going to need more of your lips around my cock."

I tapped on his chin. "We'll see."

I wanted it too, but if he ignored me again all day and made me ride with the two bores, he could suck himself off.

❖

Perhaps it should have been no surprise, but Weston started the day far less grumpy than usual. After we dressed, we grabbed a quick breakfast and he actually spoke to me instead of silently glowering at everyone in his vicinity.

We didn't flirt. By tacit agreement, that didn't happen when we were working.

Well, except for the time he got me off in his office. But we'd been alone with no witnesses so that didn't really count.

Marisol, Dev, and Jeff were waiting for us at the first factory, like yesterday. The men acknowledged me this time, but Marisol's gaze barely flitted over me. She was all about Weston, immediately latching on to his side.

I didn't have to stick around to see if he was going to ignore me in favor of her. Melinda from HR whisked me away for my first interview with Cherise, an avid mountain hiker.

Today was already going much better. Cherise was sweet and enthusiastic. A manager on the factory floor, she told me a lot about her job first then we talked about her hobby. She'd brought all her Andes gear with her, and I made a mental note to send her more when I got home.

As our interview wound down, she walked me out of the meeting room to show me around the factory floor.

"Do you see the Andes field team a lot?" I asked.

She rolled her eyes. "All the time. They spot-check us every other day." She laughed. "At least, that's what it feels like. We all hold our breath when they're here."

I nodded at the suits, almost a football field away from us. "Have you been here when Mr. Aldrich comes through?"

"Yeah, of course. He used to stop by a lot more often." She leaned closer to me. "I think he and Ms. Davies broke up, so he doesn't fly out to California as often as he used to. At least, that's the rumor."

"Oh?" I blinked at her and let my gaze shift to Weston, deep in conversation with the general manager of the factory. I couldn't read Marisol's expression from this distance, but I was certain she was hanging on to his every word.

I'd asked him if he'd had sex with her. He hadn't answered.

Which had been answer enough.

It didn't matter, not really, except I couldn't help wondering if I'd been a consolation prize last night when he couldn't have Marisol.

Cherise shook her head. "I shouldn't have said anything. You're so easy to talk to, I forgot you work for him for a minute."

I reached out, squeezing her upper arm. "It's fine. Don't worry about it. I work for his company, not *him*, you know? I don't think you said anything wrong anyway."

Her lips were pressed tight with worry. "It was gossip about my boss."

"Harmless," I assured her. "Can you introduce me to a few people? Would that be okay?"

She tore her gaze from Weston, still frowning. It took her a moment to snap out of her worry. "Oh, sure. No problem."

I met up with the suits in the parking lot. We had one more visit to make today and an hour drive to get there. Weston scanned me from head to toe then spun around and headed toward his car. I stayed back, watching to see what would happen while expecting to be stuck with Dev and Jeff again.

As expected, Marisol walked straight to Weston's car. As she reached for the door, he cleared his throat.

"Actually, Elise will be riding with me today."

Everyone seemed to hold their breath, waiting for him to offer more of an explanation, but he swiveled on his sleek, fancy shoes, brushing past Marisol and opening the passenger door. When I didn't move, he raised an eyebrow and gestured for me to get in.

Marisol also hadn't moved, forcing me to slide by her. Weston laid a hand on the center of my back and waited until I was seated to carefully close my door. I watched Marisol speaking to him in the side-view mirror, but Weston quickly dismissed whatever she said and walked away.

Climbing into the seat next to me, he checked his mirrors and drove out of the parking lot, Dev, Jeff, and Marisol still standing there.

"I don't think she's happy."

Weston hummed. In agreement? It was hard to tell.

"How was your visit?" he asked, changing the subject. His super-power.

"Interesting. You should send Cherise a whole Andes wardrobe. She takes a lot of pictures of her hikes for her social media. She has over thirty-thousand followers on Insta. It would be really good advertising."

He turned his head and gave me a disconcertingly warm smile. "Can you email Renata Cherise's information? She'll take care of it."

"Already done."

He reached over the console to squeeze my leg. "Very nice work, Elise."

"Thank you."

His hand remained, inching higher. I was wearing pants, so I didn't know where he thought he was going.

"Weston—"

"Shhh."

He reached the top of my thighs and slid inward, tucking his fingers into the rounded crease at the apex, grunting with satisfaction as he nestled in.

"I like this." He curled his fingers into my flesh, testing the give. "I'm going to be putting my face here later."

"Oh, are you?"

I tried for haughty, but that was difficult with Weston appreciating a part of my body I wasn't sure *I* even liked.

"I am."

So certain, but I couldn't blame him.

I was pretty much a sure thing for the rest of this trip. I'd already crossed the line, why deny myself something that was *so good*? The consequences would be there whether we stopped now or ten orgasms from now.

"By the way..."

He glanced over. "Yes?"

"You and Marisol were a couple, right?"

His fingers clamped down on my thigh, and he exhaled a hard, heavy breath. "We were, but we haven't been anything to each other besides colleagues for some time."

"Okay. Thanks for sating my curiosity."

The insecure beast in the back of my mind wondered how Weston could possibly be attracted to me when he had been with a woman like Marisol. We were not the same. When Weston put his hand on her thigh, he probably slipped right through.

He was looking at me instead of the road. "You don't look so sated. This was why I didn't want to answer you yesterday."

I turned to him. "What do you mean?"

"Are you, or are you not, comparing yourself to her?"

"What woman wouldn't?"

"There's no comparison."

I snorted. "No kidding."

He squeezed my thigh almost too hard. "Stop that bullshit, Elise. You know you're fucking gorgeous. You and Marisol are nothing alike. Quite frankly, I wouldn't want you to be anything like her. There's a reason we aren't together."

My fingers curled around his flexing wrist. "You're going to leave bruises."

"Good. Then you'll see them and remember it was your thighs I couldn't wait to bury my hand between. You'll remember I'm going to be walking around the next factory, trying to hide an erection while counting the minutes before I can get back to this spot and replace my hand with my face."

"Oh."

The corner of his mouth hitched. "Yeah. Oh. So get anyone else out of your head. They're out of mine."

Biting down on my bottom lip, I slowly melted into my seat. His hold on me loosened slightly, but he didn't let go.

And I didn't want him to.

Chapter Eighteen

Weston

I WASN'T HAPPY.

It was impossible for me to pretend otherwise, so Marisol was scrambling to smooth over the scowl on my face.

Brian Lewis owned one of the factories that produced Andes' patented filler. He'd been with me since the beginning when I'd been nothing more than a rich kid with a lot of ideas. There was a time I'd trusted him implicitly.

But as Andes had grown, so had his business. Where we had once been a priority, we were now being pushed to the side.

Which was not acceptable.

"Excuse me." Marisol stopped speaking, and everyone turned to me. "Did we not discuss this on the phone last week, Brian?"

Brian was ten years older than me, red-faced and round-bellied. He had peaked in high school but wasn't self-aware enough to recognize no one was impressed by his piddling claim to fame for scoring the most touchdowns in a single game.

I could have ignored all that, and had for years, but his excuses were making me despise everything about him. He was lucky I'd walked into the factory in a good mood.

"Now, Weston, I explained we're in the process of hiring more staff. In the next month, we'll be doubling our third shift and—"

I held up a hand. "When you signed contracts with us, there were no contingencies for your staffing shortages. It isn't any of my business that you've overextended yourself. That's not something I need to know, and to be perfectly honest, not something you should be spreading around. It doesn't make you look good."

He guffawed, his gaze bouncing around my colleagues when his sole focus should have been on me. They couldn't help him. He'd landed himself here, he had to figure his way out. It wasn't going to be with lame excuses or explanations. Action was the only acceptable solution to me.

Maybe I should have cut ties with this man years ago. He'd gotten comfortable with me, and I him, but it wasn't like me to bring personal relationships into my business. I supposed nostalgia was to blame. Brian had taken a chance on an upstart business, and that meant something.

"Look, Weston, it's all under control. We're only slightly delayed in production, which I understand isn't acceptable to you, but I can offer a discount on this next shipment to make up for it."

I stared at him, my patience paper thin. I didn't like being spoken to like I was being handled. I wasn't a tantruming toddler.

"Of course we understand," Marisol soothed. "Let's get that discount written down, though. Verbal promises are only as good as the legal contracts they're repeated on."

Everyone chuckled but me. There was nothing amusing about one of my managers speaking for me, especially when she wasn't even close to correct.

"*We* actually don't understand." I nodded to Marisol, Jeff, and Dev. "You can go. Brian and I need to have a private conversation."

"Go?" Marisol repeated.

"Go. You're no longer needed." Swiveling on my toe, I strode into Brian's office, not doubting for a second he would soon follow.

While I waited, I took out my phone, texting Elise.

Me: *Where are you?*

Elise: *Hello to you. I'm outside on a picnic bench with Elias and Cameron. They're telling me about their rock climbing weekends. Where are you?*

Me: *Hell. Be ready to leave within a half hour.*

Elise: *I might not be finished by then.*

Me: *Be ready in half an hour, Elise.*

Elise: *Please.*

Me: *What?*

Elise: *Weston, you might be my boss, but if you also want to be the guy who puts his dick in me tonight, say please.*

Me: *I swear to god, if the men you're with see you talking about getting dicked down, I will spank your ass until you can't sit on it.*

Elise: *Only if you want to be spanked in return.*

Me: *Why did I think texting you would calm me down?*

Elise: *Awww, you did? That's kind of sweet. And just so you know, I walked away from the table to talk to you so no one is seeing the filthy things I'm saying about your beautiful dick.*

Me: *Thank you.*

Me: *Please be ready in a half hour.*

Elise: *You're welcome. And I'll see what I can do. xx.*

A half hour later, I walked outside, intent on finding Elise so I could blow out of this place and get her back to my hotel room. Instead, I found Marisol waiting for me.

"What was that about?" she asked.

Marisol didn't get angry as a general rule. She expected life to go her way, and when it didn't, she became genuinely confused.

Despite our breakup and mutual flaws, I still liked her and respected her professionally. She wouldn't have her position if I didn't.

And until recently, a trip like this would always end in us sleeping together.

I had absolutely no desire to go there with her anymore.

Exhaling, I pinched the bridge of my nose. My meeting with Brian had only served to drive a spike through my skull. After our contract ran out, I would have my production teams search for a supplier to replace him. Our history wasn't enough to save our business relationship.

"You know I hate when anyone speaks for me." I dropped my hand and tucked it in my pocket. "Did you wait around for me to tell you that?"

Her red lips curled into a smirk. "That, and to allow you to ask me to dinner."

I frowned, scanning the parking lot. "Did you send Dev and Jeff away?"

She stepped closer, her hand sliding up my chest. "Of course. It would have been impolite to ask them to wait when I'll be riding with you."

"I have Elise with me. I had no intention of giving you a ride."

Her tongue touched her top lip. "Oh, her. I completely forgot about her." She waved the thought of Elise off. "That's fine. I don't mind if she's in the car."

My frown deepened, as did the ache in my head. "What did you expect me to do if you minded? Leave her here to fend for herself?"

Marisol huffed a little laugh. "I saw her flirting with the factory boys. I'm sure one of them would be more than happy to give her a ride."

A furious laugh shot out of me. "You have to be joking, Marisol. Tell me you're joking. Do you have any idea who Elise is to me? Do you remember anything I ever said to you?"

Instead of waiting for an answer I really didn't care to hear, I strode toward the side of the building, which I knew from memory was the location of the picnic tables. Before I could reach the corner, Elise and two men came around it. She was laughing at something one of them said, her cheeks a deep pink.

My mood had already been black, but seeing her with two men crowded around her, interested in her, sent me into a cold fury.

"Elise," I barked.

She stopped walking, her eyes flaring wide as she finally noticed me.

"It's time to go." When she didn't move right away, I swore I went blind for a second. The spike in my head dug deeper, and frustration dragged me under. "Right now."

My tone was sharp and commanding. Too harsh for Elise, but I felt driven to it. She knew from our texts I was frustrated, yet she was dragging her feet, not coming to me when I needed her to.

Finally, she said something soft to the two men before starting toward me. I only exhaled when she was by my side. Her anger was palpable, but she kept her lips pressed together and her professional face on, even when Marisol joined us on our walk through the parking lot.

I wasn't able to hide my feelings, nor was I willing to play polite when Marisol had the gall to cut off Elise so she could reach the passenger door first.

"Elise is in the front with me," I intoned. "If you want me to drive you back to your car, climb in the back."

Marisol spun away from the door, her lips popping open. "Weston?"

I opened the back door for her. "If you'd asked first, I would have told you the only seat I had available was the back one."

She stared at me for a long beat, her deep-brown eyes sweeping over me as if trying to read how serious I was. Elise was behind me, but I had to take care of this problem before I gave her my attention.

Marisol flipped her black waves behind her shoulder and marched forward to duck into the second-row captain's chair. She folded her arms across her chest and stared straight ahead as though she'd never been so wronged in her life.

I closed the door on her and reached for Elise. "Come on."

"She could have taken the front seat."

I huffed a long breath. "Don't give me shit right now. She wasn't invited into my car, you were. You don't sit in the back seat."

She stuck her lip out, and it was all I could do not to bite it. "You're very annoying and grumpy."

"I've had an extremely frustrating few hours. Please don't add to it."

Her pout instantly morphed into concern. "What's up? Is there anything I can do?"

"No." I brushed my hand over her arm. "Nothing other than sticking with me on this trip even when I'm acting like your grumpy boss."

Her eyes danced with amusement. "I'm used to that, so I can do that."

The ride back to the hotel should have taken two hours. Instead, it lasted a hundred years. Elise tried to engage Marisol in conversation, but she didn't bite. Instead, she brought up vacations she and I had taken, restaurants we'd dined in, made blunt insinuations about what we normally got up to on my trips to California.

I caught Elise giggling softly, trying to cover it up with her hand. That was the only reason I didn't burst into flames and lose my shit on Marisol. Elise wasn't bothered, so I contained myself and turned up the music, putting an end to further inane chatter.

Marisol was conveniently parked near the hotel. I dropped her at her car, telling her I'd see her in the morning, and drove away, sighing with relief.

"We're going to dinner," I told Elise.

"Are we? I'm pretty tired."

I sent a glare her way. "Shut up."

She laughed softly. "Not likely."

I reached across the car, sliding my fingers into my new favorite place at the crease of her thigh.

"Thank Christ for that."

Once we ordered, Elise relaxed into the back cushion of her bench, glancing around the diner. A small, soft smile lifted the corners of her mouth.

"What?" I groused.

Her gaze shot to mine. "Are you grumping at me already?"

"No." I raked my fingers through my hair. "Yes. I don't like not knowing why you're smiling."

That made her laugh. "If you must know, I was thinking this place isn't very like you."

I leaned forward, clasping my hands on the table. "You don't like it?"

I'd brought her to the diner I'd invited her to last night. It wasn't anything special to look at, but the food was more than decent, and it was the kind of place no one would bother us.

"No, I do. I'm surprised you do, is all." She cupped her mouth to whisper to me. "I don't think they have any Michelin stars, West."

West.

Heat surged through my veins. She only called me West when I was fucking her. Hearing it outside the bedroom ignited a Pavlovian response. It took me a few seconds to convince my body now wasn't the time or place to bend her over and slide into her.

"You don't think much of me, do you?"

A rush of pink heated her cheeks. "That isn't true. I was kidding. I don't think you're a snob, far from it. But you have to admit you're used to the finer things in life. I see the suits you wear every day. And you live in a penthouse. Don't pretend you're just an average Joe."

"You're not wrong. I do like luxury and won't deny it, but that's not the only thing I can appreciate. If it were, I would have missed out on a lot. I would have walked right by this diner without coming in and that would have been a shame. This place makes one of the best huevos rancheros I've ever had."

"You'll have to give me a taste."

"I will give you anything you want, Elise."

Her teeth dug into the corner of her bottom lip, and the pink in her cheeks intensified. She looked younger, sweeter. The blood that had been lodged in my cock flowed directly to my thrumming heart. There had never been a day I hadn't cared about her. Even when she was living in another state for three years, I kept track of her.

As much as I wanted to fuck her again and again, I would never lose sight of who she had always been to me. The sex would end when we went home, but she was Elliot's sister, which meant I would protect and care for her always.

Our waitress stopped by with our drinks, and afterward, we both went quiet. I was going over the meetings I had the following day, and Elise took out her phone, most likely reading texts or emails.

A soft laugh burst out of her. Her eyes lifted to mine. I cocked my head in question.

"Nothing." She shook her head. "My old coworker, Brandon, ran into Patrick at a bar last night."

"And?"

My stomach tightened at the mention of her ex. One minute in his company, and it had been obvious he hadn't been worthy of her. If I'd been a betting man, I would have put my money on Elise wising up and leaving him within a year. Since it had taken her four times that, I'd been lucky I wasn't.

Her gaze flitted to her phone and back to me. "Brandon pretended not to speak English when Patrick asked him if he knew where I was. And Brandon's boyfriend apparently got in on the act by translating what Brandon was saying."

"What did he say?"

"Well, Brandon doesn't actually speak another language, so Cliff had to make everything up. He told Patrick Brandon arrived from Croatia two weeks ago and had grown up in a monastery, never seeing a woman besides his mother."

I blinked. "What did Patrick say to that?"

She shrugged. "He was angry and confused. I don't really want to know what he said, which I told Brandon."

"You're never going to speak to him?"

"No. There's nothing for us to say to each other."

Something in my stomach soured. I couldn't put a finger on why, though. "Really? You don't even want to yell at him?"

"I'm not really a yeller, you know. And I don't think he deserves a chance to try to explain away what he did to me. It might have been immature of me to cut out of there like a ghost in the night, but when I decided to go, it felt like I had to do it immediately or I wouldn't survive."

My brow lowered as I watched her. She didn't like talking about this. This guy was still hurting her, whether she wanted to admit it or not.

"What about what you deserve?"

She tucked her hair behind her ear. "What do you mean?"

"Don't you deserve closure?"

"Closure isn't real. There's no door between pain and happiness. No matter how many conversations I have or don't have with Patrick, I still have to walk through the way he hurt me. If I deserve anything, it's to not be hurt by the man I once loved."

"Once loved? You don't anymore?"

Her hand wrapped around her glass of iced tea. "When I loved him, it was without vital information. Once I found out who he truly was, that love became null and void. I know that sounds cold, and maybe it is, but it's how I'm able to cope with life's bullshit. And you know I've had more than my fair share."

I pushed a long exhale out of my nose. She'd done something similar to me. One day, I was her second brother. The next, I barely existed. Maybe it was the memory of those long, icy years making me so uneasy now.

As much as I despised Patrick, I couldn't help feeling for him. The arctic side of Elise Levy was an impossible place to be after years of living in her sunshine.

"You have. You and Elliot have been doled more unlucky hands than most people." Reaching across the table, I took her free hand in mine, rubbing her knuckles with my thumb. "When I inevitably screw up, I ask that you give me a chance to make it right instead of giving me the ghost treatment. Can you promise me that?"

Her nose scrunched, but she curled her fingers into mine. "It depends on how deeply you screw up. If you push me off a cliff, I'm definitely ghosting you. Literally." She grinned at me, growing more serious when I couldn't find it in me to smile back. "I don't want to go back to the years when I avoided you. For our sake, and Elliot's. I can't predict my reaction to a hypothetical screwup, but I can promise to try, okay?"

I huffed a dry laugh. "I know that's all I'm going to get out of you, so I guess it'll have to be okay."

Dinner arrived. My huevos rancheros, Elise's tomato soup and grilled cheese. She was inordinately pleased with her meal, which settled my twisted stomach. I liked seeing her pleased, any way it happened.

I held up a forkful of egg, pico de gallo, and fresh avocado. "Open."

She leaned forward, parting her lips to accept the bite of my dinner. Her lips closed around my fork while her gaze stayed on mine. Slowly, I slipped the fork out, watching her taste my favorite dish. Pleasure suffused her cheeks with color.

"I'm right, aren't I?"

She nodded. "Delicious. Thank you for bringing me here."

"Thanks for sharing it with me."

She picked up her spoon, pausing before scooping up some soup. "Did Marisol come here with you?"

I scoffed. "Once. She wasn't impressed."

"How long were you together?"

I cocked my head. "Is it my turn to expel my relationship details?"

"What's fair is fair, Westie."

"Please stop hanging out with Miles."

"You'll have to discuss that with him. He's a little obsessed with me." She shook her spoon at me. "Don't try to distract me. How long were you with her?"

"Two years seriously, give or take."

"How long unseriously?"

She'd picked up on my wording. No surprise there. "A year."

"So, three years." She tore off the corner of her sandwich. "That's a long time. I didn't know she existed before this trip."

I raised a brow. "Did you keep up with me while you were in Chicago?"

"Somewhat. Elliot mentioned you from time to time. He never said anything about beautiful Marisol, though."

I couldn't fight the smirk tugging at my lips. "That's because Elliot tried to pretend she didn't exist. Compartmentalizing is a Levy talent."

"My brother wasn't a fan of beautiful Marisol?"

"Don't call her that unless you want me to refer to you as Stunning Elise."

She stopped chewing to cover her grin with her hand. "That *does* have a lovely ring to it."

It did. And it was fitting.

"No, Elliot didn't like her. He said if I stayed with her, she would change me in ways that would make him not like me either."

"My brother, the smooth talker."

I shook my head. "He's blunt, but he tells the truth."

"But you didn't listen."

Heaving a deep sigh, I wiped my mouth with my napkin. "It took me some time to come to my senses. She lived in California for the duration of our relationship. It made it easier for me to close my eyes to a lot of the reasons we would have never worked."

"That makes sense. You had reunion sex over and over. It would be hard to give that up."

My jaw tensed at her casual reference to me fucking another woman. I didn't feel so casual when I thought of her with any other man.

"You're right. It was easier to stay than go. Plus, there was a part of me that wanted to prove Elliot wrong."

"I bet he took your breakup well." She pressed her lips together to hold back a grin.

"Excuse me for calling your brother an asshole, but that asshole threw a ticker-tape parade when I told him we were over."

"Very comforting," she quipped.

"I didn't need comforting." Even if I had, the idea of Elliot offering comfort was laughable.

She kicked me softly under the table. "Didn't you love her?"

I chuffed, picking up my fork. "Do we need to keep talking about this?" I scooped a large bite of my quickly cooling dinner into my mouth. Elise was determined to keep me talking.

"You asked me all sorts of prying questions, Westie. It's only fair I get to ask the same. You must have loved her to be with her for three years."

I scooped another large bite onto my fork. "It was something like love. I thought I wanted to marry her, but when we ended, I wasn't heartbroken."

"Marriage? Wow."

"We would have been divorced within a year if we'd even made it down the aisle."

I'd been toying with buying a ring. Looking back, I couldn't even remember why. I supposed it'd felt like the next natural step.

When I'd brought up the idea of marriage, Marisol told me until I'd found a way to love her as much as my company—not more, but equally—she couldn't marry me.

There had been no tears. We'd gone back to her house, like always, and had spent the night in her bed. When I left the next day, I'd been relieved. When I thought of my calendar and all the time that had been freed up without a girlfriend to consider, I realized she'd been right.

I wasn't heartless. I *had* missed her. But the fact was, I got over that quickly.

Today had been my final straw with Marisol. The way she dismissed Elise, then tried to stake some type of ridiculous claim on the drive home, had turned me so far off of her, all my warm feelings had withered and died right then and there.

I put down my fork. "That's enough of that topic. I can think of far more interesting things to discuss."

"I don't know. Prying into your personal life is awfully fun for me."

"I'd rather be prying into your pants."

A laugh burst out of her, and this time, I joined her.

"That was awful," she said through giggles.

It had been. The worst line that had ever left my mouth. But the payout had been far too great to give a damn.

CHAPTER NINETEEN

Elise

WHEN WE RETURNED TO my hotel room last night, Weston had been all over me, fucking me over the desk and again in the shower. He'd been rough and intense, slapping my ass and nipping at my flesh.

I had been the same. I'd sucked him until my lips were numb and my jaw was sore, but it hadn't been enough. My fingertips had mapped out the dips and divots of his muscles. I explored him and he explored me.

We'd been ravenous for each other. And each time we came, it seemed like we might be sated, only to start over again. It was hours before our bodies finally gave out.

I had never once experienced anything like it. Falling asleep naked, wrapped around him, him wrapped around me, was another first for me.

Naked.

Asleep.

In his arms.

Letting him stay had been a mistake. Now, I knew what it was like to wake up with him, to be roused from a heavy sleep by his lips on my shoulder.

Morning with Weston meant warm kisses and silky caresses. He was taking care of my body without much effort from me. Sleepy orgasms and the most delicious lazy fuck. It was perfect.

Addictive.

My face was buried in my pillow, fingers curled into the sheets.

"Pretty girl, I need more days waking up like this." Weston's face was next to mine, his chest against my back, hips between my spread legs as he leisurely slid in and out of me.

"How many times do you think I can be inside you before we fly home tomorrow?" he whispered beside my ear. "Every spare minute I have, I'm going to spend either inside you or eating you, baby."

I smiled into the pillow. "As long as you leave some time for me to suck you."

He grunted, slamming into me with more force. "You really love sucking cock, don't you?"

"Your cock, West. I love how you feel on my tongue. Almost as much as when you're inside me."

The groan that he emitted came from somewhere deep in his chest. "Oh fuck, Elise. How are you so perfect? Your pussy feels like it was custom made for me, and your dirty little mouth says exactly what I want to hear. I'm not gonna want to give you up."

"You have me now," I murmured.

He pressed into me, putting more of his weight on my back. The mattress was soft, so we sank together, one writhing, rolling form. Weston's mouth only left me to whisper dirty things in my ear.

Our bodies slapping together echoed off the walls. As time passed, no end in sight, Weston's skin heated mine, our perspiration mingled, and we slid easily against each other.

He was so thick and long, filling me, stretching me, rubbing the spots he'd made tender inside me. The dull pain only served to highlight the pleasure coursing through me.

Lazy didn't mean delicious. Languid didn't mean he hadn't woken every one of my nerve endings. Weston knew how to fuck, and his skills were catered to me, down to his breath on the back of my neck.

I shuddered beneath him, an orgasm rolling through me from nowhere.

"West," I cried weakly. "I need you so much."

"That's it, baby." He swiveled his hips, grinding into me. "I'm here. Take what you need."

I whimpered and rubbed my face into my pillow as my inner walls fluttered around him. He grunted beside my ear, desperation tinging the guttural sound.

"Come for me, West," I coaxed. "Let me feel it."

Rearing back to his knees, he took hold of my hips, lifting them from the mattress. Languid slipped into heated, wild pounding. His hips slammed into my ass, fingers digging into my flesh. My nails scrabbled against the sheets, and my head tipped back from the pillow as the orgasm he'd given me spiraled into another.

My moans were hoarse and loud, drowned out by the sounds of our fucking and Weston's frenzied grunts.

He pushed in deep, so deep, my eyes flew open, and I nearly screamed at the raw, needy feel of him hitting the end of me. He stayed there, pulsing, bellowing my name. I panted and thrust back.

I was floating.

Hot and sticky.

So, so satisfied.

Weston didn't make me love my body, but when we were together, the switch that made me hate parts of it flipped off. His mouth and fingers and cock, the way he looked at me and said filthy things to me, stripped me of my insecurities and allowed me to be nothing more than a sexual, sensual being.

It was exactly what I needed right now.

How was I supposed to give this up after tomorrow?

⚬

We were up and dressed, ready to leave for the day, Weston sharp and intimidating in his sleek suit for his meetings with his Asian supply managers, me outdoorsy and athletic in my leggings, T-shirt, and Andes fleece vest for my rock climbing adventures.

Weston frowned at me. "I'm not happy about this."

I smoothed his lapels and brushed imaginary dust from his shoulders. "As you've told me many times, and it's been duly noted. You'll be spending the day with your ex-girlfriend who wants to ride your dick, and I'll be watching a bunch of sweaty men climb rocks and assert their manliness. We can take our jealousy out on each other tonight."

He scoffed, but I saw the hitch of his mouth before he turned away. He'd been sticking to his story that his wariness over me going rock climbing with the men I had interviewed yesterday was out of concern for my safety. Weston Aldrich did not admit to being jealous.

But it was obvious, and we both knew it.

We also knew it was useless. We didn't belong to each other outside of my hotel room, and this time tomorrow, we wouldn't even have that.

I grabbed his hand, pulling him back toward me. "Kiss me so I don't forget about you."

He took my face in his hands, scowling fiercely. "If you even try to forget about me, I'll tattoo my name on the inside of your eyelids."

And then his mouth was on mine, giving me the kind of kiss I'd have to be dead to forget.

<hr>

I spent the morning and early afternoon going back and forth between taking notes and being awed at the human body's ability to defy gravity.

Elias, Cameron, and ten other athletic humans in their climbing group were showing off for me, I was sure of it. They scaled sheer rock faces with inch-deep fingerholds like they were Spiderman.

Elias, a guy around my age who was basically a big ball of energy, came over to where I was sitting and watching. He had a nice smile and an easy laugh.

He held his hand out to me. "Come on."

"Why?"

"You're going to climb."

"No, I can't do that."

He shook his hand. "Come on. You don't know if you don't try."

He had a point, and since I'd been getting back to trusting and loving my body, I sighed and took his hand. What was the worst that could happen? I'd fall on my ass? If I did, I'd never see any of these people again. Besides, they'd spent a good portion of their time out here falling and brushing themselves off, why couldn't I?

He took me to a boulder he said was for beginners. It was ten feet tall with a craggy surface. I stared at it, wondering how they expected me to climb it.

A few others from the group came over, pointing out all the spots I should put my fingers and toes as I climbed. Then, they told me to try.

Just like that, I was expected to climb a giant rock.

So I did.

And I fell.

Again and again, my ass collided with the mat on the ground.

Every single time, they cheered for me.

And every single time, I got a little higher.

I was aching, surely bruised, but once I got going, I didn't consider giving up once.

Cameron snapped pictures of me five feet off the ground and showed me when I dropped down. To my surprise, I'd been smiling like a lunatic.

"You're a badass," he proclaimed. "If you had more time here, I'd have you scaling this with your eyes closed."

Laughing, I swiped sweat from my forehead. "Maybe I'll come back."

Elias slid next to Cameron, throwing his arm around his friend. "Did I hear you say something about coming back?"

My eyes widened. "I said maybe. No promises were made. I'll have to hitch a ride with the CEO, and he's known for being grumpy."

Elias rolled his eyes. "That cat never smiles. Is everyone at Andes like that?"

I waved my hand around. "Hello, Andes employee. I smile, and Mr. Aldrich does too. Besides, don't you see the Andes' field team all the time? They can't all be frowning grumps."

"Nah." Cameron rolled his head on his neck, the cracks loud enough to make me wince. "We used to see them all the time, and they were serious as shit. I don't mind them not coming around anymore. We gotta keep the vibes up, you know?"

"What—?"

Elias reached for my hand, cutting off my question, and pulled me toward the boulder again. "Stop trying to distract us. You're not finished. We still have hours of daylight left. I'm determined to get you to the top."

I crinkled my nose. "I don't know…"

"I do." Elias pointed to the rock. "Get on it, girl."

I could think of a hundred excuses not to get back on, but despite my aching arms, sore butt, and broken fingernails, I bought into Cam and Elias's enthusiasm.

In the words of Cam, I was going to conquer this bitch.

Chapter Twenty

Weston

Elise was in the shower when I let myself into her room. I shed my clothes on the walk to the bathroom. It had been a long day, filled with meetings I couldn't cut short, despite my desire to do so.

When I reached the bathroom, I stopped in my tracks to stand outside the shower stall, watching Elise. Her head was tipped back, rinsing her hair. My dick throbbed as I took in her delicious, lush curves. Her gorgeous big tits. Her soft, round hips and sloped stomach. That ass that felt absolutely unbelievable when I was taking her from behind.

That ass that was covered in bruises.

What?

Tearing open the shower door, I dropped to my knees to examine her.

She screeched, spinning away from me. "Weston! What the hell?"

Gripping her hips, I tried to turn her. "What is that?"

"What?" She swatted at my hands. "Get up, you scared the shit out of me!"

"Why does your ass look like you just had the spanking of a lifetime?"

She went still, then slowly peeked over her shoulder at her backside. "Oh. It looks worse than it feels."

"Explain."

Her fingers hooked the underside of my chin. "Come up here and I will."

Sensing I wasn't going to win this right now, I rose to my feet and crowded her space until her breasts were flattened against me.

"Explain, Elise."

She hooked her arms around my neck, bouncing on the balls of her feet. "I went rock climbing today, and I fell a lot. You should have seen me, West. Actually, I have a video and some pictures. It took me a long time and a lot of falls, but I made it to the top of a ten-foot boulder. Can you believe that? *Me.*"

Her excitement and explanation eased some of my boiling concern, but I did not like seeing her pretty skin marked up by anyone but me. I did not like knowing she'd endangered herself around people she barely knew. I did not like that she'd shared this obviously incredible experience with the men from the factory.

"You could have broken something." I slid my hand down her back to gently cup her ass. "I'm not convinced you didn't."

"I'm not in any real pain. It's just that I bruise easily, like a peach. All my falls were onto a mat. I really wasn't trying to hurt myself." Her lips touched the center of my chest. "Tell me you're proud of me."

I squeezed her cheek, and when she didn't wince, I was able to breathe slightly easier.

"There's never been a day I haven't been proud of you." Dipping down, I captured her mouth in a slow, licking kiss. My heart hadn't stopped thrashing. I wasn't certain I was exactly pleased with her right now, but I needed her kiss like an anchor in a storm.

Her lips kept me from drifting into blackness.

I stayed in her sweet softness.

Eventually, I let her mouth go, and we finished washing ourselves. Shower off, I dried her, then quickly rubbed myself down with a towel while she combed through her wet hair at the vanity. I stepped up behind her, circling my arms around her to cup her breasts.

We looked good together. The top of her head aligned with my jaw. Her olive skin was a few shades darker than mine. My fingers spread wide over her breasts. Her dark-red nipples peeked out from between them. I was straight, while she was all curves. Her pink lips were plush and turned up at the corners. Light danced in her deep-brown eyes. My mouth and eyes were flat and intent, concentrating on Elise.

The contrast between us—our shapes, our shades, our expressions—was art. Sensual, erotic art.

"You're gorgeous," I told her.

She let her head fall back and reached up to cup the back of my neck. "You are too."

"We look good together."

A sigh fell from her. "I know."

I rolled her nipple between my fingers and smoothed my other hand around her back, pressing on her.

"Bend forward for me."

She caught my eye in the mirror and her bottom lip between her teeth. She was wary. Uncertain.

"Elise. Bend forward. Let me see what you did to yourself."

"Bossy," she murmured breathlessly.

Slowly, she bent in half, resting her breasts and elbows on the counter. I dropped to my knees behind her and pushed her legs apart so I could see all of her. Not just the mottled and bruised skin that made me feel like an untethered madman but the peak of pink nestled between her thighs. That made me feel mad too, but not in an unhinged way.

Trailing my fingers along her slit, I kissed each and every bruise on her round ass.

"You damaged yourself, baby." I dragged my tongue along the edge of the valley between her cheeks. Goose bumps sprung up in my wake, and Elise shuddered. "Was it worth it?"

"What?" she breathed.

"Hurting yourself." I licked along the other side. She was so soft, driving me out of my mind. "Was it worth it?"

"Yeah. It was worth it before you got down on your knees for me. This is a really, really good bonus."

"I'm the bonus?" I thrust two fingers inside her. "Not the main event?"

She mewled, arching her back. "It was a really big rock, West."

"Was it?" My thumb found her clit. "That's special. Did it make you come harder than you ever have in your life?"

She laughed and moaned all at once. "That would have been strange."

I kissed my way up her back and clamped down on her shoulder. Her ass pressed into me as she rocked on my hand. I licked her neck, jaw, and ear, making a mess of her. Her sounds of pleasure echoed off the tiles.

"I'm coming, West."

As she started to let go, I pulled my fingers out and slid my cock in their place. Her head reared back, hitting my shoulder. I cupped her throat, rubbed my thumb along the hinge of her jaw, and dipped down to lick inside her open, gasping mouth.

"I think you need a reminder," I said against her lips.

She turned her head, nipping at my bottom lip. "I do?"

"Yes." Jerking my hips, I slammed into her. "Look at us, baby."

She turned back to the mirror. Our eyes met. Desire flared between us in our reflection. There had never been a time when I had been more attracted to a woman. It was madness what simply looking at her did to me.

"See what I do to you?" I stroked her hair, gathering it away from her face. "This is the main event. You and me, like this. Nothing's bigger, is it?"

She shook her head. "No, nothing."

"When I'm inside you, it's you and me. Nothing else matters."

"It's the same for me."

"This body is important to me." I slipped my hand from her jaw down to her breast, kneading it hard. "It kills me to see you hurt when all I want to do is make you feel good."

"You do. Better than anything I've ever experienced." She pushed off the vanity, meeting each one of my thrusts, taking me deeper, harder. "Please, West. *Please.*"

"Do you want more, beautiful?"

"Mmmhmm. More, please."

"Anything, Elise. Anything you want, I'll give it to you."

Later, after we left the room for dinner and a drink at the hotel bar, after I'd told her the boring, tedious details of my day and she'd shared the heart-stopping pictures and videos of hers, after we'd showered and fucked again, after a movie and a blow job on the couch, after pajamas and yawns and running from the end of the night, we gave in and tucked ourselves under the covers.

We rolled toward each other, and I stroked her cheek with my thumb. "Are you good with everything?"

Her lids were heavy as she blinked at me. "Everything?"

"Yes. Everything between us ending tomorrow."

"Mmm." She pressed her cheek to my hand. "Yes. It has to, doesn't it? I don't want to sneak around, and telling Elliot would be—"

"Impossible."

It would destroy our friendship, that I knew. He would see me going after his sister as a betrayal. There was no gray area for Elliot. Right was right. Wrong was wrong.

The rules were unspoken, but they were stamped all over Elise Levy.

Off-limits.

No-go zone.

Even if that weren't true, I had enough experience with relationships to know I was bad at them. I would never hurt Elise, which meant we could never be more than a lost weekend.

She was sleepy and unbothered, nuzzling my palm as her eyes drifted closed. Perhaps she wouldn't even want more than what we already had.

"Don't worry about a thing, Westie. Go to sleep."

"I'm not worried."

Regretful, not worried.

She rolled into me, her head on my shoulder, fingers splayed on my stomach. I pulled her closer, arm wrapped around her.

She was soft, fitted against me like she'd always been there.

This was temporary.

Ending soon.

But for now, tonight, Elise was mine.

⚜

The flight back to Colorado was subdued, but at least Elise sat beside me. With my hand tucked in the crease of her thigh, I spent most of my time reading emails and reports, glancing over at Elise intermittently.

She read a paperback for half the flight, absently stroking my hand and wrist every once in a while.

With a sigh, she closed the book and her eyes.

"Finished?" I asked.

Her lips tipped up. "Yeah."

"Good ending?"

Her eyes fluttered open, and she turned to me. "A happy one."

I smirked. "Fiction then."

She dragged her hand down my face. "Shush, you cynic."

"Realist. How many happy endings do you personally know about?"

"Plenty. Aren't your parents married?"

I shifted in my seat, squeezing her thigh. "They're not a prime example of everlasting love, Elise. Try again."

My parents' marriage was for show. They may have loved each other at one time, but I had no memory of affection between them.

These days, they shared a home, but their lives were entirely separate. I was fairly sure that wasn't the kind of happy ending in Elise's books.

She tapped the divot in her chin. "Rebecca."

"Should I know who that is?"

"You should since she works for you. Rebecca is married to her high school sweetheart, Sam. She still blushes when she talks about him. So, I'd say, yeah, happy endings are real."

"Hmmm." I angled my upper body toward hers, my nose brushing hers. "I think I need a bigger pool to believe it."

"We're not in California anymore, West. What are you doing?"

"We're not home either." My lips brushed hers. "Give me another hour or two."

"Aren't I out of your system yet?"

Cupping her jaw, I sucked her bottom lip between mine. "Getting there. Another hour or two and I'll forget what you sound like when you come. It's already getting hazy."

"Wow, I feel sorry for you." She licked the seam of my mouth with the tip of her tongue. "I've completely forgotten what you feel like in my mouth. In fact, I'm not entirely certain who you are."

"Strange that you're kissing me."

"Well, you started it. I thought it would be rude if I pushed you away."

With a huff, I fell back in my seat. She grinned at me before picking up her phone and opening the Kindle app.

"Do you have another book to read?" I asked.

"Mmmhmm. I downloaded a horror story." Her eyes flicked to mine. "Don't worry, there's no happy ending. I read spoilers. Everyone dies except for the hero, who spends the rest of his days all by himself in a big, empty penthouse, counting his money."

I pinched her inner thigh, making her squeal. "I'm reporting you to HR for insubordination."

She narrowed her eyes. "Do your worst, Mr. Aldrich."

•

Though it pained me, I always hired a driver to take me to and from the airport. The idea of leaving my car in the elements made me too twitchy.

This time, I patted myself on the back for my foresight. As soon as I climbed into the back seat beside Elise, I had her face in my grasp and my mouth on hers.

She made a yelp of surprise, and her hands flew to my wrists, but when I licked her lips, she sank into the kiss and let me in. The drive home wasn't long enough to do anything more, but I intended to use the last of our time alone wisely.

Elise had other ideas.

She pulled back, panting, rubbing her fingertips over her wet lips. "Weston, don't."

"Tell me why not."

She let out a long sigh. "You know. We can't do this here. Drawing it out will only make it harder."

I took her chin between my fingers, scanning her face. "You've given me no indication that ending this is hard for you."

"Obviously it is." She pulled her face back out of my grip. "We had fun, but I now know a side of you I didn't before and it's going to be hard to shut that off. I will, but it won't be easy."

"I will too. It's better that way."

Her head bobbed sharply. "It is."

I took her face in my hands again, rubbing my lips over hers. "What harm would one more time do? I don't think I can shut this off until I have you again."

She shuddered, resting her forehead on mine. "Weston...it's not smart."

"Nothing about what we're doing is smart, Elise. Tell me yes. Tell me you'll come up to my place and let me have you." I rolled my forehead back and forth on hers and pressed on her bottom lip with my thumb. "I fucking need you, baby. Give me today."

Her breath swept over my mouth as she exhaled. "I—"

"Don't say no."

She pulled back, her dark eyes latching on to mine. Her fingers stroked the thick stubble on my jaw then lowered to slide along my throat.

"One more time," she whispered.

The feeling of relief that crashed over me was shocking in its strength. But I didn't stop to analyze it or ponder why. I had Elise in my arms, my mouth on hers, devouring her sweet lips, her curves pressed against me.

One more time.

It would be enough. I had no room in my life for anything more.

CHAPTER TWENTY-ONE

Elise

By the time our car pulled up in front of our building, my lips felt puffy and bitten. Staid and serious, Weston Aldrich could be an animal when he was in the mood, and he'd gone feral on me.

God, I was going to miss it.

At least we still had today.

Weston climbed out of the car first, holding his leather messenger bag in front of the bulge in his pants, so he didn't scar innocent passersby for life. Snickering quietly, I slid out behind him. He took my hand, helping me to stand and onto the sidewalk.

While we waited for the driver to grab our bags from the trunk, heat simmered between us. His gaze had gone molten as he stared at my swollen lips.

Fortunately, we only had to make it upstairs before we went at each other.

"Elise. Weston."

At the sound of our names, we turned to find Elliot exiting our building, a small smile playing on his lips. It took everything in my power not to jump away from Weston when we were already a couple feet apart.

"Elliot? What are you doing here?" When he reached me, I leaned forward to kiss him on the cheek. He gave me a side hug before stepping back and shaking Weston's hand.

"Are you really surprised I would want to see you after you were away for so long?" he asked.

I chuckled, despite my plummeting stomach. So much for one more time. "Three nights, El. That's barely a blip."

He rocked back on his heels, his hands tucked into his pockets. "So, I want to hang out with my sister. Do you have a better offer?"

I willed myself not to glance at Weston. "Your idea of hanging out had better involve sitting on my couch watching movies because that's all the activity I have the energy for."

He laughed, turning his attention to Weston. "It sounds like you're working your employees to the bone, Aldrich."

In my periphery, Weston went rigid. "You know me. I like to make the work environment as painful as possible and keep my employees chained down so they can never leave," he deadpanned.

Weston started for my bag, but Elliot beat him to it. "I've got Elise's things. You can head up to your place and do whatever it is you do when you're all alone."

Weston and I finally exchanged a glance. He smirked, but his disappointment was palpable. "Count my money. That's what I do when I'm alone."

"Make sure not to get any paper cuts," I quipped halfheartedly.

As much as I'd protested, I'd wanted that final time with him, and now it would never happen.

Weston stood behind me in the elevator, Elliot beside me. His hand brushed up and down the center of my back, featherlight, but I felt it to my toes.

The door slid open on my floor, his touch falling away. I twisted around to face him.

"Bye, Weston. Have a good rest of your weekend."

He nodded to me, his expression unreadable. "Thank you, Elise. You did an outstanding job on this trip. I won't forget it."

Heat rose to my cheeks. "I won't either," I mouthed before spinning away to follow my brother down the hall.

I let Elliot into my apartment, sighing past the knot in my chest. Saoirse was in Wyoming visiting her dad, brother, and sister-in-law for the weekend, so we had the place to ourselves.

He carried my bag to my bedroom, setting it down on the end of the bed. Then he leaned against the doorjamb while I set about unpacking. He knew me well enough not to question my need to organize immediately. We were the same that way.

"Tell me the truth," he started.

I raised my head from my stack of clothes. "About...?"

"How is Weston as a boss?"

"Oh, he's fine. We don't have a lot of interaction on a daily basis."

"You did on this trip, though."

"Somewhat." Oh god, I hated lying to my brother. "While we were at the factories, he did his thing, and I did mine."

His brow lowered. "He took care of you, though? Made sure you were in your room at night?"

If he only knew how well Weston had taken care of me...

"He did. I promise, he looked out for me, even though it wasn't necessary." I put my hands on my hips and crinkled my nose. "Who do you think looked out for me when I was in Chicago?"

He scoffed. "It sure as hell wasn't Patrick."

I pressed a hand to my aching chest. "Ouch. Punch landed."

Elliot's stance softened infinitesimally. "It wasn't intended as a punch. Not to you, anyway. My point was, it drove me crazy knowing you were halfway across the country with a man I couldn't trust to keep you cared for."

Dropping my eyes to my bag, I resumed unpacking. "Well, you were right about him, and now I'm back here, under your watch."

"My caring for you shouldn't make you angry. If Dad were here, he would be saying the same things I am."

"He might, but he would do it gently."

"Unfortunately for you, I didn't take after him in the gentleness department. He gave all of that to you."

I looked at my brother, sucking in a breath. He really was so good to me. It was unfair for me to be grumpy because he'd interrupted what Weston and I shouldn't have been doing anyway.

"You don't need to be gentle to be good, which you are, El. Thanks for giving a shit."

"Always, El." He crossed to me and picked up my emptied bag, placing it on the highest shelf in my closet. His version of a warm hug. "Now, what terrible movie are you going to make me watch with you?"

⸺◆⸺

Monday morning, there was a Post-it waiting for me on my desk. I laughed out loud when I read it.

Fratricide is the act of killing one's own brother.

So Weston was still grumpy about being interrupted by Elliot. To be fair, I still regretted it as well, but murder hadn't crossed my mind.

With a grin, I typed up an email to my boss.

To: westonaldrich@andesinc.com

From: eliselevy@andesinc.com

Dear Grumpy Boss,

I'm concerned about a sticky note on my desk this morning.

You might have an employee contemplating acts of violence against their own sibling. Why would one do such a thing? I can't think of a possible reason.

On another note, my own brother spent the night at my apartment after I got him drunk on White Russians and made him watch zombie flicks. A good time was had by...well, not all. Mostly me.

I hope the rest of your weekend was equally fun.

Wishfully,

Elise

After that, I was buried under piles of work, only stopping to have lunch with Rebecca and Simon and to shoo Miles away from my desk. Periodically, I checked my emails, but since I'd received no response, I imagined Weston was five times as busy as I was.

By the end of the day, I submitted my first story to Salma and had prepped my notes to write another one. I was shutting down my computer when an email came in.

* * *

To: eliselevy@andesinc.com
From: westonaldrich@andesinc.com
Dear Elise,

That does sound concerning. Might you have mistaken the intended subject of violence? Perhaps you should be looking closer to home.

One can't help wondering, what was your first reaction when you read the Post-it?

As for your other subject, my weekend started off hot but ended up cold and lonely. I'm happy yours was more enjoyable than mine. You deserve it after how hard I worked you on our trip.

Have you recovered?

Concernedly,

Weston

* * *

To: westonaldrich@andesinc.com
From: eliselevy@andesinc.com
Dear Grumpy Boss,

I probably shouldn't tell you I laughed out loud when I first read the note. Perhaps I should be concerned about *myself*.

I'm sorry your weekend didn't end as well as it started. At least you'll have the memories of the good times. I know I like to take my favorite memories to bed with me so I can think about them when I'm all alone...

Since it's now past 5:00 pm and I'm still exhausted from how hard you worked me on our trip, I'll be signing off for the night.

Have a lovely evening, Weston.

Warmly,

Elise

I shut down my computer and gathered my things. If I didn't leave now, I might have been tempted to sneak up to eight and knock on Weston's door. Since that wasn't professional or smart, I cut my losses and rode down to the lobby instead.

My phone vibrated with a text from Saoirse asking about my dinner plans. I was replying to her as I headed outside, so I wasn't paying as close attention to my surroundings as I should have.

I never saw him coming.

"Elise." My name, croaked. My arm, grabbed.

Startled, I tried to pull back at the same time my head whipped up and my eyes landed on my ex-boyfriend.

Patrick's fingers tightened on my arm, but his words were weak and pleading. "Don't run away. I flew out here to see you."

"I—" I was so shocked at his presence I had no clue how to respond. "What are you doing here?"

He'd gotten thinner, had let his beard grow thick. Had it been two months since I last saw him? Standing in front of me now, it could have been years with how drastically both his appearance and my feelings for him had changed.

"Isn't it obvious? I came to see you. I'm *here* for you, Elise, so you can tell me why the hell you left me."

We were making a scene in front of my office building. My coworkers were streaming out, peering warily at me and the loud, disheveled man. It was bad enough he was here. Adding witnesses only furthered my humiliation.

"Lower your voice, please. This is my job, Patrick."

He threw out his free hand. "Do you know how crazy I've been going? Your friends and brother almost had me convinced you were never real. Can you believe that? I guess it is believable since you're the one who removed every trace of yourself from my life. But you just said my name. You said it, so I know it was real."

"Please, just—"

"Elise," he cried hoarsely. He wasn't angry. He was utterly despondent. I hated that seeing him this way affected me, but it did. "I love you, sweetheart. I need you to talk to me. Please, just fucking talk to me."

He moved fast, yanking me into him and wrapping his arm around the back of my neck.

"Patrick, stop."

Our eyes met. His were smudged with black underneath, but they were so familiar, it hurt to look at him this close up. "I've missed you so much."

Then his mouth crashed into mine.

Chapter Twenty-Two

Weston

Leaving the office at five was outrageous, especially after being out of town for half a week. Yet, here I was, striding across the lobby, hoping I was fast enough to catch up with Elise.

When I caught her, I had no idea what I was going to do with her.

Dinner, maybe.

White Russians and zombie flicks.

Christ, was I jealous of the time she'd spent with her own brother?

It was entirely irrational, but I was. I wanted that time for myself.

Stalking out of the building, I looked left, then right. I'd found Elise, all right, but she wasn't alone. Some tall, bearded fuck had his mouth on her.

Possessiveness roared inside me. Bitter disappointment clouded my vision. She'd moved back to her lumberjack the minute she got home.

It was her right. She wasn't mine. So why the fuck did betrayal stab at my chest?

I found myself backing up, preparing to turn around and go inside where I belonged when Elise ripped herself away from the man who'd been holding her.

My vision cleared. This wasn't Thomas, and Elise didn't look happy.

He grabbed at her, catching her by the elbow. "Stop it, Patrick. This wasn't talking, nor was it welcome. You can't just kiss me. That's over."

Patrick.

I was on them before I acknowledged I was going to move. My arm banded around Elise's middle, easily pulling her from the other man's grasp.

"You heard her," I snapped. "You need to leave."

At the sound of my voice, Elise melted against me, sliding around to my side.

Her ex's eyes narrowed on where we were holding each other. I scoffed, raising my chin.

"That's right. She's mine now. You screwed up, didn't treasure her, and I got the reward." I gently moved Elise behind me and stepped into him.

He puffed out his chest like he was a big man, but I *knew* he was small. Tiny, even. I didn't mean his physical size. I was referring to his mind, his confidence, the essence of him. That was minuscule.

It had been apparent to me the first time I met him, when Elise had let her light dim so this idiot could shine. She had deferred to him, and when she'd caught herself laughing too hard or stating an opinion, she would dart her eyes to him and clamp her mouth shut.

"What is this?" Patrick snarled at me before softening to look at her. "Elise, what is this? Don't tell me you're with someone else. Don't tell me that."

"I've moved on," she replied quietly.

He thumped his chest. "Yeah, well, I should have a say in that. How have you moved on when we never broke up? I've been hunting you down to beg you to come back to me and you've been fucking someone else?"

I had to laugh. "I think Elise ghosting you was a loud and clear message that you're broken up. It isn't her fault you're too dense to understand."

"This has nothing to do with you, man. Elise and I were having a conversation before you showed up."

"What you aren't seeing is everything to do with Elise involves me. She's mine. And what I walked up on didn't look like conversation. It looked like you were forcing *my* girl into a kiss." I pointed to the corner of the building. "If you need playback, the security cameras captured the assault in real time."

"Weston—" Elise started.

"What are you talking about?" Patrick sputtered, cutting her off. "I kissed her because I missed her. I would never hurt her." He tried to peer around me to get to her, but I was a brick wall keeping him away.

"Just go, Patrick," she said sadly. "We're finished."

"I don't accept that." He shoved his fingers through his hair. "I know you saw the texts. Steve's girl told him, and I get why you're mad, but—"

"Go!" she yelled. "Don't say anything else. Just go!"

The pain lashing through her words alerted me. What the hell had this guy done to her?

Patrick staggered back. "Elise. God, I'm so sorry, sweetheart. Please, *please* let me explain."

Suddenly, I almost felt sorry for him. He was just now coming to the realization he wasn't going to get her back. Whatever he'd done, the damage had been permanent, and it was hitting him like a tidal wave.

I held my hand out to her. She slipped her warm palm into mine, and I drew her forward, kissing her temple.

"She's mine now. All taken care of. You had four years to treat her right, and you failed at the task. You made her feel so unsafe, so unwelcome in her own home, she moved across the country to get away from you. But I have her now. I recognize how lucky I am to even be allowed to stand beside her. It's too bad you didn't, but your loss is my gain. So you can go. You're not needed here."

He stared at her with wide, shining eyes. If he cried, I wouldn't have blamed him. Losing Elise had to be gut-wrenching. But from the sound of it, he'd done it to himself.

"I love you, Elise, but I can see I'm hurting you. Even if you're finished with me, I think we need to have a conversation. I can't force you, though. The ball's in your court now, sweetheart. I'll wait to hear from you." He swiped at his eyes. "And so you know, I am disgusted with myself for the way I treated you. I will never stop regretting it."

She nodded, but that was her only response. After an eternity, Patrick walked away, and I pulled Elise against my chest so she didn't have to watch him.

"Everyone will see us," she mumbled.

"Doesn't matter." I made long strokes up and down her back until her body slowly loosened and curved into mine. "I'm taking you home."

"Okay."

———◆———

Elise was in my penthouse, and I had no idea what to do with her.

I wanted her happy. I was still trying to figure out how to make that happen, but I wouldn't stop until I reached my goal.

She was wandering around my living room, trailing her fingers over the furniture and stopping to examine the art on my walls.

"You have so much space," she said, awed.

"More than I need."

"Yeah." She peered out the floor-to-ceiling windows. "It's beautiful, though. Not cold and stark."

With a short laugh, I cocked my head. "Did you assume I'd want a cold and stark home?"

She spun around, starting toward me. "I suppose I didn't think about it very hard, but no, I don't think you'd want that. You're not cold." Her hands smoothed up my lapels. "Thank you for being there for me. I'm sorry you got pulled into all that, but I'm not sorry you were there."

"Don't thank me for that."

She laughed. "Don't growl at me for thanking you."

"I didn't know I had." I swiped my thumb along her cheek. "How are you?"

"I'm fine." She groaned. "Well, not really. That was so awful. I imagined what it would be like if he found me, but that was so, so real. He's not doing well."

"But you are, aren't you?"

Her eyes were wet when they met mine, but she nodded. "I am. I've spent this time walking through it and making myself better. I don't think he's done that."

My jaw hardened at the sound of her worry. "My concern doesn't lie with him."

"I know." A slow smile spread across her lips. "You were right. You do make me feel safe."

"Good." If I couldn't make her happy, at least I could make her feel safe. "What I said to Patrick wasn't untrue, you know. While you're not mine, I do feel lucky to have you and that I get to know you again. His fuck up is definitely my most valuable gain."

Her fingers curled around my lapels, and she gave them a tug while she sighed. "Weston. God, don't say perfect things like that when I'm trying to keep hold of my feelings for you."

I smoothed my hands from her wrists to her shoulders. "I'll always tell you the truth and take care of you. As long as you know it, I don't have to say it out loud anymore."

Her gaze held mine. The shine in her eyes brought out the flecks of gold. Fucking dazzling.

"I do know." She sniffled and dropped her hands. "What do we do now, pal?"

I chuckled, though it was bitter. The last thing I wanted to be was Elise's pal. "I don't know. If you were Luca or Elliot, I'd say let's order takeout and—"

"Watch zombie flicks?" She bounced on her toes.

"Most likely a game." I shook my head. "But I'll watch anything you want."

There might not have been White Russians, but inside my head, I was celebrating the fact that I was going to get my coveted zombie flicks with Elise.

⸻◆⸻

We were on my couch, food in our laps, choosing a movie. Elise went for *Shaun of the Dead*, which I'd never seen and probably never would have if not for the woman beside me.

I gave her the pickle that had come with my hamburger. Her wide beam had been thanks enough, but she leaned over and kissed my bicep too.

She'd run home to change out of her work clothes and into leggings and a T-shirt that hung off one shoulder, revealing the strap of her bra. The wide neckline kept slipping lower, and Elise didn't seem to be concerned.

My burger went half-uneaten while I tracked the path of her shirt. Her bra was pink and, as I'd discovered, lacy. My fingers twitched to pull the neckline down another inch or two to reveal the creamy round tops of her breasts.

I wouldn't.

Elise's giggle brought my attention to the screen. A guy walked through his neighborhood, oblivious to the fires, dead bodies, and bloody handprints.

It should have been enough to turn me off, but my dick didn't care about anything other than the woman sitting beside me. Her skin, her scent, her laugh, the memory of the feel of her, her taste.

Jesus.

I closed my eyes and pictured Elliot, thinking of the time my dad knocked me down the stairs. It had been a careless accident when I was a skinny ten-year-old, more bone than anything else. My dad had been drunk and blundering, pushing me aside without much force, but since I'd been at the top of the stairs, it hadn't taken much for me to tumble.

An apoplectic Elliot had hidden me in his room for two days, bringing me bags of frozen peas and ice packs for my bruises while making detailed plans to kill my father. If I hadn't approved, his alternate plot had been to hide me in his house forever. He'd had lists with bullet points. He'd meant it.

On day three, when my mother came for me, he stood in front of me until I relented and agreed to go home with her.

There was a lifetime of those kinds of stories between us.

That was what was on the line.

If I went for what I truly wanted, I would be risking the single most valuable relationship in my life. Even if Elliot approved of me dating his sister—a long shot—if things didn't work out with Elise, nothing would be the same between Elliot and me.

With my track record and my single-mindedness, when it came to my company, failure was the most likely outcome.

And yet...

When I'd told Patrick Elise was mine, I hadn't been lying. The words leaving my mouth had been the complete truth.

The fact that it was impossible hadn't entered my thoughts.

"Are you even watching?" she asked.

I lifted my eyes from her bra. I'd been staring for a while, and now I'd been caught in the act.

"I'm watching you enjoying your movie."

She smiled with a sigh. "I'm enjoying all of tonight. I didn't know you were capable of relaxing, yet here you sit. Are you dying to check your email?"

"No. I haven't thought of it." That wasn't strictly true. Work was always on my mind, but with Elise, it was at the back, on a low simmer. That was rare for me.

I let my gaze trail over her. Her feet were kicked up on the ottoman in front of her. Her toenails were polished sky blue, and she had a small blue columbine tattooed on the inside of her ankle. "When did you get that tattoo?"

She rubbed her feet together. "It's the Colorado state flower. Saoirse took me to get it before I moved, so I'd always have a piece of Colorado with me."

Someone screamed on the TV, but I was focused on her.

"Do you want another one?"

"Maybe, if there's another moment in my life I want to mark permanently."

"Planning to move again?"

She shook her head. "No. I like being near Elliot. This is my home." She shoved at my knee. "I can't tell if you like it or not."

"Your tattoo?"

She lowered her chin, silently saying, *"Duh."*

"I do like it. It's very pretty. I remember putting my mouth on it a few times on our trip." Her cheeks flushed, and my nostrils flared at the shared memory we weren't supposed to be talking about.

I wadded up the wrapper with the remains of my dinner inside, tossing it into the paper bag on the floor beside the couch. "I'm glad to know you're not the type who'd get a man's name tattooed on you. Otherwise, you'd be spending a fortune to remove it."

A laugh burst out of her. "You can bet I'm most definitely not that type. Even if I was, getting Patrick's name on me would have never entered my mind."

"No?"

"No." She tossed her trash in with mine and shifted so her legs were tucked on the couch, twisting to face me. "I've done a lot of thinking about how I've been feeling since the breakup. What he did devastated me, and I'm still getting over that. But I realized I got over *him* a lot faster than I expected, and it's not just because I'm so deft at compartmentalizing. I think I chose Patrick because I knew when it ended, I wouldn't be broken."

"You always expected it to end? Elise, I thought you were a believer in happy endings," I admonished.

She rolled her eyes at me then poked my arm. "I am, jackass. I didn't make those decisions about Patrick consciously, but I think I always knew we wouldn't wind up together. I think half the reason we lasted as long as we did was because—like you with Marisol—I wanted to prove you and Elliot wrong. The other half was because there wasn't anything threatening about loving him. He didn't light me on fire, but then again, he didn't *light me on fire*."

I'd stopped listening the moment she'd said I was part of the reason she'd stayed with him. My brain imploded with that frustrating revelation. I squeezed my eyes, attempting to process what she'd just said.

"You stayed to spite me?"

Her nails scratched lightly on my forearm, springing my eyes open. "Is that really all you heard?"

"I'm supremely self-centered."

She huffed. "I mentioned none of this was conscious, right? I wasn't actively thinking, 'Oh, I can't dump Patrick for not taking care of my emotions because then Weston will know he was right and will gloat.' That didn't happen. In hindsight, that was very much part of it."

I reached out, running my forefinger along the pink strap of her bra.

"You really disliked me, didn't you?"

"Dislike is too strong. I had thoughts, though." She rubbed her lips together. "To be fair, I now know I was wrong and stupid. I wish I hadn't wasted so many years shutting you out when we could have been friends."

I dipped my finger under the strap to rub my knuckle along her skin. "The plethora didn't help."

She shook her head, grinning. "No, it most certainly did not."

"Do you know how much I despise hearing I was even part of the cause of you staying with that guy?"

"I can imagine."

I unhooked my finger to flatten my palm at the base of her throat. "A lot. If I didn't think I'd scare the shit out of you, my fist would be meeting drywall right now. I'm sorry, baby. I'm sorry for driving you away."

"Weston," she breathed, scooting closer. Her arms went around my shoulders, her cheek pressing against mine. "Don't, okay? I don't blame you, and I'm not mad at you. You have nothing to apologize for. I'm back, and we're good. You and me, right?"

I turned my head, our noses brushing. "I wasn't lying about you being mine."

Her lashes fluttered, and she rubbed her nose against mine. "I didn't think you were."

"But we can't."

Her soft breath floated over my lips. "If we did, it would be..."

Dangerous. Ruinous. Beautiful.

"Yeah," I sighed. "It would be."

I curled my arms around her waist, drawing her closer. "Let's watch your movie, baby. We don't have to talk about this anymore. It'll work out how it's supposed to."

She pulled back, looking me over. "That doesn't sound like you."

I gave a wry laugh. "It doesn't, but I'm hopeful it's true since I don't have any control over this anymore."

"That must be hard on you, you control freak."

I wasn't offended. It was the truth.

Sliding my hand up her back to cup her nape, I shook my head. "You have no idea."

She laid her head on my chest, nuzzling even closer.

No idea at all.

CHAPTER TWENTY-THREE

Elise

WESTON: *WHERE ARE YOU?*

I wasn't surprised to see his text, but it did make my blood heat. We'd been back from our trip for two weeks and had spent almost every evening together. Some nights, we had dinner; others, when he worked late, we watched stupid TV and snuggled on his couch.

Yeah. Snuggled.

We'd been saying we were just friends while holding on to each other like life rafts. My social life was Weston. My hobbies were Weston and more Weston.

It wasn't wise and probably not healthy, but I told myself I could stop at any time. We were just making up for the years we hadn't been close. If we didn't kiss or have sex, it didn't count.

So what if my body thrummed, and when I left his place, I went straight to bed and took care of my pulsing clit with his face on my mind and his name on my lips. So what if Weston's joggers seemed to be permanently tented?

I quickly replied, then set my phone face down on the table in front of me, giving my attention to Rebecca and Simon. They were on their second pitcher of margaritas and well on their way to getting shit-faced. They'd been asking me to go out with them for ages, and it had been on the tip of my tongue to turn them down once again, but I'd thought better of it. They were good friends to me, had been from day one, and I didn't want to lose that because I'd become mildly obsessed with my boss.

Rebecca's husband, Sam, had just arrived from his office a few blocks away, and since we were both mostly sober, we were laughing at their antics.

Right now, they were in a deep debate on whether rock could really beat paper. Simon said yes, Rebecca was adamant the answer was no. Sam had to make her sit back down when she tried to go outside to find a rock to prove her argument.

Sam picked up the pitcher. "If I can't beat them, I'm joining them." He filled his glass, then gestured to mine. "Refill?"

"Sure, thank you."

Two was my limit tonight. The last thing I needed was to show up at Weston's drunk. Tipsy would be dangerous enough.

Rebecca and Simon finished their argument and decided it was time for dancing. There wasn't much of a dance floor in this bar, but they found a spot that had previously been a walkway and declared it theirs.

"I need you to tell me how you guys got together in high school."

Sam turned away from watching his wife, a smile tipping his lips. He was a big man, but gentleness exuded from him. He had fluffy brown curls and soft, caramel eyes that melted when he was looking at Rebecca.

"I was a jock, she was a theater kid."

I grinned. "I'm not surprised in the least."

"No." He shook his head. "She hasn't lost her flair for drama."

I clinked my glass with his. "That's why we love her."

"One of the many reasons." He took a sip then got back to his story. "We didn't have any of the same friends, but we were in English together our sophomore year. She'd caught my eye right away but wouldn't give me the time of day."

I gasped. "Rude."

He chuckled. "I know, right? The truth was, I was a cocky little shit. I was on the varsity team my first year of high school so I thought I was a big man. Girls were into me, even the older ones, so I couldn't figure out why Rebecca wouldn't even say hi to me. I thought I was going to forget about her, then I saw her in a production of *Chicago* and that was it for me."

"Roxie Hart?"

His cheeks flushed. "Yeah. There's no forgetting Roxie." His grin was lopsided and adorable. "I upped my game, stopped hanging out with other girls, and focused my full attention on Rebecca, asking her out every other month while putting in the work of getting to know her. She wasn't mean about rejecting me. She kept telling me we didn't have anything in common and didn't make any sense together, so I made her see that we made sense. When the spring musical auditions came around, I got my big ass up on that stage and sang my heart out."

I snorted a laugh. "Did you land a role?"

He lifted a shoulder. "I can't sing a lick. They made me part of the company. Rebecca got the lead." He took a long swallow of his margarita. "On the last day of the play, she walked right up to me and said, 'I'll go out with you, but if you screw around and break my heart, I'll break your dick.' That was when I knew I was going to marry her."

I tossed my head back, laughing, buoyant on their story. I didn't care what Weston said. Happy endings were possible if you were with the right person.

A brush along my cheek startled me.

"What's so funny, *bella*?"

I whipped around to find Luca grinning at me. Over his shoulder stood Weston, his expression stony.

"Luca!" I cried, hopping up to hug him. "What are you doing here?"

He squeezed me tight and kissed both my cheeks. "West was in the mood for drinks. I had nothing on, so here I am. And what a treat, I get to see my best girl." He pulled me to his side so he could face Sam. "Did we interrupt?"

"Not at all," I answered.

Sam rose to his feet, all six feet, five inches of him. He held out his hand to Luca.

"Hello. I'm Sam," he said amiably.

Luca shook his hand, introducing himself, then we all turned to Weston. Sam held his hand out to him. Weston's eyes flicked down to it, his upper lip curling slightly before finally taking Sam's hand.

He was being weird.

When he took a seat across from me, rigid and staring straight at me, it finally hit me. Without Rebecca and Simon here with us, it probably looked like I was on a date with Sam.

"Hi, Weston," I said.

"Hello," he uttered.

"Remember that conversation we had about happy endings?"

His nod was barely perceptible.

"And remember when I told you about Rebecca marrying her high school sweetheart?" Again, he nodded. "Well, until just now, I'd never heard their full story. Sam just let it all out, and I have to say, I'm an even firmer believer in happy endings."

Sam patted my forearm. "Well, damn. I'm honored. Don't tell Becks, though. She'll gloat."

I laughed, my gaze flicking to Simon and Rebecca in the midst of some monstrosity of a line dance.

"I think I'm safe telling her anything tonight since she won't remember it tomorrow." Catching Luca and Weston's attention, I pointed out my coworkers. "That's Simon and Rebecca. They got a head start on the margaritas."

Luca guffawed. "Are they seizing?"

"That's dancing," I corrected.

Sam rubbed his forehead and stared at Weston. "Wait a second. You're not Weston Aldrich, are you? Rebecca's boss."

Weston's glare slowly faded with the dawning of what he'd actually walked in on and he looked at Sam without homicidal intent.

"I am. Unfortunately, I don't have the pleasure of working with Rebecca on a regular basis, but from Elise's stories, I'm missing out."

Oh, that charmer.

It worked on Sam. His barrel chest puffed with pride. "I imagine it's a good thing for me my wife doesn't work close to you." He eyed Weston appraisingly. "Otherwise, she'd probably come home and ask me to grow out my hair, maybe add some highlights and start wearing suits."

I elbowed him. "I have a hard time believing Rebecca would ever ask you to be anyone other than yourself."

He winked at me. "Yeah, you're right." Then he put his glass down and stood. "I'm going to go check on the two of them. Brace yourself for when I tell her her boss is here."

Luca blew out a breath when Sam walked away. "Thank Christ that wasn't what it looked like. I thought we were crashing your date."

"No." I sipped my margarita and glanced back and forth between Weston and Luca. "I'm not really dating anyone right now."

Weston leaned forward, his elbows on his knees. "So, you're single and free?"

"I guess so. How about you?" I asked.

His mouth twitched. "Free as a bird."

"Me too," Luca supplied. "Not that you asked."

"Don't pout," I cooed. "I was about to get to you."

A waitress stopped by, taking their drink orders. Weston's eyes were locked on me when he ordered his bourbon. I licked the salt off my lip. His nostrils flared, and his fingers flexed on his knees.

We hadn't been out anywhere together since California. I hadn't realized how difficult it would be to pretend with him. It seemed unnatural for us to be so far apart. He hadn't hugged me when he showed up, and the low ache in my stomach longed for his arms to be around me.

"How was your day?" I asked him.

"Fine. The same as always. Yours?"

My lips twitched. "Good. There was a sticky note on my desk this morning."

His brow arched. "Oh? What did it say?"

"It said stars can come back from the dead. These are called zombie stars."

Luca's brow furrowed. "Who's leaving sticky notes on your desk?"

I bit my bottom lip to stop from grinning and shrugged. "They're anonymous, but I have my suspicions."

"Zombie stars." Weston rubbed his chin. "Interesting. That sounds like your kind of star."

"You like zombies?" Luca asked.

I nodded. "I do. Well, not real-life ones."

"Of course not," Weston said dryly.

"It's kind of creepy someone at your job knows that," Luca said. "Maybe you should report this to HR, Elise."

It was almost impossible to hold back my snort, but I managed. "I'll think about it."

"It's probably some idiot desperate for your attention," Weston said.

I slowly turned my head from Luca to him. Heat flooded between us. "Is it?"

He lowered his chin and opened his mouth to speak when a shriek cut him off. Rebecca was stumbling toward us, Simon and Sam on her heels. I sat back in my chair, the knot in my stomach loosening.

⸺◆⸺

I surpassed my self-appointed limit, finishing my third margarita. It wasn't my fault, really. The six of us were having fun and talking so much, I got thirsty. And I wasn't drunk, just floaty and happy.

It was fortunate tomorrow was Saturday. You know, just in case I was actually drunk and needed time to recover.

Right now, I had more pressing matters to attend to. "I'll be right back. Ladies' room."

The restroom was empty when I entered, so I quickly did my business and washed my hands. The moment I opened the door to the bar, Rebecca's laugh floated above all the other sounds, making me smile.

"Happy?"

I hadn't noticed Weston leaning against the wall farther down the hall, away from the bar. I sauntered over to him, and when I was near, he hooked his arm around me, drawing me into his chest.

I sighed, finally getting the hug I'd been craving.

"I was ready to murder him, you know," he murmured.

"What?" I tipped my head back. "Murder who?"

"Sam. When I thought he was your date. It ripped me apart."

I sucked in a shaky breath. "I'm sorry. I'm not seeing anyone." I pressed a hand to his cheek, rubbing at the turned-down corner of his mouth with my thumb. "This is hard."

"I hate it," he groused.

"Should we stop hanging out so much? It only makes it harder."

"No." His arm tightened on me. "I want more of you, not less."

"West," I sighed, tucking my face in his throat. "I do too."

His fingers delved into my hair. His other hand slid from my waist down to my ass, kneading and rubbing, keeping me pressed tight against him. How could something that felt so right be wrong? It was easy to forget why we couldn't be together when he was holding me like this.

"Look at me, baby," he murmured softly.

Pulling back from his throat, I opened my eyes. He was right there, dipping down so we were eye to eye. He palmed the back of my head and touched his lips to mine. He was gentle, sweet, pecking lightly at first, then with more firmness, but not too much.

"I can't, Elise." He kissed me again, barely taking my bottom lip between his. I clutched at him, dizzy from the soft kisses he was raining all over my mouth.

"Oh shit."

Our heads whipped around at the same time, finding a wide-eyed Luca staring at us from the end of the hallway.

"Oh shit," he repeated.

Weston wouldn't let me pull away. He kept me locked against him, even as he pushed off from the wall.

"Hi, Luca." My voice came out small and nervous. My heart thumped hard in my chest. This could be bad. I wished I was fully sober to face this.

Luca scrubbed at his face then marched toward us. "Hi, *bella*. What kind of trouble have you gotten into?"

"There's no trouble." Weston went taut, as if he was prepared to battle Luca if he had to. "It's no concern of yours."

Luca's gaze slid back and forth between us. "What isn't a concern? Tell me what I walked in on because, to be quite honest, this doesn't look like a drunken make-out session."

Shuddering, my lashes fluttered to my cheeks. "It's not. We're—" What the hell were we? I didn't even know how to begin to explain us to Luca.

"We're together," Weston declared.

I asked, "We are?" at the same time Luca yelled, "You're what?"

"Together," Weston confirmed.

Luca pulled up straight, shaking off some of his alcohol-induced haziness. "I'm assuming Elliot doesn't know about this since the city isn't burning."

"It's new," I told him.

Incredibly new. Like a minute old. And I hadn't even agreed to anything.

So why was I holding on to Weston?

Oh, because I liked him saying we were together. I wanted that to be real. If he was just saying it for Luca's sake, I'd take a page out of Rebecca's book and break his dick, only he wouldn't get a warning.

Luca crossed his arms, assessing us. "You'll tell him. I won't lie to him."

"Give us a little time," I pleaded. "We won't sneak around, but I'm not ready to face my brother yet."

"You won't have to lie," Weston said with certainty. "He won't ask, so there won't be a reason to. When Elise and I feel the time is right, we'll tell Elliot."

Luca stared at him for a long moment before scoffing. "He's going to be so pissed." He rubbed his jaw like he was thinking. "I'll be pissed if you fuck her over, West."

Weston's hold on me tightened. "I would never do that."

Luca shoved his fingers through his hair and cupped his head, muttering curses. He paced back and forth in front of us, battling something internally.

Finally, he stopped, nodding like he came to a decision. "I never saw this coming, but I can't say I'm not thrilled to death about it, for both of you." He wagged his finger between us. "There's something right here. It fits. The two of you fit. Although, I'm second-guessing all the times you referred to Elise as a sister."

Luca chuckled. Weston didn't.

"Feelings evolved. I've never lied about how I feel, though. There was a time she was like a sister to me, but that faded and now she's something else."

Luca's humor dropped away, replaced by a look of understanding. "I get it, Weston. I know you wouldn't have gone there with Elise unless you were serious."

I cleared my throat and wrested myself away from Weston. It was difficult to be taken seriously when I was plastered to his chest.

"I would love it if you two didn't talk about this like I'm not here. The thing is, Weston and I haven't really had a chance to define anything yet, so can you give us that chance, Luca? I know you're in a tough spot, and I hate that you are, but—"

He held his hand up. "I don't like Elliot being in the dark about something so big, but if I hadn't walked back here when I did, I would have never guessed there was anything going on between you. So, I'll take the blame for bad timing. You two crazy kids figure yourselves out. I'm going to go to the bathroom and pretend like I didn't see a thing."

He started to turn, but I called out to him. His brow winged in question.

"My birthday's next weekend," I said.

His grin was small but sincere. "I know it is, *bella*."

"Well, Saoirse is throwing me a little party on our rooftop. You should come."

He rocked back on his heels. "As much as I would love to be there—not just for you, but to meet your elusive friend after all these years—I'll be at my parents' next weekend for their fortieth wedding anniversary."

"You'll be missed," Weston deadpanned.

I thought maybe he wasn't happy Luca was involved now. Or maybe he was being sincere. Weston's innate grumpiness made him hard to read at times.

Luca disappeared into the restroom, leaving Weston and me alone.

I heaved a sigh, worry worming its way into my stomach. Weston dipped down, brushing his lips over mine. When he pulled back, there was a trace of a grin on his mouth.

"Come home with me."

I nodded.

We were really doing this.

Chapter Twenty-Four

Elise

As soon as Weston closed his apartment door, he was on me, his hands in my hair, his mouth slanting over mine. The way he was kissing me was nothing like the sweet pecks in the bar. He'd been freed from his restraints. All the rules he'd been following had fallen away. His teeth scraped over my lips. His tongue licked into my mouth, deep, tasting. I moaned and fell backward, hitting a wall. Weston followed me, pressing himself flush.

My nails dug into his chest, wildness overwhelming me—*everything* about what was happening overwhelming me. We'd been finished with this side of our relationship. Just friends. Then everything had changed.

I was trying to catch up, but Weston wasn't giving me a second to think.

Did I even want to?

This man was who I wanted. Friendship was never going to be enough, not with how close we had become and how strong my feelings were for him.

"West," I moaned against his lips.

"Yes." He tugged my hair and pushed his thick cock into my belly. "I've been waiting to hear you say that again."

"West." My lashes fluttered. He kissed my nose, then bent his head to lick a line up the side of my neck. My knees were weak, but he had me propped against the wall. Anchored.

His hand was in my dress, beneath my bra, squeezing and rubbing my nipple. I worked at his buttons, frustrated there were so damn many on his dress shirt. I was close to ripping it off when I got the last one undone and could drag my palms over his heated skin.

Suddenly, he straightened, meeting my eyes. He took my head in both of his hands, taking a long time to stare at me. I felt the weight of his gaze in my chest, so heavy and filled with a thousand words. There was vulnerability Weston almost never showed. It hit me hard.

"I'll be your friend, Elise, but I can't be only that. It's impossible."

I pushed up on my toes and pressed my lips to his. "I missed you so much."

"I missed you too. You have no idea."

We'd spent every spare moment together but had held ourselves apart. Now that was over.

Weston took me to his bedroom, shedding his clothes like old skin along the way. We'd avoided his bedroom in all the time we'd spent together. I hadn't even set foot inside. Later, I'd explore it. Right now, the man sitting on the edge of his bed, pulling me between his spread knees, was my entire focus.

Weston tugged the bow at my hip, and my wrap dress fell open. He shoved it the rest of the way off, leaving me in my black satin bra and emerald-green lacy boy shorts.

He gripped my hips and rubbed his forehead on my stomach, releasing a shuddering breath. Then he kissed the indent of my belly button. I had never been comfortable with another man paying any attention to my stomach, but everything was different with Weston.

When we were alone, there was only us. Two people who craved each other. There was no part of him I wouldn't kiss or savor, no part that didn't turn me on and make me want him even more, and I knew from experience he felt the exact same way.

Weston didn't do things he didn't want to. He didn't lie or pretend. If he told me I was gorgeous and kissed my soft stomach, it was real.

"My beautiful fucking girl," he murmured as he edged down my underwear, kissing my exposed skin.

The fabric pooled at my feet, and Weston angled forward, kissing the top of my slit. I widened my stance, letting him in. His tongue breached my lips, teasing my clit. The barest touch and I had to hold on to his shoulders so I wouldn't fall.

I really had missed him.

He lay back, bringing me with him to straddle his face. There was a moment of shyness, where I felt ungainly and overlarge, but Weston took me out of my head, gripping my thighs and pulling me to his mouth. The satisfied groan he released when my pussy met his lips erased my doubts.

He put me where I was because he wanted me there.

He made *me* want to be there.

My fingers curled around the top of his headboard, needing to hold on as his skilled tongue swiped over my soaked flesh. Like everything Weston did, he lapped at me with slow, measured precision. If I were brave, I would have peeked at his face. I was dying to see his expression. But this position had made me vulnerable, and I wasn't ready to add another layer to it, so I closed my eyes and concentrated on what he was doing to my body.

His moans of pleasure.

His soft, insistent strokes up and down my legs.

The flick of his tongue on my clit.

His determined, unending devotion to licking every inch of my pussy.

My orgasm collided with me in a sudden burst, lighting me aflame. I cried his name and writhed over him, still careful not to drop down too low. But he obliterated my care, yanking me firmly onto his mouth and chin.

Weston was an intense man, which he brought to the bedroom and multiplied infinitely. His attention to my pleasure, to *me*, made me feel lucky, sexy, sensual. Being his sole focus was incredible. One orgasm wasn't enough for him. He sucked on my clit until I was shaking and my bones were weak.

He rolled me onto the mattress, fitting his hips between my thighs. His thick cock slid through the dripping mess he'd made of me. Opening my eyes, I found him staring down at me with tenderness. I reached up, slicing my fingers through his hair then scratching the scruff on his jaw.

His cock slid into me easily, my inner walls pliant and stretching to accommodate him. He hissed when he was fully inside me, but he never took his eyes off me.

"This good?" he breathed.

"Perfect, West."

He shuddered, his eyes closing for a moment. "You undo me, Elise."

The truth in his words resonated. I believed him because he did the same thing to me. There were a thousand reasons we shouldn't have been together, but when we were, they were all dismantled and stashed away.

He slowly slid out, taking his time working his way back in. And he went on like that, showing me what this was going to be. Weston was in no rush now that he had me, and the truth was, I could have spent a hundred years making slow, deep love with him. The way he looked at me when he was all the way inside me...he took my breath away.

It was a heady thing, being the subject of his attention.

His hips rotated in a deep circle, hitting parts of me that were tender and sensitive. I gasped, clutching his flexing shoulders, and brought my knees up alongside his hips to let him in even farther.

"Do you feel like you're mine now?" he murmured.

I nodded, breathless from his deliberate, unflagging rhythm.

"I want to hear your words, baby," he demanded softly. "Say it."

"You make me feel like I'm yours."

"Are you mine?"

I nodded again. His brow pinched. I knew what he wanted.

"I am. I am yours."

A satisfied smile, then his mouth slanted over mine. His kiss was just as languid as his slick thrusts into my body.

When he let go of my mouth, he inched his face back so our eyes could meet.

"You haven't demanded it, because you're a better person than me, but you should know I'm yours too, Elise. There is no one else—and there won't be."

He brushed the hair from my face, sweeping his eyes over me.

"Good." I lifted my legs higher, wrapping them around his waist. "I want you to be mine."

It was crazy that he was. This was *Weston*. My Weston...what had been my fantasy a long, long time ago was finally true. He really was mine.

Something snapped in him. His head dropped to my throat, his mouth latching on with deep, hard sucks. I knew he was making his mark, and I should have cared, but I didn't.

His movements picked up speed, and my hips rose to meet each pump. He hit me deep and hard, taking my breath away. At the same time, he continued to devour any piece of skin he could get to. Biting and sucking, he groaned like my flavor was the best he'd ever had.

My fingers were tangled in his hair, stroking his shoulders, the taut line of muscles along his spine. My beautiful man, I couldn't get enough of touching him. Weston may have marked me to claim me, but I was claiming him too. Every inch of his skin that I touched, I stamped with possession, an invisible signature he could feel and I knew was there.

We writhed together in his sheets, kissing and holding on as our bodies collided and retreated until there was no going back. He slammed into me, and I tossed my head back, moaning from the pleasure-pain of having him so deep inside me. My inner walls flexed, pulling a guttural groan from him, and then we both let go.

I came, wet and visceral, so hard, I shook from it. He jerked once, then twice, plunging in as deep as he could go and stilling there. His cock throbbed, coating my insides as he emptied himself.

No condom.

It was a fleeting thought, one I didn't care about.

Weston took my face in his hands and kissed me deeply, his tongue slipping into my mouth. I slid my palms up his arms, little aftershocks shaking my body as we kissed with no destination but each other.

Eventually, when we were breathless and our lips were red and swollen, we shifted to our sides. My thighs were coated with his release. It would start to bother me soon, but not yet.

He pressed his thumb into the center of my chin then stroked his knuckles along my cheek and brushed errant strands of hair off my face.

"I don't want to miss you the way I have for the past two weeks. That's finished now, Elise."

"It is," I agreed, rubbing his stubble. "I don't want to miss you like that either."

Thick emotion coated my chest. I sucked in a breath and pinched my hip to stop myself from tearing up, but it was almost impossible. We'd crossed lines in California, but this was something different. We were embarking on untested grounds, knowing there would be shaky parts but doing it anyway.

"It was when you were nineteen. Spring break."

My brow pinched. "What was?"

"When I saw you as something other than a sister."

My mind raced back to that spring break. I'd gone on a trip to Mexico with a bunch of girls then visited Elliot for a couple nights before I went back to the dorm. Weston had been there, of course. He had been a semipermanent fixture in the Levy home.

I had taken a thousand pictures of my first time snorkeling and casted them to the TV in the living room so I could show Elliot. He'd tried to get me to snorkel with him on vacations when we were kids, but I'd been too afraid.

"The bikini pictures?" I guessed.

His mouth twitched. "No, though they didn't help. It was you."

"Me? I've always been me."

"You walked in wearing a yellow sundress. It was still cold as hell in Colorado, but there you were, all tan and happy, like you'd stepped off the beach. I remember hearing the front door open and walking out to help you with your bags. The second I saw you, I was literally staggered. I thought, *that is my Elise, set on fire.*"

My mouth fell open. "I—I don't know what to say."

He smirked. "I was twenty-three, almost twenty-four, and felt like the biggest perv checking you out. *Then* you tortured me with the bikini pictures, and I had to conceal an erection from both you and your brother."

My eyes widened. "You left and stayed away the rest of my visit."

His nod was solemn. "Do you have any idea how horrified I was? All you were doing was living your life in your own home, and I was salivating over you."

I almost laughed at his expression. He really thought he'd done something wrong. I would never tell him what had changed, because I didn't think he'd like knowing. I'd lost my virginity in college to a guy who appreciated my full figure. His stark, blazing attraction to me had flipped my own perception of myself. I'd gone from a self-conscious high schooler to a college girl finally exploring and claiming her sensuality.

"I wasn't a child, West. You're only four years older than me."

"But those four years had always been monumental. They made it so I never saw you as a possibility."

"And then you did."

"Yeah," he breathed. "You have to understand, I was running Andes then. Wearing suits every day, making million-dollar decisions, in charge of thousands of people's livelihoods. I was twenty-three, but the difference between us had still been light-years. You were Elliot's baby sister, and I was the CEO of my own company."

I nodded. "I get it now. I'm sorry I made you hard."

He chuckled. "That really screwed with my head, you little brat."

I laughed, throwing a hand out. "I know, and I feel for you, I do, but I don't know what to say. You've surprised me."

He pulled me tight against him, smiling as he touched his lips to my cheek. "I wanted you to understand this isn't sudden."

"I like knowing that." I grew serious, tipping my head so I could see him. "It's not sudden for me either."

"The timing is right." He sounded so sure I had no choice but to believe him.

"Can we give it two weeks before we tell him?" I asked.

His breathing shuddered. "The longer this goes on and he doesn't know, the harder it will be."

I threaded my fingers through his. He brought our joined hands to his mouth, pressing a kiss to my knuckles.

"I know, but I think we owe it to ourselves to really become a couple before facing him. I want to know we're solid first."

Heat flared behind his eyes. I could tell he didn't like my wording, but he nodded.

"We'll give it two weeks before we go public, but I'm speaking to HR now." His tone brooked no argument, and truly, I had none since I hadn't even considered HR and office ramifications.

I groaned. "What will people at work think of me?"

His cheek twitched. "If they think anything other than you are a creative writer and a hard worker, they can share those opinions directly with me."

I snuffed. "Oh, sure. I bet you'll have a line of people waiting to spill their inner thoughts about our relationship."

"As long as they stay inner, they can have their thoughts."

From the straight line of his lips pressing tightly together, he didn't mean that at all. If Weston could have policed people's thoughts, he would have. Miles had been right. Weston was both controlling and nosy.

Well, I liked him anyway.

Sighing, I tipped my face up, and Weston answered my request with a soft kiss.

"Can I stay here tonight?" I asked, nuzzling into his throat.

"Elise." His long exhale sounded irritable. "You're my girlfriend. Do you not understand what that means?"

Girlfriend. Ah, swoon.

"Maybe," I answered. "But you can elaborate if you wish."

He chuckled against the top of my head. "It means I always want you in my bed. And if you're not in my bed, I'll be in yours. I don't intend on asking if I'm welcome."

I snorted a laugh at his pushiness, but I was pleased. "You *are* welcome."

"Good. Now, be quiet and rest because I'm nowhere near done with you."

And suddenly, I wasn't tired at all.

CHAPTER TWENTY-FIVE

I EMERGED FROM MY office at five thirty. Renata eyed me with suspicion as she packed up her things.

"Are you sick?" Her eyes narrowed to slits.

"I'm not. Why?" I looked down, checking if I was disheveled in any way. I doubted it. Disheveled wasn't a state I normally found myself in.

"You've been leaving early the past several days."

I checked my watch. Five thirty-one. "Are you leaving early?"

She crossed her arms defensively. "Of course not. I haven't left early since—I can't remember a time I left early. We're talking about *you*, Weston Aldrich. I happen to know you're in the office until seven on a good night."

"I have somewhere to be."

She cocked her head. "Or someone to be with?"

I nodded. "That too." Then I decided I might as well tell her, since Renata was the person who kept my personal ship running. "I've been seeing a woman. Elise Levy. We're serious."

Saying that and having it be true sent a shot of adrenaline up my spine. I hadn't gotten over the fact that Elise was mine. Willingly mine.

Something happened to Renata's face. Her mouth morphed into a shape I'd never seen on her before. Was it a smile?

God, *was it*?

"That's fine, Mr. Aldrich. Very fine news." Then, under her breath, but barely, she muttered, "Much better choice than the last one."

She hadn't been a fan of Marisol and had never hidden that fact. Apparently, still wasn't.

"I agree. So you understand why I've been leaving the office earlier than before. I have a reason to be home."

The work was still there. Tonight, I'd have to spend a couple hours in my home office, most likely after Elise fell asleep. Having dinner with her and soaking her up was worth losing a couple hours of my own sleep.

I would adjust.

In the past, my relationships hadn't worked because I hadn't been willing or even had the desire to shift my priorities. With Elise, making space for her was an automatic thing, not a hardship.

The ease with which I was shifting my life around surprised even me.

Over the past week, we'd developed a ritual. I drove Elise home, then she'd go to her place for an hour or two to change and spend time with Saoirse. I'd attempted to protest, but she'd told me she refused to be a girl who disappeared on her friend just because she had a boyfriend, and I'd objected to the "just" in her statement.

There was no "just" about us being together.

Elise had chosen to laugh at how possessive I was over everything about her, including her time, so it was good she thought I was kidding when I told her I wanted her to move her desk to my office. If she had any idea how much it bothered me that I couldn't witness every single one of her breaths, she would have run far and fast.

I was at the stove when I heard her letting herself in with the code I'd given her when she'd agreed to be mine. I was still working on acquiring a key to her place. Moments later, her pillowy breasts were pressed against my back as she wrapped her arms around my middle.

"Are you cooking for me, Weston Aldrich?"

She moved beside me, leaning her hip on the counter. I angled sideways, cupping her crown to draw her closer, touching my lips to hers.

"Don't get excited. This is one of three meals I can make proficiently."

"So, you didn't learn any life skills when you were younger? Expected to skate by on your pretty face?" she quipped.

I pecked her again. "This pretty face landed me you, didn't it? Which proves it was all I needed."

"Flatterer." She leaned her forehead against my arm, and I could feel her smiling.

"My mother isn't much of a cook. She grew up with help so she never learned. Then she raised me the same way. I'm lucky I know how to do my own laundry."

Her palm flattened on my back, running from between my shoulder blades to the base then slowly working back up again.

"With your three meals, and my four, we have an entire week's worth of dinners. Elaine wasn't raised with help, but she married my dad, who was a boss in the kitchen. He did all the cooking."

In the silence after her words, I heard the rest of the story.

Her father had died.

Homemade dinners went with him, as did her chance at learning from him.

Elaine had never tried making up for his absence.

Everything Elise knew in the kitchen, she'd taught herself.

I turned off the stove and took her in my arms. "We're two smart, self-starting people. We can teach ourselves."

She bounced on her toes and cupped my nape. "We're going to learn to cook together? I love this idea. I'm going to pin recipes for us."

Her enthusiasm made me laugh. "Go easy on me. No more than ten ingredients, including salt and pepper."

"I thought we were two smart, self-starting people? Where's your confidence?"

"It went up in the flames with the lasagna I attempted to cook exactly once."

She laughed, but I wasn't kidding. A fire extinguisher had been involved, and I still had no idea what had gone wrong.

"But I wasn't with you," she pointed out. "It'll be completely different this time."

I believed her. With her, everything was different.

⸺◆⸺

It was past two in the morning when Elise padded into my office. She'd put on clothing since I'd left her in my bed sleeping. A T-shirt that fell to the tops of her thighs and the underwear she wore that showed off the bottom half of her ass. They were plain cotton, but fuck, I got hard every time I saw her in them.

I pushed back so she could sit on the edge of my desk in front of me, her legs between mine.

She raked her fingers through my hair, slowly shaking her head. "What are you doing, sir?"

I caught her hand, bringing it to my mouth to nibble her palm. "Working."

"When I fell asleep, you were in bed with me. I don't like that you keep sneaking out and I wake up alone."

"I didn't realize you noticed."

Her eyes narrowed. "I noticed."

I pressed my lips to the inside of her wrist. "I've carved out time for you because I want to be with you more than I want to be doing anything else. But the world keeps turning, which means I have to catch up. I'm almost done."

She swiped her thumb under my eye. "You're tired. You can't burn the candle at both ends."

"I *am* tired, but my body is trained to run on little sleep. I'll turn in soon."

She worried her bottom lip between her teeth. "I don't like this, West. Maybe I should spend some nights at my place so—"

"Absolutely not. Don't suggest it."

She huffed. "Then you're going to have to find a way to delegate. I need my man to be energetic. What use are you to me if you're running on fumes?"

She was working me, and she was doing it right. If she'd just pleaded for me to turn in, I might have been able to resist. But implying I wouldn't be able to satisfy her...that got me out of my chair.

I pushed her legs apart, stepping between them. "Do you know it's now officially your birthday?"

Her breath caught. "It is, isn't it?"

"Happy birthday, baby. I'm glad I get to be the first one to say it."

"Thank you, Westie. It's going to be a good year, I can feel it."

Her lids were heavy. She needed rest. So did I. But I wasn't quite ready for sleep yet.

I took her mouth with mine. She was warm in my arms, her lips soft and pliant. The kiss was a slow, languid slide.

Her hands slipped under my shirt and up my back. Elise had a thing for my back and always found a way inside my shirt. I'd taken to untucking them as soon as I got home to make it easier for her.

"Lie back." I helped her ease back on my desktop. She stared up at me from under her thick lashes, and my heart did a wild thump in my chest.

I gripped the hem of her T-shirt and gathered it in my fist until her breasts spilled out. Saliva pooled in my mouth. My cock thrummed. "Christ, you're gorgeous."

Her lips tipped, then she hooked her thumbs in her panties, arching her hips so she could tug them off. I helped her, tossing the navy-blue cotton to the side and falling back in my chair.

I lowered the chair to the right height and leaned in, kissing her slick core.

"West," she cooed. "Don't tease me."

"I won't."

My palms were on her inner thighs, holding them apart. My face was buried in her sweet cunt. She was wet and soft, except for her little clit, which was a hard bead under my tongue.

She was the sexiest woman I had ever seen. Her pussy, the best tasting, the prettiest. I thought about it in meetings. I wanted to be angry with her for making me want her this way, but it was impossible when she let me have her despite my irrationality.

My tongue made wet, lapping sounds through her arousal. Fingers slipped through my hair, gentle but insistent.

"That feels so good, West," she breathed out. "Don't stop."

Never.

For the rest of my life.

Let me die eating this pussy.

Everything about this woman was decadent. Her natural scent was rich and creamy. I buried my nose in her flesh and inhaled as I licked her. I stroked her inner thighs, smooth and silky, and reached up to play with her breast.

She arched when I rolled her nipple between my fingers. She was close, rocking her hips, pressing into my mouth.

The bottom half of my face was coated in her, and my cock throbbed with jealousy. I went deeper still, my scruff scratching against her. I needed this.

The gentle fingers in my hair curled, tugging at me to bring me closer. My lips closed around her clit with firm suction, and I plucked at her nipple.

Her hips rose and fell in waves while shaky breaths pushed through her parted lips. She moaned my name and yanked my hair. Her orgasm was pretty and desperate. I lapped up every moment until she was limp and her cries faded into soft whimpers.

I stood, pulling her to a sitting position. "You need sleep."

"You do too." She slipped her hand into my joggers, pressing against my erection. Then she wrapped her fingers around me, pumping me slowly. "It's my birthday."

I took her face in my hands, my forehead against hers. "Does my baby want a birthday fuck?"

She nodded. "Please."

We pushed my pants down together, and within seconds, I was gliding into her soaked pussy. She leaned back on her hands, offering a view of her rounded curves that drove me out of my mind.

I shook my head. "This is going to be fast."

"Because you want me so?"

Pushing into her until our pelvises were flush, I ground against her swollen lips, rotating my cock inside her. Her head fell back, and she let out a long, ragged sigh.

"I don't want to tell you how badly I want you. It would scare you."

Instead of answering, she hooked her hand behind my neck and brought my mouth to hers. We kissed, breathing each other in as my movements picked up speed. She held on to my neck, nipping at my lips, and I kneaded her tits, her stomach, her hips. My hand roamed, needy for more of her, while my cock powered into her again and again.

I wanted to hang on. God, did I want to last. But I was so fucking desperate for her.

In the back of my mind, I knew why, but I shoved the reason aside and focused on my beautiful girl. Focusing on Elise was all I could do, and it was my downfall.

Her parted lips.

Breathy sighs.

Thick thighs squeezing my hips.

Bouncing tits each time we collided.

Sinking into her soft flesh.

I told her she undid me, and I couldn't think of anything that had been more true. My control, my thoughts, my convictions, they all unraveled around her until I was living and breathing for the sole purpose of belonging to her.

One last thrust, then I held myself deep inside her, spilling everything in me. Her lips hovered over mine as I grunted and panted, then she sat up the rest of the way, holding me in her arms.

"Everything's right," I said.

"It is."

It wasn't until we were back in bed together, Elise drifting off to sleep, that I let the worries about tonight creep into my head.

Her party. We'd be seeing Elliot. Pretending we weren't together, right in front of him. I was uneasy about lying to him. But Elise wasn't ready to tell him, and her birthday party wasn't the place.

One more week, it would be out in the open.

We just had to get through tonight.

Chapter Twenty-six

Weston

THE NIGHT WAS CLEAR.

The air was warm.

Decorations were over the top.

Elise was happy.

My brother was trashed.

Elise was dancing with Saoirse, Rebecca, Simon, and the random girl Miles had brought. I was sending him death glares.

At least Miles's state of inebriation was taking my mind off the fact that I had to pretend to be *just friends* with Elise. It sucked, and I did not see the wisdom behind it. Lying would only compound Elliot's anger when we told him.

Elliot and Sam had some common ground, discussing Denver real estate development. While everyone was busy and happy, I walked up behind Miles. He was pouring himself another drink.

"You don't need that," I hissed.

"It's a party." He grinned at me, tipping the cup into his mouth. "You should have fun, Westie."

Westie. It grated on me every time he said it. Even worse, that he and Elise were such great pals, he'd gotten her into the habit of calling me that too.

"Do you even remember whose party this is?"

Miles blinked at me. "Of course. I'm here to celebrate my best friend, Elise Michelle Levy."

"Best friend?" I scoffed. "You're not a very good friend, stumbling around, making a fool of yourself. How old is your date?"

His unfocused eyes slid to the woman in hot pink who'd accompanied him. "Sabrina is older than me, Westie. She's your age, old man. And the only reason I'm stumbling is because I twisted my ankle when Sab and I went rock climbing this afternoon. I'm mildly blitzed. I wouldn't get trashed at Lisie's party. I might miss the cake."

I crossed my arms over my chest. Now that I looked at him, he wasn't as wasted as I'd originally assumed. Nowhere near sober, but not about to black out.

"Did you go to a doctor for the ankle?"

He waved me off, taking another long pull from his drink, which looked like straight vodka. "Nah. I'm self-medicating. I'll go tomorrow if it's not any better." He chuckled to himself. "By the way, not a good idea to go climbing after eating an edible."

Any hope I'd had for him fizzled out in that instant. "You knew better."

He winked at me. "Sometimes you have to do stupid shit and learn your lesson afterward. That's what makes life fun." Then he threw his arm around my shoulders. "Now, tell me what we bought Lisie."

I tossed him off me. "You came to her party without a gift?"

"You are, without a doubt, the most uptight person alive. Of course I got her a gift. I wanted to know what you got her."

My jaw was going to crack from how hard I was clenching it. "New hiking boots."

What I didn't say was I also bought her twenty pairs of those cheeky panties that drove me insane and a gift card to her favorite lingerie store so she could buy fifty more pairs or whatever else she wanted. Those gifts were for her, but they were most certainly for me too.

I'd also given her a Suunto Sports Watch to wear hiking, a cashmere robe, and Merino wool socks.

Then there was the body cream she had a small sample tub of and loved but told me it was too expensive for her to buy. I'd bought her two, one for my place, one for hers.

She'd been mad at me, but I'd told her they were nonrefundable so she'd have to get over it.

She swiftly forgave me when I gave her the gift I'd bought during the hours I was in my office while she'd slept last night. Cooking lessons for the two of us, along with all new cookware.

Miles rubbed his hands together. "Oh, I bet she liked that. Did you know she saw a mountain lion on one of her hikes?"

I would have laughed if it didn't irk me that she'd revealed anything about her personal life to Miles. Not that I didn't trust Elise around him. I just didn't think he deserved to know her.

"Did she? She should be careful."

Elise was unwrapping presents, cooing over everything with nearly the same amount of enthusiasm as she had when she'd opened mine. I could have gotten over it had she been closer. Instead, she was on the other side of our group, a big table between us, taking great care not to look at me for too long or pay me much attention at all.

It went without saying, I was not happy.

Miles shoved his gift at her. Since the time we spoke, he'd been drinking steadily. His only saving grace was the fact that Elise didn't seem to be bothered by it.

Elise opened his present, holding up a gold chain with a chunky gold *E* dangling from it.

She gasped. "Miles! This is gorgeous. I love it so much. Thank you."

He puffed his chest out, his face flushed. "Remember back in high school, when you had that *E* necklace? I thought you might like a grown-up one."

She squeezed his arm. "I remember. That was incredibly thoughtful."

"Wait a minute," Sam chimed. "You two went to high school together?"

"We did," Elise answered.

Sam leaned forward with interest. "Give me the history. What were you guys like? Did you ever date?"

My fingers curled, but Elise burst out laughing. "No. That's hilarious. We very much did not date."

Miles nodded, his head bobbing loosely on his neck. "Yeah. Ellie and I have been besties forever." Then he frowned. "Wait. I can't call you Ellie anymore. Sorry, Ellie."

The hair on the back of my neck prickled. Elise had told me not to call her Ellie. I'd wondered why at the time but had dropped it. Miles knew, though. He knew something about her I didn't.

Elise waved him off. "It's fine."

Sam turned to her. "Wait, what's wrong with Ellie? It's a cute nickname."

Miles tried to snap his fingers, but when he couldn't, he pointed at her. "Right? It is a cute nickname, but I had to go ruin it. I ruin everything." His head dropped and Elise reached for him, but he flung her hand off and stumbled to his feet.

Elliot and I exchanged a glance. He lifted a shoulder. Neither of us understood what was going on, but my gut told me it wasn't good. My gut told me to shut my brother up before he continued his path of destruction.

I got to my feet, but Miles was already ranting.

"I thought it would be funny, you know?" He shook his head. "Maybe I didn't think that. Maybe I didn't think at all. I saw you on the first day of school. You had a sparkly headband on, and you were laughing with friends. Friends, Lisie. You had friends, but *I* was supposed to be looking out for you when I had no one."

He was staring right at Elise, red-faced, his chest heaving. "So, I called you that. Ellie the Elephant, and they laughed. Then I had friends. People laughed with me, they wanted to be around me."

My mouth fell open, trying to wrap my head around what my brother was saying.

Elliot's chair scraped back. He circled the table to get to Elise, who looked like a deer caught in headlights. She was frozen, eyes wide, watching my brother.

We all were.

There was no way he was saying what it sounded like. My brother was a fuck up, but if he did this…if he was cruel to her, even once…

"I'm sorry, Lisie." He viciously yanked at his hair. "It snowballed, and I lost control of it. I made you miserable, but I wasn't happy either."

"Just say it. You bullied Lise in high school," Rebecca screeched, cutting right to the chase.

Miles turned his head, nodding.

With his confirmation, my brain switched off.

I had no idea how I got to him. One second, I was on the other side of the table. The next, I was on top of him, my fists pummeling into his face, his chest, anywhere I could hit him. He barely tried to block me, taking it because he knew he deserved it.

"You hurt her? You hurt my Elise?" All I saw was red as I screamed in his face. "I trusted you and you hurt her?"

Arms wrapped around me, pulling me off him. It wasn't just one man. It took Simon and Sam to pry me away from Miles. As soon as my weight was lifted, he sat up and scooted backward.

"I told you to watch out for her," I yelled. "What did you do, Miles? What did you do?"

"I messed up," he cried. "But she forgave me. Don't you forgive me, Lisie?"

The fact that he looked at her, addressed her in my fucking presence, was so audacious, I could have sworn I was hallucinating.

"Don't look at her. Look at me. Tell me why you bullied the girl I told you to watch out for." I slapped my chest. "I told you to protect her when I went to college. I fucking trusted you."

Miles staggered to his feet, leaning heavily against the back of a lounge chair. In my periphery, Elliot had his arms around Elise. Her other friends were crowded around her.

She was protected like she should have been all those years ago.

Miles's gaze lifted, meeting mine before falling away. "Sometimes there isn't a good reason. Sometimes people do bad shit they regret."

"Not to Elise. You don't just do bad shit to her and think I'll *ever* be okay with you again. That is *my* girl, and she is ten times more important to me than you will ever be, Miles."

He swallowed hard. "I know that."

Him not defending himself or making a joke of the situation only made me angrier. I needed to fight him. If I didn't, I would have had to ask myself how I'd missed this. My own brother had taken part in hurting my beautiful Elise while I'd been off at college, relieved to be gone.

"You know that, yet you fucking bullied her? I didn't think a lot of you before, but now—"

"Weston, stop," Elise cried. "Don't say something you can't come back from."

She wouldn't be happy with me for speaking to him this way, but she was a far better person than I was.

Miles raised his head, his face flushed. "You think I didn't know that? The second you met the Levys, I didn't even exist to you. And guess what? I was jealous. In my warped child's mind, they took my brother from me." He threw his arms out, but they quickly flopped at his sides. "You left, and there was no one to protect me, but you told me to protect *her*. I wanted to hate her, and I tried to. I was fucking awful to her. There's no excuse, and I can't make it right or change what I did. So, you can write me off, fire me, never see me again. That's what you want anyway."

I shook my head. "No. You don't get to be the victim here."

Elliot broke away from his sister, taking Miles by the shoulders. Elliot's control was like iron. He had to be homicidal but kept it locked down. He was doing it for Elise.

"You need to leave. This is my sister's birthday, and now you've ruined yet another thing for her."

He shoved Miles, not hard, but he was wobbly enough on his feet that he stumbled forward, ending up in front of Elise.

"Lisie..." he croaked.

She reached out, stroking his cheek. "I really wish you hadn't done this."

"I didn't mean to. I'm sorry."

She nodded. "I know you are, but you should go now."

He glanced around at everyone with wild eyes, like he didn't really know what he should have been doing. That was when Saoirse took over. Wrapping an arm around Miles's poor date and hooking her other arm in Miles's elbow, she walked them both to the elevator.

Elliot rounded on me as soon as my brother was out of my sight.

"Care to tell me why you keep referring to my sister as yours?"

His arms were folded over his chest. Face blank. He knew.

"Elliot, stop." Elise went to him, standing in front of him so she was between us, even though we were still feet apart. "We were going to tell you next week."

He wouldn't look at her. "Why is my sister saying 'we'? You should have been the one to come to me." His jaw rippled. "How long have you lied to me?"

That was a complicated question, and my mind was still half blacked out with rage. Tears rolled down Elise's cheeks, and I was about to lose it.

I made eye contact with Rebecca. "Take her away," I said through clenched teeth. "She doesn't need to be here for this."

Simon and Sam were still at my side. I nodded to them too. "Take her, please."

"Weston, no, please—Elise swiveled to her brother then me—"this doesn't have to happen. We can all talk."

Elliot's gaze remained firmly on me. "He's right. This is between Weston and me."

She sniffed, wiping her cheeks, and it killed me. Absolutely killed me not to hold her and tell her it would be okay. I couldn't make any kind of promises to her right now, and I had the feeling if I tried to touch her, Elliot would toss me off the roof without even blinking.

"If you hurt each other, don't bother coming to me afterward." She pointed back and forth between us. "That's for both of you. I will never forgive either of you if you do."

I wouldn't touch Elliot, but I had no idea where his head was. "I'll see you as soon as I can."

A shudder racked her whole body. She turned away from me, pressing a hand to Elliot's chest.

"If you're mad at him, you have to be mad at me too. Remember that."

Then she left with her friends around her.

Bereft and confused, I sank into my original seat and picked up my drink. I needed to blunt some of tonight's revelations. If I thought too hard about the dramatic change Elise went through between when I left for college and when I came back...

No.

I'd have to confront that later, when I could look at Elise and assure myself she was okay.

Elliot took the chair across from mine, his fingers curling around the arm so hard they were white at the tips, and his knees vibrated with tension.

He stared at me with a steady, level gaze. "I can't decide who I'm more angry at, you or Miles."

"You didn't know what he did to her?"

He lifted a shoulder. "I knew she was teased and having a hard time. But our mother was unwell, our father was gone, I had moved away, so I didn't..." He clamped down, turning away. "I should have known, but once I was gone, I didn't want to go back. Not because of Elise. Never her."

"I know."

When I first met Elliot and he brought me home, the Levys were warm and bright. Their mom was eccentric, kind of off the wall, but in a lovable way their pragmatic father balanced out. They talked, laughed, hung out together. Even Elliot. And I had been accepted into their fold.

Things changed once their father died, but I was so far entrenched I stayed through the chaos and darkness. I stayed for Elliot and Elise, but myself as well, because no matter how shitty the Levy household was at times, it was always preferable over my own home.

"I need to know exactly what he did to her." He rubbed his hands down his shaking thighs. "Then I'll be able to decide what action needs to be taken."

"I can deal with my brother."

"I don't know that I trust you to do that." His gaze turned razor sharp. "Did you touch her when she was a kid?"

My head blew back like he'd physically hit me. "No." That was all the denial he was getting from me. He should have known better than to even ask.

"When did it start?" he pressed.

"When she came back to Denver. But it's been there for a while now, at least for me."

"Whose idea was it to keep it from me?"

"It was mutual. We were planning to tell you next week."

He angled forward. "It was Elise's idea, wasn't it?"

"It was mutual."

He huffed something close to a laugh. "I know my sister as well as I know you. She considers everyone's feelings when making decisions, while you make up your mind and act. There is no way on this planet waiting was a mutual choice. You deferred to Elise in this."

I blew out a breath, letting my beer bottle swing between two fingers. "Does it really matter?"

"It does to me. I'll forgive Elise for anything. You don't have that luxury."

I grimaced, knowing I could lose him, but I wasn't going to say what he wanted me to. "The choice was mutual. The brunch Elise asked you to put on your calendar next weekend was when we were going to tell you."

He stared at me for a long time then gave a slight nod. "What would you have said?"

I'd thought about this since things started with Elise. How I would explain. How much was any of Elliot's business. He was her brother, but he'd been a parent to her also.

"I would have told you we're in a serious, committed relationship. That my intentions for her are not short term. I would have explained thought and consideration went into the decision we made to be together, including your feelings, but in the end, our feelings for each other were paramount."

He lowered his head, pressing two fingers to the space between his eyebrows. "Admirable you're willing to get serious, but why did it have to be my sister?"

"It couldn't have been anyone *but* Elise."

"She's too good for you."

"I don't deny that."

He glowered at me. "You know, yet you let this happen?"

"I didn't let anything happen. It was a decision. I've also made the decision that Elise is my priority."

He scoffed at that declaration. "Interesting, but forgive me if I don't believe you. You weren't able to do that with the last one."

If I hadn't been so on edge, I would have laughed. He still disliked Marisol so much he wouldn't say her name.

"It's not about ability. It's a choice and a desire. Nothing I can say now will convince you I'll be a good partner to Elise. I can't show you the future. But I do think you know me well enough to understand when I decide I'm going to do something, I don't back down or accept failure."

He finally lifted his head. "Do you love her?"

A rush of...not panic, but a strong, overpowering emotion hit me. I swallowed down the knot in my throat. "That's not something I've told her yet."

"But do you?" he pushed.

Another swallow. "I've loved Elise for as long as I've known her. It's evolved over the years, and what I feel for her now is vastly different from what I felt for her when we were kids."

"It's love, though."

I nodded. "I'm not saying it to you before I say it to her."

He chuffed. "Never thought I'd be having this conversation with you."

"Neither did I." I scrubbed at my jaw, antsy to get away but needing to know Elliot and I would be okay. "I'll be good to her."

"I really don't want to end our friendship, but I will always choose my sister over you if that's what it comes down to."

I heaved a heavy breath and told him the stark, honest truth. "I understand that because I would choose her over you too."

He blinked at me and stayed silent, obviously contemplating my words. I thought about what I'd said too. It had come out before I even considered it, but if push came to shove and I had to choose, Elise would be it, hands down.

"As you should." He pushed back from his seat and stood. "I'm going to see my sister now."

I bit my tongue to stop from telling him I should have been the one going to Elise.

"Don't give her shit," I warned.

He lowered his chin, giving me another long, heavy look. "She's always been the most important person in my life."

With that, he turned and walked away, leaving me with no idea what he was thinking.

At least I was no longer burning with rage. There was no room for it, not when I was filled with a consuming worry that I wouldn't be Elise's choice after Elliot got to her.

Chapter Twenty-Seven

Elise

When the knock finally came, I ran for the door. Not caring which man of mine was on the other side, I threw open the door and lunged with my arms open.

Elliot wrapped his around me and backed me into my apartment.

"I'm sorry," I said into his shoulder.

"You have nothing to be sorry for."

As soon as he said it, the tears I'd been keeping on a tight leash began to flood out in uncontrollable rivers.

"You didn't kill him, did you?"

"No." His big palm cupped the back of my head. "I considered it, but no."

I pushed back from him, lightly slapping his cheek. "Don't even suggest it."

He attempted to be stern with me. "Then don't ever keep things from me. I don't like knowing you're even capable of subterfuge."

"Obviously, I'm not very good at it since you figured us out the first time we were in the same place together."

"He said your decision to keep me in the dark was mutual."

I wrinkled my nose. "Not at all. He was the one who warned me the longer we hid it, the worse it would be when you found out."

"I knew it." He let go of me to stalk farther into my apartment. "You convinced my best friend to lie to me, which he's never done. Maybe I should be worried about the type of influence you'll have over Weston."

I cocked my head. "You don't seem mad."

"I'm...not sure what I am. I don't like the lying."

"Believe me, I don't either. It's unnatural for me to lie to you. But I wanted us to have time, just in case you disapproved, to make sure Weston and I were solid enough to stand up to that."

"I can't say I *do* approve." He folded his arms over his chest. "Elise, do you have any idea how much he works? He won't be able to give you the time and attention you deserve. That bothers me, and I think, over time, it will bother you too."

"He's been coming home early." I felt the need to defend Weston, though Elliot wasn't wrong about his track record.

Elliot nodded. "That's good. But when does he do the work that he should have done in the office?" When I didn't answer, he went on. "I'm assuming he brings his work home. A man like him doesn't change, even if he wants to. I want more than that for you."

"But I had a man who gave me his time and attention, and he still wrecked me." I pulled on Elliot's arms, unfolding them, and squeezed his forearm. "Look, I know who Weston is. I'm not blind. I'm choosing him, and he's choosing me. We'll work out what we want our relationship to look like, but believe me when I tell you I'm happy with him. Happier than I could have imagined."

His mouth pressed into a firm line. I understood where he was coming from. Elliot and Weston had been cut from the same cloth, but where Weston had remained bendable, Elliott had been dipped in iron. He was uncompromising and assumed Weston was the same way. In the past, I may have agreed, but now that I knew Weston on a deeper, more intimate level, I didn't. Weston's two a.m. office visits were bad, and there was no way he could keep them up, but we were new. It would take time to find the right balance. The fact that he was choosing to spend time with me over work said a lot. It gave me confidence that we could figure this out.

Elliot's eyebrow winged. "In other words, I should keep my opinions to myself?"

"No, of course not. Your opinion is always welcome, as long as you know I'll tell you when you're wrong."

"When have you not?"

"Never." I sucked in a breath. "Well, if you want the entire truth, Luca knows. He saw us kissing last weekend."

"Now that"—Elliot shook his finger at me—" makes me angry. Luca will never let it drop that he knew before I did."

"He told us we looked good together."

Elliot flinched, looking away. "For your sake, I'm trying to be okay with this. Don't push it."

I took my brother's hand in mine. "Come and sing 'Happy Birthday' to me. Saoirse made a red velvet cake and it would be a shame to let it go to waste."

Saoirse had retreated to her room for privacy. When I called her name, she came out and joined us to sing and cut the cake at the kitchen table. I made the same wish every year: that everything would work out the way it was supposed to.

Elliot ate his cake, even though he rarely ate sweets. He even complimented Saoirse.

"This is good. Have you considered baking professionally?"

She waved him off. "Of course not. Then it wouldn't be fun." She unfolded her long legs from her chair and bent to kiss the top of my head. "Happy birthday, Lise. I'm bummed your party got cut short, but I'm glad I got to spend it with you."

I leaned my head against her hip. "Thanks for being a goddess."

She left Elliot and me alone again. He stared at me for a long time while I dragged my fork through the frosting on my plate. I was antsy to speak to Weston, but at the same time, I needed to know things with my brother were settled.

"He paid for your college."

My head shot up. "*What*? Who did?"

"There was no money left when Elaine died. I had no idea until I came back and took over, but our mother's financial situation had been dire. I was going to sell the house to support us, but West stepped in. He used his trust fund to pay off the house. He seeded my first business. And when it was time, he paid your tuition. I tried to be prideful and deny him, but he wouldn't allow it."

I was in shock. My mouth fell open, but I had no idea what to say. We'd never been wealthy, but I also had never been worried about money, even in those post–Dad years when Elaine went off the rails. I guessed I should have been paying more attention.

"He never told me."

Elliot smirked. "No, he wouldn't have. He asked me to keep it to myself. He didn't want you to know what a shit show our mother was." He shook his head. "He's been protecting you for a long time. I suppose I'll have to trust that he'll keep doing so."

He rose to his feet and pulled me up into his arms. "Happy birthday, El. I love you."

"I love you too, El."

He let me go, taking a step back. "I'm going, since I know you're about five minutes away from tossing me out so you can go to him."

I snorted. "Maybe ten."

He ruffled my hair, but he didn't quite smile. "I don't like change."

Elliot eschewed change so much through elementary and middle school he'd been like a cartoon character, owning multiples of the same pieces of clothing so he could wear the same outfit daily, only changing with the seasons. Fortunately for us all, he had a much better fashion sense these days.

I smiled at him. "I know you don't."

<hr>

I let myself into Weston's place, finding it quiet, which wasn't surprising. I carried a plate with a slice of cake on it through his apartment, searching him out. A glow came from his office, unsurprisingly.

I peeked through the crack in the door. Weston was hunched over his desk, his fingers clasped behind his neck. His computer was on, but he wasn't reading the screen.

"Hi," I called softly, pushing the door open.

He shot to his feet, storming toward me before I could take one step into the room. He took my face in his hands, tilting my head to one side then the other, then he grunted and kissed my forehead, the tip of my nose, and my lips.

"You're here."

"I'm here," I confirmed. "I brought you cake."

"I thought he'd convince you to stay away from me."

I crinkled my nose at him. "Well, you don't know either of us as well as you say you do. I would never allow Elliot to change my mind about you and he loves you. He would never try to trash you to get me to break it off."

He blew out a breath, his gaze raking over me like he was confirming I was really here.

"Fuck," he gritted out. "I was sitting here, no idea what was happening, going out of my mind."

"I'm sorry." I pressed my lips to his in a long, lingering kiss. "I had to make sure everything was okay with Elliot before I came to you. I hate that you were alone."

I put the cake down on a nearby table so I could wrap my arms around his neck. He yanked me against him, his palms smoothing down my hips to my butt, then he buried his face in the crook of my neck.

"He told me you paid for my college," I whispered.

He stiffened but didn't let me go. "You weren't supposed to know."

"I was going to say I can't believe you did that, but I can. Thank you, Weston."

"You don't have to thank me, baby."

We held each other for a long time. His breath was hot on my skin while he stroked me from the center of my back to the bottom of my ass. As time ticked by, I melted into him.

"It's okay," I cooed. "It's all okay. We can just be us now."

He released a shuddering breath and raised his head. His mouth slanted over mine in a soft, deep kiss. His tongue slid along mine, claiming me with every gentle flick. His relief was palpable. He'd really been worried I wouldn't come back to him. That hit me hard in my chest. I put everything into kissing him back, into showing him I was just as deeply into this as he was. That this was something big and real for me, and it would take a lot more than my brother's disapproval for me to walk away.

"You can't leave me," he murmured against my lips. "Do you understand? You can't disappear on me. You can't leave."

Another hit.

"I won't, West. I'm here with you. I won't disappear."

He kissed me again, walking me backward toward his bedroom. When his mattress hit the backs of my knees, he kept walking, so we fell together. He pushed my skirt up, and his fingers slipped into my panties.

"Wet."

I nodded. I was. Heavy emotion mixed with desire had filled me with need.

He reared back, sweeping my panties off me, then unzipped his pants to free his cock. Falling over me, he rubbed himself between my thighs.

"I have to have you," he said against my ear.

I threaded my fingers in his hair. "So have me."

In one smooth motion, he thrust into me, filling me completely. My neck arched as I moaned, my fingers curling around his strands.

Weston cupped my face, holding me as he moved in and out of me. He went deep with every thrust, and I felt him all the way to my chest. The zipper of his pants scratched against the back of my thighs, but if he stopped, I would die, so I ignored it, focusing on him.

He never stopped watching me. He held my face like if he let me go, I'd disappear.

"I'm here, West," I told him breathlessly. "I'm yours."

"Mine," he grunted. "Don't leave me."

"I won't."

His mouth covered mine again, and he hitched one of my legs over his arm so he could find his way even deeper inside me. I held on to him, giving myself to him, showing him with my body I was his for as long as he wanted me.

Later, we watched a movie in his living room. Weston ate his cake and made me make another wish. This time, I wished for Weston to believe I was in this for the long haul.

He idly stroked my bare thigh while my head rested on his shoulder.

"Were you ever going to tell me about what a piece of shit my brother is?" he asked softly.

"No. Miles and I settled things when I first started at Andes. It's history."

"Not to me."

With a sigh, I lifted my head. "Miles was a dick in high school, but he wasn't the worst by far. What he said tonight was true, he got people to like him by making them laugh."

"Don't defend him."

"I'm not. He was absolutely wrong, and he knows that. Miles was part of the reason those years were miserable for me, but since he and I hashed it out, I'm over it. I can't drag high school shit around for the rest of my life. I'm satisfied he feels like a dick for how he behaved, so I don't really need a pound of flesh from him. It's over, and we're sort of friends now."

His hands flexed, and I could tell he wished he was wrapping them around his brother's neck.

"You can't be friends with him, not when I'm planning on killing him."

"You're not killing anyone." I rubbed his scruffy cheek. "I think you need to have a conversation with him, though. Did you hear the rest of what he had to say? He felt abandoned. I kind of think he still does."

"Fuck him," he groused. "He *is* abandoned, as far as I'm concerned."

I pressed my lips together, frustrated. "Does it not matter to you that I'm over what he did?"

"No. You shouldn't have had to get over anything."

"I shouldn't have, that's true, but that's not how it worked out. And Miles...I don't know. He's made it his mission to befriend me. I *like* him. Maybe if you guys really talked, you'd grow to like him too."

He glowered at me. "We'll never be like you and Elliot."

"No, probably not. But Elliot and I are trauma bonded."

He let his head fall back on the couch cushions, heaving a sigh. "You're really not going to let me kill him, are you?"

"No."

"I want to."

Laughing, I tucked myself under his arm and curled into his side. "I know you do. It means a lot."

"I'd do anything for you, Elise."

Maybe Weston telling me he'd kill his own brother for me shouldn't have felt like a romantic declaration, but it had. When Weston Aldrich said he'd do anything for me, he meant it.

Something deep and achy came awake in my chest. It stretched and bloomed while we snuggled on Weston's couch, the last minutes of my birthday slipping away. Though this day hadn't gone quite as I'd expected or hoped, I'd begun and ended it in Weston's arms, and that trumped everything else.

CHAPTER TWENTY-EIGHT

Weston

To: ELISELEVY@ANDESINC.COM

From: westonaldrich@andesinc.com

Dear Elise,

Unfortunately, I have to cancel our lunch plans today.

It seems going camping for two days without cell service means when I come back to reality, reality is waiting for me.

Luckily, I made sure to enjoy every minute of our camping trip.

The outdoors will never be the same.

Regretfully,

Weston

To: westonaldrich@andesinc.com

From: eliselevy@andesinc.com

Dear Grumpy Boss,

That *is* unfortunate. I was very much looking forward to our lunch plans. Lucky for me, another Aldrich has volunteered to take your place.

Miles says hi, by the way.

Those two days were worth the slap in the face, right? Mine probably wasn't as harsh as the one you experienced, but I'm hitting the ground running this morning.

Worth it, though. I've never felt more peaceful than I did this weekend with you.

I hope you have time to take a breath today.

Wistfully,

Elise

One breath. That was all I had time for. I sat back in my chair, sucking it in as pictures of our weekend flashed through my mind. I'd taken Elise to my spot, and she'd been all in. We spent two solid days hiking, fishing, and fucking under the stars.

She was easy to be with. So damn easy that when we were apart, which was more often than I liked, everyone else struck me as drudgery.

It had been a month since her birthday. For Elise and me, that month had been smooth. Without the looming deadline of telling Elliot hanging over our heads, we'd been able to let ourselves sink into our relationship.

Things between Elliot and me were getting better. He was wary, and rightfully so since he'd had a front row to my past relationships. Two weeks ago, he'd nearly knocked me out at the gym.

I put my phone down on the mat next to the weights, cursing under my breath. Disappointment sat like lead in my gut.

"Troubles?" Luca asked.

"I've got to fly out to California tonight to meet with our lawyers tomorrow morning," I answered.

Elliot had stopped lifting, tuning in to our conversation.

"Why is that a problem?" Luca shrugged. "That sounds like a typical day for you."

"Elise and I are supposed to be starting cooking lessons. I'm going to have to miss them. I have to be in California to meet with my team tonight."

Elliot scoffed, wiping his face with a towel. He didn't say anything, but I could almost hear his mind going.

"Oooh, cooking with Elise?" Luca bounced on his toes. "Tell me where it is. I'll go with her."

"No," I barked, immediately and violently opposed to the idea. "It's for her and me."

"Then you should be here to go with her." Elliot dropped his towel and approached where Luca and I were by the weights.

"If I could, I would. Believe me, I'd much rather be here with Elise than out there dealing with supply chain problems."

His frown deepened. "Two weeks and you're already letting her down. I warned her this would happen, and here we go. I have to say, it's sooner than I expected."

"Come on, Elliot. Elise will understand," Luca chided.

"Sure she will. That's who she is." Elliot met my gaze in the mirror. "Will you be spending this evening with Marisol instead of my sister?"

I stiffened at his question. I loathed giving him the answer. "She's the supply chain manager. Of course she'll be there. If there was any-thing I could do about this, I would—"

Elliot took a step toward me, his jaw like iron. "You are the CEO and owner of the company. These people work for you, West. If you want to spend your evening with your girlfriend instead of your ex, you can and should make that happen. All I see is a man not willing to change or bend. My sister will be the one who changes and bends, and in the end, neither of you will like what that turns her into. This is your opportunity to set a precedent. Don't bullshit me and don't bullshit yourself."

Heavy, hot breath heaved out of his nostrils as he stared me down. I was at a loss. That was the most I'd heard Elliot speak at once in all the years I'd known him. My mind was scrambling to take it all in.

"Elliot—" Luca started, but Elliot just shook his head and brushed by us toward the locker room.

Bending down, I grabbed my phone and stared at the email from the lawyers. It struck me I hadn't questioned their need to meet first thing tomorrow. I was so used to handing over my schedule to others it hadn't fucking dawned on me to do anything different.

I was an idiot.

"He's right."

Luca cleared his throat, looking away. "Yeah."

My brow crinkled with incredulity. "You didn't say."

"You're a grown man. I didn't think I needed to tell you not to brush off your girlfriend."

"I wasn't brushing her off. I would never." Heaving a sigh, I raked my fingers through my sweaty hair. "Shit."

Then I fired off a text to Renata, telling her to shift my meetings forward so I could fly in and out in one day and would be here tonight.

I looked up at Luca. "Done."

He cocked his head toward the locker room. "You might want to inform Elliot before he bursts a blood vessel."

I wouldn't call myself a changed man, but that conversation with Elliot had opened my eyes to how I was running my daily life. When I'd told him so, all he'd said was, "About time." But he didn't knock my teeth out that day, and since then, we'd shared a few meals together. Things were getting back to a semblance of normalcy between us.

I also hadn't missed a cooking lesson with Elise yet. We were still shockingly incompetent cooks, but we were having fun screwing up.

Canceling lunch with Elise today had been a twist in my gut, but it had been a pipe dream in the first place. I'd warned her this morning it would have to be quick if it even happened, to which she'd assured me she could find another date if I stood her up.

Of course it was my brother.

I hadn't spoken to him beyond a cursory greeting in the elevator since Elise's birthday. Elise may have forgiven him, but I didn't know I had it in me to do so.

My phone rang. "Yes?"

"Good morning, Mr. Aldrich. Nice weekend?" Renata asked.

I rubbed my forehead. It was a bad sign that my head was throbbing at nine in the morning.

"Great. What can I do for you?"

"Brian Lewis is on the line. He sounds pissy."

No doubt he did. He must have heard we were in the process of negotiating with a new supplier. As soon as our contract ended with him, we'd be cutting ties.

In the past, I would have taken his call because of our history and some misguided sense of obligation. The truth was, in my position, there was no need for me to deal with the minutiae of all the Brian Lewises Andes worked with. These days, my time was far too precious for me to give it up to him.

"Please inform him Glenna will be handling West Coast operations from now on and put him through to her assistant if he'd like to make an appointment to talk to her."

"I—" Renata paused. Papers shuffled. "Well, okay. I'll do just that after I put in my earplugs. That man has a temper."

"If he yells, hang up. You don't have to handle that."

I could almost hear her smirking. "Don't worry, Mr. Aldrich. You pay me more than enough to handle a grown man's temper tantrum. It's the most entertaining part of my job."

◆◆◆

I was at the end of the longest conference call of my life when the door pushed open and Elise appeared, holding a small paper bag. My chest tightened at the sight of her in her swishy navy skirt and silky white button-down with a bow around the collar. She hadn't given in to the Andes, Inc. culture of wearing active wear to the office, and I secretly hoped she wouldn't. Seeing her in her sexy librarian attire never failed to make me sit up and pay attention. Both me and my cock.

She crossed the room and perched her plump ass on the edge of my desk, waiting for me to finish my call.

I half listened while slipping my hand up her leg, her skirt gathering on my arm as I ventured higher. She didn't even try to stop me, her mouth curling and legs parting to let me stroke the velvet skin on her inner thighs.

The meeting ended as my fingers stroked the lace of her panties. I may have said goodbye, but I couldn't guarantee it. Elise pressed the "end call" button for me. That much I knew.

"I brought you sushi." She placed the paper bag closer to me. "I'm assuming you were planning on starving yourself."

I bent forward, pressing my face into the creamy flesh of her thighs. "You keep me well fed."

Her fingers slipped into the back of my hair, and she laughed softly. "Real food, Westie. You can't eat me right now."

I raised my eyes to hers. "I beg to differ." Pushing her legs far apart, I fit my face between them and breathed in the heat emanating from her. "Christ, you smell good."

She gently shoved my head away, tsking playfully. "Renata told me you have fifteen minutes. Make me happy by eating sushi while I keep you company. You can eat *me* tonight."

This woman knew exactly how to work me, and I always wanted to make her happy, so despite the fact that the only thing I was hungry for was her pussy, and despite the aching erection tenting my pants, I sat up and opened the bag. Elise tried to slip off my desk, but I gripped her thigh, keeping her in place.

"Stay."

Her mouth curled. "I'm staying. I was just going to sit in a chair."

"Stay here. I had you by my side all weekend and now I'm not used to you being far away."

"You're sweet."

I scoffed, opening the sushi. "You're the first person to ever claim that."

"I'm glad you saved it all for me, then."

Popping a piece of salmon sushi in my mouth, I slid my hand up Elise's skirt again. She smirked at me and closed her legs, trapping me there. I didn't mind.

"You went to lunch with Miles?"

She nodded. "He was there when I read your email. He offered, I accepted."

"And?"

"And what?" Her head tilted. "We had a good time. He was telling me about the new visual concept he helped design that's rolling out in the US stores this fall. He's really talented, you know. He has a sharp, artistic eye."

I chewed harder than necessary on the next piece of sushi. Elise saying anything positive about Miles got under my skin. He didn't deserve her company, let alone her praise.

"He draws okay," I said drolly.

Her brow arched. "It's a lot more than that or you wouldn't have him working here. I wish you'd talk to him. I can tell he's bummed the little connection you guys had before has been severed."

"That was his doing."

She slid her hand over mine, weaving our fingers together. "This isn't the time to talk about this. We have ten minutes before you have to get back to the grind. I'm asking you to consider speaking to Miles. I'll be there if you want."

I glowered at her, annoyed my brother had taken up a third of our limited time together.

"Why don't we talk about what we're going to do this weekend to top the last one?"

She picked up a piece of tuna sushi, dipped it in soy sauce, and fed it to me like it was the most natural thing in the world. To her, it was. Elise was a carer, and she was damn good at it. And since I was competitive to a fault, the way Elise was compelled me to try harder, to be better for her.

"We have the fundraiser Saturday," she reminded me.

"That's right." My gaze swept over her. My beauty. "I was going to say I'm not looking forward to it, but then I realized you'll be dressing up for me."

"For you?" She laughed.

"Mmm. Don't pretend you didn't pick your dress out with me on your mind."

Her teeth were digging into her bottom lip. "You have no idea what my dress looks like."

"If you're in it, it'll be sexy."

"Weston," she sighed. "You really are sweet."

"To you and you only."

"Good. Now, eat your sushi so I can go back to work knowing you're not withering away."

Something in my chest tugged me forward toward Elise. A visceral urge to grab her, press my face to her middle, and not let her leave this office. The need was so fervent I had to hold on to the arms of my chair to stop myself.

"Go, before I don't let you."

She slipped off my desk, angled down, and touched her lips to mine. "I'll see you tonight, Westie."

I growled. "Stop spending time with him."

She giggled and kissed me again. "Bye, grumpy."

Then she disappeared through my door, and I heaved a long breath. Before her, Andes was my life. It had never bothered me to skip obligations to spend more time at the office. Then Elise came along and, without even trying, dismantled everything I'd thought to be true about myself.

It was a dizzy, disorienting feeling, but I wasn't fighting it.

Not when it meant I could have Elise.

I could prove Elliot wrong and be the man she deserved.

Chapter Twenty-Nine

SAOIRSE PEEKED HER HEAD into my room. "Your Prince Charming has arrived, and he looks positively delicious."

I turned to her, smoothing my palms over the skirt of my burgundy gown. My nerves were fluttering. "Am I suitable?"

Her breath caught. "Oh, babe. You look like a pinup. So stunning. Weston is not going to know what hit him."

Laughing, I shook my hands out. "I don't know why I'm so nervous."

She crossed the room, taking my hands in hers and rubbing them gently. "It's like your big couple debut. I get it. But you have to remember this is *Weston*. He'll be by your side the whole way. It's going to be romantic as hell."

"It's *Weston*," I murmured to myself. The flutters still happened, but they were for him instead of nerves. "Is he wearing a tux?"

She nodded, her eyes rounding. "He is, and he's looking like James Bond, the Daniel Craig era."

I sucked in a breath. "Okay. Let me go look at my man."

My floor-length gown swished as I strode out of my bedroom in my strappy heels. This dress had been more expensive than my rent, but being on Weston Aldrich's arm at a black tie fundraiser called for a splurge. I wanted to look good for him, like we belonged together.

I turned the corner, and there he was, standing in the middle of my living room. I wondered if he'd waited there to give me space to make an entrance.

"Hi." My teeth dug into my crimson-painted bottom lip. My heart flipped in wild circles. My man was gorgeous, always, but in a tux? Weston Aldrich put every other man to shame. And the way he was standing, his hands tucked in his pockets like he was casual, his heated eyes and tight jaw telling a different story, made me want to drop to my knees and tell him he could do anything he wanted to me.

"Hi, baby." His gaze trailed over me, from my red toenails to my pin-curled hair. "Come over here. I have something for you."

My movements were automatic. He called, and I answered. With each step I took toward him, the high slit in my skirt revealed my leg all the way to midthigh. The boning in my bodice straightened my spine, pushing my breasts out, making me feel graceful and sensual. And from the hunger in Weston's eyes, I looked that way too.

After an eternity, I reached him. He took my hand, kissed my knuckles, then spun me around. His mouth was beside my ear. His lips pressed to the shell, then his tongue darted out for a taste.

"You are the most beautiful creature I've ever seen, Elise."

I shuddered, my lashes fluttering against my cheeks. "Thank you, Weston. You make me feel that way. And you"—I turned my head so our eyes met—"look absolutely dashing tonight."

"Thank you, baby."

His arms circled around me, and in his hands was a black box, which he flipped open. Inside, resting on black velvet, was a diamond pendant that had to be antique. Diamonds arranged in a star motif framed a dangling, cushion-cut diamond. From the bottom, more diamonds dangled in something like a sparkling fringe. It was unique and extravagant. No one had ever given me anything like this, nor had I seen something so beautiful up close before.

"I cheated slightly and asked Saoirse about the neckline of your dress. I wanted to make sure I bought something you could wear tonight." His mouth was beside my ear again. "Do you like it, baby?"

My entire body was trembling as I attempted to hold back tears. I would not ruin my makeup before we even left the house.

"It's exquisite, Weston. Put it on me?"

His fingertips trailed over my neck. The pendant rested heavily on my chest as he slid the thin chain around to my nape. When he was finished, his lips touched the back of my neck, then he spun me around, his eyes flaring at the sight of his necklace on me.

"You should be dripping in diamonds," he told me. "How did I get so lucky to have you?"

I touched the pendant then cupped the sides of his neck, tipping my face up to his.

"You have made me feel so special and the night has barely started. Thank you for the necklace. I don't think I'll ever take it off."

"That's the first of many. You'll have to rotate."

He pressed a lingering kiss to my cheek, then my throat, ending with a featherlight kiss to my lips.

"Your mouth looks incredible with that color on it, but I hate it right now." He glared so hard at the lipstick on my lips I almost laughed.

I held it in for his sake, but I *did* smile. "I'm keeping track of all the kisses I owe you. I'll make up for it later."

He took my hand in his, looking grumpy but somehow happy too. "Good. I won't forget that promise."

Andes gave grants to many environmental charities, and tonight's fundraiser was in support of the largest land trust in Colorado.

My nerves were back at the forefront when Weston and I walked into the lavish ballroom filled with filthy rich people in their finest attire. He'd told me on the drive here there was someone he would need to speak to, but other than that, he would be by my side the entire evening.

A waiter swept by. Weston snagged a glass of champagne and handed it to me. I held the stem between my fingers and lifted a brow.

"None for you?"

"No." His hand curved over my shoulder. "I'll have something harder from the bar."

We wandered over there, Weston stopping to greet multiple people on the way. He introduced me to everyone, but names went in one ear and out the other. I was a little bit high on how proudly Weston announced me as his girlfriend to all the stately men and women we spoke to.

We found Luca at the bar, flirting with the bartender. If Weston was James Bond, Luca was the ravishing villain the audience was secretly rooting for. His dark hair fell over his forehead in an artful swoop. Thick stubble lined his chiseled jaw. A playful smirk pulled at his full lips.

Weston's tux was classic, whereas Luca's was modern and stylish. Navy blue with contrasting black lapels and black piping down the cigarette pants, not many men could pull it off, but Luca did in spades.

As soon as Luca spotted us, he yanked me away from Weston, taking my hand to twirl me in a big circle.

"*Bellissima.*" He shook his head as his eyes swept over me. "You're something special tonight, Elise."

Blushing, I pressed my face to my shoulder. "Thank you. Did you see the necklace Weston gave me?"

He leaned in and definitely peeked down my cleavage. "Stunning. Though I think West could afford something bigger."

Weston shoved his shoulder. "Eyes to yourself."

Luca held his hands up. "She invited me to look."

I spread my hand over the tops of my breasts. "At my necklace, *Luca*. Which I think is perfect, by the way. If he had given me something bigger, I don't think I would have been able to wear it in public. I'm not used to jewelry this extravagant."

Weston's arm circled my waist, and he lightly kissed my temple, his whiskey in his other hand. "Get used to it."

Luca grinned at both of us. "I like this. Too bad Elliot isn't here tonight to see you two looking like you stepped out of a fairy tale. He sends his regards, by the way."

"More importantly, he sent his check," Weston added.

"My brother, the philanthropist."

The three of us chatted for a while until Luca saw someone he knew. When I checked where he was headed, I laughed. Of course his trajectory was the gorgeous blonde in red. His very own Bond girl.

Weston and I found our table. I set my bag on the chair, but I wasn't ready to sit down yet. He grabbed another glass of champagne for me when my first one was empty. A band was playing surprisingly recognizable rock music from a couple decades ago.

"There's something I don't know about you."

Weston skimmed his knuckles along my bare shoulder. "Is there? Let's rectify that. What would you like to know?"

"Do you dance?"

His mouth tipped. "Not often. You?"

"Not often enough. This band is good."

"They are." He pulled me close, his hand splaying low on my back. "Will you dance with me tonight?"

"I thought you'd never ask." I leaned into him, hoping he'd kiss me, despite my lipstick, but Weston stiffened, his attention on something in the distance. I turned in his arms, trying to see what he was looking at. A sultry woman in black strutted toward us, her dark eyes gleaming and laser-focused on Weston.

Marisol.

Weston had prepared me for her presence here tonight, but my stomach still soured when she joined our group and pressed her cheek to Weston's in greeting. She shook my hand as though we were meeting for the first time.

"Lovely dress."

"Thank you. Yours too." That wasn't a lie. I didn't think I liked this woman, but I couldn't deny she was nothing short of stunning.

Her smile was tight and went no further than the barest tilt of her lips.

"Weston, Dominic Peters and his COO, Charlie Platt, are here and ready to have a chat now. Do you think I could steal you away for a bit?"

"Give us a moment, please," he answered, pulling me a few feet away from Marisol.

Weston's hand skated down my arm, and his eyes bored into mine. "Will you be all right if I step away and take care of this?"

"Of course." He'd warned me he'd have to be the boss tonight. "Go, have at it. I'll drink champagne and mingle."

He stared at me for another moment then shook his head. "You are truly the best, Elise. I'll try not to let this take long, but Peters likes to hear himself speak, so—"

"It's fine. If I get bored, I'll hunt down Luca. But I doubt I'll get bored."

"Okay." He kissed my forehead then dipped his head to take a deep inhale of my hair. "Be good, beauty."

Watching him walk away with Marisol twisted my stomach into knots even though I didn't doubt for one second he was fully mine and she had no hold over him. They met up with two other men near a set of doors then all four exited the ballroom entirely.

Exhaling, I raised my drink to my lips. He'd be back as soon as he could. Until then, I'd make the most of my evening.

It was nearly an hour before Weston returned. Over that time, I had gone from happily watching the glamorous people milling around to being miffed to feeling abandoned. When he took the seat beside me and kissed my cheek, I frowned at him.

"I'm sorry, baby," he murmured. "That took longer than I expected."

"Longer than I expected too." Though the last thing I wanted was to get in a fight with him, I also wasn't going to pretend I was happy with being neglected for so long.

He shifted in his chair, angling his body toward mine, his warm breath brushing my ear as he spoke quietly. "Events like these are for charity, but they're also where connections are made and deals are brokered. Can you give me patience tonight? I might have to speak to Peters again, if he gets his head out of his ass. Otherwise, I'm all yours."

I slid my narrowed eyes to his. My night out with my Prince Charming was turning out to be less Cinderella's ball and more like my senior prom when my date kept sneaking outside to smoke weed with his boys.

"If you don't dance with me, I don't think I'll forgive you."

"Elise"—he took my hand in his, his arm draped around the back of my chair—"if I don't dance with you, I'll never forgive myself."

I managed to settle down and enjoy myself for a while. Weston introduced me to our tablemates, the ones who'd basically ignored me until he arrived. They weren't my people. Most were old enough to be my parents, but they were clearly all enamored with Weston. I tried to be mad about it, but I sort of got off on watching my man being fawned over.

On the inside, I was preening. They might have wanted a piece of him, to be able to tell their friends they'd had dinner with *the* Weston Aldrich, but at the end of the night, he would be only mine.

After dinner, Weston asked me to dance. On our way to the dance floor, we were waylaid by Marisol and a silver-haired man in a classic tuxedo. He had to be seventy years old if he was a day, and he was wearing a pair of cowboy boots on his feet.

Something about him set me on edge.

"Weston, I'm ready to talk brass tacks if you are." This must have been Dominic Peters, the man who'd already stolen Weston from me once tonight.

I braced myself for it to happen again.

Weston's fingers flexed around mine. "I would love to do that, Dominic, but we were on our way to the dance floor. I made a promise to my—"

Marisol shook her head and made a strangled sound. Dominic Peters held up a hand.

"My plane is taking off in two hours. We can schedule something when I'm back home, but I'm not sure when I'll have the time for this discussion."

Weston's gaze slid to mine. I gave him a closed-lip smile. This was where I was supposed to play the good CEO's girlfriend and happily give him up again without making him feel guilty.

"I'll be fine on my own," I told him, though I didn't really mean it. "Do your thing."

His fingers loosened then slipped from between mine, dragging up the back of my forearm. "I'll be back as soon as I can," he murmured.

"It's really fine. Who even wants to dance?"

His calloused thumb rubbed my elbow, then he kissed my temple. "I do, Elise. I'll be back."

Luca sank down in the seat next to mine. "*Bella.*"

"Hey."

"Where's West?"

I shrugged. "No idea."

It had been...a long time since Weston left me. I had gone from watching couples swirl around the dance floor in waves of silk and satin to watching the minutes tick by on my phone.

"I noticed you sitting alone but thought he was getting a drink. When he wasn't back the next time I checked, I decided to come see what was going on." Luca laid his hand on my shoulder. "How long has he been gone, Elise?"

"Mmm...I've lost track."

I stopped checking because it was making me nauseous.

He frowned and cursed under his breath. "This isn't the first time he left you tonight either."

"He and Marisol are discussing a possible contract with a supplier. It's important."

I felt like a robot, saying the things I was supposed to say as Weston's girlfriend. I couldn't quite pinpoint my real emotions, though. Angry, sure. Hurt, definitely. But confusion seemed to trump both of those, at least for now. How could we have started the night so beautifully to have it go like this?

Luca's brow pulled into a heavy, straight line. "I am baffled. Are you okay?"

The band switched to one of my favorites songs, and my chest panged. "I don't know. No, probably not. I wanted to dance."

Luca lifted my hand from my lap, rubbing his thumb over the top of it. "I'm not Weston Aldrich, but I do all right on the dance floor. Can I give you a spin?"

For the first time since Weston walked away, I perked up. "I would really love that, Luca."

It wasn't surprising Luca was suave on the dance floor. He spun me and swung me, making me laugh and ignore the ache in my chest. The music slowed, and he reeled me in, one of my hands in his, the other around my waist. He was a gentleman with me, keeping space between us while I was in his careful arms.

"How are you?" he asked, sweeping me with his concerned gaze.

"Disappointed. I had been looking forward to tonight. If you weren't here, I think I would be ordering an Uber right now."

A crease appeared between his dark brows. "If you want to go now, I'll take you home."

I sighed. "One more dance, okay?"

"Anything you want."

Luca led me through the exquisitely dressed people, twirling me and making me feel floaty. One dance turned into two, and then I lost count.

When the music slowed again, Luca smirked, something devious lighting his expression. "Our picture has been taken quite a few times since we hit the floor."

"Has it?" I'd noticed a few members of the press and some photographers circling around the room, but I hadn't thought much of it since I wasn't anyone interesting. Luca was, though. As the bad boy heir to a motorcycle dynasty, Luca often made it into the press simply by showing up places and looking like he did.

"Mmhmm. It's going to absolutely burn West up when pictures of the two of us dancing are published everywhere."

I wanted to be delighted by that, but it only made me sad. Pictures with Luca were fine, but pictures with Weston would have been even better. Tonight was supposed to be our night, but it had been derailed quickly and completely into something that was making me second-guess everything.

Luca noticed I wasn't laughing with him and he held me tighter, squeezing my hand in his. "He's messing up with you right now, but you have to understand, Weston's like a machine when it comes to his company. I'm going to speculate he has no idea how long he's been gone."

"Well, I do." The knot in my throat made my words soft.

"Yeah, you do." Luca was so gentle with me, swaying me to the slow, rhythmic beat of a ballad. "I'm sorry for that."

I let my eyes close and gave myself over to Luca for a moment. He'd probably left his Bond girl to take care of me. I would let him go at the end of the song so he could find her. One of us deserved to have a fun night.

Then Luca stopped moving and I was being tugged in another direction. My eyes flew open as I collided with Weston's chest. Luca's hand was still on my back, a look of concern shooting from his dark eyes.

"I've got her now," Weston said lowly.

"It's about time." Every trace of Luca's trademark humor had dropped. "You should be thanking me for taking care of Elise instead of treating me like an enemy." His attention turned to me. "Are you okay? Offer stands to take you home."

"I'm *here* now, Luca. Elise doesn't need a ride." Weston swept me away from Luca as if he was trying to steal me. The only thing stopping me from pushing away from him was that I wouldn't make a scene.

Luca stayed focused on me. "Elise?"

I shook my head. "It's okay. Thank you so much for keeping me company."

Weston was positively rigid, and I could feel the rumble in his chest when Luca pecked me on the cheek.

"Anytime, beautiful," he murmured. "I'm always here for you."

He didn't bother saying anything to Weston before he walked away, but that had been statement enough.

"Elise," Weston ground out. "I'm—"

"I'd like to go now." I flattened my palms on his chest, staring at a spot somewhere over his shoulder because I couldn't bring myself to look at him right now. "If you're not ready, I'll take an Uber."

He flinched at that. "On what planet do you think I would let you leave here in an Uber? Of course I'll drive you home." His hand slid from my shoulder to cup my neck. "But are you sure you're ready to leave? We haven't danced or—"

"I'm ready."

I wasn't a woman who yelled or threw fits when I was hurt. Instead, I withdrew. I had been closing in on myself since Weston left me behind, but now that he was back and seemingly oblivious to my turmoil, I couldn't find it within me to even try to express how he'd made me feel.

So, I turned, freeing myself from his hold, and calmly walked away.

At this point, it was unimportant if he followed.

Chapter Thirty

Weston

The glowing screen in my Tesla jarred me. I swiped my thumb over the time. It had to be wrong.

If it was right, I'd been gone from Elise for nearly an hour. That was impossible. There was no way I'd fucked up so monumentally.

My head was throbbing from listening to what had felt like hours of bullshit from Peters that amounted to a big problem I was going to have to handle.

This wasn't how I'd envisioned the night going.

"Elise." I reached across the center console, taking her cold hand in mine. "I'm sorry, baby. I never meant to be gone that long. The deal with Peters is unraveling because he doesn't think our strict oversight is necessary. We're up against a rock and a hard place with the end of our contract with Brian Lewis—"

I cut myself off. Elise was staring placidly ahead, and if she was listening, I couldn't tell. Not that anything I was saying mattered.

"That shouldn't have happened tonight. The minute I recognized what was going on, I should have told him I'd meet with him another time."

I brought her hand to my lips, kissing her knuckles one by one.

"I fucked up, baby. I was being the CEO of Andes instead of your boyfriend and that was absolutely the wrong choice to make. It will never happen again."

Worse, I'd walked away from Peters angry at his blustering and carried that attitude across the dance floor, straight to Luca and Elise. The sight of her tucked in his arms, her eyes closed, Luca smirking like the cat who'd caught the canary, had nearly blinded me with rage.

I'd reacted before thinking, and now, I didn't just have to find a way to make it up to Elise, Luca was due an apology too.

At the moment, my focus had to be on Elise—where it should have been this evening.

"Talk to me, baby."

She blinked, turning her head slightly toward me. "I don't really want to talk. I'm tired."

I squeezed her hand tighter, holding it against my lips. "I'm sorry." Silence.

When we finally arrived home, she rushed out of my car and to the elevator, slapping the button for her floor. With a growl, I hit the code for the penthouse and banded my arm around her waist to hold her back flush with my front.

"I'm going home," she uttered.

"Not tonight. You're coming with me."

"Weston—"

"If I let you go right now, you'll disappear." I held her tighter. "I'm not letting you disappear."

When the doors opened on her floor, she shimmied from side to side, attempting to loosen my hold, but there was absolutely no way she was sleeping in her apartment.

"I don't have the energy to fight you," she whispered as the doors slid shut.

"The last thing I want to do is fight with you."

Once we were inside my apartment, I locked the door and leaned against it. Wariness of what was to come slipped down my spine.

Elise stalked through the entry, pausing to bend down and slip off her heels. She carried them with her to the bedroom, her dress flowing behind her.

I followed.

She was fumbling with the zipper on the back of her dress. Stepping up behind her, I gently nudged her fingers aside and unzipped her, pressing kisses to the bare skin of her shoulders. She crossed her arms over the front of her dress so it didn't fall, then broke away from me to go into my walk-in closet.

I followed again, yanking off my bow tie and shrugging off my jacket.

Elise had taken off her dress, leaving her in a bloodred corset and matching panties. My breath hitched. My stunning, sexy girlfriend was standing there in lace and my diamonds, and she wouldn't even look at me.

"Elise—"

She pulled on a pair of joggers then started working on the hook and eye closures down the front of the corset.

"Please don't try to make me talk about this now." Her eyes lifted, sweeping over my face before lingering somewhere around my chest. "If you give me some space, I'll be able to have a conversation. Right now, though...I'm closed down and don't think I could stand to listen to you try to explain away what you did tonight."

My chest constricted with the weight of her honesty. I knew her well enough to recognize she'd gone cold. I would give her time, but space wasn't really an option for me.

Tonight had begun with Elise slipping on the exquisite lingerie she'd no doubt chosen with me on her mind. I should have brought her home, undressed her, and taken my time appreciating what was underneath.

My inability to set aside my job for one fucking night had catapulted us to the opposite end of the spectrum. The corset fell open, and Elise threw it aside, covering her breasts with her arm while she shook out a T-shirt and tugged it over her head.

While she went into the bathroom, I sank down on the end of the bed, my head in my hands. Patterns of my past were repeating. My past failures mocked me.

Nights like this had ended a couple short-term relationships. I'd brushed myself off and moved on.

Most of the time, I hadn't even paused to mark the end.

I would not let Elise go. I refused.

Balance was possible. It had to be.

She padded out of the bathroom, her face washed, curls brushed out of her hair. As she walked by me, I snagged her around the waist and pulled her to me, pressing my face to her middle, holding her tight.

She was stiff at first, but her muscles slowly uncoiled, and her fingers sliced through my hair in languid strokes. Neither of us said anything. She didn't want to talk, and quite fucking frankly, I needed to get my head together, so I didn't say the wrong thing when she allowed it.

I rose to my feet and cradled her face in my hands. "Are you sleepy, baby?"

She exhaled, her parted lips rosy and chewed on. "I'm just...ready for tonight to be over."

"I'd like to do it over." I rested my forehead on hers. "Tell me what you want."

"You won't give me space, so what's the point?"

"Space isn't the answer. Ask for something else."

She worried her bottom lip with her teeth then sighed. "Zombies."

"Should have known."

We spent the rest of our waking hours watching zombie movies on my couch. Elise let me hold her, but she didn't speak or touch me the way she always did. I had her, but not really. By the time we went to bed, I was going out of my mind.

But I bit my tongue until it was bloody. I hadn't given her the night she deserved or the space she'd requested. Silence was all I had in me, even if it killed me to do so.

***

I woke up to a nightmare. Pictures of Elise and Luca dancing the night away were all over social media. I knew this because Luca had personally emailed me links.

She looked breathtaking, and it killed me because she hadn't been in my arms.

If I knew Luca, he took great delight in rubbing my face in my screwup.

I had one chance to fix it.

With a tray of coffee in one hand and a bag of pastries in the other, I kicked my front door closed. When I turned around, Elise was standing a few feet away, rubbing her eyes.

"Good morning, baby. I have coffee."

She covered up a yawn with her hand and eyed the cups on the tray. "Is that from Patterson's?"

"Mm-hmm. I had it delivered."

As soon as I set the tray down on the kitchen island, she plucked her iced coffee from the cup holder and opened the drawer where she had started keeping a stash of metal straws.

I set the pastries on a plate. She chose a chocolate croissant and carried it with her coffee to the table.

I followed with my cherry Danish and steaming cup, taking the chair across from her.

"Sleep well?" I asked.

"Better than I thought." She sipped her coffee. "You were tossing and turning."

"Yeah." I dragged my fingers through my hair. "Spent a lot of time thinking."

"I might have slept through it, but I didn't notice you leaving the bed to go to your office."

I huffed a dry laugh. "I'm not letting you out of my sight until you're mine again."

She leaned back in her chair, wiping her mouth with her napkin. "If you don't want me out of your sight, can you tell me why it was so easy for you to do at the fundraiser?"

"No." I shook my head. "It wasn't easy. I didn't want to do anything other than spend the night with you on my arm, but I'd already agreed to talk to Peters, and with the direction our negotiations were going, it wasn't something I felt comfortable backing out on. I kept thinking once I handled him, I would be able to get back to you and give you my full attention."

"I understand you have obligations. But you made me feel like an afterthought, and I was expected to grin and take it."

"You're my first thought, Elise. *Always*. I know my actions directly contradicted that, but it's the truth."

I got up from my chair, rounding the table to crouch beside her, and took both of her hands in mine.

"I fucked up. I genuinely lost track of time. It was not a conscious decision to be away from you as long as I was. That is absolutely no excuse, but I need you to know I didn't purposely set you aside. I know the result is the same and I made you feel unimportant, but you are unequivocally the *most* important person in my life."

I brought her hands to my mouth and finally caught her eyes with mine.

"Nothing like that will happen again. Please forgive me so I can make it up to you."

Her eyes narrowed. "How could you possibly make it up to me?"

"Would you dance with me?"

Her lips were pursed. If I thought for a second she'd be happy about it, I would have kissed her. We weren't there yet, so I held her chin and rubbed my thumb along the crinkled bottom one until her mouth relaxed.

She gripped my shirt with both hands and sighed. "You really disappointed me, Weston."

"I'm so sorry, baby. Remember that second chance I made you promise to give me when I inevitably screwed up? This is it. I'm cashing it in."

"So soon?"

"Yeah." I stood and pulled her with me. She was still clinging to my shirt. I slipped my fingers through the back of her silky hair. "I'm surprised I lasted this long."

I wouldn't have had Elliot not told me what an idiot I was being. It was unfortunate he hadn't been there last night. Then again, I really shouldn't have needed him sitting on my shoulder, telling me not to leave Elise alone for an unacceptably long time.

I took each of her wrists and wrapped them around me, then I gathered her in my arms. She was finally looking at me, meeting my gaze. Her big brown eyes blinked up at me, and words were trapped in my throat. There was a lot I wanted to say. A lot I was feeling. But as I stared down at her, at the face I'd known for most of my life but had never gotten used to seeing, I could only think of one thing.

"I need to tell you I'm completely in love with you."

Her fingers curled into my back. "What?" she breathed. "You are?"

"I know the timing is wrong for telling you this. I'm not trying to manipulate you into forgiving me. It's the simple truth."

She chuffed at that. "There's nothing simple about you being in love with me. Jeez." Her forehead knocked against my chest, then she tipped her head back and furrowed her brow. "Really?"

I nodded solemnly, bracing myself to be told to fuck off.

"Well"—she licked her lips, and her fingers dug into my back a little harder—"if you love me, you should dance with me right now and I'll consider forgiving you."

My phone was in my hand before she finished her sentence. Music was playing in the next moment. Something slow, so I could hold her against me the way Luca got to.

After a minute of dancing that was more like swaying, Elise spoke. "It was worse because you were with her."

My head fell forward. God, what a massive fuck up. If she'd been off with Patrick—

No.

That I couldn't contemplate.

Not right now. Possibly not ever.

"I get that. I feel nothing for her, but I completely understand why that compounded an already bad situation."

"You were angry when you saw me with Luca."

"I was." My hand made long, smooth strokes up and down the length of her back. "The meeting with Peters was an exercise in frustration, then I saw you in Luca's arms and it was more than I could reasonably handle."

She rubbed her face back and forth on my chest before laying her cheek over my heart. "It might be wrong of me to feel or say, but I'm glad you were jealous. You deserved to feel a stab in the gut from seeing me spending time with another man."

"Elise—" My hold on her tightened, and my jaw clenched.

"I would never purposely provoke that side of you. That's not who I am. But" she lifted up on her toes so her nose was even with mine—"knowing you *were* jealous makes me feel wanted by you."

"I want you every second of every day. Do you know how often I want to tear a hole through the floor of my office so I can watch you all day?"

Her eyes rounded. "No. How often?"

A dry laugh burst from me. "A lot. I curse the fucking ground for keeping us apart."

"That's a little crazy, Westie."

Westie. I never thought I'd be relieved to hear her call me that. That meant I had a chance.

"I'm telling you, Elise, I really love you."

The corners of her mouth curved. "You can't do that to me ever again."

"I won't." I rested my forehead on hers. "My work has been my life for a decade. It's important to me, but not more than you."

"Prove it," she challenged.

"I will." Somehow. Some way. "Be patient with me?"

Breaking myself of a ten-year habit I'd structured my role in my company around would take time. That wasn't Elise's problem, and I refused to lay my burden at her feet.

"As long as you don't forget about me."

"Never." That I could easily promise.

Her sigh brushed my lips, then she tilted her face, so it was her lips brushing mine.

"I love you too, you know. It scares me how deep I am with you and how easy it would be for you to devastate me."

Her admission pummeled me straight in the solar plexus. The beauty and ugly of what she said dug into me until all I could do was hold her against me and bury my face in her hair, breathing her in.

"Don't be scared. I've got you."

She sniffed and clung to the back of my shirt. "You put yourself between me and a mountain lion. I believe you."

"Overgrown kitty cat," I muttered.

She laughed then yanked on my hair to raise my head. Her mouth was waiting for me. I'd wasted a lot of opportunities in my life, I would not waste another second not kissing Elise.

CHAPTER
THIRTY-ONE

Elise

THROWING MY HEAD BACK, my laughter echoed off the elevator walls. "I wasn't in charge of the pasta, so it can't be my fault it was ruined."

Weston tugged me into his side. "You were distracting me. Our teacher is going to fail us. Do you know I've never failed anything in my life?"

"That's because you never took cooking lessons." I nibbled on his proud, scruffy chin as we ascended to the penthouse. "I'm not surprised you've never failed, you overachiever."

He clucked his tongue and shook his head. "Taken down by gummy pasta."

I grasped the lapels of his jacket. "We're awful cooks, but we had fun, didn't we?"

He took my face in his hands and slowly looked me over. The corners of his mouth hitched, and so did my breath.

"I can't think of anything more fun—outside the bedroom—than destroying every single dinner we've attempted to make in Chef Sandra's class."

"Love you," I whispered.

"Love you too, baby."

It'd been almost two weeks since the gala. Weston had been making a concerted effort to be an attentive boyfriend, even in the midst of dealing with supplier issues in California. There had been a couple days I'd barely seen him, but he'd let me know I was on his mind through emails and texts and then curling his long body around mine in bed at the end of the day.

We'd just finished our final cooking lesson, and although we hadn't learned a thing, I wanted to sign up for another. Weston was so very capable in every aspect of his life except this one. Aside from the three meals he'd perfected, he was a terrible cook.

So was I.

But damn, did we have fun trying and failing.

It was also a relief to know Weston wasn't perfect at everything. A relief for me, not him. He really, really didn't like not being able to master something.

Our mouths were latched as we stumbled into Weston's apartment. He dug his fingers into my hair, keeping me in place so he could devour my lips with his. He always kissed me like it was our last.

I tugged his shirt from his pants and glided my palms over his taut abs, sighing into his mouth. His abs flexed, and I circled my arms around his waist, stroking the line of muscle along his spine. He made me dizzy with desire, and it hadn't lessened over time. If anything, it had only gotten stronger.

A throat cleared. "Now might be the time to let you know I'm here."

Weston immediately pushed me behind him, and I peeked around to see the intruder. Miles was kicked back in the living room, his legs stretched out in front of him, ankles crossed, a bottle of water in one hand, a paperback in the other.

He put the book down and wiggled his fingers. "Surprise."

Weston folded his arms over his chest. "You're not welcome here."

Since the threat of danger was gone, I ducked around Weston. "I think what Weston means is we didn't know you'd be here tonight."

"I meant what I said," Weston intoned.

Miles flinched, and his pained expression wound its way around my gut. He and Weston had never been besties, but the distance between them was lined with spikes and guarded by bloodthirsty crocodiles. It seemed almost impossible to bridge.

Rubbing the back of his neck, Miles scooted to the edge of the couch. "I texted, but by your arctic welcome, I'm assuming it wasn't read." When Weston didn't respond, he went on. "Look, I've been staying with Mom and Dad while my place is being renovated—"

Weston went rigid behind me. "What place?"

Miles cocked his head. "Uh, the townhouse I bought a year ago. I emailed you the listing. You even replied, 'looks good.' It needed a top-to-bottom reno, so it obviously didn't *look good*, but I assumed you were saying you saw the potential." His brow pinched. "You don't remember?"

I glanced back at Weston. His nostrils flared as he glared at his brother. Then he shook his head once.

"Ah, okay." Miles nodded, his jaw rippling. "I sort of wondered why you never mentioned it again."

I was torn, which was strange. I should have been on Weston's side, not just because I adored him, but because of my history with Miles, but Miles's turmoil and need to be seen by his big brother was palpable.

"None of that explains what you're doing in my home." Weston's tone was dry and impatient.

Miles stood and kicked the duffel bag beside the couch. "I was hoping I could crash here. Like I said, I've been staying with Mom and Dad, but I can't do it anymore. Dad's been around a lot more than normal and all they do is fight."

"That's nothing new." Weston was unimpressed.

"No, I know." Miles cupped the back of his neck, glancing between the two of us. "Dad's been bringing his girlfriend to the house. So that's new."

If Weston had been rigid before, he was solid now.

"What the fuck?" he uttered.

Miles nodded. "It's like World War III in that house. I've had a lifetime of ignoring their fighting, but even I can't disassociate my way out of our mother pounding on Dad's bedroom door with a fireplace poker."

"Christ. Did you try to stop her?"

Miles grimaced. "Nah. I learned when I was thirteen not to put myself between them." He dragged his finger along the scar in his eyebrow. "That's from me taking a hit from the wineglass meant for Dad."

Weston made a strangled sound. "You never told me that," he accused. "She threw a wineglass at him? How did I not know about this?"

The corner of Miles's mouth hitched into a sardonic half smile. "You had the Levys, I had the Aldriches."

"What does that mean?"

"It means you were able to escape the chaos that is our parents' marriage, but I was left behind with them." Miles toed his bag again. "They haven't calmed down in their old age. If anything, they've lost the inhibitions of their youth. I won't be surprised if they kill each other one of these days. It'll be very *War of the Roses*. In the end, they'll be lying in a pile of rubble, their hands around each other's throats."

Weston's arms slipped around my shoulders, and he pulled my back to his chest. His body vibrated with tension. I wished I could take it away, but he and Miles needed to have this conversation. If Weston wanted me here as a buffer, I'd be that for him, but this had to be between the two of them.

"You should have told me about the glass," Weston admonished. "How was I supposed to help you if I didn't know?"

Miles gave him a steady glare. "I had four stitches and you didn't ask what happened. Should I have given you a written account of the events? Is that what would have made you care?"

"I cared."

Miles scoffed. "You showed it by disappearing." He bent down and picked up his bag. "Whatever. I get that I'm in the way here. I'll grab a hotel room."

My heart ached for him. I had known they hadn't come from a warm and fuzzy home, but it had never occurred to me Miles had been left behind to endure the very things Weston had been escaping. Had it occurred to Weston? It didn't seem like it.

"Miles," Weston gruffed. "You opened this Pandora's Box, you get to stick around and sort through it with me. Put your bag down."

Miles's expression slipped from disgruntled to hopeful puppy. "I can stay?"

"We'll see." Weston squeezed me before letting me go to take my hand in his. All of us sat down on the sectional sofa, Miles on one side, Weston and me on the other, that chasm roiling between them.

Miles started talking, releasing a deluge of two decades of his parents' drama. He'd been stuck in the middle, defending their mom while also stopping her from maiming their father, who'd spent the majority of his time cheating, drinking, and spending his massive trust funds. Their mother would baby Miles, take him on lavish trips, pull him from school in the middle of the day for adventures so he would be on her side. Their father vacillated between threatening and completely forgetting Miles existed.

"You left me with them," Miles accused.

Weston rubbed the center of his forehead. "Mom doted on you. She *still* does. I didn't think—"

Miles shrugged. "You were a kid too, and you were selfish. I get that."

My lip was being chewed to death, and my hand was being crushed between Weston's. The worst ache was my chest, though. Elliot and I were so close. We'd been there for every one of each other's milestones. Neither Miles nor Weston had that. Weston had run while Miles had stayed, growing resentful over each passing year.

"And I get you were angry at me for being selfish." Weston leaned forward, a crevice between his brows. "I don't think I can forgive you for taking that anger and directing it at Elise. That was for me, not her. She never did anything to you and you fucking—"

"I know." Miles's shoulders drooped. "It's not something I'm proud of, especially now that we've gotten to know each other and we're friends." His eyes flicked to mine. "We are, right?"

I nodded. "You annoyed me into acquiescence."

He smirked. "My superpower."

Weston turned to me. "I don't think I'll ever be able to comprehend your level of evolution. You're the injured party, yet here you are, laughing with the villain in your story. How can that be?"

Miles flinched, and to be honest, on the inside, I did too. I had to remind myself this was fresh for Weston. I'd had years to come to terms with everything that had happened, Weston hadn't.

"I can't stay angry forever, Weston. I'm choosing to move on and let it go. It's especially easy now that I understand where Miles was coming from and what he was dealing with."

Weston brought my hand up to his lips, touching it gently. "That's one of the big differences between you and me—I can absolutely stay angry forever."

I let out a soft giggle. "I would never try to take your anger from you. I hope you're hearing what Miles is saying to you, though."

He switched his attention to Miles. "I'm hearing it. I was a neglectful, shitty brother. I screwed up, and I'm owning that right now. That doesn't mean I can snap my fingers and get over what he did to you. He knew you were precious to me and purposely sought you out to bully you. You'll have to forgive *me* for not being all right with that."

"No one expects you to," I told him. "But maybe over time..."

"Maybe." Weston's mouth pressed into a hard line. I wasn't optimistic he would ever soften toward Miles.

Miles's expression lightened, clearly more optimistic than me. "Maybe isn't no."

Weston remained unamused. "You can stay here, but no longer than a week. If you're annoying or bother Elise, you're out immediately."

Miles winked at him. "Got it. You don't want me staying long enough for squatter's rights to kick in. That makes sense."

Weston rose, pulling me with him. "Jokes, huh? Are you sure that's the route you want to take?"

I pressed on his chest. "Shhh. That's enough. Nothing has to be resolved in one night."

Miles flopped against the couch cushions, misery pulling at his features. "Humor has been my fallback for a long time. Sorry."

Weston grunted. He was obviously finished, which was fair since he'd been far more patient and open than I would have expected. The fact that he hadn't thrown Miles out at first sight was huge for him.

"Are you good to set yourself up in the guest room?" I asked.

Miles nodded. "Westie's let me stay here more often than I care to admit."

"'Let' isn't how I'd put it." Weston's fingers flexed on my hip. "One week, Miles."

He nodded glumly. "Message received."

⸻◆⸻

Weston and I were in bed, facing each other, his fingers gliding through my hair in long strokes. My lids were heavy, but I fought off sleeping in case he wanted to talk.

And he did.

"I shouldn't have left him behind," he murmured.

"You didn't know."

His hand stilled, flattening on my cheek. "But I did. Not about the violence, no, but our home wasn't warm or loving. I found that with your family and never wanted to go back. I should have brought Miles with me."

"You were a kid."

"I didn't even think about him. That's the raw, ugly truth."

"And yet, he's still here. He still wants to be your family."

He shuddered, his thumb spreading to graze the curve of my bottom lip. "I can't even look at him right now without wanting to kill him for using you as his whipping boy when he should have been lashing out at me."

"Then look at me. See *me*, West. I'm alive and well."

"I see you," he whispered. "You're all I see anymore."

That made me smile. My grumpy man was capable of being incredibly sweet.

"I love you."

His forehead rolled over mine, and he released a ragged sigh. "I love you too, Elise. I wish I could give you what you've given me. All I have is a dysfunctional family and a company I poured my blood, sweat, and tears into for the last decade. It's not enough."

"Good thing I don't want anything other than you." I dragged my nails along his scruff. "Keep giving me you the way you have been and I'll be a happy girl."

"That's all I want. You happy."

He didn't understand he held the key to that. Diamond necklaces and cooking lessons were beautiful and special, but when it came down to it, Weston's time and attention were all I would ever need from him.

Chapter Thirty-Two

Weston

AFTER A SOLID WEEK of negotiations, Andes officially broke ties with Brian Lewis and the insufferable blowhard Dominic Peters. Marisol's team had found us a third supplier more than willing to follow our terms in order to land the contract.

Miles was still in my guest room, but he wasn't bothering me as much as he typically did. That was due in part to him lying low. He was keeping his mouth shut and his dirty socks in his room. But I couldn't discount the fact that I was actively attempting not to be annoyed with him. I had never given him a chance to be anything other than my fuckup little brother.

This weekend, I might even carve out some time to spend with him.

I was shutting my computer down, my mind already out of the office, when Renata knocked on the door.

"Yes?"

She pushed it open. "There's a reporter from the *Times* on line one for you."

I frowned at her. Renata knew I didn't give interviews unless they were scheduled and vetted well in advance. "Why? Send them to PR. I don't have time to talk to reporters."

"Weston..." the way she wrung her hands had me sitting up, alarm bells ringing, "I really think you should speak to her."

I reached for the phone but stopped myself. Impetuousness wasn't my style. Acting without planning would only lead me to disaster.

"What is this about?"

Renata approached my desk, worry deepening the ever-present creases in her face.

"She said her name is Ellis Frey. I looked her up when I put her on hold. She's an environmental reporter who was nominated for a Pulitzer two years ago for investigative journalism." Renata heaved a breath. "She told me the *Times* will be running a story about our suppliers disposing of waste improperly and illegally. She'd like a quote from you, but it's running no matter what."

My spine froze into an icicle. "Impossible."

"I think you should speak to her."

"I will. I'll tell her what a load of bullshit this is." My hand went to the phone. "Thank you, Renata. You can go home."

She spun on her sensible heels and walked out, closing the door behind her.

I picked up the phone.

It was two in the morning when I crawled into my bed and wrapped myself around Elise. Her hand went to my face.

"What's wrong?" she rasped.

So fucking much. But the thought of telling her nearly sent me into a panic.

"I don't want to talk tonight, baby."

"Okay."

My mouth found hers in the dark. Need for her swept over the anger and confusion that had been consuming me the past several hours. Holding her, touching her, was the only thing keeping me stable.

Pushing her nightgown up and off, I buried my face in her throat and let the weight of her breasts on my chest soothe my rapidly beating heart.

"I need you."

Her fingers slid through my hair, and her legs fell open. "I'm here, West."

She was soft and so warm. I'd woken her up, and without hesitation or question, she'd come to me. Right now, I was a sinking ship, and she was the band that kept playing through impending disaster—comfort and distraction before the inevitable, painful end.

Her eyes were shining when I brought my head up. "Panties off. Let me feel you."

Nodding, she reached down and slipped them off. Climbing to my knees, I dragged my briefs down, revealing my hard, aching cock. She propped herself on her elbow to wrap her fingers around me. Her palm was hot, grip tight, as she pumped me.

"West," she cooed. "Come here."

Elise was my destination. She was the reason I'd left my office instead of spending the night at my desk attempting to solve the unsolvable. If I could just have this reprieve, I would be able to face what was coming, the potential destruction of everything I'd built.

I fitted myself between her thighs and fell over her. My cock wedged between her slick folds, sliding back and forth, grazing her clit with each pass.

My arm tunneled under her neck, fingers delving into her hair as I slowly sank inside her. Our eyes were locked, breaths passing between us, skin to skin, pounding heart to pounding heart.

We rode each other in the quiet. There were no words that would sound right, and I couldn't form any with the knot of need lodged firmly in my throat.

She touched my face. I stroked the downy skin of her shoulders and jaw. Our lips met in a firm press, parted, then met again. Her eyes held a thousand questions, but something in mine must have made her kiss me instead of asking.

Her knees pressed into my sides. I went deeper, plunging farther. We were as close as two people could be, and still, I was greedy for her.

She came with a sigh and a moan, her body holding mine deep. I rubbed my lips over her bowed throat, absorbing the vibrations from her pleasure.

If I could have stayed like this forever, just the two of us in the dark where nothing outside could creep in, I would have. Above all else, I would have chosen this.

As hard as I tried to keep going, to fight off the ending, my body answered Elise's call. I held her face as I poured into her, whispering that I loved her against her lips. She held me close, keeping me between her thighs as we rolled to our sides.

We'd traded positions. I was the one who always held her, but it was as easy as breathing to let her cradle me in her warmth.

"I love you, West," she murmured.

"Love you too, baby. Go to sleep."

She nodded, her cheek on mine. "You too."

It didn't take long for her breaths to even out and her arms to slacken. I stayed awake for a lot longer, keeping her close, wondering how I was going to survive what was coming my way.

Chapter Thirty-Three

Elise

I FOUND OUT THE news at the same time as everyone else.

Andes was under investigation by the EPA for the disposing of toxic chemicals in nearby water sources. This came after an article exposing the practices at Brian Lewis's factory, which had been going on for years.

After spending the weekend alone while Weston was in lockdown in his office, I had expected the worst. What I hadn't expected was for him not to tell me what was going on. We'd barely spoken since he'd woken me in the middle of the night to make love to me.

As hard as I tried not to make any of this about me, it was impossible not to be hurt. To have to open up the *Times* to find out what was going on with my own boyfriend was a dagger to the heart.

I sucked it up, put my supportive pants on, and texted him.

Me: *I read the article. I'm here when you need me. I love you so much, Weston.*

An ass plopped down on my desk. "Did you read that bullshit?"

I placed my silent phone face down and looked up at Miles. "I did. I'm absolutely sick for him."

"It's utter bullshit. Andes runs regular checks at each of their suppliers. There is no way something like this would slip through the cracks. Obviously, someone at the *Times* is smoking too much and their brain cells are misfiring. Weston's going to own that paper when he's through with them." Miles waggled his brows. "How does The Aldrich Times sound to you? Miles Aldrich, editor in chief. I have no clue how to run a paper, but it can't be that hard."

Despite the boulder sitting heavy in my stomach, I laughed. "I encourage you to follow your dreams."

"It's only been my dream for the last minute or so, but I appreciate the support." His expression grew serious. "Tell me how he's doing. I haven't seen him at home."

I lifted a shoulder. "I haven't seen him either. I don't know how he is."

His brow dropped low over his concerned gaze. "What? You haven't even talked to him?"

"Nothing more than a quick text to let me know he was dealing with an emergency at Andes. That was Saturday morning."

Miles's hand curled into a ball. "That's not cool."

It wasn't cool, but I felt the need to defend Weston. Andes had been his life for so long, having it threatened and attacked had to be killing him. I wished he'd let me be there for him. *That* was killing me.

"He's dealing with something huge, and he's not used to sharing his burdens."

"Nope." He shook his head. "Not an excuse to leave you hanging. I don't like it."

"I don't either, but I'm not going to go storming into his office demanding attention."

"You shouldn't have to demand it."

I sighed. "Can you go away, please? You're making me more upset."

His righteous indignation slipped away. "Oh no, I'm sorry, Lisie. God, I'm an idiot."

"You're not. I get that you're angry on my behalf, but I don't need that."

He hopped off my desk to round it and slung his arm over my shoulders. "Let me take you to lunch today. I promise to be on my best behavior."

I tossed his arm aside and leaned away. "I'll let you know if I'm in the mood. Right now, I'm too grouchy to consider it."

He backed up a step or two, holding both hands up. "Okay, okay. I may be dense at times, but even I can read the undercurrents. Just to say, I'm here for you if you want company."

"Thanks, Miles."

He finally left, and I turned over my phone. No response from Weston. My text hadn't even been read.

It was midnight when a text rolled in. I'd been tossing and turning for an hour, sleep nowhere in sight. I guessed I'd been waiting to hear from him.

Weston: *Sorry it took me so long to reply. I've been in meetings with lawyers and haven't touched my phone all day. This isn't going to end anytime soon.*

Me: *You don't have to be sorry. Are you home?*

Weston: *Just got home. I'm about to crash.*

Me: *Want me to come up and crash with you?*

Weston: *I want that, but I know I won't get the sleep I need if you're here. Besides, I'll be up at dawn for more meetings.*

Me: *Okay. I understand. Can you at least try to keep me apprised of what's going on with you? I don't love being in the dark.*

Weston: *I'll try, but, baby, right now, my priority is Andes. My head is there, so if you don't hear from me, that's why. Love you. Goodnight.*

Me: *Love you too. xoxo*

I clutched my phone to my aching chest. I'd been longing to hear from Weston all day, so why did I feel worse now that I had?

———◆◆◆———

I rode the elevator up to eight, chewing on my lip. My stomach was a riot of butterflies. I couldn't quite understand my body's reaction. Dropping by to see Weston had become a regular thing, so why was I nervous today?

Probably because it had been days since we'd been face to face and our conversations had been brief and sparse. He was buried in meetings with lawyers and his executive board. I knew that, and I was being as understanding as I could, reminding myself again and again this wasn't about me.

Renata was on the phone when I approached her desk. Her movements were harried. Her mouth was pulled into a deep frown as she nodded at what the person on the other end was saying.

Her eyes flicked to mine. I pointed to Weston's office and mouthed, "Is he in a meeting?" She shook her head, her attention reverting back to the person she was speaking to.

I knocked lightly on Weston's door, waiting a beat before pushing inside.

My heart dropped at the sight of him. He was at his desk, his head hanging in his hands. He didn't look up as I crossed the room. He only reacted when I laid a hand on his shoulder and said his name.

His head jerked up, and the purple smudges under his eyes took my breath away. Weston never looked anything less than put together, even in the middle of the wilderness during our camping trip. Right now, he was ravaged.

"West," I sighed.

He stared right through me for a moment before snapping out of his daze. "Elise. What are you doing here?"

"Checking on you." I motioned to the paper bag I'd set on his desk. "I brought you lunch. I assumed you weren't stopping to eat."

His exhale was ragged with exhaustion. "If you'd called, I would have told you I'm having a working lunch in a few minutes with my lawyers. You wouldn't have wasted your time coming up here."

"Oh." His tone was more curt than he'd ever taken with me. It hit me like a load of bricks. "If I'd called, would you have even answered?"

His brow lowered, a deep crease forming at the top of his nose. "Look, I don't know what you want me to say. I'm in the middle of trying to save Andes. Do you understand how many jobs are on the line if I can't pull a rabbit out of a hat? If I don't answer the phone, it's because I'm busy. This is my sole focus, which I explained to you last night. I can't worry about answering your calls right now."

My hand dropped from his shoulder like I'd been scalded.

I guessed I'd actually been *scolded*. I couldn't remember a time I'd felt so small. Probably high school, eating lunch in the bathroom so

I didn't have to try to choke down my food to the chants of "Ellie the Elephant."

"Okay. I get it. I'm going to go." I picked up the bag, crinkling it with my curled fingers. "If you need anything, let me know."

"Elise." He leaned back in his chair and gave me a long, thorough once-over. "I'll text you tonight, all right?"

"Sure." I swallowed down my hurt feelings. This wasn't about me. If I kept telling myself that, maybe I'd start to believe it. "Bye, Weston."

Renata was off the phone when I left Weston's office, appearing just as run ragged as he was.

"How'd it go?" she asked. Her wry expression said she knew exactly how it had gone.

I took a deep breath and offered her a smile. "Do you like sushi?" I lifted up the bag. "I have extra."

She grabbed it from me. "I'm so hungry, I'd eat a rat. My boss isn't giving me a break."

My laugh was forced, but I was trying. "Well, let me know if you're hungry tomorrow and I'll grab you something when I go to lunch. It's no trouble."

"You're a good one, Elise." She shook her head. "He's not himself at the moment. What's happening with the EPA and in the press is a personal attack in his mind. Weston's entire ethos is being called into question. He's not just defending Andes, he's defending himself."

I wasn't sure how to respond to that. And it turned out I didn't have to. Weston's voice came through the speaker on Renata's phone.

"Renata, I told you I'm not taking visitors." His harsh bark rattled down my spine. Was I a visitor?

Renata quickly picked up the phone, glancing at me then away. "I understand that, but I assumed there was an exception for—"

He cut her off, and although I couldn't hear what he was saying, the droop on her face told me everything. This phone call was in direct response to her allowing me access to him.

She hung up and avoided my gaze. "Thanks for the sushi, honey."

"I'm not an exception, am I?"

With a heavy sigh, she folded her hands on her desk and finally met my eyes. "I told you, he's not himself. The decisions he's making do not reflect how he feels about you."

"Sure. But he's still making them."

Her mouth pressed into a thin line. There was nothing left to say. My boyfriend had just barred me from his office, and we both knew it.

———◆———

At midnight, I received my text. I stared at his name on the screen, my thumb hovering until it turned black. It was a relief when it went away. I put my phone face down on my nightstand, covered my head with my blankets, and made myself shut my eyes.

In the morning, after a few hours of broken sleep, I allowed myself to read Weston's texts.

Weston: *Home now. About to crash. Bad day.*

Weston: *Are you asleep?*

Weston: *Goodnight, baby.*

He'd sent me one more this morning.

Weston: *Check in with me when you get this so I don't worry. Too much going on to be worried about you, baby.*

That I was crying before getting out of bed was a bad sign of how the day was going to go. I swiped the tears away from my eyes.

The bitter part of me wanted to let Weston be worried since I was consumed with it. But I wasn't that petty.

Me: *I'm fine. Don't worry. I hope today's better.*

I didn't check my phone again until I'd showered and dressed for work. He'd read it but hadn't responded. Dread sat like lead in my gut. Nothing about what was happening felt right. Weston was in crisis, and instead of leaning on me, he was holding me at arm's length.

Or maybe he was pushing me away entirely. That was what it felt like.

Saoirse was in the kitchen when I plodded in. As soon as she saw my face, she filled a mug to the brim with coffee and slid it across the counter to me. When I saw it was the one I'd bought her at the farmers' market, with a picture of an opossum and the words "Eat trash and hail Satan," I nearly sobbed. This was her favorite mug. She never shared it.

"You feel sorry for me," I accused.

She cocked her hip. "Your boyfriend's being a dick, so sorta."

"He's not a dick. He's just—" I broke off. I hadn't decided exactly how I felt.

Saoirse came at me with her arms out. I let her hug me but absolutely refused to cry. My makeup was done and I didn't have time to redo it. This was where I made my stand.

She pulled back, resting her hands on my shoulders. "He's being a dick, honey. There's no disputing that. I get what he's going through is huge, but you're here entirely in the dark. It's not right. He can't just set you aside when life gets tough."

"You're right, and I'm not going to try to deny it. But what can I do? I can't exactly storm into his office and demand attention. That's not my style. Even if it was—" I choked on my own words. It took me two attempts to clear my throat so I could get them out. "I'm barred from his office anyway."

I almost crumpled then. Saoirse's sympathetic expression made me want to fall into her arms and spend my day there. I wasn't this girl, but the thing was, Weston had made promises the last time I'd forgiven him for choosing his job over me, and I'd believed he'd keep them.

He hadn't.

Reality was a Mack truck.

"Lise—"

I shook my head. "No, it's fine. I'm fine. I have to go to work. I'm sure everything will be okay."

She sighed like I was the saddest thing she'd ever seen, and I sort of felt like it. If Patrick had simply stopped talking to me for days on end then told his assistant I wasn't allowed to visit, I would have told him to go fuck himself, no matter the underlying reason.

But this was *Weston.*

The exception to every rule.

I wasn't ready to give up on him yet.

My midnight texts kept coming, but that was my only correspondence with Weston for the rest of the week. Work was busy, and in my off-hours, Saoirse practically danced on her head to distract me from my quickly fading boyfriend.

I read the news and listened to gossip around the office. People worried but were certain Weston would fix everything. They said this while wringing their hands and updating their résumés "just in case."

Sympathy softened me toward Weston. His mantle was heavy. Everyone was looking to him now, and that had to be a difficult weight to stand tall under.

My patience was a finite thing, though, and it was wearing thin. One week of neglect and being set aside for Andes, and I was more than hurt. Weston was ruining us more every day that ticked by.

His midnight texts were a slap in the face.

I wanted to run up to the penthouse and scream, "*You banned me from your office!*" But I wasn't the screaming kind. I was the folding kind. The "quietly pack it away" kind. The "remove myself from a situation, flattening me little by little" kind.

When the weekend came around again, I trudged to the farmers' market with Saoirse, but even her buoyancy couldn't keep me afloat. I took my phone out when she was distracted and texted Weston, even though I'd promised myself and her I wouldn't.

Me: *Hey...I know you're busy, but I thought maybe I'd see you, even for a little bit. Are you at the office?*

Without waiting for a reply I knew down to my bones I wouldn't be getting, I stuffed my phone back in my bag, my stomach roiling with shame over asking for scraps.

Saoirse bumped into me, drawing my thoughts from my heartache. "Babe, look what I got for you." She held up a glass jar in the shape of a beehive with a little bee on top.

"What is it?"

"You put honey in it and use this little swirling stick to serve it. Isn't it adorable? I bought it for you because you're the bee's knees."

I took the container from her, choking back sudden tears. "This is the sweetest present I've ever been given."

There was no hiding from Saoirse. She cupped my cheeks with both hands and kissed my forehead.

"Don't you dare cry in the middle of the farmers' market or I'll start crying too, and then I'll never be able to come back and ask for the honey guy's phone number."

"Why don't you ask for his number now?"

She waggled her brows. "I'm keeping him in suspense. This is my second weekend flirting with him. One more, I think, and he'll be ripe for the plucking."

Just like that, she'd managed to keep my tears at bay and make me laugh.

⁙

By evening, I hadn't heard from Weston. In one of the rare moments I wasn't being watched over by Saoirse, I took my keys, shucked my pride, and rode the elevator to the penthouse.

I let myself in and stopped in the doorway when I wasn't met with the silence I'd been expecting.

"Hello?" I called.

The television went silent. "Lisie?"

"Miles?"

I ventured down the entryway and Miles appeared, his hands on his hips, a happy grin on his face.

"Hey. I didn't expect to see you. Did Weston send you to make sure I wasn't trashing his apartment?"

That answered whether Weston was here. I was disappointed, but I would have been even more so if he had been here, hanging out, ignoring my texts.

"No, he didn't send me." My keys dug into my curled-up hand. "Has he—is he at the office?"

Miles's cocked his head, his brow crinkled with confusion. "Wait—you know he's in California, right? He left this morning. You *do* know that, right?"

Everything in me wanted to tell him yes, of course I knew that. But I was too taken aback to even pretend. My shock must have been written all over my face because Miles crumbled right along with me.

"*No*," he whispered. "He didn't."

"I don't know where he is," I confirmed.

"Shit." Miles came at me, scooping me into his arms the way he always did. "I'm sorry, Lisie. I don't know what he's doing."

I sucked in a shuddering breath and let my forehead fall on his shoulder. Deep inside, I knew this was coming, but now that it was here, I couldn't believe it.

This was my limit.

I loved Weston. I'd given him time, space, and understanding because of that. But this...this was too much. He got on a plane, flew states away, and I hadn't even been a factor.

This wasn't like when Patrick's betrayal had slammed into me like a tidal wave. Weston's destruction had been done by slowly and steadily chipping away at me until I was all raw nerves, cracked bones, and shriveled trust.

We were over without even a whisper of a conversation.

I stumbled back from Miles, my eyes blurry with tears. "I'm going to go."

"You don't have to. Stay with me."

"No." I swiped at my cheeks. "I can't be here anymore."

Just like his brother had, Miles let me go.

Chapter Thirty-Four

Weston

I was living in my own personal nightmare. The reports coming out of Brian Lewis's factory made my stomach turn. The fact that Andes hadn't been aware of his illegal disposal didn't excuse it or make up for the long-term damage that had been inflicted on the environment.

We should have known.

What had happened was the very antithesis of the foundation of my company. Having the smallest footprint possible was my biggest pride.

But the old proverb is absolutely true. Pride does indeed goeth before the fucking fall.

Marisol had been talking nonstop since I'd climbed into the car with her this morning. Since she was in charge of the West Coast supply chain, she was shouldering part of the blame for missing what Brian had been doing and had been actively working on damage control alongside me.

The car pulled up in front of Andes' headquarters. I got out first, then took Marisol's hand to help her out. We were on our way into the office for yet another set of interviews with EPA officials.

Marisol's hands were flying as she went over what was going to be happening in the next few days. "Mark in field relations will be visiting the—"

I wasn't listening. Elise rounded the corner of the building, heading toward the entrance. As if she sensed me approaching, she turned her head, and our eyes locked.

She stopped walking. I caught up to her a moment later.

"Elise."

Her lips flattened. "Weston."

Not a warm greeting. Not that I deserved it.

But god, I craved even a minute of Elise's warmth after more than a week of nothing but misery.

"Would it be possible to talk?" she asked.

It was on the tip of my tongue to tell her yes, but I glanced at Marisol first. She held up her wrist and tapped her watch then flicked her hardened gaze to Elise.

"I'm sorry, but I have a meeting—"

Elise shook her head. "It's about work and will only take a minute."

Relief settled in my chest. She'd given me a reason to say yes. Work I could make space for. Everything else had to wait. I couldn't let myself even stop to think if there would be anything waiting for me at the end.

"I can give you that. Follow us up to eight."

Elise stood as far apart from me as she could in the elevator. Marisol did the opposite, to my ever-growing annoyance. Silence waged war in the small space. When we finally arrived on the eighth floor, I couldn't get out fast enough.

I opened my office door, allowing Elise inside. Marisol tried to follow. When I stood in her way, her mouth fell open in shock.

"You're not letting me in?"

"No. Go work in the conference room," I bit out. "I'll be out in a few minutes."

Her perfect brows arched. "If she wants to talk about Andes, I don't see why—"

"No." I closed the door and turned the lock.

Elise was standing next to the chairs in front of my desk. I took longer than I should have drinking her in, but I was hungry for her. I'd lost track of how long it had been since we were in the same room. It felt like weeks but couldn't have been more than a few days.

Elise launched into what she had to say without preamble. "I remembered something one of the guys I'd interviewed said. I'm not sure it will help, but I thought you should know in case it does. Cameron Gilles mentioned the field team used to come around all the time, but he hadn't seen them in a long time and didn't miss them."

I had to close my eyes to process what she was telling me. "Cameron Gilles? Who is that?"

"He works at Brian Lewis's factory. He's one of the men who took me rock climbing."

"And while you were rock climbing with *Cameron*, he told you he hadn't seen the field team in a long time?"

"He did. It was an offhand comment while we were joking about other things, but I went back to my notes to make sure, and that was what he said."

I folded my arms over my chest, anger simmering in my blood. "And this is the first time you thought to tell me?"

"Yes, it is."

My hands tightened into fists. "Christ, Elise, if you would have told me this a month ago, all this—"

"I'm sorry, Weston, but out of context, I couldn't have known how important it was. It only makes sense now, which is why I'm in your office."

Though what she was saying was completely rational, I had to work to rein in my temper. There she was, looking beautiful and sad and so fucking far away. If I could have crossed the room, I would have shaken her or held her or fucked her. Maybe all three. But then what? Andes was hanging by a thread. What I wanted didn't come into play. Not now.

"Is that it?"

She blinked, her shoulders falling. "I guess it is."

She started for the door, and I stepped aside, holding my breath. If I caught her scent, I feared I'd give in and lose sight of what I had to be doing.

At the last second, she whirled around to face me. "I heard you telling Renata not to allow me into your office."

I flinched at her admission. I hadn't done that to be cruel. I'd done it out of necessity. "I'm sorry you heard that. But you have to understand—"

She held her hand up, and it was dangerously close to touching me. "And then, as if that wasn't bad enough, I knocked on your door Saturday morning. Miles answered, and he was the one to tell me you'd gone to California. You left the state and didn't bother telling me." Her tongue darted out to lick her lips. "What are you *doing*?"

"I'm trying to save my company, Elise. I thought you knew that."

"No, Weston. What are you doing with me?" She huffed a breath. "I'm not even a consideration, am I?"

Phones were ringing on the other side of the door. Voices of people coming to work, attempting to rectify the disaster happening to *my* company. My plate was full, and I'd just been given one more thing to add to it.

I was cracking, being pulled in so many directions, my head was spinning.

And the woman I loved, the woman I'd made promises to, was in front of me, rightfully hurt, needing me.

I was fucking up, like I always did, and there was nothing to be done. There was no trading one disaster for another. Right here, right now, I had to choose which one to tend to.

"I can't do this with you. We'll talk when I'm out from under this, but it can't be now. People are waiting for me so—"

Her fingers grazed along the arm of my jacket. "I was waiting for you."

There was finality in her gentle words. Past tense. A death knell delivered like a basket of kittens. It would have killed me if I had let it, and I couldn't do that.

"I told you before we started I was no good at this. I warned you, didn't I?" My anger resurfaced, but even I didn't know where it was directed. It was just...there. Thick and suffocating.

"I guess you did. I'm sorry I didn't listen." She backed up until she hit the door, then she fumbled with the knob. "And don't worry about talking once this is over. I think we've said all we needed to. I hope it all works out. Andes is a good company."

She was gone in the next second, and the sense of wrongness hit me like a ton of bricks. I almost chased her, but I had no idea what I'd say if I caught her.

My phone vibrated in my pocket, and I yanked it out to check the notification. Elise's picture lit up my lock screen.

Fuck.

Black coated my vision, and I hurled the phone against the wall, the loud crack like music to my fucking ears. The urge to pummel my fists through the drywall nearly overtook me. My body listed forward, my hands ready to pound something into oblivion.

Why did she have to do this?

Why couldn't she have given me the time to take care of what I needed to?

I shoved my fingers through my hair. There was no time for this. Andes was too big. *I'd* built it into something too massive to let my personal feelings affect my work.

One minute.

That was what I gave myself to pull it together.

When the minute passed, I strode into the conference room and glanced around at my team of lawyers, board members, and Marisol.

Attention was on me, as always.

"I think it's time we discuss our California field team."

Chapter Thirty-five

Elise

"She's a seven at best." Simon puckered his lips.

"It's all smoke and mirrors. Without that red lipstick and all that hair, she'd be a solid four." Rebecca puckered her lips at Simon, both of them imitating Marisol the Beautiful, who'd been at Andes the past three days.

We were sitting outside in the plaza in front of the office. They were shit talking to make me feel better. It wasn't working, but I appreciated the effort.

"I don't care about her."

"Of course not." Rebecca's arm wrapped around my shoulders, and Simon squeezed my knee.

It was the truth. My heart had been decimated by Weston all on his own. Marisol hadn't been a factor, nor was she. If he went back to her, I felt sorry for her. To willingly be with a man incapable of choosing the woman he said he loved was a form of self-hatred.

I'd spent too many years hating myself to ever go back to that.

"Tell me more about Wyoming," Simon insisted.

"I'll tell you about it when I get back," I promised.

Last night, I'd been slipping into the kind of melancholy I hadn't experienced since I was a teenager. My limbs were heavy and achy, and when Saoirse tried to speak to me, her voice sounded like it was cutting through water.

That was when she decided we were going to her family's ranch in Wyoming for a long weekend. A change of scenery, fresh air, and cowboys were her answer for my heartbreak. I only agreed because once the weekend showed, Elliot would inevitably hunt me down. I'd been avoiding him too long, but explaining to him what had happened was the very last thing I wanted to do.

Weston could do that. He'd made this choice. He could tell my brother what he'd done.

"Just don't stay away forever," Rebecca pleaded. "I don't know if I can go back to the days when it was just me and Simon at lunch."

He threw a piece of bread at her. "You're an absolute slunt."

A laugh burst through the shards of glass in my chest. "A slunt? What is that?"

Rebecca covered his mouth with her hand. "Our dearest Simon just called me a slutty cunt. I've told him many, many times only Sam's allowed to call me that—and *only* during sexy times."

Another laugh. It felt like my sternum was cracking. "These are things we never needed to know about you and Sam."

She shot me a wry grin. "Sam is a filthy man. I hope you're happy for me."

Simon threw another piece of bread at her. "Shut up, wench."

She wagged her finger at him. "Now *that* you're allowed to call me."

While they bickered, three people exiting the Andes' building drew my attention. In the middle, walking stiff as a board, her chin held high, was Marisol. She was surrounded by two men, security guards. They were gripping her elbows, and every couple steps, she tried to jerk free of them.

"Oh shite," Simon muttered. "She's being escorted out of the motherflipping building."

"What in the world...?" Rebecca cut herself off, obviously as fascinated by the scene unfolding in front of us.

"I don't know what's going on," I whispered.

As they got closer, Marisol's protests carried across the plaza. "Stop touching me like I'm some kind of criminal. I'll have you arrested for assault. This is inhumane."

The security guards remained silent. They'd probably heard all this before.

"Where is Weston Aldrich? When he finds out you've treated me this way, you'll lose your pathetic rent-a-cop jobs."

"Ma'am, as we told you already, our orders came directly from Mr. Aldrich," one of them informed her.

Simon was practically vibrating beside me, but he was quiet as a mouse, not missing a single word.

"This is absolutely ludicrous, and I refuse to believe a word you say. I need to speak to Weston. I demand it." Marisol tugged her elbow free and tried to spin back around toward the building, but she was stopped before she took a step.

"Ma'am, if you don't leave Andes' property, we'll have to call the police. If Mr. Aldrich wants to talk to you, I'm sure he'll be in touch."

The threat of arrest finally made her stop fighting. A car pulled up to the curb, and the guards helped her into it. They stood there, waiting until the car had driven away before retreating into the building.

Rebecca blew out a heavy breath. "Wow. I'm going to need to know what that was all about, stat."

My stomach was a mess of writhing worms. I pressed down on it and swallowed hard.

"We'll read about it in the news," I uttered.

"Screw that, I'm heading inside. You know someone has the tea." Simon squeezed me in a side hug. "Would you like me to text you when I find out?"

I shook my head. "No. I don't need to know."

He sighed. "All right. Have a great time in Wyoming. Kiss a cowboy for me, love."

The thought of kissing anyone but Weston made me want to scream, but I smiled at Simon and promised to tell him all about my trip when I got back. Rebecca waited with me until Saoirse arrived to drive us to the airport, then she hugged me and told me everything would be okay.

I didn't believe that for a second, but at least I was getting out of there, giving in to my instinct to run far, far away from the source of my pain.

Hundreds of miles between me and Weston Aldrich.

It wasn't forever, but it was all I could give myself at the moment.

Chapter Thirty-six

Weston

I walked into Andes Thursday morning, and it felt like a hazy film had been wiped away.

The piece of information given to me by Elise had been the start of uncovering the nefarious, destructive conspiracy that had been going on right under my nose. Once that initial thread was pulled, it all came unraveling in a surprisingly swift and complete deluge.

The past three years, the lead of my California field team had been accepting bribes from Brian Lewis to falsify his inspection reports. He actually hadn't set foot in that factory in more than two years. Without oversight, Brian had been cutting corners to save money, illegally disposing of waste into the environment.

When my field team went to inspect Dominic Peters's factory during our negotiations, he'd been offered the same deal: cash in hand to look the other way, allowing Dominic to ignore our strict policies.

No doubt he would have accepted, but our negotiations had gone awry and Andes had contracted a third factory.

Dominic Peters proved to be the underhanded, duplicitous scumbag I had first appraised him as. When he didn't get our business, he decided to get even by going to the press.

Through all this, Marisol had been beside me, most likely shaking in her boots while playing the supportive friend. The fact of the matter was, she'd been in charge of the field teams on the West Coast and all this flying beneath her radar was impossible to believe.

My team scoured her computer, uncovered proof of her negligence, and she'd been escorted from the building, her access to both Andes and me revoked. The last acknowledgment she would ever receive from me was my signature on her letter of termination.

A lot of people's lives were going to be turned upside down, some ruined, but I couldn't help being relieved. Now that we knew exactly what we were dealing with, we had a path to recovery.

And now that the haze was gone, a sudden and acute sense of clarity washed over me.

I had made a massive mistake with Elise. I had been aware that I was, but I'd been on a single-minded mission to save Andes. I hadn't had the mental headspace to halt the ball I'd started rolling.

I got off on the seventh floor. Now wasn't the time to beg for her forgiveness, but I couldn't spend another day in my office without at least seeing her. Absent the haze that had been keeping me apart from everything but my goal, the pressure in my chest became intolerable.

Without Elise, I couldn't breathe properly.

She was my breath of fresh air. My body had become dependent on her. How could I have gone two weeks without breathing her in? It was inconceivable.

To my great fucking disappointment, Elise's desk was empty, her computer screen black. I was late arriving at the office. Most people were already working. *She* should have been working.

I strode around the floor, checking the break area and stairwell, not finding her. Eyes were on me, including Elise's friends, Rebecca and Simon, who were huddled together near the collab table. They straightened when I approached them, their whispered conversation cutting off abruptly.

"Hello," I greeted.

They mumbled greetings back, with none of the friendliness I was used to from them. But then, they were Elise's friends. They'd no doubt heard how badly I'd neglected her.

I cut to the chase.

"Do either of you know where Elise is?"

They exchanged glances. Rebecca blinked at me.

"I'm sorry, who?"

I cocked my head in confusion. I needed to sleep for about thirty hours to catch up on all I'd missed. Had I said the wrong name?

"Elise Levy. Do you know why she isn't at work?" I pressed.

Simon scratched his chin. "I wish I could help, but I really don't know who you're talking about."

I pointed at her empty desk. "Elise. The woman who sits at that desk every day. Where is she?"

Rebecca tossed her hair over her shoulder. "I really don't understand what you're saying." She turned to Simon. "Do you?"

He shrugged. "Not a single clue."

Understanding dawned on me. Violence rose in my blood. They were giving me the same treatment Patrick had been given by Elise's friends in Chicago.

"That's enough," I bit out. "I'd like you both to remember who you work for. I won't be disrespected in my own company."

Rebecca lifted her chin. "I don't think it's appropriate to threaten your employees because they won't discuss their coworker."

Simon linked arms with her. "I agree. If there's nothing else, we're busy."

They walked away from me without another word. But then, there was nothing left to say. I shouldn't have been in a position to beg my employees to tell me where my girlfriend was.

And yet...

Where the hell was she?

Once I was in my office, I asked Renata to check with Elise's direct boss, Salma. She reported back that Elise had taken two days off and would be back Monday. She did *not* tell me where she was.

I spent the rest of the day fucking *floundering*. My concentration was shot, and the pressure in my chest only mounted as the hours slipped by.

It wasn't as if I had nothing to do. It was that I couldn't bring myself to care anymore, not now that I'd fully wrapped my head around the bomb I'd dropped on my own life.

I went through the motions to get through the day. As listless as I was, and as badly as I ached to tear out of here and hunt Elise down, there were still calls and meetings that required my presence, if not full attention.

By the time I walked into my apartment that evening, my chest felt like there was a herd of elephants stomping on it. I kicked off my shoes, leaving them where they landed, and yanked the tie loose from my throat.

Miles was at my dining room table, a few take-out containers scattered around. His mouth fell open in surprise when I sank down into the chair across from him.

"You're home early," he muttered around a mouthful of lo mein.

"Where is she?"

He swallowed hard and wiped his mouth with a paper napkin. "Now you're asking?"

My fingers flexed on the table. He knew. "Tell me where she is."

"Have you bothered calling her? Asking her yourself?"

I swiped my phone awake and slid it across the table. He picked it up, squinting at the chain of unanswered texts, then put the phone face down and slid it back.

"She isn't around." He met my eyes with a hard glare. "That's all you're getting from me. If she wanted you to know where she was, she would have told you. I guess since you broke up with her—"

I slapped the table, black shrouding the corners of my vision. "I didn't break up with her. Goddammit, I would never break up with her. I couldn't—"

"You ignored her for almost two weeks, Weston. You don't have to say the words 'I'm dumping you' for it to be true. You withdrew from the relationship, and since a relationship requires two people for it to exist, I'd say yours is over."

I shot up from my chair, shoving my fingers through my hair. "Fuck, fuck, fuck. That's not—"

"Don't say it isn't what you meant to do. You made a choice, and that was to give everything to your company. Own that shit, Westie. That's who you are."

I opened my mouth to explain what had been going on but fuck that. Miles worked there. He had to be well aware.

"I had to give everything to Andes. There was no other option."

He shrugged. "All right. Well, as someone who's never been in a serious relationship, I'm not going to sit here and dole out advice."

I heaved a sardonic laugh. "Thanks for that."

He held up his hand. "But from a layman's perspective, you're a complete piece of shit."

"You have no idea what you're talking about."

"Maybe." He balled up his napkin and tossed it on his plate. "But I do know I've been staying here a while, and I saw you going to bed every night alone. How many nights did you spend alone before all this went down? I'm guessing none. I'm guessing you were with Elise, then suddenly, boom, something big happens and you won't have anything to do with her."

"I *told* her I couldn't have distractions—"

Miles winced. "Yeah, again, I'm no expert, but calling your girlfriend a distraction is not the vibe. And you know what? I'm glad she's not around. If this was your plan of approach, you would have failed miserably. *I* want to dump you, and you know, I'm not your girlfriend."

"Why are you here?" I rammed the heel of my hand into my forehead. "Don't you have somewhere else to be? I said a week. It's been a hell of a lot more than that."

"I didn't think you noticed." He got up from the table, gathering his dishes. "Don't worry, I'll be gone soon. Then you can be all alone with the love of your life, Andes."

Two weeks of frustration and all of the anger I'd been tamping down swelled until I couldn't stop myself from exploding. One second, I was pacing behind the dining room table. The next, I had my brother shoved against the wall, my fist reared back to slam into his face.

His eyes locked with mine, and he raised his chin as if to give me a clearer target.

"Shut up," I hissed. "Why do you always have to talk? You don't know anything."

"I know what I'm seeing. You're screwing up, and for what? What, Weston?"

I leaned into him, pressing him hard into the wall. "What would you have me do? Let my company fail and end up like Dad, a lazy drunk who doesn't care about anyone but himself? Would that be better?"

"Is that your only choice? One extreme or the other? You end up alone either way." He pushed me off him and backed away, his hands up in defense. "For being an asshole and laying your hands on me, you can clean up the mess you made me make. I'm going to my room."

His dishes and food were scattered all over the floor. I stared at them blankly, Miles's parting shot rattling around my head.

You end up alone either way.

You end up alone either way.

You end up alone either way.

I got out the broom to sweep up the noodles and rice and acknowledged Miles was right. In my efforts to be nothing like my father, I'd become just as destructive as he was.

Now what?

I could crawl to Elise and beg for her forgiveness, but my hands were empty, and my promises meant nothing anymore since I'd already broken the ones I'd sworn I never would.

It eviscerated me to even think it, but how could I not wonder if Elise was better off without me in her life?

She deserved someone who would be able to always choose her.

Maybe my absence was a favor to her.

None of those thoughts sat right with me, but that didn't make them any less true.

It had been a while since I'd made it to a gym session. Friday morning, I finally had the time. When I walked in, Luca jerked with surprise. I nodded to him, continuing toward the weights, where Elliot was lifting.

He watched me approach in the mirror. Expression unreadable, his muscles flexed as he curled a dumbbell to his chest.

"Hey," I greeted him. "How are you?"

He dropped the weight in the rack and walked away without a word. My head fell forward, shame heavy on my shoulders.

He was pissed, and rightfully so.

I'd hurt his little sister. If I were him, I'd tear me apart.

Luca sidled up beside me. Leaning his back against the mirrored wall, he watched as I picked up a weight.

He lifted his chin. "You dig yourself out of your hole?"

"For now." My eyes slid to him. "It's been a hell of a time."

"I wouldn't know since I don't read the newspaper."

"You're in line to take over a multibillion-dollar company. You should, at the very least, read the financial section."

He folded his arms and made a chuffing sound. "Right. Good advice. I was referring to the fact that I haven't heard a word from you. Radio silence for two weeks is absolute bullshit."

I dropped the weight back in the rack. "I'm sorry if your feelings were hurt—"

"My feelings aren't hurt. I'm used to you dropping off the face of the earth to tend to your priorities. I count myself lucky I don't depend on you for any type of emotional support because I would have been waving like a flag in the wind. The thing is, *I* would have been there for you. You know that, right?"

I cupped my nape and heaved a sigh. "Thank you. I do know that. I wasn't thinking about seeking support while I was in the middle of it. Now that we're starting to come out on the other side—"

"You finally remember the rest of us?" He shook his head. "Elliot's categorically displeased with you."

We both looked across the gym. Elliot was running full out on a treadmill. His fierce expression and the tightness in his shoulders most likely had nothing to do with how hard he was pushing himself.

"What does he know?"

"That you broke up with Elise—"

"I didn't break up with her." Miles's words vaulted to the front of my thoughts. I had withdrawn. There was no denying that. "We didn't end things officially. I don't want to end things."

"Wow." He turned his head, his gaze unfocused. "For a smart, successful man, you really are a bumbling fool. You dumped her and broke her fucking heart. Have you even faced that?"

My heart hammered against my ribs. This wasn't anger, though. A wave of panic mixed with helplessness slammed into me.

"That wasn't my intention. I didn't think—"

"No, I know what you were thinking about."

He didn't say it, but we both knew where my thoughts had lain.

"I don't know how to be any different." That was the stark, raw truth. This had been my entire identity for so long, changing was incredibly fucking daunting.

But the alternative, losing Elise forever, was unacceptable.

And I might have already done that.

"Then you need to figure it out. At this point, you haven't only lost Elise. Where she goes, Elliot goes too."

With that parting shot, Luca sauntered off, heading toward the treadmills.

I had a lot to think about. Serious changes to make if I wanted a chance at making things right with Elise. And Elliot, for that matter.

What Marisol said to me when she rejected my marriage idea had been laughable then, but now it struck a powerful chord. I was proud and loved what I'd built with Andes, but compared to my love for Elise, one didn't come close to touching the other.

It was Elise. It had always been Elise.

I still wasn't convinced I was good enough for her, but I was certain if I lost every other thing in my life and only had her, I would have absolutely everything.

I had a lot of work to do. Luckily, work was the one thing I was good at.

Chapter Thirty-Seven

Elise

Going to Wyoming had been the right decision.

I still felt like a vital part of me had wilted, but while I was there, I didn't have time to concentrate on the loss. The ranch wasn't only a ranch, it was a luxury resort. So when Saoirse and I weren't brushing horses and cooing over newborn calves, we were getting massages and spa treatments. Then we visited with her brother, Lock, and his wife, Elena. They had two kids who were all over the place, entertaining and sassy.

The dread only returned when we touched down in Denver.

That part of me was still wilted. My heart ached so badly I kept touching my chest, expecting it to be tender, but this ache was deep down.

I told myself at least the worst was over. I couldn't be rejected again. It had already happened.

Now, I was about getting on with my life.

I had no choice.

Rebecca greeted me with her signature flair when I passed by her reception desk. I'd brought her back a postcard of cowboys wearing nothing but boots, covering their dicks with their hats. She told me it was going on the front of her refrigerator so Sam would pick up on her newfound cowboy kink and invest in some chaps.

I stupidly thought everything was going to be okay, but when I sat down at my desk, I was proven wrong.

A single Post-it.

As harmless as those fluffy white caterpillars with toxic pin-cushion hair.

I shoved it with my pen. I did not want the thing on my desk.

But it wasn't budging, and my eyes weren't avoiding the neatly written black print standing out in stark relief on the square of yellow paper.

A study showed that couples' heartbeats synchronize
when they're together.
No wonder I'm out of sync without you.
I love you.

What the hell was this?

Tears sprung to my eyes. My teeth dug into my bottom lip to keep them from spilling over.

I crumpled up the note and tossed it in the trash. But having it in the small can under my desk was too close, so I picked up the whole thing, carried it to the break room, and dumped my trash into the bin there. Then I strode back to my desk and turned on my computer.

My hands were trembling as I typed out an email response to that utter nonsense.

To: <u>westonaldrich@andesinc.com</u>

From: <u>eliselevy@andesinc.com</u>

Weston,

Please refrain from leaving anything on my desk unless it pertains to Andes. It's incredibly unprofessional to bring personal matters to the office. You have the luxury of an office where you can hide your reactions. I am sitting in the middle of my coworkers, forced to read a *love note* from the man, my boss, who effectively gutted me.

This is not fair, and if it continues, working at Andes will be untenable for me.

- Elise

I stared at the email for several minutes, my stomach churning madly. Then I took a deep breath and deleted it all. If I opened up contact between us, he'd take it as permission to continue, and I didn't want that.

I had no idea what Weston was doing now. He'd made it abundantly clear he couldn't be in a relationship with me. I truly had thought that would be the end of everything. But while I was in Wyoming, he'd texted me nonstop. Saoirse had eventually taken my phone from me.

All these thoughts would be saved for later, when I was home with a glass of wine and Saoirse to yell our frustrations to the universe. Another deep breath and I tucked it all away.

Everything was going well until noon. My stomach growled, notifying me it was time to grab Simon and Rebecca for lunch. Before I could shut down my computer or make any move, the distant ding of the elevator shot like a bullet to the part of my brain that told me it was time for *flight*.

Moments later, Weston Aldrich strode through the creative floor. His long, lean legs carried him toward me so swiftly I hadn't been able to brace myself for his presence.

He stopped in front of my desk, his fingertips pressing on the edge.

"Hello, Elise."

I blinked up at him, focusing somewhere over his shoulder. "Hello."

"I was wondering if you'd join me for lunch today."

He might as well have slapped me for how violently I flinched. "What?" I wheezed.

"I'd like to have lunch with you. Will you join me? I made reservations—"

I shook my head. "No, thank you. I'm not interested."

He went still, the tips of his fingers turning white from how hard he leaned on them.

"Please."

His forceful plea was what did it. Finally, I forced my eyes to his. It was a mistake. My agony reflected back at me, which didn't make any sense. He had chosen this. Why was he here, acting like this was just as torturous for him as it was for me?

I could have thrown what he'd said to me when I'd tried to bring him lunch back at him. I could have been cruel and mean, telling him he'd wasted his time coming here and should have just called.

But I'd never allow myself to lash out because I was hurting. Elaine had worn her pain like porcupine needles. Becoming my mother was my worst nightmare. Weston wasn't going to turn me into her.

"Are you looking for closure? I've told you my opinion on that." I gestured back and forth between us. "What you're doing now is only prolonging the process of moving on. We don't need to see each other. I don't want to."

He pressed his palms flat on my desk and bent forward, his voice low and urgent. "No one is moving on, Elise."

My breath hitched, but I held strong. "This is inappropriate."

"Come with me."

"No."

He shuddered. His shoulders shook, and his eyes squeezed closed for a few seconds. I understood that feeling. I'd had it for weeks now.

"Tonight, then."

I stayed firm, even as his pleas sliced through me like the sharpest blade.

"No, Weston."

He opened his mouth to speak, to beg, I guessed, but Simon and Rebecca crowded in next to him, and Simon actually nudged Weston's side with his elbow.

"Read to go, Lise?" Rebecca chirped.

"Lunch is on me today, love," Simon added.

I grabbed my phone, leaving everything else behind, and vaulted up from my chair. "I'm ready."

I left Weston standing by my desk, but not before I caught his bereft expression.

What was he doing? And why now, after everything?

—◆—

Two bouquets of pink flowers waited for me at home.

I frowned at them, then at Saoirse. "Two? Really?"

"Actually"—she plucked the card from the smaller bouquet—"this one is mine. It says, '*To Saoirse. Thanks for taking care of my girl when I didn't. I heard you like flowers too. Enjoy.*' So, yeah. Weston's trying to win me to his side."

"Are there sides?"

She shrugged. "I guess that's up to you. Does he feel like your enemy now?"

"I feel like he's a stranger." I squinted at the flowers, which were too pretty for me to throw away. "I'm not reading the card."

"Do you want me to read it?"

"No. Yes." She reached for the card. I grabbed her arm, stopping her. "No. I don't want anymore 'I love yous' from him. They don't mean anything."

"They mean something."

I narrowed my eyes at her. "One bouquet and you're on his side?"

"I thought there were no sides."

I had to laugh. "I don't even understand what's happening right now. Why is he sending us flowers?"

She raised a shoulder. "The only way you'll find that out is if you talk to him. Don't you want to at least tell him what you think of him?"

"I don't, no. That won't do anything for me besides pick at wounds. I just want this to all be over."

My bottom lip started to quiver, and a wave of despondency swept me under. I'd had time to get used to it, but there were still instances where I couldn't wrap my head around our ending. This was one of those times. I hoped it was a terrible dream and I'd wake beside Weston. He'd hold me and assure me he'd never choose anything over me.

That wasn't happening. He'd already done the choosing.

Chapter Thirty-Eight

Elise

WESTON WAS EVERYWHERE.

He left another Post-it on my desk. This one equally gut-wrenching.

Baader-Meinhof phenomenon is a frequency illusion in which something you notice for the first time starts to "appear" everywhere.

I'm under no illusions about you. From the moment I fell, you are all I see.

That would have been bad enough, but Weston was nothing if not dedicated to his pursuits. I supposed since Andes was crawling out of its crisis, he now had time to pursue me, setting himself up at the collaboration table, which happened to be across from my desk.

He'd greeted me when I'd walked in, watched me read his note, and flinched when I ripped it up and tossed it in the break area trash can.

At lunchtime, he approached my desk and spoke in a low, private tone. "Will you have lunch with me today?"

My fingers didn't pause on my keyboard. My monitor had never been so interesting.

"No."

"Please."

"The answer isn't going to change."

"Don't you think we should have a conversation?"

"No."

I had never been more aware of my surroundings. Weston and I hadn't been out loud about our relationship, but he hadn't kept it a secret either. For the most part, my coworkers had an idea we had been together. Now, they were all getting to watch the aftermath play out.

"Elise. You can't—"

"I can." Finally, I flicked my eyes to him. I wouldn't meet his gaze, but I gave him a long look. He was wearing the navy-blue suit I'd once told him was my favorite. There was not a chance that was by accident. Weston was too deliberate.

He scrubbed at the thick scruff on his jaw. "You're ghosting me. That's what this is. You said you wouldn't do this."

I sucked in a sharp breath at his accusation. He didn't get to say that to me. He wasn't the one who'd been wronged here. I'd reacted to his actions.

"You ghosted me first, Weston."

I pushed back from my desk and walked right by him. There was no way I could stay. As I rode the elevator down to the cafeteria, I considered I might not get to stay at Andes at all if Weston didn't back off. I'd take my dead-end job back in Chicago over *this*.

Weston had cleared out by the time I'd made it back to seven, but he'd left me something behind: a dill pickle spear in plastic wrap with a note that said, "*This came with my lunch. Don't let it go to waste. Talk soon. I love you.*"

I ate the freaking pickle.

Then I had to hide in the bathroom to have a cry.

It wasn't just a pickle I was crying over. It was the reminder of our history. He'd been giving me his pickles forever. Weston had been part of my life for so long, the prospect of truly cutting ties with him overwhelmed me with sorrow.

I wavered in those moments. Would it have been so bad to listen to him? He was clearly sorry. If he said the right words, I could take him back, and this wretched emptiness in me would be filled with him.

But what happened next time Andes needed him? How could I go through this again?

The answer was easy. I couldn't.

I dried my tears and went back to my desk, newly resolved to continue working to get over Weston Aldrich.

⸺⬦⸺

He wasn't making it easy. Weston worked at the collab table for at least part of the next few days, asking me to lunch each day and leaving me love notes. More flowers were delivered at home. He pleaded for a conversation.

I told him no. I ripped up his notes, shoved his flowers into Saoirse's room. Each time he came to me, the stone thickened around my heart. I had to do it. If I didn't protect myself, he would have gotten to me. When it came to Weston, I wasn't strong.

Thursday, when I returned to my desk, there was a gift bag waiting for me. Shifting the tissue paper aside, I peeked at the contents and frowned.

An empty jar.

Okay. Confusing.

I sat down in my chair to read the note he'd left with it.

There is a shelf where I keep the jars with their hearts. I always take the hearts. Leaving them behind to rot seems wrong, somehow.

My morals are my own. Don't judge me.

Earlier, I gave her her own jar. She asked me why. I told her to put it on a shelf. Anytime she wants, she can pluck my heart from my chest and put it in her jar. My heart is hers, after all.

It slowly dawned on me where these words had come from: the book I'd been reading when Weston and I had flown home from our trip.

It had been a dark romance about a serial killer who had fallen in love for the first time. I'd swooned when he'd told her his heart was hers.

But how had Weston known?

A warm breath touched my ear a beat before he spoke. "If those crazy people get a happy ending, we should too."

He pulled back after whispering in my ear and moved to my side, leaning over me to bring us face to face.

"Did you read my book?"

He nodded. "I want to know everything that's going on inside your head. That one was dark, baby."

"I don't—" He couldn't be sweet and considerate. It was too late for that. To pull out the big guns now, when we were finished, was unfair on every level. "I don't think you want to know what's going on inside my head right now, Weston."

Murder.

Death.

Kill.

Heartbreak.

"I do. Every angry, beat-up thought, I want it. How can I fix it if I don't know which parts to aim for?"

"You don't. Please go. I can't do this here."

If he didn't stop, I would cry, and one crying jag at work was enough for the ages.

"Okay." His fingers grazed my hair. "I love you, Elise."

I shuddered but kept my mouth clamped shut.

He tapped the lid of the jar. "My heart is yours, after all."

Then he sauntered away as if he hadn't just given me a jar to contain his heart. As if he wasn't continuing to wreck me every single day.

⸺◦⸺

I made it through the week. Barely. Friday rolled in like a lamb, gentle with Weston's conspicuous absence from the collaboration table.

There was a note, of course.

> *They say Plato invented the concept of soul mates.*
> *I say your parents invented mine.*

For some reason—a reason I wouldn't let myself dwell on—I couldn't bring myself to rip that one up. I shoved it in my drawer. Unfortunately, I couldn't shove it out of my mind.

Soul mate.

He thought I was his soul mate.

He knew I was the girl who read romance novels for the happy endings and believed in things like soul mates and happily ever afters. Calling me his soul mate was cruel. A direct hit to the thick wall surrounding my heart.

Miles stopped by when I was at my most vulnerable. Instead of perching on my desk, he pulled up a chair and plopped right beside me.

"How's it going, Lisie?"

"Your brother is torturing me. How are you?"

He laughed under his breath. "If it's any consolation, he's been climbing the walls all week."

"That doesn't console me. I don't want any of this."

"Yeah, I get it." He leaned his elbow on my desk. "You want to talk about something else?"

I turned away from my monitor. "Sure. What if you tell me how you're doing? Is your house ready to move into yet?"

"My house is a money pit. I don't know why I bought it. I'm not really a house person. It just seemed like something an upstanding grown-up would do."

"So sell it."

His brow dropped. "That didn't even sound judgy."

"It wasn't. Obviously, I'm no expert in real estate, but I'm a strong believer in cutting your losses when things aren't working."

He huffed. "That's your one personality flaw."

"What?"

"Cutting and running. You peace out when things go south instead of fighting. It's funny because I used to think you were braver than anyone I knew. Now I'm realizing you're just as afraid as the rest of us."

I swallowed back the lump in my throat. Miles really could aim right for my most tender parts, even after all these years. This time, I was pretty certain he wasn't even trying to hurt me.

"I never said I was brave." Oh, great. Even my voice betrayed me, coming out thick and raspy.

"Shit." He took my hand in his. "I'm sorry. I still think you're rad, Lisie. I'm just saying it's a relief to know you're fallible."

I let him hold my hand, which said a lot about my shaky emotional state.

"What you're saying is you think I'm messing up by leaving Weston even though he left me first."

His thumb stroked along my knuckles. "I'm not saying any of that. I'm surprised you won't speak to him. That seems like fear to me, but what do I know?"

I leaned closer to him to whisper. "I am afraid, Miles. If I could find a way to forgive him, how could I possibly trust he would never do this to me again? Sometimes acting on fear is a good thing. Nature gave us fear to protect ourselves from danger."

"You make sound points. There's also something to be said for conquering your fears. We wouldn't have fire if a couple cavemen hadn't conquered their fear of burning alive. Would you rather be living in the dark, Lisie? I wouldn't."

I pulled back, giving myself some space. "I thought we were supposed to be talking about you."

He lifted a shoulder. "Can't blame me that my thoughts keep coming back to my favorite couple."

I rolled my eyes. "Let's talk about why you think you need to own real estate and conform to some grown-up mode. What's that about?"

The corners of his mouth lifted into a smirk. "You get to psycho-analyze me now?"

I mimicked his shrug. "What's fair is fair."

"No, Lisie, you don't have the time for all my neuroses. Let's leave it at growing up with a loser father and an overachieving brother shaped me into a lazy yet ambitious amalgamation of a man."

At the quiet chirp of my email notification, I reached for my mouse in an automatic response, glancing away from Miles to check if the message was something I needed to deal with urgently. The address made the blood drain from my face.

"Oh shit. Is that your ex?" Miles leaned into me, his chest pressing against my shoulder. "What's he want?"

"I have no idea."

The subject line said *my explanation*. Apparently, Patrick wanted to explain himself, and since I'd blocked him everywhere else, he'd found my work email.

"Click on it. Let's see what the idiot has to say."

I elbowed him. "Go away."

He tugged on my arm, spinning me toward him. "Hey, I'm kidding."

I stared at Patrick's name on my screen. This had to be a joke. I'd spent the week dodging Weston, and now my other ex was invading my space. When did it end?

"I know." I cupped my forehead. "I don't understand why he sent this."

"I guess you won't know until you read it."

I slid my eyes to him. He was watching me warily. "What if the reason he hurt me doesn't matter anymore?"

"Doesn't it?"

My lips were so dry licking them didn't help. "I don't know."

Eventually, Miles left me to my thoughts. Patrick's email sat in my inbox like a land mine. If I clicked it, it could end up being inert...or it could blow up in my face.

I forced myself to stop thinking about it for the rest of the day. But as five o'clock drew near, I ended up staring at my inbox again, this time with resolve.

Squeezing my eyes shut, I clicked.

CHAPTER THIRTY-NINE

To: WESTONALDRICH@ANDESINC.COM

From: eliselevy@andesinc.com

Weston,

If you have time, I would like to talk. Meet me on the roof at six tonight? If that doesn't work, please let me know when will.

-Elise

I had almost missed it. I'd been in the process of packing up for the day and something had told me to check my inbox one last time.

There it was.

Elise was going to give me an opportunity to speak to her after stonewalling me for over a week. Not that I didn't understand why she'd done it. She had every right to lock herself away from me. That didn't mean I hadn't been utterly bereft without her.

I made it to our building's rooftop fifteen minutes early. She arrived on time, and I rose from the chair I'd taken at the same table we'd sat around on her birthday. Her gaze landed somewhere around my shoulder. Mine roved everywhere, greedy for her.

She'd changed into a Chicago T-shirt, and I couldn't help but feel like it was a subtle threat. She'd moved across the country once before, she could do it again. Chances were, she'd picked the first T-shirt available and I was overthinking things, but this was what I'd become.

A madman for her.

"I brought you a beer." I gestured to the sweating bottle on the table. "If you want it."

"Sure. Thanks." She slipped into her chair at the end of the table. I reclaimed my chair to her right. Our knees touched when I scooted in. She moved hers away.

Her thumbnail dug into the label on her bottle. I held mine between both my hands, spinning it in slow, tight circles.

My pulse skittered in erratic waves from the panic and fear coursing through me.

"How are you?" I asked.

She huffed softly. "It's been a long week."

"Long few weeks."

"Yes." She glanced up from her beer, still not making eye contact. "Andes is...going to be okay?"

There were dark smudges beneath her eyes. Twins to the ones beneath mine. She looked beautiful, stunning even, but sad. So damn sad. I'd done that to her. I'd sucked the sunshine out of her, leaving her cold and dim.

"Yes. A lot is still happening behind the scenes, but the EPA investigation is being dropped, which is a massive relief." There was a lot more to it than that, but I wasn't about to waste this time with Elise by talking about Andes.

"That's really good." She tucked her hair behind her ear and exhaled. "I got an email from Patrick today."

I went still. "Did you? What did he have to say?"

"I don't know. I decided not to read it."

"Yeah?"

I had no clue what I was supposed to say here. My first instinct was to call IT and have them block Patrick from our servers. My second was to break into her inbox and read what that khaki-wearing motherfucker dared to send to *my* girl.

I ended up deciding to be quiet and let her speak.

"I was thinking about what Miles said on my birthday when you asked him why he'd bullied me. He said sometimes there isn't a good reason for the bad shit people do and wind up regretting. And as I was considering reading Patrick's email, I realized there was no explanation he could offer that would make more sense to me than the one Miles gave. I don't *need* an explanation from him. It won't make a difference to how I feel about what he did."

The label on her bottle had been nearly picked off. Mine was almost empty, bitterness coating my tongue.

Before Elise, I'd never thought of myself as a jealous man. I now understood it was because I'd never been with a woman I belonged to the way I did to her. I was hers, which meant she was also mine. My mind would not accept anything less. So, hearing about Patrick, and even my brother, was nails on a chalkboard.

These thoughts were irrational, and they were mine to deal with. I was in no position to command her to scrub every man she'd ever met from her memory. Though, in a perfect world, that was what I'd do.

None of the thoughts streaking around my skull would convince Elise I was a man she could take another chance on, even though I was. The one thing I was one-hundred-percent certain of was: I would always choose Elise.

And it was her time to speak and mine to listen.

She had more to say.

I angled forward, stealing a few inches of the space she'd put between us.

She sucked in a ragged breath.

"But I need an explanation from you, Weston. I want you to tell me how you were able to push me aside. How did you feel when you ordered Renata to bar me from your office two minutes after I'd been inside it? What were you thinking when you flew to California without telling me you were going? Did you know you were leaving me when you crept into my bed in the middle of the night and fucked me? I want you to explain that to me because I don't understand how you were able to do any of it."

The angry flush in her cheeks was visible in the low evening light. It jabbed at my chest so hard I folded forward, bracing my palms on the table.

She was giving me the floor to explain, but I didn't know where to start. How could I possibly give reasons for all the ways I'd hurt her? There was no denying I had done those things, and there was no prettying them up.

"I never meant to leave you, Elise. Not when I came to you that night, not ever."

A divot carved between her brows. "But you did."

I wanted to fight her on that, but she was right. Intentional or not, I *had* left her.

"I did. I pulled back from you. It wasn't something I decided to do, but that doesn't change the fact that I did it. Before you, I've never prioritized anyone above Andes, nor have I wanted to."

A shudder racked through her body. "Believe me, I know."

"I know you do, baby. It kills me that you know." I rubbed the spot between my brows, gathering my thoughts. "That day you brought me lunch, the second I saw you, all I wanted to do was fall into you. I'd been holding steady by keeping my distance, but it's impossible for me to think about anything else when you're in front of me."

"Yet you sent me away."

"I was holding on by the skin of my teeth, Elise. My company was crumbling around me, and when you walked into my office, I didn't give a shit about anything but you. That couldn't be an option for me at that time. I *had* to give a shit. That was why I asked Renata for no visitors. Not because I didn't want to see you. It was because seeing you was all I wanted."

She slammed her bottle down on the table. "Then you should have said that. You should have told me what you were feeling. If you'd said, 'Elise, I love you so much that you drive me to distraction when you're around, so I have to stay away from you while I handle this crisis,' I would have been patient. If you'd said *anything*, I would have supported you. That's what you do in a relationship. But not you. That's not what you did. You dropped out of my world without a single warning. You flew to California with *her*—"

"She's nothing to me. I don't know how to make you understand that." I raked my fingers through my hair, tamping down the frustration in my veins.

"How did you feel when you found out I'd left town? Did you wonder if I'd gone to Patrick even though I've told you over and over my feelings for him are long gone?"

My hand dropped heavily to my side. Her eyes were finally on mine, shining but steady. The challenge was crystal clear. She had me.

"I felt like I was being ripped apart. No one would tell me where you were. I still don't know."

It was on the tip of my tongue to ask if she *had* gone to him, but I bit the urge back. She hadn't gone to him. I knew that. But when it came to Elise, logic and reason flew out the window.

"Then you might have an inkling of how I felt when I'd knocked on your door only for Miles to inform me you'd left the state without a word to me. He pitied me, Weston. Your brother felt sorry for me because of how poorly you treated me."

Another jab. I deserved every one. Before I'd walked out onto this roof, I had known I'd royally blown it, but seeing my beautiful girl like this, miserable in her righteous anger, showed me this was far worse than I'd let myself acknowledge.

"I'm sorry."

"It's too late."

"I love you, Elise. I fucked up. I know that. I tried to fit you in around Andes, but I should have been fitting Andes in around you."

Her head jerked back with what I could tell was surprise at my blunt honesty.

"That's exactly what you did. Your company is the love of your life. I could never compete with that, and I shouldn't have to."

"That's unequivocally untrue. You're the love of my life."

She turned away, the shake of her head telling me she didn't believe me. I'd done nothing to *make* her believe me, so that made sense.

"When I was eleven, my dad got bored with his life of fucking around, so he bought out a Denver-based camping supply company. It wasn't a huge business, not on the scale of Andes, but they employed a few hundred people. Within a year"—I snapped my fingers—"my father grew bored of being in charge and having responsibilities. He broke the company apart and essentially sold it for scraps. All those people lost their jobs and a decent business disappeared almost overnight. I watched it all as a kid and promised myself I'd make up for it. I'd build something here and never be anything like my father."

Her mouth had flattened into a hard line. When she finally looked at me again, her dark eyes were made of stone.

"I don't want to hear about Andes anymore."

"Elise—"

"Should I tell you about all the times my mother let me down? Should I bring up my dead father? My fear of abandonment? Your story about your dad explains your obsession with your company, but *mine* explains why I will never be able to allow myself to be chosen second."

"You'll never be chosen second again." I reached for her hands, but she yanked them back, cradling them to her chest, protecting herself.

From me.

"I love you, Elise. I love you more than Andes. I have missed you like an amputated limb. None of this makes sense without you."

"We've had this conversation before, Weston. You made me promises after the gala that you broke so easily. Why would I believe anything has changed?"

I felt it. The ephemeral hold I had on her was slipping away. All the hope I'd been pinning on this one conversation was hanging in mocking tatters. But I'd been stupid to think a conversation would fix weeks of neglect and unfulfilled promises.

"Because I lost you." Staggering to my feet, I backed away from the table, no idea where I was going. If I sat still for another second, I'd explode. "I lost you, and I can't *breathe*. I've never cared at the end. Not once. But I know I'll follow you to the ends of the earth. There's no one else for me."

Her only reaction was to stare at me, slowly blinking, picking at the last scraps of label on her full beer bottle. With her chin tipped, the hanging twinkling lights glinted off her face. The sorrow pulling at the corners of her mouth and the redness outlining her eyes shattered me. Fury aimed at myself, at my actions, ignited at the base of my spine. My bottle exploded on the ground before I even realized I'd thrown it.

Elise jumped, whimpering with fear. Then she was on her feet, tripping backward to get away from me.

"Tell me you've stopped loving me," I pleaded, following her footstep for footstep.

She shook her head. "Don't."

"I know you love me. You wouldn't have asked me to meet you if you didn't."

"It doesn't matter. I *can't* love you.

"It does matter. That's all that matters."

I had closed the distance between us in a second, winding my arms around her in a breath. Cradling her head in my palm, I buried my nose in her hair and breathed for the first time in weeks. She mewled but didn't push me away. She was limp in my arms, letting me hold her, but making no move to hold me back.

I was losing again, and I had no idea how to stop it from happening.

"I love you." I kissed her silky hair. "I love you the most."

"Stop it," she whispered.

"I know you don't want me to talk about Andes anymore"—she stiffened when I said it. God, how I'd messed up—"but there are steps I've taken this week to ensure nothing like this will ever happen again. Concrete, measurable changes. If you don't want to hear them now, I'll email you what I've done and you can read it when you're ready."

"I don't think I'll ever be ready."

"Then I'll be waiting forever." My lips lingered at her temple. "I love you, baby. You are my destination. It's why I came to you in the middle of the night and why I'll keep coming back, even if you push me away."

Finally, her arms moved. She grasped my shirt, her nails clawing my back as she clung to me. I held her tighter, her soft body sinking into me.

"I don't know if I can believe you, Weston."

I nodded against her hair. "I know. But I'm going to keep coming until you do."

"You should let me go."

"I can't."

She allowed me to hold her as she trembled. There was a chance this would be the last time I got to do this. We both knew it, but neither of us spoke it.

"If I could go back to that night, I would have told you everything," I murmured. "I would have let you in."

"I wish you had."

The sun was almost beyond the horizon when she stepped out of my arms and got on the elevator alone. I stayed on the roof to watch the stains of orange and pink fade to black.

Then I went back to the penthouse and into my office. I had an email to write and the love of my life to convince I was worth one more chance.

Chapter Forty

Luca and Elliot were already at the table when I arrived for brunch. Luca smacked a big kiss on my cheek, and Elliot hugged me tighter than usual.

I'd kept my distance from him, which hadn't been easy. If he had seen me at my darkest, he would have lost it. Elliot didn't care about many people, and I had always known for a fact I was his number one. He had moved heaven and earth to get me away from Patrick without asking a single question. I was afraid of what he would have done had he known all the ways Weston had rejected and hurt me, so I'd chosen to only tell him we'd broken up due to his work commitments.

When Elliot pulled away and cupped my face, there was evident strain around his searching eyes.

"How are you?" he asked.

"I'm okay."

A stretch of the truth, but if I told him I'd never been so brokenhearted and felt like sleeping for the next decade, he would have been...angry. Not at me but at the source of my despair. The last thing I wanted was to drive an even bigger wedge between my brother and Weston.

The empty fourth chair at the table was evidence enough of how drastically things had changed.

"I ordered you a coffee, *bella*." Luca nodded to the steaming cup in front of me.

"Bless you." I picked it up in both hands, sipping the smooth but strong drink.

"I thought you were bringing your roommate," Luca added.

I set my cup down, a small smile twitching on my lips. "She's impossible to pin down. Today, she's helping a friend she met in pottery class paint the walls of their new business."

Elliot grunted. "How many friends does she have?"

I laughed. Elliot had never understood Saoirse. "Everyone she meets is a new friend. I'm her only best friend, though."

If I had explicitly told her I wanted her to be here today, she would have ditched her new pottery friend in a heartbeat. I never doubted the meaning of my best friend title.

We ordered our food, and the topic moved on to Elliot's most recent trip to Singapore. He'd bought me a lariat-style necklace with a golden orchid hanging from it. It was an upgrade from his usual gifts, but I supposed he'd felt sorry for me and it was his way of cheering me up. The necklace was beautiful, and I put it on right away, but it did nothing to fill the hollowness in my chest.

Luca folded his hands on the table. "Elliot and I received an email from Weston this morning."

Elliot jerked. "We don't have to talk about this."

"What did it say?" I asked.

Elliot patted my arm. "It doesn't matter."

"It does. I want to know what it said."

Because there was an unread email from Weston in my inbox too. It had arrived last night, a few hours after I left the rooftop. I hadn't been able to bring myself to read it.

Luca's gaze dashed from Elliot to me. "He laid out the changes he's making within Andes executive management. It's pretty extensive. They're adding a new oversight branch that will report to the COO, not Weston."

Elliot folded his arms. "It's about time. He's run that company the same way since the beginning, when it was just him and Renata. He deals with the minutiae as if he's not the CEO."

"Why did he send that to you guys?" I glanced between them.

"He wanted our opinion on his plan," Elliot answered.

Luca's mouth hitched. "He asked if we thought it would be enough."

My brows rose. "Enough?"

Luca's half smile grew into a full-blown smirk. "To convince you it won't be the same this time."

"Is it enough?"

Luca answered first. "It's good. I never thought I'd see the day Weston was willing to give up some control over Andes."

Elliot picked up his coffee. "It makes sense if you think about it. Weston wasn't able to see the big picture because he was bogged down by the details. He missed things he shouldn't have. That's what led him here. It put his company in jeopardy, which he won't want to repeat."

Luca slapped his arm. "He would have kept doing the same thing. You know why he's restructuring. Don't pretend you don't."

Elliot brought his cup to his mouth. "I'll believe that when I see it."

"Have you spoken to him?" I asked.

"No, and I won't." He set his cup down and flicked lint off his sleeve.

"You won't?"

Elliot leveled me with a steady, blunt gaze. "No. He knew when he chose to be with my sister I would pick a side if it fell apart, and it wouldn't be his. A discussion won't solve anything. I would be surprised if he expects to have one."

Elliot never pulled punches, and I felt this one more than any other he'd lobbed at me. Weston and I had been so careless, falling in love and damning the consequences. And now, here I was, staring the consequences in the eye.

A lifetime of friendship could be thrown away.

"And if I forgive him?" I pressed.

"If he does something to prove to you he's worth forgiving, we'll be right." He angled forward suddenly. "I see your gears turning. You can't be in a relationship with him for my sake. That will never work."

"Obviously. I just wanted to know where your head is."

Luca chuckled. "Elliot would never admit it, but he's been off-kilter the past week. He actually walked out of the gym locker room dressed for work in a black suit with brown shoes."

I winced. "Elliot would never."

Luca's head bobbed. "He did."

Elliot turned, the hinge of his jaw jumping and ticcing. "I never said I was happy with the current circumstances."

Luca mouthed, "Off-kilter."

The topic moved on to safer pastures while *my* gears kept turning. Truthfully, they hadn't stopped since the roof. The way he'd looked at me, owning up to everything he'd done wrong, holding me like he couldn't stand another second apart, the email waiting in my inbox…

It wasn't only last night, though. All week, he'd been relentlessly present, which I was certain hadn't been easy for him considering everything going on.

Our waiter dropped our food off. I'd skipped breakfast and ordered a chicken salad sandwich. I went for the pickle first, and Luca chuckled.

I raised a brow.

He winked and watched me, amused.

"What's so funny?"

"You and your pickles."

Elliot almost smiled. "She's been a maniac for them since she was little. Our dad used to sacrifice his pickles to Elise every time we went somewhere and one was on his plate."

Luca tapped his chin. "I'd wondered why I'd caught Weston sliding you his pickle when we had lunch last month."

I shrugged. "He always has. He doesn't like them."

Luca chuffed, and Elliot stared at me, unblinking from across the table.

"What?"

"El." Elliot shook his head. "He watched Dad do it, and when Dad was gone, Weston took his place. That's why he always gives you his pickle."

"I—" I looked back and forth between them. Elliot had started eating as though he hadn't dropped a gigantic bomb on me. Luca was still watching me, something soft and sympathetic playing on his features. "I didn't know."

Luca reached over and squeezed my forearm. "He wouldn't have wanted you to know."

Because he had always loved me.

Not in the same way he did now, but Weston's love for me had been a presence in my life for as long as I could remember. Through my stone-cold bitch phase and his plethora through living in Chicago. Even now, I didn't doubt he still loved me.

Brunch went on for an interminably long time. I'd been looking forward to being with Elliot and Luca, but now, all I wanted to do was leave so I could roll what I'd just learned around in my mind.

And read the email.

When I was finally headed home in the back of my Uber, I took out my phone, scanning over Weston's plans for Andes. From my cursory, untrained glance, Weston wasn't playing around.

At the bottom, he'd written me another quote from my book.

"Lying in a pool of blood—my own, for once—it's her face I see. I'm not so lucky that she would actually be here. A hallucination is all a man like me can ask for. I reach for her. Her fingers are solid when I expected ephemeral.

"Are you real?"

She weaves our fingers together. "As real as you are."

"I'm dying."

"If you're dying, so am I. I refuse to let you go."

"You're the only reason I would stay."

"I should be dead already, but I'm nothing but a servant at her command. If she tells me to stay, I will. If she asks me to be a better man, I'll turn myself inside out to do it. There's nothing I would not tear the world and myself apart to give her. All she has to do is ask."

Those weren't Weston's words, but I wanted to believe he meant them.

As soon as the Uber stopped in front of my building, I bolted, running for the elevator. I had to see him, even though I wasn't quite sure what I would say.

At his door, I shoved my key in the lock without considering whether I should. Before we fell apart, I'd always let myself inside without knocking.

"Weston?" I called.

There were plates on the dining room table. I wrinkled my nose at the leftover food. It wasn't very like Weston to leave his table a mess, but then, I hadn't been myself lately either.

He wasn't in the living room. I started toward the hallway where the bedrooms were and heard noises. The TV? It didn't sound like it.

Two more steps down the hallway cleared up what I was hearing.

Animalistic moaning.

Guttural grunting.

"Harder. Please, more."

"Yeah, baby. That's right."

Blood drained from my face. My hopes pooled at my feet.

Oh god. He'd moved on. After everything he'd said about waiting forever, he hadn't even waited twenty-four hours.

I stumbled backward, somehow managing to steer myself toward the door.

We were over.
Really, truly over.

Chapter Forty-One

ALMOST BLIND FROM THE tears spilling in heavy waterfalls down my cheeks, I tore open the door...and ran smack into the man standing on the other side, his key poised in his hand.

"Elise?" Weston caught my arms, holding me steady. "What are you doing here? Are you crying?"

I sucked in a breath, not quite understanding what I was seeing. "How are you here?"

"I'm coming home from the office." His palms slid up my arms to cup my face. "Why are you crying, baby? What's wrong?"

I tried to explain. "I heard...I thought..." I swallowed hard. My stomach was a mess of panic mixed with utter relief. "I thought you were with someone else."

His head jerked. Astonishment flooded his features as if the suggestion was preposterous. "Why would you think that?"

"I heard..." I waved my arm toward the bedrooms. "I heard fucking."

Weston's gaze snapped in the direction I'd gestured to. "Miles," he hissed. "Stay here."

He stalked off, disappearing down the hallway. There was a loud slam followed by Weston bellowing Miles's name. Then he yelled something about burning the sheets.

He returned to me, red-faced and in a hurry. "Come on. I shut his door, so you won't have to see the horror I just did."

His hand closed around mine, and he pulled me to his bedroom, closing the door once we were inside.

"I was gone for three hours." He pressed on the door. His head dropped. "Three hours, and he found someone to fuck. Jesus. Can I kick him out yet?"

A little snort escaped me. I couldn't help it. Weston looked so disgusted I could only imagine he saw Miles's pasty ass pumping away.

His head shot up. "Is this funny to you? It's your fault he's here."

I sputtered another laugh, and Weston's shoulders fell, the tension in him bleeding away. The corner of his mouth hitched.

He closed the space between us and snagged me around the waist, tugging me against him. "You're here."

My hands flattened on his chest. "I'm here." Then a wave of madness came over me, so I pushed him. Like the stubborn brick wall he was, he didn't budge. "Why did you never tell me you like pickles? How could you have given me all your pickles when you like them? Why would you do that?"

I'd been laughing a moment ago, but now I was crying again. Weston had to be confused by my wild outburst, but he gathered me in his arms without question and held me through it.

"Baby." His lips were at my temple, fingers stroking my hair and back. "Who told you that?"

"Luca. And Elliot told me you started giving me your pickles when Dad died."

Warm breath fanned across my skin as he exhaled. "That's true. I'd give you anything, you know. Pickles are no big deal."

"It is a big deal. Why should you go without something when you like it? I would never knowingly take something you like away from you. Never."

He pulled back, and the look he gave me was devastating. "You took you away from me, and I more than like you."

"I didn't want to go."

He nodded, slow and heavy. "I know, baby. But you're here now."

"It was the pickles that did it."

His head cocked. "Not the hours and hours of planning that went into restructuring my executive team?"

My lips twitched. "That was a little bit of it."

"Are you...?" He held my face, stroking my chin and bottom lip with his thumbs. "Are you coming back?"

I kissed his thumb, and he went still. "You light me on fire, Weston."

His brow pinched. "I want that to be a good thing, but I'm not sure it is."

"You scare me. That's the truth. But your brother said a few things to me yesterday, and I can't really stop thinking about them."

"I'm not sure I want to hear anything Miles had to say."

"Well, it's part of why I'm here, so..."

"Ah, damn." He scowled at the door. "Will I have to thank him after this?"

Despite everything, Weston's innate grumpiness still made me laugh. "I don't know. Maybe."

"Come here." He pulled me over to his bed, sitting on the end of it, and tugged me down next to him. "Tell me, baby."

Weston's eyes were pinched and tired, but hope was dawning behind them. The scruff on his jaw was thicker than usual, and his hair was wild like he'd been yanking at it all day.

My heartstrings were being plucked hard, and the urge to skip this conversation so I could lean into him and tell him everything would be okay was almost overwhelming. But not talking had gotten us here, and I never wanted to be here again.

"Miles said if a couple brave cavemen hadn't conquered their fear of burning alive, we'd still be in the dark. I don't want to be in the dark, Weston. So, I have to get over being afraid of the way you light me on fire, because I want the light, and I want you." He opened his mouth to speak, but I pressed two fingers to his lips. "But this is it, you know? This has to be it. Don't take me back if you can't live up to your end of the deal."

"I'll live up to it," he swore, kissing my fingertips before taking my hand in his. "Plans are in motion. Change doesn't happen overnight, not for a company the size of Andes, but it's happening. It should have happened a long time ago, but I never had a reason. Work was my life."

"Impossible to compete with."

"There's no competition, Elise. My life now revolves around you and what we're going to build together. For a while, I lost sight of my goal. A long time ago, I vowed to be nothing like my father. To be better than him. That pushed me to build Andes and watch it flourish. But I don't only want to be better at business. I want to be a better man than him, to take care of my family and put them first. You're my family. You'll always come first."

"Weston—" This man, he knew exactly how to love me.

He took my chin between his fingers, tipping my face to his. "I don't want to live through the last few weeks again."

"It would kill me if I had to," I told him.

The look he gave me was filled with promise and determination. "I won't let that happen. I never want to live another second where you're not mine."

"I'm yours." Had I ever not been his in one form or another?

"We belong to each other, and I will do everything in my power to watch us flourish."

"I will too."

His exhale hit my lips moments before his mouth did. Soft and sure, we melded into a kiss that felt like it had been decades coming. His fingers were in my hair, and I grasped his shirt. We did nothing more than kiss and kiss, so much relief pouring between us. Being apart had been as unnatural as breathing underwater.

This was right.

Weston close, loving me like forever, me loving him right back.

His forehead rolled against mine. Our lips separated by a breath.

"I love you," I told him.

"Never once doubted it, baby. I love you the most, you know."

I closed my eyes, accepting that to be true.

Sparks flew when we kissed again, igniting us, but I wasn't afraid of this fire.

Not anymore. I didn't have to be.

After all, this was *Weston*.

EPILOGUE

Weston

One Year Later

"YOU NEED A NEW jar. This one is getting full."

Elise came up behind me, where I'd been studying the odds and ends she'd artfully placed on the shelf in her home office. Her arms wound around my middle, and her cheek pressed against my back.

"You write me a lot of notes. It was bound to get full."

I rubbed my hand on hers. "Is that a complaint?"

"Never. If you stop writing me notes, I'll complain."

Loosening her arms, I turned around to face her. "I don't foresee that happening."

"Better not."

She tipped her head back, giving me her mouth. I pressed mine to hers, groaning at the feel of her lush lips. Over a year of kissing her, months of living together and seeing each other on a daily basis, and I hadn't gotten used to having her.

Time was ticking. We had to be on the road soon. "Are you all packed?"

She snuggled in closer, her cheek on my shoulder. "Mmm...yes. You?"

I dragged my nose through her silky hair. "I am. What are the chances my brother is ready?"

Elise sputtered a laugh. "Slim to none."

A year of her being mine, and she hadn't gotten tired of me. It was astounding, really. Being my partner came with baggage. The big job, the tendency toward grumpiness, the wayward brother.

A crash sounded from the living room, followed by Miles yelling he was okay.

Fuck me and my wayward brother. He'd moved out months ago, but he always managed to find an excuse to worm his way back in, and I must have lost my mind because I let him.

"Should I go check on him?" Elise asked.

My arm tightened. "No. Stay. We're spending the weekend with him. That's enough."

I felt her smile. "You invited him. This was your idea."

"Yeah," I breathed out. "Sometimes I make mistakes, this being one of them. He caught me in a moment of weakness. Made me nostalgic for our childhood camping trips."

"Fortunately, this camping trip comes equipped with alcohol and edibles." She winged her eyebrow. I kissed it.

"You're cute, but I'm not convinced. Did I tell you about the time Miles tripped on LSD—"

"And you had to carry him back to the car? Yes, once or twice."

"You know all my stories."

She shook her head. "Then I guess we'll have to keep making new ones."

Breaking away from me, she moved to her dresser to rummage through one of her drawers. I sat down on the corner of our bed to watch.

We were getting ready to go on a two-night camping trip with Miles, Luca, Saoirse, and Elliot. It had been Elise and Saoirse's idea. They had spent the last few weeks planning activities for us.

I had a plan of my own.

It was supposed to happen at sunrise tomorrow. Elise and I would get up and walk down to the creek near our campground. We'd be alone. Maybe it'd be chilly and she'd snuggle into me. I'd get down on my knee and ask her to be my wife.

Her ring was burning a hole in the front pocket of my backpack.

Elise spun around, holding a pair of fuzzy socks and her e-reader.

"I almost forgot this. I would have kicked myself."

I smiled at her, my little reader. "You're planning on reading all weekend and not giving me any attention?"

She walked over to me, tossed her things down on the bed, and braced herself on my shoulders. Like it was magnetized, my hands went to her ass, tucking into her back pockets.

She bent down to kiss me. "As if I could ignore you."

"Come here. I'm needy," I growled against her mouth.

"Weston...we have to go." Even as she protested, she lowered to her knees, straddling my lap. "I'm here."

"Yeah, you are." Wrapping my fingers around her wrist, I brought the underside to my lips and kissed the tattoo she'd gotten a few months ago. The fine-line drawing of the head of a mountain lion that looked like a heart at first glance had been a surprise to me. It was

Elise's commemoration of the beginning of *us*. Catching a glimpse of it never failed to make me feel like I had escaped gravity.

I kissed her wrist again then nodded to her e-reader. "What's happening in the book?"

She dug her teeth into her bottom lip. "The heroine is falling for the villain. He's horrible."

After a year together, I knew all about her books. I hadn't read a whole one since that first time, but I'd peek inside them to see what got Elise's motor running.

"Did he kidnap her?"

She snorted. "Yeah. And he murdered her boyfriend."

I pushed her hair away from her face. "Ah, romantic."

"Right? The boyfriend murdered the hero's whole family, so he had it coming."

"Oh yeah, that makes sense."

She swatted at me. "Don't make fun."

"I would never, baby." I kneaded her ass and touched my lips to her throat. "You know how much I love you?"

"Half as much as I love you."

I cocked my head. "You're mistaken, Ms. Levy. I love you the most. You make me feel crazy sometimes. I want to stalk you, kill everyone who looks at you, chain you to me."

Her smile was slow and devious. "So, what you're saying is you're a dark romance hero?"

"I'm saying I'm yours. Will you be mine forever?"

Her lashes fluttered, brushing her cheeks. "Mmmhmm."

I pulled my head back from hers, and the plans I'd made for how I was going to do this slipped away. I didn't want to wait a second longer.

"Elise."

"Yes?"

"Will you marry me?"

Her lids popped open wide. "What?"

"I have a ring. It's in my backpack. I'll give it to you when you say you'll marry me."

Her mouth fell open. "What?"

"You said that."

"Are you asking me to marry you?"

"Why are you so shocked? I love you. I'm never going to stop loving you. I want you to be my wife." My brow dropped. "You haven't said yes."

"I'm just really surprised, Weston. We're going camping!"

Fed up with not getting the answer I wanted, I flung her off me and onto her back, wedging my hips between her spread thighs. She smiled up at me.

"Say yes," I ordered.

A delighted laugh burst out of her. "Yes. Obviously yes! I can't wait to marry you, West. I love you so much."

Closing my eyes, I lowered my forehead to hers. "Thank god. You had me worried for a second. This wasn't how I wanted to do it. There was going to be a sunrise, a walk—"

"This was perfect." Her arms wound around my shoulders. "I love that you couldn't wait."

"You're going to be my wife."

"You're going to be my husband."

"Soon."

"Soon," she agreed.

My eyes opened, finding hers locked on mine. "Are you happy, baby?"

"The happiest I've ever been."

Even with my brother bumbling around in the living room and the two upcoming days of next to no privacy with Elise's brother sleeping in the next tent, I'd never in my life been this utterly, wholly content. I had the friends, the family, the success, and most importantly, the girl of my dreams.

Maybe happy endings weren't so unbelievable.

PLAYLIST

"Everything is Free" Flock of Dimes

"Better Now" Post Malone

"Baggage" Rare Americans

"Worst of You" Maisie Peters

"Cold Cold Man" Saint Motel

"Kill The Director" The Wombats

"Something in the Orange" Zach Bryan

"Very Few Friends" Saint Levant

"No Right To Love You" Rhys Lewis

"Ivy" Frank Ocean

"Better Days" Dermot Kennedy

"This is what falling in love feels like" JVKE

"Blossom" Dermot Kennedy

"Please Notice" Christian Leave

"Glue Myself Shut" Noah Kahan

"Love of My Life" Harry Styles

"I Should Live in Salt" The National

"Homeward" Dermot Kennedy

"I'm With You" Vance Joy

https://open.spotify.com/playlist/0y5WVhWBI7Mt5U6BW3G eCA?si=c042a5f94cd34c43

Stay in Touch

Join my reader group to chat about books with my readers and find out news about my books first!

https://www.facebook.com/groups/JuliaWolfReaders

THANK YOU TO...

I HAVE BEEN CHOMPING at the bit to write an office romance for years, but I have a confession to make: I've never worked in an office. Not once. My first career was a hair stylist, then I became a stay at home mom, and now I'm here, writing books for you. Luckily, my husband has worked from home since 2020, so I've been able to observe an office job live and in person.

There are a lot of meetings. *A lot*, guys.

I have to thank my husband for talking me through the inner workings of an office, and helping me plot the business side of this book.

Thank you to Alley Ciz, Laura Lee, and CoraLee June for always being there for me to chat, vent, and help me pick cover photos. Same for my necklace chat girls.

Thanks for beta reading, Jenn!

To my editor Monica and proofreader, Rosa, I couldn't do this without you guys.

Kate, my sweet Kate, you are always making me my favorite cover, and you did it again this time.

To my readers, thank you for coming on this ride with me. From rock stars to bullies and now to billionaires, you guys are here for it and I am here for you.

About Julia

Julia Wolf is a bestselling contemporary romance author. She writes bad boys with big hearts and strong, independent heroines. Julia enjoys reading romance just as much as she loves writing it. Whether reading or writing, she likes the emotions to run high and the heat to be scorching.

Julia lives in Maryland with her three crazy, beautiful kids and her patient husband who she's slowly converting to a romance reader, one book at a time.

Visit my website:

http://www.juliawolfwrites.com

Julia's Books

<u>Dissonance</u>
Blue is the Color
<u>Times Like These</u>
<u>Watch Me Unravel</u>
<u>Such Great Heights</u>
<u>Under the Bridge</u>
The Never Blue Duet
<u>Never Lasting</u>
<u>Never Again</u>
The Sublime
<u>One Day Guy</u>
<u>The Very Worst</u>
<u>Want You Bad</u>
<u>Fix Her Up</u>
<u>Eight Cozy Nights</u>